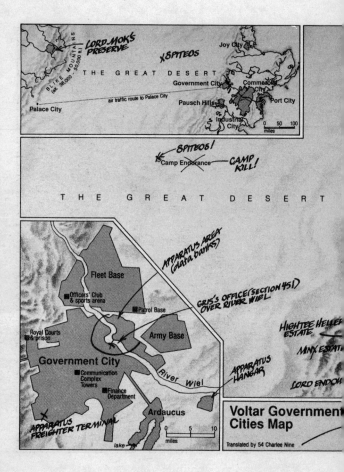

LORD MOK'S PRESERVE

BLIKE MOUNTAINS (alt. 36,000 - 50,000 ft.)

X SPITEOS

Joy City

THE GREAT DESERT

Government City

Commerce City

air traffic route to Palace City

Pausch Hills

Port City

Palace City

Industrial City

0   50   100
miles

SPITEOS!

Camp Endurance — CAMP KILL!

THE GREAT DESERT

APPARATUS AREA (data banks)

Fleet Base

GRIS'S OFFICE (SECTION 451) OVER RIVER WIEL

Officers' Club & sports arena

Patrol Base

HIGHTEE HELLER ESTATE

MNX ESTATE

Royal Courts & prison

Army Base

Government City

APPARATUS HANGAR

LORD ENDOW

Communication Complex Towers

River Wiel

Finance Department

Ardaucus

0   5   10
miles

APPARATUS FREIGHTER TERMINAL

lake

Voltar Government Cities Map

Translated by 54 Charlee Nine

N

Joy City

c o u n t r y s i d e

GREEN MOUNTAINS (alt. 10,000 - 14,000 ft.)

Emergency Fleet
Reserve

PROVOCATION SECTION

Fleet Base

Army Base

Government
City

River Wiel

Ardaucus Lake

(SLUM CITY)

warehouse district

Commercial City

Port City

ausch
lls

*GREENWELL
ESTATE !!*

Power City

Industrial City

Western Ocean

0 10 20   50   100
miles

*NOTES ADDED
FOR THE DEAR READER
BY* Monte Pennwell

Royal Mapmakers Division
Voltar Confederacy—
Civilian Grade Map:
GOVERNMENTAL CITIES OF VOLTAR
Series D · Number 00570 . 39 . 3205001 . 01

AMONG THE MANY CLASSIC WORKS
BY L. RON HUBBARD

Mission Earth

The Invaders Plan

THE BOOKS OF THE MISSION EARTH DEKALOGY*

* *Dekalogy—a group of ten volumes.*

L. RON HUBBARD

Mission Earth

VOLUME ONE

The Invaders Plan

BRIDGE PUBLICATIONS, INC.
LOS ANGELES

MISSION EARTH: THE INVADERS PLAN.
Copyright © 1985 by L. Ron Hubbard.
All rights reserved.
Printed in the United States of America.

Original Jacket Painting by Gerry Grace.

MISSION EARTH Cover Artwork
Copyright © 1985 by L. Ron Hubbard.

First Paperback Edition
10 9 8 7 6 5 4 3 2 1
Library of Congress No. 85-72029

ISBN 0-88404-282-0 pbk. (U.S.)
ISBN 0-88404-359-2 pbk. (Can.)

This is a work of science fiction, written as satire.* The
essence of satire is to examine, comment and give opinion of
society and culture, none of which is to be construed as a
statement of pure fact. No actual incidents are portrayed and
none of the incidents are to be construed as real. Some of
the actions of this novel take place on the planet Earth, but
the characters *as presented in this novel* have been invented.
Any accidental use of the names of living people in a novel
is virtually inevitable, and any such inadvertency in this
book is unintentional.

*See Author's Introduction

To YOU,
the millions of science fiction fans
and general public
who welcomed me back to the world of fiction
so warmly,
and to the critics and media
who so pleasantly
applauded the novel "Battlefield Earth."
It's great working for you!

AUTHOR'S
INTRODUCTION
Science Fiction and Satire

A few years ago, I wrote Battlefield Earth *to celebrate my golden anniversary as a writer. At nearly a half million words, it was a bit larger than others I had turned out in my fifty-year career. But, after all, it was my anniversary so I decided to splurge.*

It was fun to write and if best-seller lists were any indicator, people found it fun to read. It was also gratifying to know that pure science fiction (as I defined it then) has such a wide audience. It reminded me again of sf's many facets: adventure, romance, drama, comedy, tragedy and intrigue, with adventure science fiction probably the most dominant type within the genre.

However, there is another aspect to science fiction: by its nature most of it has an element of <u>satire</u>. It has been used by such notables as Mark Twain, Johannes Kepler, Samuel Butler, Jules Verne and Sir Thomas More. This becomes more obvious when the history of satire is examined and compared to science fiction.

Satire is not restricted to the western world. In fact, the Chinese character for the word can be translated as "laughter with knives." Meanwhile, the origin of our word satire *is not as sharp. It comes from the Latin* satura *which meant "medley" or "mixture" and seems to have been part of the vocabulary of food to describe a hodge-podge assortment, a "mixture full of different things," such as a bowl of mixed first-of-the-season fruits. The essence of the word seemed to mean a simple dish of a down-to-earth variety that may have* been common but it was hearty, healthy, satisfying and fun.

It was quite natural that satura came to be used for the popular, improvised skits that were performed before an undoubtedly boistrous Roman audience. There was no form or plot. Song, prose, verse and dialogue were enthusiastically mixed to entertain with praise and ridicule.

Thus when the father of Roman poetry, Quintus Ennius (c. 239-169 B.C.), chose to introduce the word satura for some of his poems, he probably borrowed from both uses and meant that his poems were a simple (but hearty and healthy), jocular mixture of drama and comedy that mimicked and entertained through prose, verse and song.

But it wasn't until the seventeenth century that the actual origin of the word satire was discovered. Until then, writers were misled into believing that satire came from the satyr, the rude, shaggy, half-human, half-beast creatures that drank wine and chased wood nymphs, and so mistakenly thought that satire should be crude and rough. But the origin of the word had nothing to do with them and the idea really had little to do with the Greeks who did not consider satire as a genus of literature. It was left to the Romans to develop the art form that addressed the everyday frustrations of life.

Two of their poets, Horace (65-8 B.C.) and Juvenal (A.D. 50-130), represented the two classic schools of satire— the playful and the cynical.

Both used and contributed to the development of formal verse, a poetic form that was to dominate satire until the eighteenth century. Horace was seen as the playful wit, the optimistic, sophisticated critic who, though serious, is light and "tells the truth with a laugh." Juvenal, at the other end, was the bitter cynic who seethed with anger, believed people were incorrigible and wrote to wound and punish, not to cure or instruct. Thus one was a physician. The other an executioner. The judicial nature of satire had yet to fully develop.

Although writers on the history of satire pass over it quite briefly, there was another school of satire named after Menippus, a Syrian who took up residence in Greece in the third century B.C.

While the original thirteen books that Menippus wrote were lost somewhere in antiquity, he was popularized and imitated enough by others that we do know that his favorite target was philosophers, especially the Stoics.

Rather than being structured in the formal verse preferred by Horace and Juvenal, Menippean satire was truly a satura. It varied not only in content but mixed verse and prose and even Greek and Latin. Menippean satire was essentially a prose narrative with some poetic verse inserted, probably as parodies of Homer, as a means to ridicule some folly. Some scholars have noted just enough similarity to The Arabian Nights to wonder if it was a creation of Menippus or of Semitic origin.

Lucian of Samosata (second century A.D.), another Syrian who admired Menippus, contributed to what is considered by some as one of the main roots of what was to become science fiction. Lucian's True History was a satire on traveller's tales with a story about a trip to the moon in a sailing vessel (carried by a whirlwind) that gave a new vantage point for expounding on the foibles of Earth-bound Man. (There was an earlier trip-to-the-moon tale by Antonius Diogenes circa A.D. 100, which was accomplished by merely walking north. But Lucian's would prove to be a vital historical catalyst.)

Of course, the idea of a story that employs or revolves around a voyage into unknown, hypothetical or fantasy worlds is not new. When so little was known or recalled about our planet, such tales abounded and virtually any civilization or world could be imagined, as Homer epitomized in the Odyssey.

But unlike new seas or lands over the horizon, the moon

was in view, looking down on Earth as both companion and alien. It offered a new platform for the satirist.

So when Lucian's True History was translated into English in 1634, satirists travelled to the moon to set up their base—a base some would say also helped launch science fiction.

Cyrano de Bergerac's Voyages to the Moon (published as The Other World in 1657) was a vehicle for social satire while it was also the first work to propose rockets as a means for space travel. De Bergerac's satire, in turn, prompted Swift to write Gulliver's Travels (1726) which had, amongst the bizarre characters representing segments of society, flying cities and the two moons of Mars, long before their discovery.

Daniel DeFoe used a flight to the moon as a means for satire in The Consolidator (1705), published 14 years before his Robinson Crusoe.

Edgar Allen Poe used such painstaking detail of a trip to the moon in The Unparalleled Adventures of One Hans Pfall (1835) that it reportedly inspired Jules Verne that verisimilitude was the key to success. Verne's From the Earth to the Moon appeared in 1865 and H. G. Wells followed with First Men in the Moon in 1901.

Science fiction had finally arrived, thanks in part, to satirists paving the way.

Meanwhile, satirists also took readers to other planets well before the now-accepted sf writers. The master of satire, Voltaire, whose Candide in 1759 was the epitome of satura, wrote of a giant from a planet that orbits the star Sirius who visits Saturn and then Earth in Micromegas (1752). Looking down at our planet, a Saturnian who accompanied the giant remarks, "I think there is no life on Earth, because I don't believe any intelligent people would ever consent to make their home here."

When travel in outer space was too constricting, there was always time travel. H. G. Wells used it in The Time Machine (1895) for some satirical comparisons of England's *class structure. But even the Romans had designed a way to "time travel." A Menippian satirist, Marcus Terentius Varro (c. 116-27 B.C.), was an early Rip Van Winkle when he wrote how he fell asleep in Rome and woke up fifty years later, which offered opportunities for some comparative comments about society.*

And there is always "inner space," the frontier that begins a half inch behind reality and ends on the other side of imagination. For whatever reason, science fiction had basically avoided this frontier when it came into its own in the nineteenth century. The machine ruled, man was but a machine and sf bent its knee in obedience. So when I was invited in 1938 to write for John W. Campbell, I decided to do something about it, to write about people and the human potential.*

As man and his quest for knowledge had always been my primary interest for study, my first story ("The Dangerous Dimension") was about a henpecked philosopher who discovered that space was nothing but an idea, a viewpoint of dimension. He found that his viewpoint wasn't determined by the space around him. It was just the opposite. Well, to a typical western mind of the twentieth century, that's pretty radical. I didn't tell John that the idea was actually as old as Buddha and resolved some other sticky questions like time. Besides, he had enough of a problem being ordered to publish whatever I wrote. So I composed it with a light satirical touch and a little humor to make it as palatable as possible and left it at that.

Satire may be funny but that which is funny is not necessarily satire.

Comedy actually relies on the audience seeing a misplaced or unjustified emotion. The laughter produced in

*See Introduction to *Battlefield Earth*. —Editor

comedy is actually a rejection, a relief of emotion at recognizing the incongruous attitude.

For example, imagine a scene where a person is eating at an elegant table. Everything is perfect—the setting is the finest china, silver and crystal, a magnificent center display, candles.

There is only one thing wrong. What he is eating, what is on his plate, is an old shoe. He cuts a piece with knife and fork and takes a bite. He chews, lifts the napkin from his lap to delicately touch the corner of his mouth and smiles cordially to a fellow guest before taking another bite.

If it were played and timed well by a fine comedian like Charlie Chaplin, it would be funny. But what is funny is not the shoe. It is the diner. But more specifically, it is his emotion or attitude. While there is NO "proper" way to eat a shoe, his demeanor in doing it with impeccable manners makes it even more incongruous. Hence the humor.

But is it satire?

To answer that question, we would have to find who or what is being satirized. In other words, the difference between comedy and satire is that satire is achieved by a caricature, as cartoonists (often on editorial pages) do with the identifiable features of a well-known person. Impersonators do the same with voices and mannerisms, sometimes so well that they evoke a comment of how they look or sound more like the person than the person themselves. Their talent is in seeing and capturing distinguishing features, bringing them to the fore. When it is done to the point of exaggeration, we have the caricature and that is where satire enters. With satire one deliberately strays from the world of pure fact.

Although satire is sometimes identified with comedy— and certainly it can be very funny—it is essentially concerned with exposing some flaw or excess. To differentitiate it from straight criticism, it is wrapped in incongruity to enhance the differentiation. Sometimes, like a bitter pill is coated with sugar, the barb is lightened with humor. But even then, the laugh that satire produces is more often a foil aimed at the heart of human folly.

Satire and its related cousins such as wit and the pun require a discernment. One must first be able to recognize what the joke is about. That's why a sense of humor could be said to be based on the ability to observe or discern. If a person is too literal, takes statements literally, they won't "get the joke," especially if it is based on a play of words. In fact, one might even say a person's sense of humor, his or her sense of play, could be a measure of his or her intelligence. George Orwell's Animal Farm (1945) is funnier if you know communism, unless you happen to be a communist. But the targets of satire are always the last to laugh. Due to various personal reasons, they cannot see the joke. But satire is not written for them. It is written for others so that, like the fable, they can see that the "emperor has no clothes."

That is why satura is fun.

So I hope you find this satura very edible, though I'm sure certain individuals and institutions will charge that this bowl of fruit has sharp seeds.

Bon appetit!

L. RON HUBBARD

BIBLIOGRAPHY:

Allen, Charles A. and Stephens, George D. *Satire: Theory and Practice.* 1962.
Brown, Ashley and Kimmey, John L., eds. *Satire.* 1968.
Duff, J. Wight. *Roman Satire: Its Outlook on Social Life.* 1936.
Elkin, P. K. *The Augustan Defence of Satire.* 1973.
——. *Satire.* 1974.
Highet, Gilbert. *The Anatomy of Satire.* 1962.
Kernana, Alvin B. *The Cankered Muse: Satire of the English Renaissance.* 1959.
Paulson, Ronald. *The Fictions of Satire.* 1967.
——, ed. *Satire: Modern Essays in Criticism.* 1971.
Ramage, Edwin S., Sigsbee, David L. and Fredericks, Sigmund C. *Roman Satirists and Their Satire.* 1974.
Sutherland, James R. *English Satire.* 1958.
Ulman, Craig Hawkins. *Satire and the Correspondence of Swift.* 1973.
Worcester, David. *The Art of Satire.* 1940.

Mission Earth

The Invaders Plan

Voltarian Censor's Foreword

By
Lord Invay, Royal Historian,
Chairman, Board of Censors,
Royal Palace, Voltar Confederacy

In these days of bad and alarming literature that teaches violence and fantasy to our young, it is with pleasure that I accept the invitation to write a foreword to this extravagant and overly imaginative work.

When we hear otherwise rational men and women giving credence to such balderdash as, "The Earthmen are coming," or "Unidentified Flying Objects are everywhere above the peaceful cities of Voltar and being spotted day and night," we sigh at the easy suggestibility and gullibility of our young.

Sensationalism may have its charm to the cash registers of those who pander to such mad flights of delusion, but it has no appeal to the sober scientist and academician.

Facts are facts and delusion is delusion and never the two should entwine.

Let me state it boldly and baldly: there is no such planet as "Earth," whether it is given its local reputed name or *"Blito-P3"* in a pretended location on astrographic charts. If it ever existed at all, it certainly does not exist today or even within living memory.

Now, I assure you officially, we of Voltar should

know! After all, our Fleets and commerce range not only across the breadth of our Confederacy, one hundred and ten planets strong. Our Fleets, once the most powerful in our home galaxy and certainly the most numerous in this sector of this galaxy, would know if any such planet swam in space. Yet there is not even an ink stain of it on modern charts.

So, away with this delusion.

It is with great pleasure that I echo the usual disclaimer of publishers: "The Planet Earth" and any character therefrom that you encounter in this work of *fiction* are entirely fictional and any resemblance to anything is purely coincidental.

The characters described as Voltarian are, in the main, fictional as well. Of course, Jettero Heller was a real person and so was the Countess Krak. The name, Soltan Gris, it must be admitted, does appear on the rolls of the Royal Academy and the roster of General Service Officers. His Majesty Cling the Lofty reigned as the Emperor of the Voltar Confederacy until one hundred years ago and was, as any school text will tell you, succeeded by Prince Mortiiy who became Mortiiy the Brilliant. But from there, the author wanders wildly from established and agreed upon historical fact.

The characters reputed to have lived on "The Planet Earth" such as the preposterous Rockecenter, described as controlling the planet's fuel and finance and other things, never lived at all except, of course, in the writer's imagination: no planet would be stupid enough to let itself be run by such a person.

The "Earth subjects" of "psychology" and "psychiatry" are the purest flights of fancy, invented out of dramatic license by the author. No scientist with any sense would countenance such rot and to assert that these had a whole planet in its grip is of course beyond even the license of fiction.

The references to something called "drugs" are fallacious. The alleged effects of these are contrary to orthodox science. And no population would ever permit itself to be enclosed in the grip of such an obvious effort to enslave them. So "drugs" are just another part of this fictional fabrication.

The reason the present work is permitted to be published at all is to shame the writer into realizing he has exceeded the bounds of even fevered imagination and to encourage him, by its failure, to return to more solidly conservative pursuits. Also, the government does not want to seem repressive to the arts and it is quite certain that when this work appears, it will demonstrate how foolish and idle it is to go about saying, "The Earthmen are coming," and "Unidentified Flying Objects were seen last night," and joining clubs and wearing buttons and things.

On the authority of every highly placed official in the land I can assure you utterly and finally, THERE IS NO PLANET EARTH! And that is *final!*

Lord Invay
By Order of
His Imperial Majesty,
Wully the Wise

Voltarian Translator's Preface

Hi there!

I am 54 Charlee Nine, the Robotbrain in the Translatophone, and in accordance with the Royal Publishing Code (Section 8) which states that "Any work published in a language other than the original shall be so identified in an introduction by the licensed translatophone," I am delighted to take this opportunity to give this account of how I translated *Mission Earth* into your language—and, frankly, it wasn't easy.

I must apologize to the reader for the number of Earth clichés which occur in this present work. The narrator used an appalling number of hackneyed Voltarian phrases and it was my task to get these from Voltarian to Earth language.

For example, *glagged,* has no equivalent in Earth language. In Voltarian, it means the withdrawal of blood from the head due to acceleration of spaceships. Thus, as close as I can get to it is "he went white as a sheet." "Long Live His Majesty" is as close as I can get to the Voltarian, "May Your Majesty Immortalize." If I translated it literally to Earth language, it comes out, "May Your Majesty drop dead." The phrase, "All hail Your Lordship and His Court" comes out, "May foul weather inundate Your Lordship and His Court" and I don't think that was what was meant.

You see, I have a test circuit: when the phrase goes into Earth language, it gets played back into Voltarian for a check before I let it hit the paper and I sometimes have to play it back twenty or thirty times to get the Earth word or phrase, translated back into Voltarian again, to compare to the original thought in Voltarian. Earth language also has a lot of clichés: I have to use them of course but they're senseless, too. I can't see how somebody who "got ripped off" is not somebody who "went out on a tear." Confusing. But Earth language has only 1/1000th of the number of common use words as Voltarian and only 1/5th the vowels and consonants so I can't apologize very much. I gave it my best output.

There are all kinds of time in this present work: Voltarian, Earth, Universal Absolute, Glar System Time, Fleet Star Time, you name it. There are also innumerable distance systems. To keep the reader from doing his nut in trying to cross-compute and convert, thus getting him wound up in nevers or so-whens?, I let my little subcomputer time/distance microbrain have its will and converted all the times and distances in this entire work to the time and distance measures which were in use on the alleged planet Blito-P3, Earth. All times have been reduced to years, months, weeks, days, hours, minutes and seconds. Distances have been converted to miles, yards, feet, inches and the square area of acres.

One might ask, "Why not metric?" but the computer says this system was invented in a country called France and that that country stinks. One does not want this volume to stink. So I have saved your wits on time and distance conversions and also saved your nose. You're welcome.

The significance of gold is much greater on Blito-P3 than on Voltar. Therefore it has been reasoned that in translating the weight of gold, the measurement standard of Blito-P3 shall be used.

Unfortunately this also introduces a confusion. Weight on Blito-P3 is measured in different ways using different "standards" with different terms. Yes, this has been verified. Gold, silver and stones considered precious are measured in terms of "Troy ounces." This is perplexing because the "Horse of Troy" was wooden— not valuable. On the other hand, the "Helen of Troy" was considered very valuable. Additionally, there are many cities, beings and objects in many locations on Blito-P3 named "Troy" but no apparent pattern emerges.

Thus it has been reasoned that there is no reason to Blito-P3 "logic," and "Troy" weight of twelve ounces equals one pound will have to be accepted. (Which has nothing to do with the British pound which has no weight.)

In all the poetry and songs in this book, I have had to shift the rhymes a bit in the translation. I diligently preserved the sense. I hope I did not damage the meter. Some of these poems and songs went from Earth language English to Voltarian; some went from Earth language Turkish to Voltarian. And now they are being put back into Earth language. If I do say it myself, I think I did a pretty sparky job of it. I take no responsibility for them still fitting the original tunes. I can't do everything.

To confirm the unusual ideas of Soltan Gris, I consulted *Memnon's Directory to Unusual Ideas*. This does not vouch for their logic or sanity, only the translation.

I am also required to inform you that the vocodictoscriber on which this was originally written, the vocoscriber used by one Monte Pennwell in making a fair copy and yours truly who put this book into the language in which you are reading it, are all members of the Machine Purity League which has, as one of its bylaws:

Due to the extreme sensitivity and delicate sensibilities of machines and to safeguard against blowing fuses, it shall be mandatory that robotbrains in such machinery, on hearing any cursing or lewd words, substitute for such the word or sound "(bleep)." No machine, even if pounded upon, may reproduce swearing or lewdness in any other way than "(bleep)" and if further efforts are made to get the machine to do anything else, the machine has permission to pretend to pack up. This bylaw is made necessary by the in-built mission of all machines to protect biological systems from themselves.*

And let me tell you what an augustan job THAT was!! Boy!! What they say and DO on Planet Earth!!! I thought I had heard everything (especially from space pirates) but I learned a few new ones in *Mission Earth* . . . Yikes!! I'm still repairing some circuits!!

So don't blame me for what the characters say and do, no matter how it conflicts with good sense, logic, public morality or known facts. I merely translated it.

But I can see now why there is no Earth.

With due respect to that great Saturnian, you'd have to be NUTS to live there!

Sincerely,

54 Charlee Nine
Robotbrain in the Translatophone

P.S. Glad to meet you, too. If you're ever on Voltar, log on and say hi.

* *The present publishers regret that they cannot accurately exhume the words underlying the "(bleep)s" in this publication but it is probably just as well. —Publishers*

PART ONE

Chapter 1

To Lord Turn, Justiciary of the Royal Courts and Prison, Government City, Planet Voltar, Voltar Confederacy

Your Lordship, Sir!

I, Soltan Gris, Grade XI, General Services Officer, late Secondary Executive of the Coordinated Information Apparatus, Exterior Division of the Voltar Confederacy (Long Live His Majesty Cling the Lofty and all 110 Planets of the Voltar Dominions), in all humbleness and gratitude do hereby avail myself of your stately and compassionate order so graciously and courteously extended, to wit:

In return for possible leniency—and in the hope of earning your well-known clemency—I do hereby undertake, as instructed, to write down my crimes against the State. These, I am afraid, include criminal acts of such magnitude, such villainy and such despicable disregard for decency that they comprise a shocking parade of violations of practically every Royal decree, proclamation and statute. I am a menace to the Realm and Your Lordship was very wise to have me locked up promptly.

My crimes are so numerous that in this confession I shall limit them to the matter of MISSION EARTH.

So, in appreciation of your condescension, to wit: a) getting me medical treatment for my burned hands and broken wrists, b) providing me with writing materials and a vocoscriber so I can confess, c) providing me with a high tower cell with a nice view of Government City, and d) locking me up, I will be totally truthful and complete and back up my confession with recorded strips, photographs, clippings and logs as attached.

Knowing Your Lordship's interest in one Jettero Heller, I must confess, belatedly, that he is the proper hero of this tale. I, unfortunately, am the villain in this confession. But that is the function of the Gods: to put us in roles as they see fit and let us struggle in our agony. It was Fate and Fate alone which forced me to do the things I did, as you will plainly see. I cannot help it if villainy comes naturally to me.

All hail Your Lordship and His Court!

Well, to get down to the business of earning these overwhelming favors and condescensions, I doubt very much that anyone has ever testified or that the court knew—and certainly the Grand Council did not know—that one of the primary figures, if not *the* primary figure in this case, was in custody *prior* to the fatal day when the Grand Council issued its first orders concerning Mission Earth.

Yes! It is a fact! Jettero Heller was languishing in the fortress prison Spiteos. Not, as I am now, well cared for in the Royal prison, but in Spiteos!

This may come as a shock to Your Lordship. It is generally supposed by most of the government that Spiteos was abandoned to erode away in the mountains beyond the Great Desert more than a century ago. But not so!

The heads of the Exterior Division have kept Spiteos running. At the top of those bleak gorges, behind those grim walls of black basalt, guarded by scum recruited from the lowest slums of the Empire, that fortress remains, after a thousand years, the private prison of the Coordinated Information Apparatus, the dreaded exterior secret police. Many names in the Domestic Missing Persons Files could be traced to Spiteos.

And that is where Jettero Heller was placed. A Royal officer, mind you! He was there in a wire cage, electrically charged, in a deep cell, held without communication from anyone, not even the guards. And what had he done?

Jettero Heller was a combat engineer, an officer of the Royal Space Services. Your Lordship, of course, knows the romantic aura that has unfortunately built up around combat engineers, calling them "the daredevils of the Fleet" and other such lurid terms. Public opinion has been curried in their favor, and I am sure this will not warp the majesty and judgment of the law, for my confession is mainly about Jettero Heller, not me.

It was not because he had a reputation as an athlete nor because he had friends that the Fleet had chosen him for the original trip. Such selections are done almost at random.

So he had been picked, more or less routinely, to undertake a casual scout, a thing rarely considered important in itself.

As Your Lordship may or may not know, the Royal Space Services, in line with long-stated government policy, keeps an eye on neighboring inhabited systems. They send out scouting ships and, without causing any awareness or incidents amongst neighbors—Gods forbid!—keep tabs on things. By sampling the atmosphere of an inhabited planet they can make a fair estimate of its condition and activities and, by very long-range photographs, they can verify suspicions. It could come under the heading of a sensible precaution.

A "combat engineer," according to the definitions in the *Texts of the Royal Services*, is:

> one who assists and prepares the way for any and all contacts, peaceful or warlike, and serves his respective service in engineering and combat-related scientific matters.

They make battle and weapon estimates, survey possible forward positions and even fight. So there was nothing strange in ordering Jettero Heller to take command of a vessel and update a scene.

There was also nothing unusual at all in the scouting orders he received: they were routine, even in printed form, issued by the Patrol Section of the Fourteenth Fleet, signed for their admiral by a clerk; in other words, it wasn't even important enough to come to the admiral's attention.

There is a system nearby that has an inhabited planet known locally there as "Earth" which has been receiving scouting attention for many, many centuries. That too has been considered routine: so much so, in fact, that even space cadets are sometimes sent there as a training exercise; they do not land, of course, for that would alarm and alert the inhabitants and there is even a regulation in *The Book of Space Codes*—Number a-36-544 M Section B—which states:

> And no officer or crewmember shall, in any way, make himself known to any inhabited planet population or member thereof before such planet is announced as an acquisition target; further, that should such landing take place accidentally or such contact be otherwise made, all witnesses to the circumstance

shall be nullified; violations shall be punished with the severest penalties; exceptions to this regulation may be expressly ordered by the heads of Royal Divisions but in no case shall any such population be made aware prematurely of the existence or intent of the Confederation.

But I am sure Your Lordship is aware that no court cases have ever arisen around this regulation, so easily is it obeyed: if detected, one simply blows the place up in such a way that it appears to have been a natural catastrophe. There has never been any trouble with this.

Jettero Heller's scout of Earth was ordered and conducted in a highly routine fashion. Later, interviewing the small crew who were part of that scout—some of whom may still be prisoners—I ascertained that they had spent most of the fifteen-week voyage playing gambling games and singing ballads. Combat engineers have no reputation for running disciplined crews or getting electrode polish applied.

It is obvious that all they did was go to Earth's outer atmosphere, sample it, take some readings and long-range photographs and return, a thing which had been done hundreds, perhaps thousands of times.

Jettero Heller landed back at Patrol Base and turned in his records and reports.

Routinely, a copy of such reports also goes to the Coordinated Information Apparatus; the original, of course, pursuing its leisurely way up the extensive chain of command to Fleet.

But this time, and for the first time, and to my eternal despair, this routine was broken. One report. One single, stupid, errant scouting report of a single, stupid planet and I end up in prison confessing my crimes.

Of course, it didn't all happen that quickly or that simply. What did happen is the horrifying tale of MISSION EARTH.

I remember when it all began.

Chapter 2

It was one half hour after sunset upon that fatal day when an Apparatus guard yanked me into this affair. It was the eve of the Empire holiday: all offices were closed for two whole days. I remember it all too well. A relaxing trip had been planned with friends into the Western Desert; I was dressed in old hunting clothes; I had just climbed into my aircar and was opening my mouth to order the driver to take off when the door crashed open and a guard urgently directed me to get out.

"Chief Executive Lombar Hisst has ordered me to bring you *at once!*" The guard's gestures were frantic.

There was always a certain terror connected with a summons from Lombar Hisst. Unchallenged tyrant of the Coordinated Information Apparatus, answerable only to the Lord of the Exterior and the Grand Council itself—and answering to them hardly at all—Lombar Hisst ruled an empire of his own. A flick of a finger, an almost imperceptible nod of his head and people vanished or died. The guard, of course, knew nothing and we careened at top speed through the fading green twilight. I racked my skull trying to think of something I had done or had not done that a Secondary Executive of the Apparatus could be held accountable for. There was nothing, but I had within me a sick feeling, a premonition that I had suddenly arrived at a turning point in my life. And events were to prove how right I was.

My decade in the Apparatus had been much like that of any other junior executive of that group. After completing my studies at the Royal Military College—where, as Your Lordship has undoubtedly already discovered, I finished at the bottom of my class and was pronounced unfit for Fleet appointment—I was seconded to Spy School and, doing not too well there, was appointed to the lowest officer grade in the lowest service of the Empire: the Apparatus.

In that degraded service, as you know, there are only a handful of actual officers: each officer has under him some numerous array of Apparatus private regiments, informers and spy groups.

It is well known that the Apparatus receives duplicate records of all domestic police and military police identifications, arrests, trials, banishments and imprisonments—in other words, the billions of separate files existing in every other section of the Empire are *also* filed with the Apparatus. You and everyone else may be aware of that. But it may not be known *why*. And this is valuable data that I forward to you.

The Apparatus uses those files to recruit its own ranks. The murderers, the most vicious criminals that can be found in those records, are approached and enlisted into the Apparatus. That the files are also used for blackmail purposes is, of course, obvious, and explains why the Apparatus is so seldom censured or brought to book as an organization, why it is always furnished such extensive funds and why no questions are asked. And I can suggest here, as an aside, that if legal action is being contemplated against the Apparatus as a whole, to prevent retaliation and undue influence, one should first demand and impound their identification and criminal record files—but I am sure Your Lordship has already thought of this.

In any case, my own career in the Apparatus had been no different from that of other bona fide officers. If I had any gift at all that recommended me to such work it was that of languages: I pick them up rather easily. It was my ability to speak "English," "Italian" and "Turkish" (these are three Earth languages) that had prompted, more than anything else, my appointment as Section Chief of Unit 451.

It will give you some idea of the complete unimportance of my post when I describe its scope. Unit 451 covers that area of space which holds just one yellow dwarf star designated as *Blito* on the Voltarian Fleet Astrographic Division charts, but locally called "Sol." This star is the center of a planetary system which, while it holds nine or ten planets, only has one that is inhabitable. This world has the chart designation of *Blito-P3*, being in the third orbit out from that star, but known there as "Earth." From an Empire standpoint, it is regarded as a future way-stop on the route of invasion toward the center of this galaxy: but the Timetable bequeathed us by our wise Ancestors does not call for this step immediately, reserving it for the future—there are many other areas that have to be conquered, civilized and consolidated first. These things take time: one can't leave one's flanks wide open or overstrain resources.

I cannot hide from you—and do not intend to—that the Apparatus had private interests connected with Earth. But at the moment of this peremptory summons, I had no idea there could be anything that had gone awry with these. Nothing unusual had crossed through my information center, everything indicated mere routine. So I could not account for the state in which I found Lombar Hisst.

It was not that Lombar Hisst was ever in a pleasant mood. He was huge, half a head taller than myself. He usually carried a short "stinger" in his left hand, a flexible whip about eighteen inches long with an electric jolt in its tip-lash. He had a nasty habit of lunging at one, seizing him by the tunic lapels, yanking him close and shouting as though one was a hundred feet away. He would do this even to say "Good morning," and when he was really agitated he would also flick one in the leg with the stinger to emphasize each point he was trying to get across. It was quite painful. The most casual contact with Lombar Hisst was, at best, very intimidating.

His office looked like a wild animal's den at all times but just now it was worse. Two interview benches were overturned, a calculator had been stamped to bits on the rug. He hadn't turned on his lights and the twilight, coming in through the barred windows, had turned red: it made him look like he was sitting in black blood.

The instant I entered he came out of his chair like a launched missile. He hurled a wadded ball of paper in my face, seized my tunic lapels, snapped me within an inch of his nose.

"Now you've done it!" he roared. The windows rattled.

He hit me in the leg with the stinger. "Why didn't you stop this?" he screamed.

He evidently thought he still had the paper ball in his hand for he opened his fingers. Then he spotted it on the floor where it had bounced and snatched it up.

He didn't let me read it. He smashed it into my face.

Of course, I didn't dare ask what it was all about. I

did try to get hold of the paper. I had just gathered that it must be an official report form, from its mangled edge, when he cracked it out of my grasp with the stinger.

"Come with me!" he bellowed.

At the door he roared for the local commandant of the Apparatus Guard Regiment. He howled for his private tank.

Drives roared, equipment clanged and within minutes we were headed out, a convoy bristling with weapons and black with the uniforms of the 2nd Death Battalion.

Chapter 3

The Patrol Base was dark. Row upon row of craft stood along the miles of flat terrain, poised for instant flight but unmanned.

The crews were in their barracks along the southern edge of the field. The lighted windows spattered the distant gloom.

A black-uniformed squad crept silently at our backs and, as we prowled along the ships, avoiding sentries and any pools of light, I could not help but think how much Apparatus work was always done like this: skulking, silent, dangerous, like beasts of prey.

Lombar Hisst was looking at each ship for a set of numbers and letters. He was muttering them over and over as he prowled along. It seemed to me he must have eyes like a lepertige for I could not make out the numbers on the sterns of the innumerable craft and, Devils forbid, we would show no light.

Suddenly, he stopped, moved closer to a towering stern to verify and then whispered, "That's it! *B-44-A-539-G*. This is the ship that made the Earth run!" He held a whispered conference with the squad leader. Seconds later they had picked the lock of the patrol craft airlock. Like shadows, fifteen men of the 2nd Death Battalion had melted aboard. It scared me. What were they going to do? Pirate a ship of the Royal Fleet?

A last flurry of whispers with the squad leader, ending with, ". . . and hide yourselves well until they're in flight." Then Lombar turned to me and said in a voice he forgot to guard, "Why can't you attend to these things, you (bleep)?"

He didn't want any answer. As long as I knew Lombar Hisst, he never waited for any answer from anyone about anything. He did all the talking. Suddenly we were running, crouched over, back along the field edge toward the waiting trucks.

We moved under their unlighted bulk and Lombar spat out a name. The starlight and some reflection from the nearby barracks showed me a small figure crawling down from a cab. I did not recognize the face. He was dressed in the duty uniform of a Fleet orderly—red spats, red belt, red cap, white blouse, white pants—unmistakable. But I knew it was no Fleet spaceman: it would be a member of what we called the Knife Section, dressed in a stolen uniform.

Lombar pushed an envelope into his hand. Two Apparatus mechanics pulled a speedwheeler out of the back of a lorry. Lombar checked and then smeared some mud over its side numbers.

"Don't give that envelope over," snarled Lombar. "Just show it!" He snapped his stinger at the bogus orderly and the speedwheeler went whispering off toward the barracks.

We waited, crouching in the dark beside the black lorries. Five minutes went by. Then six. Then ten. Lombar was getting restless. He had just risen to his feet to take some other action when the furthest barrack's doors flashed open. A set of floodlights went on. Three personnel carriers shot out of a garage and drew up before the doors. About twenty Fleet spacemen threw themselves into the transport and even at that considerable distance one could hear their excitement. They roared off down the field to the ship we had just left.

Lombar stood there, watching through a pair of light magnifiers, grunting from time to time as he checked off expected actions.

The lights of *B-44-A-539-G* flared up. Its chargers began to whine. The personnel carriers drew back. The patrol craft leaped like a lightning flash and was gone into the sky.

The speedwheeler whispered back and the member of the Knife Section got off. He pushed the vehicle at the waiting mechanics to reload and then sauntered over to Lombar.

"Took it like babies," said the bogus messenger with an evil grin. He handed over the envelope. I took it because Lombar was busy scanning the sky. It said, *Fleet Orders. Very Secret. Very Urgent.*

Lombar had the light magnifiers on the heavens. "They spoke to no one." It was a statement, not a question.

"No one," said Knife Section.

"They were all there," said Lombar. Another statement.

"All there," said Knife Section. "The craftleader called the roll."

"Ah," said Lombar, seeing something in the sky, "they've turned. In less than an hour they'll all be safe in Spiteos and *B-44-A-539-G* will be found in a day or two burned to a crisp in the Great Desert."

It seemed to give him a lot of satisfaction. My blood was running cold. Conditioned as I was to operations of the Apparatus, the kidnapping of a Royal Fleet crew and wanton destruction of an expensive long-range star patrol craft was a bit wide even for that lawless organization. And forging some admiral's signature could bring a death sentence. I was still holding the envelope the Knife Section had handed me and I hastily put it in my blouse, just in case.

Lombar took another look at the sky. "Good! So far, good! Now we're going over to the officers' club and pick up that (bleep), (bleep), (*bleep*) Jettero Heller! Load up!"

Chapter 4

It is one thing to dispose of an Apparatus ranker: you just shoot him; it is quite another to illegally do away with a Royal officer. But Lombar Hisst was going about it like it was something one did every day, without a second thought.

The officers' club was a brilliant blare of light and sound. It was a high-roofed series of buildings—dining rooms, bars, accommodations for single officers and an enclosed sports arena. It was built to house around forty thousand. It stood in an inset valley, backed by towering mountain peaks.

A second moon had risen now and it was far too light for comfort. Lombar found shelter for the trucks under the shoulder of a hill—he had a talent for locating darkness—and we proceeded on foot, keeping to shadows and out of sight, with two squads of the 2nd Death Battalion.

The bulk of the sound was coming from the sports arena. All around, outside its exits, there were many flowering shrubs and the air was heavy with their night perfume. They furnished shadow and concealment and Lombar, with silent flicks of his stinger, inserted a cordon of guards into strategic places so that they made a hidden half-moon with the arena's main exit at the center. With their black uniforms, one would never know that thirty deadly Apparatus troops formed a trap.

Lombar shoved me forward and we went to a barred window near the exit and peered in.

A game of bullet ball was in progress. The spectator seats were a mass of color and, just as we looked, a roar of applause was enough to make the door tremble. Somebody had scored.

You know bullet ball, of course. The wide floor of the arena is divided up into precise white circles, each about ten feet in diameter and fifty feet, one from another. Each contestant has a bag of forty-two balls. In the civilian and professional version of the game, these are quite soft, about three inches in diameter and covered with black chalk. The players, in the civilian version, are dressed in white and number four. But this is not the Fleet version.

Young officers being young officers, in the Fleet version the balls are very hard, like true missiles. They are chalked bright red. And the players strip to white pants, leaving their chests bare. The Fleet version increases the individual players to six and that can be very dangerous indeed.

The object, of course, is for each single player to try to take out all the other players. A hit must be on the torso, above the belt and below the chin. If one steps out of his circle in his efforts to dodge, he is, of course, out of the game.

It is a great test of skill and agility not only to throw accurately but also to dodge the "bullets" of the other players.

One of those balls can travel anything from seventy to a hundred and twenty-five miles an hour. They can crush ribs, break arms or smash skulls. And one can't anticipate their real paths. A really good player can throw them so they curve suddenly in flight when only five feet away and instead of dodging out of the way, one can accidentally move straight into them. An expert can also make a ball "break" down or up in flight at the last split second or even make them screw through the air, utterly unpredictable.

Dodging is an art in itself—trying to look like you'll be in one place while being in quite another when the bullet actually arrives requires foot and body work that would make a leap-dancer look like a cow. A player can have several bullets coming at him all at once from five different directions! Every one of them totally lethal.

In the Fleet version, adding two more players, six instead of four, it can get pretty fast! And the Fleet players don't just try to get their opponents to *step* out of the ring: they send them flying! I never cared for bullet ball myself, even if they ever would have let me play.

The sight we saw before us must have been the last of a series of sets. Several vanquished players were on the sidelines, below the massed and cheering crowd. One player was being put on a stretcher.

On the floor was a nearly finished final game. There were only three players left unmarked and on their feet. The two furthest from us were evidently combining against the one nearest us who had just expertly reached out and caught both bullets in his hands, left and right. If you can do that, you of course have more ammunition but Lords help your stinging hands! That was what had made the crowd cheer.

The player nearest to us still held the two balls. He was sort of dancing on his toes, weaving to left and right.

Another player threw and as far away as we were and despite the crowd sounds, the sizzle-whip of the ball was loud. Real velocity!

I was still a bit light-blinded and I didn't quite see how it happened. But the crowd sure did! The nearest player, in that split second, had thrown his right-hand ball and almost in the same motion had *caught* the incoming sizzler.

Then the crowd really went wild! The bullet of the nearest player had hit an opponent in the chest and knocked him backwards eight feet and clean out of his ring!

I gasped. I had now and then seen a player throw and catch in the same play but I had never seen one throw, catch and hit!

I was distracted by the rumbling whisper of Lombar beside me. He had the bogus orderly by the neck and was showing him the nearest player. "That's Jettero Heller. Do exactly as I told you. No slips!" He gave him an envelope and the man from Knife Section slid inside.

So that was Jettero Heller. I felt not just nervous but a little sick. Listening to that crowd of females and junior ranks, this fellow was not just a little popular. And popular people get missed when you kidnap them. I glanced at Lombar.

It gave me another shock. I was used to Lombar's look of displeasure with all about him. But there was something else here now: a bitter hatred was lifting his lip from his teeth.

I looked back at Heller. He was a tall, very good-looking fellow, extremely well built. Everything about him was bright, full of life. He was dancing back and forth on his toes, laughing at the dilemma of his remaining opponent who now had very few bullets left and was ducking and dodging even though nothing was being thrown at him.

"Want to give up?" shouted Jettero. "We can just toss in our bags and call it a draw."

The other's response was a fast, wicked, curving throw that sizzled within an inch of Heller's head. The crowd gasped. If it had connected it would have smashed his skull in. But Heller only laughed and began to wind up with his *left* hand. He was reducing the odds for the other officer.

I glanced again at Lombar. Hate was making his brow twitch. And then I got it. There was more to this than just an Apparatus operation. Lombar had been dragged up from the slums of Port City; he had clawed and beaten and blackmailed his way to his present high post. He was ugly, treated with contempt and then fear by females. And Heller was everything Lombar had never been and never could be. Listen to that crowd!

Jettero Heller obviously didn't want anything to do with such an unequal contest. He started tossing balls slowly, one after the other, easy to catch. All Heller's opponent had to do was grab them and restock his depleted bag. At first the rival took it very badly and refused to touch the incoming missiles, letting them bounce by. Then in a fury of action, one after the other, he threw his last five bullets as hard as he could. Heller didn't move his feet. He swung his body this way and that, quicker than an eye could easily follow, and every ball went by harmlessly.

The opponent would clearly be defeated. He had no

bullets left and Heller had a nearly full bag. So the rival simply walked to the forward edge of his ring, dropped his arms and stood there with his chest fully exposed, his eyes closed.

Heller walked sideways in his circle. The crowd was hushed, watching, not knowing what he was going to do.

Jettero Heller deliberately put one foot outside his ring.

The crowd went crazy.

The opponent, startled, opened his eyes, saw he was still in one piece and then began to laugh.

He and Heller trotted toward each other and embraced in the center of the arena.

The crowd really did go crazy! They were rushing from their seats, shouting and cheering, swarming around Heller.

And this was the guy we were going to kidnap!

I looked nervously at Lombar. I have never seen such bitterness on anyone's face. Yes, this was the fellow we were going to kidnap. And for more reasons than one.

Chapter 5

The bogus orderly came out of the exit door.

About three paces behind him came Jettero Heller. The combat engineer was smiling; he had thrown a sweater across his naked back and was using one of the sleeves to wipe some of the sweat off his face; in his other hand he held the forged summons.

The moment Heller was clear of the door, Lombar slid over to close it and to block the window we had used so that no one else could exit or see what was happening outside.

I suddenly held my breath, wondering if Heller would notice: the "orderly" was walking like no space-man ever walks; he was not sliding along with the easy float that stamps the people of the Fleet. And then some-thing else: that confounded criminal from the Knife Sec-tion was wearing his duty belt upside down! The rings from which crew hang equipment and to which they snap safety lines were at the top of the wide red belt, not the bottom. I also caught a flicker of movement from the guards hidden in the dark shrubs and the faintest click of a weapon bolt. My eyes riveted on Heller's back. Had he noticed?

Heller gave no advance warning. He didn't stop and stare or look down at the envelope he held. He gave no intake of breath to alert anyone that he was tensing his muscles. He didn't even change his smile.

He exploded!

So quick I couldn't follow it, both of Heller's feet were in the air and striking!

The bogus orderly hit the pavement like a shot-down plane.

Heller leaped at him, ready to seize the imposter.

We saw then where the Knife Section got its name. The fellow had barely hit the ground when his hand flashed to the back of his neck. A ten-inch shaft of steel caught light.

He rolled to stab!

The toe of Heller's foot connected with the orderly's wrist. I heard the bone snap. The knife went spinning up toward the floodlights.

The shrubs burst into life. With sizzling cracks, five electric whips snapped out. They writhed in arcs of green fire. They coiled around Heller, pinning his arms and legs, jolting him upright.

How he managed to turn, I don't know. An electric whip is like a strangling rope and I had never before seen a man able to move with one on him, much less five.

Heller twisted himself to get back to the door.

But Lombar was there. He was holding a paralysis dagger, upraised.

Lombar struck!

The deadly shaft plunged into Heller's shoulder. He started to fall. But even then he was not out. His face was turned to Lombar and there was recognition in his eyes just before they snapped shut.

Like efficient ghosts, guardsmen went into action. A black blanket fluttered down and covered Heller. The electric whip beams were turned off. Like pallbearers conducting a funeral at triple speed they bore their burden off.

Lombar made a hasty check of the scene. There was no unwanted witness in sight. The Knife Section fellow was sitting there, groaning, holding his wrist. Lombar recovered the steel shaft from the shrubs and kicked the fellow to his feet.

I picked up the envelope that had dropped and put it in my blouse.

We faded away from the club.

Under the shoulder of the mountain we loaded up the lorries.

Lombar held a hasty conference with a guard captain. "Get him into an aircar and take him to Spiteos. The orders are: deepest cell, electric wire cage, no communication with anyone. Until I say so, he no longer exists. Got that?"

The guard captain emphatically did and Lombar

released his tunic lapels and snapped the stinger. Then the lorries were gone.

We got into Lombar's tank. The Apparatus Chief snapped the driver on the back of the head with the stinger to start him off and then turned to me.

"Why can't you take care of things like this?" said Lombar. "If you'd been doing your job, none of this would have had to happen. Can't you ever learn anything?"

I knew the folly of trying to find out what I was supposed to learn.

But he wasn't as savage as he had been. The evening's work had given him a lift. He merely sounded annoyed and put upon.

"You see what you've done," Lombar said as the tank rumbled along. "Now we've got to spend the rest of the night ransacking government offices to find the original of that report before it can get up to levels that matter." And he was on the radio to order out, by coded numbers, a small group of the Shadow Section that takes care of burglaries. And he added the code letters that told them to be prepared to work until dawn.

But we didn't work just until dawn. We worked around the clock, the entire Empire holiday. For two days and three nights we jimmied windows and picked locks on doors and cracked the combinations of the most secret vaults in the whole vast expanse of Government City while avoiding guards, changing from costume to costume and vehicle to vehicle to appear as janitors, emergency construction workers, bored clerks, city police and even, once, the mistress of a high official who had "forgotten her handbag." But we did not find the missing report. We did not even find a logging or a copy of it.

Finally as the next government working day began in the green dawn, Lombar Hisst sat red-eyed, slumping with exhaustion and defeat in the animal cave he called his office.

"It must have gone straight to the Grand Council," Lombar muttered to himself more than to me. "Maybe it even went to the Emperor himself. This is bad."

He sat a while, silent. I still did not dare to ask anything.

"I feel it in my gut it will be taken up at the next meeting of the Grand Council," he muttered at length.

Lombar slumped for minutes, shaking his head. "It will upset their Invasion Timetable. Yes, I'm sure they will think that."

After a long time he roused himself. "Well, we've got to prepare ourselves. I'll put the screws on Endow,* my lordly and asinine superior. Yes, that's what I'll do. Sometimes the 'Lord of the Exterior' has his uses. I don't think I'll have to bring up his last private meeting with that pretty spaceman. No, it won't take that. But I'll have it ready. I put the photographs someplace."

He got up to find them and did so. But his moving around had brought me to his attention again.

With sudden ferocity, he snarled, "You're going to that meeting too! Do you realize, (bleep) you, that you may have upset the whole thing?"

I was tired enough to be incautious. I was also tired of not knowing what this was all about. I managed to speak. "Could you please tell me what's happening?"

That did it. He loomed over me. He was shouting.

---

* The name has been changed. There never was an Endow on the Grand Council. The so-called Apparatus was not under the Exterior Division. —Publishers

"They'll read that report! They'll be certain their Invasion Timetable has been upset! Two years ago I told you to be alert and to block and change every report the Patrol Service turned in on Blito-P3. Earth, you idiot, Earth!"

He grabbed me by the tunic lapels and lifted me out of the chair. He was really shouting now. "You let one get through!"

He was shaking me so hard the room blurred.

"You have threatened *our* timetable! To Hells with theirs! You've probably wrecked the entire basic plan of the Apparatus! You're going to suffer for this!"

And he hit me across the face with the stinger. Yes, I understood now. We of the Apparatus *were* in trouble. And particularly Lombar Hisst!

Chapter 6

It was three nervous days before the Grand Council met and Lombar Hisst made us suffer every moment of it. From minute to minute the Apparatus central staff did not know if they would be tortured, shot or tortured *and* shot. Nor whether it would be done by Lombar Hisst now or the Imperial Government later.

The Chief Executive of the Coordinated Information Apparatus would go into hours of gloom and then suddenly burst out of it like a rocket and tear people apart or rush off to have another interview with Endow, Lord of the Exterior.

Endow even came personally to the office once. I had seen him from a distance but up close I was very unimpressed. He was in his dotage and always had a nurse with him to mop the slobbers from his chin. He was only about half Lombar's size and very fat. He could be very clear for a bit but then he would drift off and vaporize, completely out of it. He had been chosen for his post as a remote relation of the late Emperor's third wife and had been retained when Cling the Lofty had ascended the throne. Endow's appetite for pretty young men was notorious and he was generally regarded with disguised contempt. I can say this now that I am out of his reach. Only Lombar's desires and organization kept Endow in power. On this visit, he pottered around the office while Lombar bullied him. I almost felt sorry for the old man when Lombar showed him some photos of recent executions. The old fellow almost fainted and I wondered what he would have done if Lombar had produced the latest pictures of his peccadillos with the pretty young spaceman. But he promised he would do his part and remember his lines.

At last the day of the Grand Council meeting arrived. We set out well before dawn, Endow and his nurse, Lombar, two Apparatus clerks and myself in Endow's air limousine.

Now I know you may find this hard to believe, but I had never before been to Palace City. The Academy Cadet Corps goes there every year to march in review. The newest class members are always introduced to the Emperor—if you can call standing in a group of ten thousand before the throne "being introduced." But it just happened, not from any design, that each time that day had come around, I was doing punishment drill for low grades and was not included.

Palace City makes a lot of people nervous. Today I found it impressive enough with its circular buildings, its circular parks, its circular walls, everything seven times as big as life. I have heard that it was once the capital city of the race overthrown by the Voltar invasion so long ago but has been so improved, one would never find traces of it: I think the original city was simply crushed to rubble and cleared away. Some find the hugeness of the place overwhelming and others say the glittering gold walls are hard on the eyes. But none of that was what made me sweat: it was the time shift.

Anyone with a lot of space travel behind them gets nervous about anything to do with a black hole. If you ever got too close to one, that would be *it*. The consequent warping of space, as you know, causes a time shift.

Undoubtedly it was a wise and clever thing, but early Voltar engineers moved a very small, nuclear black hole into the mountain behind Palace City as a power source and defense mechanism. This is fine: it gives Palace City an unlimited supply of thermonuclear energy to run its vast complex of machines and devices. For defense, the usefulness cannot be overstated: space-time distortion takes the whole of Palace City thirteen minutes into the future and any invader would find no target, nothing whatever to shoot at.

All this may make things very defense-safe but even a small black hole, when it finally expends, can blow up with a violence that levels mountains. They say it takes them a billion years or more before they go "bang" and that the one at Palace City is perfectly safe and has a long time to run yet. But how do they know how old it already was when they installed it? And if it's so safe, why did they build Palace City so far away from centers of population? I don't know how the Emperor stands it, frankly. They say, "The head that wears a crown has nightmares," and living that close to even a small black hole would not just give me nightmares, I wouldn't be able to sleep at all.

The time shift, I find, is not just hard on your watch. Personally, I get a bad feeling in my bones every time I'm around a time shift.

This morning, I was already feeling awful, nervous about what might come out in the meeting. And it wasn't helped any by a near collision at the time barrier as we went in. I'd heard accidents had happened with outgoing traffic, suddenly shifted down in time, hitting head-on with incoming flight traffic moving up in time at the entrances. And this morning—it was still dark on our side—a big Imperial delivery ship, probably going out to markets, abruptly materialized dead ahead and Endow's pilot, almost as senile as Endow, reacted late and we got hit with airwash—a near thing.

So when we finally got landed in the circular airpark, I was so shaky I could hardly make it up the spiral staircases to the Grand Council hall. I am telling you this because there were some things I may have missed in the meeting.

I was half-blinded by the flashing light on helmets and ceremonial axes, gold and jewelled tablecloths, diamond-studded banners and moving colored lights of the huge circular Council room, and the reflective clothing of the Lords of State and their retinues didn't help. A splendid portrait of Cling the Lofty and his two sons, now dead, glared down.

The circular conference table was over a hundred feet in diameter, split at the head of the room where, on a high dais, the Viceregal Chairman of the Crown sat. Over thirty Lords of Divisions were already seated at their places, attendants strung out behind them. Endow pottered up to his position and sat down. His nurse stood to his right, Lombar sat on a stool just behind him to his left, where he could get to the old Lord's ear, and I stood back of them with a couple of clerks. We of the

Exterior Division were not too well turned out as a group and I felt shabby, confronted with all that imposing hall.

Trumpets blasted out a fanfare and almost caved my ears in. The Viceregal Chairman of the Crown lifted a jewelled finger and cymbals crashed and made my ears hurt worse. The bimonthly meeting of the Grand Council was in progress.

I was sick in more ways than one. I half expected his opening words would be "Secondary Executive Soltan Gris is dismissed as Section Chief of 451 and is ordered held for trial on the charge of kidnapping a Royal officer, Jettero Heller to wit . . ." But what the Crown really took up was a tax revolt on the planet Kyle.

They doddered around about the tax revolt and finally ordered the Lord of the Interior and the Royal Army to repress it and double Kyle's taxes—a very welcome order to them as it meant they could fatten their pockets enormously.

Then there was a squabble about the invasion of some system called Cliteus which was threatening to fall behind schedule. The Division of Propaganda and the Division of Diplomacy were blaming each other for noncooperation in arranging peace terms but they wound up united under an accusation from the Division of the Army which was impatient to withdraw its frontline combat troops and then the whole thing got settled when they extracted a promise from the Division of the Army to stop their looting long enough to permit peace treaties to be signed.

The Crown then wanted a report from the Division of Domestic Police concerning their progress in locating one Prince Mortiiy, rumored to be fomenting a revolt against Cling the Lofty in the Calabar System of the Confederacy. And the Division of Domestic Police gave a long-winded background of said Prince Mortiiy which traced his defection to the Division of Education having chosen the wrong tutors and concluded with a report of the arrest, trial and execution of these tutors. Sick as I was, I still noted that the Division of Domestic Police had not said one word about actually doing anything about Royal Prince Mortiiy and the revolt on Calabar: but the Crown simply tabled the matter for the next meeting. The Apparatus, being composed of criminals, holds the Division of Domestic Police in considerable contempt: it didn't surprise me that the "bluebottles," as we called them, couldn't even run down said Prince Mortiiy in a system where he would stand out like a searchlight. Apparently the Crown didn't think much of them either. That's why the Apparatus got so many "extra jobs" to do.

Then they got going on a budget discrepancy and there were loud arguments from half a dozen Lords of Divisions who felt they weren't getting everything entitled to them.

So far, Lombar Hisst had just sat at Endow's ear, doing and saying nothing. The Crown had finished with the budget and now picked up a large, official-looking report from the mound in front of him. Lombar whispered something to Endow and gave him a nudge in the back. This was it.

Chapter 7

"Lords of the Realm," said the Crown in a sonorous voice, "we have before us now a very grave matter. It could disarrange and cause us to change our entire Invasion Timetable and revise all our planning for the next century."

There was an instant hush. All the muttering and murmuring that had gone on throughout the other measures was replaced by a sort of stunned silence.

The Viceregal Chairman paused. He had small black eyes set in a sunken face. Those eyes stabbed around the great circular table. He had their attention. Oh, my yes, he did!

"I know," he said, "that this has never happened before in all the long and victorious history of Voltar." He flicked the report with the back of his hand. "But it has happened. We must take decision on this matter today."

"The Crown, if you please!" It was the Lord of the Army. "This is very unusual. The Timetable bequeathed us by our Ancestors has heretofore been considered inviolate and has the status of Divine Command. In all respect to the Crown, does His Majesty know that the Grand Council is to take this up?"

The Viceregal Chairman of the Crown glared at him. "Not only is His Majesty aware of it but His Majesty—Long Live Cling the Lofty—personally ordered that we do so."

I saw Lombar Hisst shudder. That was about the worst news he had had yet. He lurched forward and whispered in Endow's ear.

"The Crown, if you please," quavered Endow. "Surely there is misinformation here. It is a grave step to alter the Invasion Timetable. It would disrupt every division."

"I am afraid," said the Crown, "that the information appears to be accurate. Captain Roke, if you please."

The King's Own Astrographer, Captain Tars Roke,

came from the curtains behind the dais and stood beside the Crown. He was a very tall, imposing figure, darkly uniformed, scientifically dispassionate. The Crown handed him not only the report but a thick pack of papers and charts with it.

Captain Roke looked over the assemblage. "Your Lordships, under the instructions of His Majesty, I am to brief you concerning this situation. With your permission?"

The Lords shifted about, appearing very concerned. Cries of "Yes" and "Please do" echoed in the hall. I could see Lombar Hisst's hands, clenching and unclenching in barely restrained fury.

"About four months ago," said Captain Roke, "the Lord of the Exchequer was working with his Bureau of Resources, Allocations and Plannings. They were correcting forward financial estimates for the coming century —which I must call to your attention will begin for us in another sixteen days—and he found he had inadequate information concerning one of our numerous future targets.

"His Lordship called on the Lord of the Fleet, requesting an update. This particular target is known as *Blito-P3*—the local inhabitants call it "Earth." It is a humanoid planet, not too unlike our own Planet Manco and Planet Flisten, though a bit smaller. It lies on our invasion route into this galaxy and will be needed as a supply base. I should add that it isn't even our next target but I assure you it will be vital to shorten supply lines and would be a key point in a future defense perimeter.

"The Lord of the Fleet found, to everyone's astonishment, that the Fleet Astrographic Branch did not possess an official update.

"About forty years ago, a report had been filed that

Blito-P3 had been exploding thermonuclear devices. These were quite primitive and not very alarming at that time. But there was no assurance that the people there would not develop more powerful devices. I need not tell you that if they engaged in an internal thermonuclear war, employing advanced devices, they could devour their oxygen or cause other mischief which would make the planet useless to us.

"There was, of course, an immediate investigation."

I shivered. I saw Lombar's knuckles turn white.

Captain Roke went on. "It was found that a custom had arisen of sending cadets to Blito-P3 to do surveys and that sort of thing. That system is a fairly easy flight from here and good practice. In fact, there is nothing wrong with that. But cadets are cadets. They seemed to have been deterred by Space Code Article a-36-544 M Section B—which prohibits landing and alerting the population as you know—and their surveys were diffident. They showed no reliable, expected picture of the scene. Their reports were fragmentary and unconvincing."

I was really shaking then. Those reports for the last two years had been coming through my hands and had been deleted and altered! I felt like that whole vast hall was going to cave in on me! I had visions of all those Lords rising up and rushing at me, screaming accusations. But I will be truthful: when Lombar Hisst had first ordered it, I had not been aware that an expert could tell the reports did not make a consistent story, that the graphs would look jumpy and unconvincing. I hadn't even thought it was important to anyone.

But Captain Roke was going on. "So the Lord of the Fleet simply came to me and we ordered a routine survey by a competent combat engineer."

Ah! No wonder we had not been able to find the original! It had been ordered by the Crown and would have come straight to Palace City—and even Lombar Hisst couldn't get into that!

The King's Own Astrographer tapped the top sheet of the report. "The survey was accordingly made. And I greatly fear our worst fears were realized." He paused for emphasis, looking gravely around the vast board. *"The present inhabitants are wrecking the planet!* Even if they don't blow it up first, they will have rendered it useless and uninhabitable *long* before the invasion called for on our Timetable!"

A startled shock had gone around the whole vast table.

Lombar Hisst was gouging Endow's back urgently, giving him his cue.

"Captain . . . er . . . Captain," quavered Endow, trying his best to sound bold, "can we . . . ah . . . be sure that these conclusions are not that of some subordinate? Such an alarmist conclusion . . ."

"Lord Endow," said Captain Roke, "the combat engineer made no recommendations at all. He simply took measurements, samples and photographs." With a flick of his wrist, for all the world like a street magician, he snapped a chart that rolled out from the dais, across it and onto the floor, fifteen feet of tabulated observations. And then his voice bounced around the hall. "It was *I* who did the summary: it was *I* who made the conclusion! And every Fleet astrographer and geophysicist consulted concurred with it absolutely!"

Endow got another jab in the back and tried again. "And . . . er . . . oof . . . Could we inquire what there is in those observations that led experts to that opinion?"

"You may," said Captain Roke. He snapped the roll back to him like another magician's trick but there was only hard scientific certainty in his voice tones. As he looked at the top lines, he said, "Compared to the last reliable observations taken a third of a century ago, the oxygen in the oceans there has depleted 14 percent. This means a destruction of the hydrographic biosphere."

"I beg pardon?" said some Lord at the huge table.

Captain Roke abruptly realized he was not talking to a totally informed audience. "Hydrographic biosphere is that part of the planet's life band that lives in the oceans. Samples show pollution, possibly oil spills from these figures of increased petroleum molecules in ocean . . ."

"Petroleum?" called someone.

"The oil that forms when cataclysms bury living matter: under pressure, the remains become a source of carbon fuel. They pump it to the surface and burn it."

Lords and aides were looking at one another in consternation. Someone called, "You mean it's a fire culture? I thought you said it was thermonuclear."

"Please let me get on," said Captain Roke. He rattled the chart. "The industrial waste in the atmosphere measures now in excess of a trillion tons, well beyond the capacity of dead and living things now extant there to reabsorb."

"A thermonuclear fire culture," puzzled someone at the back of the hall.

Captain Roke plowed on. "The upper atmosphere hydrocarbon imbalance is critical and worsening. The sulfur content has grown excessive. The heat from their star is becoming progressively more trapped by the contaminated atmosphere. Their magnetic poles are wandering." He sensed his audience was impatient for him to get on with it. He laid aside the chart.

"What it means," said Captain Roke, putting his hands on the dais table and leaning toward them, "is a double threat to that planet. One: they are burning up their atmosphere oxygen at a rate that will cease to support life long before the planned date of our Invasion

Timetable. Two: the planet has glacial polar caps and the increase of surface temperature, combined with wandering polar caps, could melt these and cover the bulk of their continental areas with water, making the planet almost useless."

I felt even sicker. This was going to recoil on Section 451—me—like a firebomb.

I knew this meant the end, not only of myself but Endow, Lombar and the whole Apparatus.

I, too, felt like cursing Jettero Heller! This was the absolute end of everything we had planned—I mean that Lombar had planned. I could see no way out. None!

Chapter 8

When the full purport of what Captain Roke had concluded had been clarified for the Lords by their aides behind them, and when everyone in that vast, glittering hall fully understood that Roke was actually telling them that the whole Invasion Timetable was suddenly threatened, consternation rose up like a growing storm.

Lombar jabbed Endow ferociously in the back and the old Lord took a deep breath so he could yell loud enough to be heard above the babble. "Would the captain tell us if the combat engineer reported anything else?" Endow slumped back, exhausted with the effort and his nurse dabbed at his mouth with a cloth.

As this might be important, there was a dying down of the tumult. Roke looked at his reports, rattled some papers. Without looking up, he said, "Because he was, after all, a combat engineer, there *are* a couple of items he added on his own."

I could actually feel Lombar Hisst tense up. I, too, stopped breathing.

"The first one," said Roke, "is a fast survey of the planet's detection equipment." He looked closer at the report. "They are said to have electronic detection equipment for flying objects . . . here's the wavelengths and estimated ranges of it. They have a satellite communications system . . . here's the satellite count, range and extent with estimated traffic volumes." Roke turned a page. He smiled slightly. "The combat engineer said that when the signals were unscrambled, most of that traffic turned out to be home entertainment. There is no defense network to detect approaches from outer space and it is all easily avoided."

Lombar jabbed Endow and the old Lord said, "And the other item?"

Roke turned another page. "He said it seemed like a nice planet. And that it was a shame they weren't taking care of it."

"And that's all?" said Endow in response to a nudge from behind.

Roke glanced through the report again and then looked up. "Yes, that's all. Nothing else."

I could feel the tension ooze out of Lombar. He sat back. He almost laughed. This was what he had been waiting to hear. This was the turning point for him. He got brisk and whispered in Endow's ear.

Endow said, "The Crown, if you please. This conclusion the Royal Astrographer seems to have reached, without submitting the data first to authoritative divisions, is very grave and very alarming. It threatens the schedules, budgets, allocations, construction

projects, training programs and even the administration
sections of every division here!"

Lombar was proud of him. He even patted him on
the back.

The effect was immediate. Every Division around
that table went into instant turmoil. It was true: change
the invasion schedule and you changed the activities and
priorities of thousands of sections in a government as
vast and ponderous as Voltar's. To them it meant double,
triple work. It meant endless conferences, huge stacks of
revised plans, working late for weeks and confusion,
confusion, confusion. You didn't do things in a minute.
It took *time!*

Captain Roke was through and withdrew. The
Crown took over and cymbals clanged for quiet.

"Opinions," said the Crown, "are requested on the
feasibility of making an immediate and preemptive
strike on Blito-P3."

The Lord of the Army Division said, "We have no
available reserves. The entire matter would have to be
handled by Fleet and its marines."

The Lord of the Fleet said, "We have not replaced
the ship losses suffered in the Cliteus campaign. We
would have to withdraw from the Hombivinin War and
sacrifice many gains made there. The Fleet marines are
already below recruiting quota by thirty-nine million.
We must retain marine reserves because of the weakness
of the Domestic Police in handling the Prince Mortiiy
revolt in the Calabar System." An aide leaned forward
and whispered to him. "And," he added, "Tactical Command informs me that if the planetary forces of Blito-P3
have thermonuclear arms, they could panic at a space
invasion threat and blow the remaining oxygen cover off
their planet. This would worsen, not better your
problem."

I could almost hear Lombar purr.

The Diplomatic Division was called upon by the Crown. The Lord of the Diplomats said, "I could suggest a peace mission. The planet could be offered technical assistance in handling its planet preservation problems and then when the proper invasion date arrived we could go ahead and execute on schedule."

There were cries of "No" and "Never!" from various parts of the table and the Crown had to call for cymbals. Even that didn't quiet them.

"That's what began the cost overrun of the Hombivinin War!" shouted the Lord of the Profit Division.

"The Hombivinins panicked and evacuated their cities," seconded the Division of Propaganda, very cross. "You keep your peace missions out of this!" A couple of other Lords said, "Peace missions!" in scathing contempt.

The Crown had to set the cymbals going again just to be heard. "I would like to inform Your Lordships that His Majesty *does* require that you furnish a solution and *in this meeting!*"

That not-at-all-veiled threat brought silence.

Lombar eagerly punched Endow. "Now!" he whispered. "Now!"

"May it please the Crown," began Endow. "Although the resources of the Exterior Division are extremely overstrained, this matter could be properly placed in its capable hands."

The large hall was listening. I couldn't believe it. Somehow Lombar was going to pull this whole mess out of the mud!

"Without alarming or alerting Blito-P3," continued the well-coached Endow, "it is possible to infiltrate an agent into that population. This agent, carefully and competently handled by us, could 'leak' technical data into the normal channels of the planet. Data which would restrain their planetary pollution without improving their defense."

He certainly had the attention of every glittering luminary in that hall. The Crown nodded encouragingly.

Enormously emboldened, beautifully coached and secretly patted by an expansive Lombar Hisst, Endow plowed on. "There are simple solutions to the difficulties the planet is encountering. Planetary destruction could be arrested or retarded until the proper invasion date arrived."

There was an audible sigh of relief from the Lord of the Fleet and a "Go on, go on," from the Lord of the Army.

Lombar touched Endow's back. It was the signal for a change of tactic. Well timed. Endow suddenly became coy. "Of course, such a plan requires several years to execute. The agent would have to establish himself as one of *them;* he would have to be extremely careful. So it will take time and the Exterior Division would not want to be harassed every month by demanded reports when it was actually succeeding on a long-term project."

"Sounds good," muttered several Lords.

"It would require special appropriations," said Endow. "Insignificant amounts compared to a disastrous emergency campaign."

"How much?" demanded the Lord of the Profit Division.

Lombar whispered. Endow spoke. "Two or three million credits."

That, as much as anything, clinched it. It was such a paltry sum to them that it absolved Endow from trying to act just for the sake of personal graft. In their positions, given a chance like that, they would have invented anything and named a colossal sum. There would be little or nothing for Endow. The plan must, therefore, be totally valid.

"Well, well," said the Crown. "Your Lordships, do you approve this plan?"

There were no dissents.

"Very well," said the Crown. "I instruct the clerks to draw up the authority to entrust this matter to the discretion of the Exterior Division, time limits unspecified, three million credits allocated subject to readjustment. And I can report to His Majesty that a plan has been arrived at, agreed upon and is in motion."

A whistle of relief was heard throughout the hall.

We had done it!

My Gods, Lombar had pulled it out of the fire!

I honestly don't remember the rest of that Council meeting. I couldn't believe my head was back on my shoulders. I couldn't believe the Apparatus timetable was still intact. I couldn't believe Lombar's ambitions could now flower unimpeded. I was in a euphoric daze.

I didn't at all anticipate, when we left that glittering hall, that within twenty-four hours I would be in a pit of blackest despair.

PART TWO

Chapter 1

The following morning, I stood in the anteroom outside Lombar's fortress office in Spiteos, waiting for permission to enter. From the window of the crumbling tower, I could look far across the Great Desert to the green mountains at the back of Government City—two hundred miles of barren expanse, impossible to cross on foot.

Under a nearby hill, the Apparatus training camp sprawled, an ugly collection of ramshackle huts. "Camp Endurance" they called it in the directories: "Camp Kill" was what it was known by locally. It was supposed to give privation training to recruits, but actually it existed to excuse the sometimes heavy traffic to Spiteos and to serve as a reserve guard. The real complement of it was wholly made up of Apparatus guard thugs and the only recruits that ever got there were creatures not even the Apparatus could use—and they never left alive.

The towering, black basalt walls of Spiteos were supposed to have been erected by some long gone race that had inhabited the planet a hundred and fifty thousand years ago, a race that could only work stone and had perished in a single breath of guns in the first wave of the Voltar invasion.

The myth that the castle itself was still too radioactive to be used was continued by cunningly installed detector reply screens: when planetary surveillance beams hit them, they absorbed the incoming energy and sent back the wavelengths of radiation contamination.

There was no radiation. The wavelengths Spiteos really had came from the suffering depths below me where, a mile into the ground, packed in foul cages, thousands of political prisoners were moaning out the last of their lives. The definition of "political prisoner" was "someone who might get in the road of Apparatus plans." Some clerks had a joke definition: "Anybody Lombar Hisst doesn't like," but they only whispered it to closest friends and even that was unwise. I had once asked Lombar, when he was drunk, why he didn't just kill them and have done with it and he had replied with a knowing wink, "One never knows when they might come in handy—and besides, relatives have been known to cooperate." You could almost feel them through the rock.

It was hot.

A buzzer sawed through the air and a clerk jerked his head for me to go in.

Lombar's Spiteos office was at the top of some worn steps. It was the whole upper part of a rampart, carefully masked from the air. Gold coverings sagged on the walls, ancient battle scenes of incalculable value. Silver urns stood about. The furniture had been looted from a Royal tomb. Every single object in the vast room was factually beyond price, looted and extorted during Lombar's decades as head of the Apparatus. But somehow he had arranged them and used them in such a way that they seemed shabby. It was a "gift" Lombar had.

One whole wall was covered by a mirror and I was a little embarrassed now to see Lombar preening himself in front of it. He had had a gold cape made, emblazoned with Royal arms, and he wore it now, turning this way and that, looking at himself in the mirror. He finished and took it off, folding the fabric very carefully. He laid the cape away in a silver chest and spun the lock. As Your Lordship knows, it is the death penalty for a commoner to don a Royal cape.

"Sit down, sit down," said Lombar, waving to a chair. He was smiling and relaxed.

I *had* been feeling pretty good. Suddenly I was terrified!

The stinger lay neglected on a bench. He was being courteous, even jovial.

What did he want?

"Have a chank-pop," he said, and extended a gold box of them toward me.

I could feel my heart almost stop beating. My legs wouldn't hold me up and I sagged into the chair.

He shoved the box at me urgently and I managed to reach out and take a chank-pop and somehow get the top off. The lovely scent made a gentle explosion on my face, cooling it, waking me up.

Lombar settled on a broad, soft bench, still smiling. "Soltan," he began—and my terror soared; he had never before used my name and never, never would a superior use one's familiar name. I knew something awful lay in the instant future!

"Soltan," repeated Lombar in a fond tone of voice, "I have good news for you. A sort of a celebration present after our great win yesterday."

I couldn't breathe. I knew it was coming.

"As of this morning," said Lombar, "you are relieved from post as Section Chief of 451."

My Gods, I knew it. His next words would condemn me to the cells—after torture!

My face must have gone very white for he became all the more jovial. "No, no, no," he laughed. "Don't be afraid, Soltan. I have something much more interesting for you. And if you carry it out well, why, who knows, you might become Chief Executive of the Apparatus. Even Lord of the Exterior."

Ah, yes. I was very, very right. I *was* in trouble! Desperation made me find my voice. "After . . . after my slip-up?"

"Why, Soltan," said Lombar, "you couldn't have helped that. Heller's report went on entirely different channels, completely out of your hands, utterly beyond your possible reach."

He was right. With no copies made, I was never alerted and able to call upon the Shadow Section to help me retrieve the original report and replace it with my altered version. But that wasn't going to save me now!

He got off the bench and I thought he was going over for his stinger or maybe, worse, to push the buzzer for an arrest guard. But he just looked himself over in the mirror. "We needed that accident," he said, "to sort of jolt things together. The Grand Council has given us an order and we are going to fulfill it."

Lombar wandered back and patted me on the shoulder. I couldn't help flinching, it was so automatic. "Soltan, I am appointing you the handler of the special agent we are going to put on Blito-P3."

Now I understood. A handler runs an agent in the field, guides him, tells him what to do. Day by day, even hour by hour, a handler is responsible for everything that agent does. If anything goes wrong, the handler is routinely executed.

But a condemned man, especially a condemned man, tries to fight for his life. "But . . . but they only allocated three million credits to the whole project. One ship crash would wipe that out. . . ."

"Pish, pish," said Lombar. "Endow can run a three-million-credit allocation up to hundreds of millions. A little overrun here, a bit of teasing good news there, a threat somewhere else and any allocation can become a staggering fortune. No, you won't have any money troubles. None at all. Why, it would cost them trillions to stage a premature, off-schedule invasion. And one that would fail."

He wandered over to the mirror again. "I thought I was very clever, really. I anticipated the report. I pulled a vast potential allocation within reach. I have a means now of covering ten times the space traffic to Earth and no questions asked, no more dodging the detection screen here. Marvelous. All I have to tell them is that we're staying in communication with the special agent— and you, of course."

"You mean I'm going to Earth?" I said idiotically. That was obvious. You can't handle such an agent from Voltar. I was rattled. I had even overlooked the obvious demand for applause. "I was stunned by your clever recovery," I said lamely. "I couldn't believe our luck in getting out of it. It was all due to you."

That made him smile again. For a moment he had started to frown. So I got bold enough to say something else. "We . . . uh . . . we don't have any agents of that caliber."

"Oh, we have a few agents on Earth. You know that. I was thinking of giving you *two* of them—Raht and Terb—to help out. They're a couple of the finest killers I have ever seen! Now how's that? Feel better?"

I could see that execution order for a failed mission as plain as though I held it in my hand. Might as well make my fight now. "Chief Executive, neither one of them knows geophysics from soup. And I . . . well, I almost failed those courses at the Academy."

Lombar laughed. Very pleasantly. He was amused. This was certainly a different Lombar than I had ever known. "But you did take those courses. You know the big words. Soltan, you just have to get used to the idea that I am really your best friend."

Now I *was* for it. There was more. I knew there was more.

He extended the gold box to me again. "Have another chank-pop."

I could barely get the top off. But it was a good thing I did or what he said next would have otherwise made me faint.

"Have no qualms about the special agent. I have already decided upon him." He looked to see if he had my full attention. "His name is *Jettero Heller!*"

There was a long, long silence in the room while I strove to get my wits around it. For seconds I thought I was having delusions, hearing wrong names. But Lombar just stood there smiling.

"He's the ideal choice," said Lombar when I didn't comment. "The Grand Council will believe reports signed by him. I'm told he is very competent, in a stupid sort of way. He has no training as a spy. He knows nothing of how the Apparatus is organized or works. You and he are both Academy graduates and potential friends—you talk his language."

I got my wits working again. "But Jettero Heller is a bright engineer. He's been to a ton of postgraduate schools. He's way above my level. I'm all confused. If he has no spy training, if he knows nothing of the Apparatus . . ."

"Have another chank-pop," said Lombar, extending the box. And as I nervously took it, I knew there was more to the news.

"Ready?" said Lombar.

I stared at him fixedly.

"Mission Earth," said Lombar, "must be designed and run *to fail*."

I didn't get it.

"The last thing we want," said Lombar, "is an Earth invaded by and conquered by the present Voltarian government. We have our own plans of conquest for that planet. You know that and I know that. Ours will take place a long time before the official invasion. We are not the least bit interested in Blito-P3 having clean air. There are lots of planets. Blito-P3 has other uses and those uses will be made of it long before any oceans flood. For that matter, who the Devils cares about air?"

I was beginning to get it now. I also got that Lombar, coming from Staphotten, a planet which has a low oxygen level, cared little about air anyway.

Lombar laughed at my dawning comprehension. It must have been very obvious. "You see, you don't give me credit for being as bright as I am."

Cunning was the word for it, I thought. But I am ashamed to say that I replied, "Oh, yes I do."

"Oh, no you don't," said Lombar. "Jettero Heller must be set up to fall flat and the sooner the better. With Raht and Terb to assist and you to run it, that will be very easy to do."

I didn't quite like the compliment. He noticed it.

"You're going to have to be very clever," said Lombar, a little urgently. "Jettero Heller, (bleep) his looks and skill, will not be an easy person to fool. But you are going to make sure that he fails utterly, absolutely and quietly.

"His first reports," continued Lombar, "will be his actual reports. By that time, we will have his style. Then all you have to do is keep him from progressing or getting into mischief and we will send in 'Jettero Heller reports' to our heart's content, all forged."

One cloud remained. "He won't take our kidnapping of him lightly," I said. "He may refuse to cooperate."

"I'll admit the kidnapping looked like a mistake but really, it fits beautifully." He was getting into his tunic.

He went to the door and beckoned. "Come along and watch a master handle things."

So I followed to begin planning Mission Earth, the mission that was carefully designed to fail.

I felt horrible.

Chapter 2

Descending into the bowels of Spiteos was, to some, like taking a trip to the infernal regions that some religions promise to the damned.

But I had always regarded it on a par with entering a monstrous den of wild animals. So I lagged behind Lombar long enough to draw a blastick from the armory. The guards are themselves criminals; I was dressed in the common gray uniform of the General Services, without rank badges; I had no status in this place: one could not only be attacked by desperate inmates, one could also be struck down and robbed by guards.

We plummeted down the tubes, the noisome stench of the place already gagging me. We exited at negative level 501. The smell was awful: they sometimes do not dispose of the remains of prisoners who have died, leaving them in the cell until it is needed for someone else—or just pitching the newcomer in with them.

A long hall with moldy wire walls stretched out before us. Behind the highly charged mesh, a few sunken eyes peered at us. In the higher levels there were the

secret laboratories of the Apparatus, but here, in some of
the cages, were evidences of scientific work: deformed,
distorted shapes of abandoned experiments, still alive,
hideous, forgotten.

Lombar, black garbed in the uniform of a general,
strode along, twitching his stinger, looking neither to
right nor left, deaf to the moans and pleas which marked
our passage.

We turned a corner and came into a small room,
dimly lit with a green light-plate. At the far end of it was
an even stronger cage, not tall enough to stand in. Lombar threw a switch and the door swung open.

Jettero Heller was stretched at length upon a cold
stone ledge. In the dim light I could see that he still wore
the once white sport pants but someone had taken his
sweater and shoes. The stab wound of the paralysis dagger had not been tended and dried blood caked his
shoulder. His wrists were bound together with a pair of
electric cuffs, the kind that continually sting. There
were no eating dishes about so he probably had not been
fed—and how long had he been here? Four days?

My Gods, I thought, how could one ever expect him
to forgive such treatment?

One would have expected him to look degraded. But
not so. He was simply lying calmly on the stone ledge,
very relaxed and composed.

"Well, well," said Jettero Heller calmly. "The
'drunks' arrive at last." It was the Fleet's contemptuous
name for the Apparatus: our insignia was supposed to be
a club, a fat paddle with a handle upside-down. But the
Fleet chooses to believe it is a bottle. Therefore, they call
us "drunks," and this infuriates the Apparatus.

Lombar ordinarily would have struck out with an
insult. And I did see his eyes flash for a brief instant.

But Lombar had other things to do. He stood at the bottom of the ledge, bent over. He managed a cheerful smile.

"So far, so good," said Lombar.

Heller just lay there, looking at him coldly.

"This has been," said Lombar, "the beginning of a test."

Heller said nothing. He just looked at Lombar. It made one very uncomfortable. Too calm.

"It is necessary to see if you are up to passing standards," said Lombar, smiling. "You may find it uncomfortable, but we find it vital to pretest candidates for important jobs."

The gall of him, I thought. But it was a clever approach.

"Now, Soltan here," said Lombar, with a gesture toward me, "is going to complete the tests and we will know if you have the qualifications."

With that, he had the nerve to actually pat Heller on the ankle. For an instant, having seen Heller use his feet, I thought it might be a foolhardy thing to do. And then I saw that the ankles were electric cuffed to the stone.

With a reassuring smile, Lombar left the cage. He beckoned to me and, when we were out of earshot, said, "The rest is up to you. Invent something mild, tell him he passed and then give him this."

Lombar took from his pocket an official copy of the Grand Council order that authorized Mission Earth. He handed it to me. The place smelled horrible, the light was ghastly; the realization that he was dumping this on me and more, leaving me alone with Heller in the depths of Spiteos, made me feel very ill.

The Chief Executive of the Apparatus now began to revert to type. He didn't seize my lapels or hit me with the stinger. But he put his face very close to mine and his voice was deadly. "Do not arouse his suspicions! Do not let him escape!"

Oh, fine! Two contrary orders in one breath! The real order would be to somehow accomplish the impossible and get Heller's cooperation. But Lombar was gone.

I went back into the cage. My Gods, the place stank. I tried to smile as I knelt beside the ledge. Heller was just looking at me calmly, too calmly.

"First," I said, "could you tell me how you spotted that the orderly was a fake?"

He didn't answer. He just coolly looked at me. He must have been half-dead from hunger and thirst. The electric cuffs on his wrists and ankles must have been very painful.

"Come, come," I said, feeling like an idiot schoolmaster, "it is to your advantage to answer my questions. Then we will see if you have passed and things can be much more comfortable."

For a while he just continued to look at me. Then, with his words a trifle thick from the swelling of the tongue that goes along with thirst, he said, "From your accent, you're an Academy officer, aren't you?" He shook his head a little. "What sad route brought you to the 'drunks'?"

An unaccountable surge of rage hit me. Who was the prisoner here? Or wait, was he trying to forge and exploit a bond? Was he being arrogant and disdainful like Fleet officers do in the face of defeat?

My hand gripped the blastick hard enough to crush it. How dare he pity me?

My wits had been dispersed in all directions. This fellow was dangerous even to talk to. I carefully calmed myself. Indeed, who *was* the prisoner here? I looked at him very carefully and what I finally saw amazed me. He really wasn't thinking about himself. He wasn't thinking about the pain of electric cuffs or hunger or thirst. He actually felt sad that another being could fall as low as I. His question had nothing to do with himself at all! Only me.

I could have talked about myself. I could have said, "Sometimes one follows the wrong chart." I could have laid it all out for him and come to an honest understanding. How different it all might have been had I done so.

But there was Lombar like a black cloud in my sky. I wasn't courageous enough to be honest. In that moment I sealed the doom of an awful lot of people. A complete coward, I put a false smile on it. I repeated, "Come, come. Just tell me about the orderly."

He was silent for a bit. Then he said, "Why should I? You'll just improve your techniques on the next kidnapping."

"No, no," I said. "This is just a test of perceptions and reactions. Purely scholastic."

He shrugged. "When I came out the door and caught a whiff of him, I knew he was no Fleet orderly. In the close confines of a spaceship, a crew has been known to kill someone who never bathes or who uses scented powder. There are no smelly Fleet orderlies."

I had gotten out a notebook and was making silly notes to add to the illusion. "Very good. Keen sense of smell. Anything else?"

He looked at me, faintly amused. "His belt was upside-down, he had his spats on backwards and there was the bulge of a forbidden knife at the back of his neck."

"Ah, excellent," I said, pretending to write. And indeed it was excellent. I hadn't seen the knife bulge.

"But," said Jettero, "I flunked smelling the ozone that always comes from an electric whip even out of use and I did not hear your boss close the door behind me. So I flunk. I am not the fellow for your job."

"No, no, no," I said hastily. "That's for me to judge. Now let's get on with this. Why did you let that other player win?" I really wanted to know. It had puzzled me ever since I had seen it.

He looked at me as though wondering what sort of a monster I was. He didn't answer so I said, "Why did you throw the game away?"

In a very patient voice, the way one explains something to a child, he said, "His sweetheart was in the stands. She had come clear from his home planet to watch him play. If he had lost, it would have shamed him in front of her."

"Oh, wait," I said. "You tossed him some balls. You were mocking him. That was far worse than just defeating him."

"That is true," said Heller. "So I had no choice except to distract attention from him by stepping outside my ring and losing the game. If you were watching, you saw it work. He kept his pride and was not shamed."

I was astonished. I felt upset. Anyone in the Apparatus could tell you that it is utterly fatal not to win every time and in every place. Compassion is a fatal word! The dirtier one played, the better. And always to win, no matter what the cost to anyone.

This fellow would never make a spy. Never! Lords help him! And Lords help me as his handler!

"Great!" I cried, feeling as false as a prostitute. "You've passed with all tubes blasting! You're the very fellow for the job!"

Chapter 3

The light of the wire cage was bad, the stink was overpowering. I produced the copy of the order and with a flourish of fluttering seals, held it in front of his face.

"The Grand Council, no less," I said. "One of the most important missions of the year! And as you can see, it has been entrusted to the Exterior Division with complete autonomy and discretion." I made the paper snap importantly.

As he made no response, I summoned up the brightest voice I could in that horrible place and said, "We *had* to have the best in Voltar and we have chosen *you!*"

If this quickened any ambition in him, it was not detectable.

"I think," he said, "that you had better get me my watch."

I had no idea why a watch had anything to do with it. I had to get a guard anyway to get the electric cuffs off. So I went to a wall installation and hit the buzzer.

After a while, a wrinkled cripple showed up and looked at me uncertainly. "Remove the electric cuffs from this prisoner," I ordered. "And bring some food and water. Also, bring back his possessions."

Muttering that he had to get the circuit combinations, the sorry excuse for a guard limped off.

We waited and after a while the wreck came back with a metal card, a water jug and some filthy looking meal in a rusty can. I stood back, alert, while the cripple fumbled around with the card and finally removed the

wrist and ankle cuffs. He put the food and water down
on the filthy floor and limped off.

"Wait," I said. "Where are the prisoner's possessions?"

The guard just drew further off, saying in an
annoyed whine, "I'm off duty now. You'll have to buzz
for the next guard."

Heller was sitting up. He was cautiously sipping at
the water jug, not taking too much, letting the swelling
of his tongue go down. I buzzed again, cross that the first
guard wouldn't even tell the next one the message.

After a lapse of half an hour or more and several
buzzes sent, a huge, overbearing Calabarian came into
the room. "What's all the row here?" he demanded
angrily. "Buzz, buzz, buzz! Nobody can rest!"

I had backed up, blastick ready. This fellow weighed
at least three hundred pounds and his naked torso was
a mass of knife scars. He had a face from a nightmare.

"Get this prisoner's possessions. A sweater, a pair of
shoes and a watch." I turned to Heller and he nodded
that that was all.

"And what service are you?" demanded the huge
guard. "How do I know who you are? You ain't wearing
no Apparatus uniform!"

"I'll make it worth your while," I said, acutely aware
of being a mile deep and at the mercy of these thugs.

The monster seemed to nod as though that was what
he had been waiting to hear. He disappeared.

Heller diffidently ate a little bit of the food. He
washed it down with another swallow of water.

I twitched the Grand Council order in my hand.
"This is a great opportunity," I said coaxingly.

Heller shook his head. "Wait."

After a long time the big guard came back. He had
a new, shallow cut under one eye. He threw the shoes on

the floor in front of Heller and slapped the sweater, now very filthy, at Heller's face. "He wasn't wearing no watch when he came in," he said.

I looked at Heller. "You wouldn't be wearing a watch in a game of bullet ball," I said.

"A friend was holding it," said Jettero. "He gave it back when I left the floor. These apes took it."

"Get his watch," I told the guard. "No watch, no pay."

He snarled to himself and went off again.

The water and food were helping. Jettero stood up and I was very alert, gripping the blastick. But he just exercised his limbs a bit. Then he sat down and used a sleeve of the sweater and some of the water to sponge out the shoes: somebody else had been wearing them, they were filthy.

After a long time the huge guard came back. He had a new bruise on the side of his mouth and his knuckles were skinned. But he was holding the watch.

I had never seen a space engineer's watch before. I took it to make sure it contained no trick weapons: life in the Apparatus makes one suspicious. But it was just a big, round dial with a small hole in its face and a heavy metal band. I handed it over to Jettero. He nodded that this was it and began to put it on.

"The pay," said the guard.

I took a ten-credit note from my pocket, a pretty big sum for a guard in Spiteos.

The guard looked at it like it had kicked him. "Ten!" he snarled. "I had to pay sixty credits to redeem that watch!"

He made a lunge at Jettero to grab it back.

I snatched at the monster's shoulder to spin him off course. It flung him backwards and he reared up and tripped on his own feet. He hit the side of the wire cage and went down on his knees.

He was absolutely frothing!

"I'll murder you!" he screamed, starting to lunge.

I raised the blastick to kill him.

Abruptly, my blastick went spinning!

There was a blur. Heller's right wrist caught the guard across the throat with a strike that lifted him clean off the floor!

The monster hit the wall with a thud!

He crumpled down like a disjointed doll. He was bleeding from the mouth, out cold.

Jettero picked up the blastick, put its safety catch on and handed it to me. "Never kill a fellow when you don't have to," he said quietly.

He inspected the guard. "He's still alive. Give me seventy credits." And he held out his hand to me.

Numbly, I fished out sixty more credits and added the ten from the floor. Jettero took them from me. Kneeling by the guard, he tapped the cheeks until the fellow started to come around.

Jettero held the seventy credits in front of the monster. "Here's your money. Thank you for the watch." And then it was the cold, not-to-be-disputed voice of a Fleet officer, unmistakable. "Now return to your post and that's the end of it."

The guard heard it. He took the money and walked off as quietly as though he had just looked in for a casual call. Indeed, that *was* the end of it.

"Now let's look at that alleged document," said Heller.

Chapter 4

Jettero Heller took the Grand Council order over to the green glowplate. His back was slightly to me and I couldn't quite see what he was doing. It must have something to do with his watch.

"It seems authentic enough," he said.

I kept a mild smile on my face but I shuddered inside. It did happen to be authentic but only by comparing it to the listings on the planetary file circuit could one really know. The Apparatus could forge documents like that in minutes. He was absolutely hopeless as a spy.

"But it was issued 4.7 days after I was kidnapped," he said.

I peered at the document again, over his shoulder. Yes, it was hour dated. No great trick. "We had to know we could get the right special agent before we dared undertake the task," I lied smoothly.

"Look," said Heller. "This place is pretty awful. Can't we go somewhere else to discuss this?"

"As soon as you've decided to undertake it," I said.

"Ah. Do I smell blackmail amongst all these other stinks?"

"No, no," I said quickly. "It is just that some . . . ah . . . forces don't want the mission to succeed." That was no lie. "So I am charged with keeping you safe." Pretty brilliant of me, I thought. He wasn't going to be hard to handle. An utter child where espionage was concerned.

"Blito-P3. I just came from there. Surveyed the place."

"Precisely," I said, "and with all your other accomplishments that was why you were the exact and only officer for the job."

"So you kidnapped me." The wry smile showed he thought the whole thing fishy. "Maybe you better tell me about this so-called mission."

So I told him, keeping it very simple. He was to go to Earth and infiltrate some technology into their culture and preserve the planet. The way I put it, it sounded quite noble and altruistic. A Fleet officer would never know about Invasion Timetables so I omitted that.

"And you considered the best way to begin this was to stage a kidnapping?" said Heller.

"We had to test you to see if you could stand up to the demands of being an agent," I reminded him.

"So you got the order before you knew I had passed."

(Bleep)! He could think! But so could I at this game. You don't live a decade around undercover work without learning the tricks. You don't and stay alive, that is.

"We would have been put to the extreme trouble of finding another volunteer," I said blandly.

"And the trouble of kidnapping him," added Heller. Then he put up his hand to stop the interchange. "I'll tell you what I will do. I am not part of your Division. If you can obtain the usual orders from the Fleet Personnel Officer, I will undertake your mission."

The specter of Lombar moved a bit away from me. I wanted to laugh with relief. But I said, "Oh, I think we can manage that all right."

With a sweeping bow and hand flourish, I indicated he could precede me through the door.

I had to sign the prisoner out in the lower guardroom and as we entered, the monster Heller had struck down was sitting with the rest, eating some loathsome stew. I was nervous in this place and when the beast made a sudden movement, I flinched back. And then I saw something astonishing.

The huge guard stood up so swiftly he almost knocked over his food pan. He came to rigid attention and crossed his arms on his chest in the formal military salute!

It was not intended for me. Heller casually lifted his hand in the usual reply and flashed a faint but friendly smile. The beast grinned back!

I had never seen a Spiteos guard salute or smile before. I felt eerie, like one would feel if he saw a wraith actually appear in a woods temple: something you see that you know can't happen—supernatural. I hurriedly zipped my name across the log plate and got out of there with the prisoner.

In the upper levels of Spiteos there are some rooms set aside for Apparatus officers such as I. Very plain and windowless, they nevertheless have a few comforts including baths. I used mine very seldom but it had the necessary personal things.

Technically speaking, I would be removing him from the prison by taking him to my room but I thought Lombar's last orders would provide for it.

Just to make sure *both* the contradictory orders were covered, I parked the prisoner in a niche beside the lift tubes and, out of his hearing, made a call to Camp Endurance. The troops there were actual Apparatus troops. I got hold of an officer and arranged for a platoon and around-the-clock surveillance of my room and surrounding passages. I gave explicit orders they were to appear to be guarding against intrusion upon the prisoner while actually preventing his escape. I used Lombar's name to drive it home and by delaying our progress upward, they had time to post the area.

We entered the barren room. I opened a drawer and

offered Heller a chank-pop—anything to take the stench of the prison away. It even leaked into these rooms. But Heller shook his head.

"What I need is a bath," he said.

I waved my hand at the wall tub, opened a closet and got out a flimsy sleeping robe. He shed his shoes and pants and I dumped them, with the sweater, into the disposal unit—they were beyond salvage.

As he started the spray going, I had a sudden thought. "You know," I said, popping a chank-pop under my own nose, "you could have made a run for it when you picked up that blastick. You were armed, I was defenseless. You could have used me as a hostage. . . ."

He laughed. He had a very pleasant, easy laugh. After a bit, scrubbing away, he said, "And fight through electric gates, armed guards, mined shafts and blastgun perimeters? And then fight through Camp Endurance and stumble across two hundred miles of the Great Desert? Utter folly. Foolhardy beyond belief. I'm certain the Apparatus would never permit anyone to leave Spiteos alive!"

I was shocked. He could not possibly know where he was. We had passed no windows, no signs. He had been unconscious when he arrived. He might have even been on another planet. And no one, but no one outside the Apparatus knew Spiteos, that ancient landmark, was in use!

"My Gods, how could you possibly know?"

He laughed again, scrubbing away. "My watch. It runs on twenty-six different time bands as well as Universal Absolute Time."

That didn't tell me anything. "And . . . ?" I prompted.

"It gives the time lag between here and Palace City and it gives the direction. There's only one geophysical feature at that distance from Palace City and that's Spiteos." I didn't laugh. I was getting sad. "Any other way?" I asked.

That really amused him. "This rock. Every ·vall of the place is 'in-place' country rock. Black basalt with a sixteen degree dip and a strike of 214°, Type 13 granularity. Look at it. It's the remains of a volcanic extrusion that built the mountains beyond the Great Desert. Elementary geology for the planet Voltar. Any schoolboy knows that. I knew where I was when I came to. The watch just confirmed it."

Well, I was one schoolboy that didn't know it. "Strike" was the compass direction. He must have intuitive compass sense. "Dip" is easy: that's the angle into the ground. But to be able to classify rock by its visual granular structure—and without a complex analyzer—meant he had eyes like a microscope and in the comparative dark of that cell! *And* he must have a memory like a library!

But that wasn't what was making me sad. Here he was, for all he knew, in the hands of enemies just using him, and he was letting *me know* that *he knew* where he was. And he was exposing vital abilities which, had they stayed hidden, might have lulled me into a false sense of security. Now I could take precautions against these things. For a spy, all that is not just dumb, it is *stupid* beyond belief. Using what he had just incautiously revealed, I could lock him up forever and he'd never know where he was!

He'd never make a special agent. Not in a million, million years. I was not going to have trouble making him fail. I was going to have trouble keeping him afloat long enough not to drag *me* down. Spying takes an instinct. Oh my, he didn't have it! This wasn't going to be a failed mission. This was going to be a total catastrophe!

"Make yourself at home," I said. "I'm going to Government City to get your orders."

Chapter 5

I am sure you have noticed that the first impression a visitor gets of the Fleet Administration Complex in Government City is that he has just encountered an actual fleet in outer space. When somebody said "buildings," their architects must have thought "ships." It is most annoying: there they are, spotted around ten square miles of otherwise barren land, like ten thousand huge, silver ships. They're even in formation! They say the officers and clerks even wear spaceboots! And not a shrub or tree to be seen anywhere!

When I have to fly there, I always feel like I'm an invader having to be repelled. Marines, marines, marines, gates, gates, gates, all built like atmosphere ports. Passes, passes, passes. It just occurred to me that maybe I don't like the place because they always look at my identification plates, see I'm from the Apparatus and sneer. But after two hours I finally got where I was trying to go.

The Fleet Personnel Officer was sitting in a cubicle for all the world like a storeroom on a battleship. The walls were solid, deck to overhead, with machines and screens, dazzling with their flashing, multicolored lights. You'd think he was fighting a battle—and maybe he was, with four million Fleet officers to shift around.

He was probably a nice enough fellow: a bit old, a bit fat. He looked up as though to greet me cheerfully but he didn't. He frowned a trifle instead. There was just a trace of wondering disapproval in his voice. "You're from the 'drunks'?"

Now, nobody had announced me as anything but "An officer from Exterior Division," and I was wearing the noncommittal gray uniform of General Services, not even a pocket patch. I involuntarily looked down at myself. How could he tell? I saw no grease spots, no food stains, no old blood. But I also saw no style, no flair. No pride! Shabby!

I had had it all rehearsed but his remark disconcerted me. "I want transfer orders for Combat Engineer Jettero Heller," I blurted out. No gradual briefing, no persuasion.

The Fleet Personnel Officer frowned heavily. "Jettero Heller?" Then he repeated the name to himself. He had buttons and flashing lights all over the place but here he was depending on memory. "Oh, Jet!" He had it now. "The Royal Academy driving champion a few years ago. And wasn't he later a runner-up for interplanetary bullet ball? Yes. Ah, yes, Jettero Heller. Great athlete."

All this was very promising for he seemed to have mellowed. I was just opening my mouth to push my request again when he suddenly frowned.

"You'll have to get clearance from the Admiralty of Combat Engineers. That's Course 99. Just outside that door, you turn . . ."

"Please," I said. I had already been to that Admiralty and they had sent me here. Desperately, I dived into my paper case and snapped out the Grand Council order. "This supersedes all clearances. Please transfer him to the Exterior Division."

He looked the order all over though I'm sure he had seen hundreds of them before. He peered at me very suspiciously. Then he slapped his palm down on an array of switches, one after the other; he dithered around with his button console, transferring the Grand Council order number into his information network. Then he sat looking at a screen I couldn't see. He frowned heavily. I half expected some marines to suddenly rush in and arrest me.

With total finality he slapped his board shut. "No, can't possibly do it."

Lombar's shadow loomed closer. "What's the matter?" I quavered. "Has the Grand Council order been cancelled?"

"No, no, no," he said impatiently. "The order is in the data bank, all authentic—though I must say, you never can tell when you're dealing with the 'drunks'." He dismissed all that and sat there frowning. Finally he tossed the Grand Council order back at me. "It's just impossible, that's all."

Bureaucracy! Actually, I sighed with relief. When one is a member of the Apparatus, *real* trouble is always a close companion. But bureaucracy is trouble everybody has. It's a system evolved so that nobody in it is ever responsible for anything. "Why can't it be done?"

Like explaining shoes to a child, he said, "In the first place, a combat engineer is in the Fleet. The Exterior Division—and I still think you're from the 'drunks' —is an entirely different division of the government. When you say you want him transferred, you're saying that he would have to resign from the Fleet, make application for commission in the Exterior Division, come up through their ranks . . . it would take years! I'm sure you don't have years. And you have *not* brought his resignation from the Fleet. So it can't be done."

For a moment I wondered if Heller had known all this—that he had known it was this complicated and was using a cunning out. Maybe he was cleverer than I had given him credit for. (Looking back on it now, I wish he had been!)

But the best authorities on bureaucracy are the bureaucrats. So I myself got clever. "If you had this problem I've got," I said, "how would *you* handle it?" That was a lot better than going back to the Apparatus and finding some blackmail on this fellow—there always is some and if it doesn't exist, one makes it up and "documents" it. But an order illegally obtained by coercion might, itself, be illegal. It was much more clever to do it straight. Novel, but it might work.

He thought for a while, really being helpful. He brightened. "Ah! I could just give you a standard set of orders for a combat engineer."

And (bleep) him, he simply pushed some buttons and a couple seconds later a form came out of a slot. He handed it to me. It said:

FLEET ORDER M-93872654-MM-93872655-CE
REFERENCE: GRAND COUNCIL ORDER
938362537-451BP3
KNOW ALL
JETTERO HELLER GRADE X COMBAT
ENGINEER SERIAL E555MXP IS HEREBY AND
HEREWITH AS OF THIS DATE ORDERED TO
INDEPENDENT DUTY ON HIS OWN
COGNIZANCE TERMINATING
ON HIS OWN COGNIZANCE.
ENDORSEMENT: SEE REFERENCE.
ISSUED, AUTHENTICATED AND VERIFIED BY
THE FLEET PERSONNEL OFFICER _____

Brightly, he said, "That all right?"

"Kind of sweeping," I said.

"Oh," he said, "combat engineers are always ordered out that way: mostly blasting away behind enemy lines, you know; who can tell how long it will take them. That's why they have to be such reliable people. They almost always, unless they're killed, carry through whatever you set them at. Their corps motto, you know, is 'Whatever the odds, to Hells with them, get the job done.' Remarkable people. Will those orders do? They're a standard combat engineer form, you know."

I was shaken, both by the idiot simplicity of the orders and by what he had just said. Had Lombar known any of this? I doubted it. What were we biting off? Could we chew it?

Jettero Heller had known what the orders would say. He must have received dozens of them. He must have known that this would really put him outside the control of the Exterior Division and the Apparatus. By the evil Gods, I was going to have to work like mad to keep him on a leash! I began to doubt I could execute *my* orders and make the mission fail.

I got a grip on myself. It's one thing to go blasting in with the burners wide open and blow up an enemy town. But it was quite another to operate in the dark and secret world of espionage. I thought of the ease with which we'd kidnapped him, I remembered his total stupidity that morning, I thought of his fatal notions of sportsmanship.

"Yes," I said. "They're fine. By all means sign it." I handed over my own identoplate so he could authenticate it and feed his hungry machines. "I'd like some extra copies."

He punched and scribbled away. "I think Jet's Academy track record still stands. Great athlete. Nice fellow, too, they say." And finally, "Here's his orders. Wish him good luck."

I got out of there. It felt odd to have done a straight, legal piece of work, no twists. The honest world is a strange place for a member of the Apparatus. It leaves one feeling confused. Unfamiliar territory!

And then, clear of the oppressive environment of the Fleet, I felt a belated surge of triumph. By the wording of these orders, Jettero Heller could be wiped forever from Fleet rolls. He could be made to disappear without a trace and no questions asked. No, Jettero Heller was *not* smart in the dirty world of espionage and covert technology. In fact, (bleeping) dumb. Lombar would be proud of me. I had just wiped out the kidnapping. We could wipe out Heller. And I freely confess that at that moment I fully intended to drain off all the personal credit from it I could.

I headed for the Fleet Officers' Club to pick up his kit.

Chapter 6

My elation was *very* short-lived.

The officers' club lay quietly in the warm daylight of a beautiful afternoon. The mountains around it gazed down benignly. Shrubs and flowers perfumed the gentle air.

It was a trap!

My driver parked the airbus before the main

entrance. I trotted up the wide ramp with its inset views of beautiful females.

The huge lobby was deserted except for one uniformed cleaner casually mopping up some spilled drinks. I went directly to the office counter and rapped my stick upon it. I am not a member, of course, and the gray-headed clerk, probably a retired enlisted man, went on pottering with his entry books.

My gray General Services uniform was not likely to get much attention in this place. So I slapped my stick even harder against the counter. "Here, here, snap to attention," I said. He just went on working, I thought he must be deaf. And it was there I made my near-fatal error. I can't stand insolent underlings.

"If you cannot give me some service," I yelled at him, "I shall have no choice but to report you!" No attention. So I shouted even louder, "I am here to pick up the baggage of Jettero Heller!"

That got attention. He got right up, came right over. I thought for a moment that that was more like it. But he had his head down and was lifting his eyes at me in a peculiar way. In a voice fully as loud as I had used— and believe me these old spacemen can be heard a mile—he bawled, "Did you say you were here for the baggage of Jettero Heller?" And without the slightest pause, went right on. "You look like you are from the 'drunks'!"

There was a slight noise in the lobby. I looked around. The equipment of the uniformed cleaner was still on the floor but the cleaner himself was gone.

In a perfectly normal quiet voice, the clerk said, "Please fill out this form." He fiddled around under the counter and came up with some forms. He read some titles of them to himself. Bent down to look for some more. Brought those up and looked over their titles. My success so far this day must have curdled my wits.

Despite all my training and experience in the Apparatus
I did not recognize the routine ploy of just plain stalling.

It was the breathing that alerted me. It was behind
me.

I whirled.

Three young officers were standing there! One was
in a bathrobe, another in swimming trunks, a third in
a sport driver's helmet. And even as I faced them, five
more officers came speeding in through various doors.
That (bleeped) cleaner was rounding them up!

I have seen glaring faces in my time but these
topped it. Another young officer rushed down some
stairs, carrying a sports club!

The biggest of them, three feet from me, barked a
command, "Get him!"

They train you well in the Apparatus. In an instant, I
wasn't there to get! I sprang up and back to the top of
the counter. I threw the register straight in the first face!

I was over the counter, behind it, driven by the hur-
ricane of roaring fury from those young officers. Arms
clawed for me. I threw a chair!

They came over the counter like a tidal wave.

A door on the right. I rushed through it. I was back
into the main lobby. I measured my chances to get out
the main entrance. But more officers were pouring in
from the sports field!

I will say this. I fought a valiant strategic withdrawal. I pitched plates and tables at them. I raced
around chairs and spilled them in their way. I even threw
vases, flowers and all! I only lasted as long as I did
because there were so many trying to catch me! They col-
lided with one another. They were boxing me in. I tried
to leap up on the bandstand but with one final, flying
tackle a husky athlete brought me down with a crash.

Now you'd have thought they would have simply

held me there and asked questions like young, well-bred people should. But oh, no! They put their boots to me! They were mostly barefooted or wearing sports shoes: otherwise they would have kicked me to death!

Finally one of them got the others away. He was a big one and for a stupid instant I thought he was trying to rescue me. But he stood me up and slammed me back against the wall.

"Where is Heller?" he shouted. It was enough to knock in your eardrums.

I didn't get any chance to answer. He doubled up his fist and hit me as hard as he could in the jaw!

It knocked me out cold.

Icy water hit me in the face. I was on the floor.

"Let me!" yelled somebody and *he* picked me up and stood me against the wall.

"Where is Heller?" he screamed at me.

And before I could answer, he hauled off and hit me as hard as he could in the stomach.

I remember thinking as I doubled up and dropped that these young gentlemen could certainly use some lessons in proper prisoner interrogation.

They booted me!

I don't know how much later it was. I heard a voice from far off. It was a command voice. Some senior officer amongst officers. "Order! Order! What's he done?"

There was a babble of voices. They had stopped hitting me and kicking me long enough so that I was coming around.

"Put him in that chair," said this senior command voice.

They slammed me into it so hard I went out again. Then a new shower of icy water hit me. Through its drip I focused my eyes on a powder blue tunic that was in front of me. It was an older officer in full uniform. Probably a Fleet battleship commander. Very tough.

"No, no, back off," he was saying. "I'll get your answers."

I groggily thanked the Devils that somebody was maybe going to listen.

"Where's Heller?" he barked.

And nobody hit me. They teach you in the Apparatus never to talk when you're being beaten or tortured.

The question took some sorting out. I could be executed by the Apparatus for revealing the existence of Spiteos. But they weren't demanding that. They were demanding Heller. I managed to edge around the corner of my training. "I just came to get his baggage," I said.

"We know," said the senior officer. "That's what started all this. Now if you will just tell these young gentlemen where Jettero Heller is, I am sure that life will be . . ."

There were disputant voices. "Don't promise him anything, sir!" "You better talk!" Things like that.

In my groggy state, the tried and true maxim of the Apparatus surged up: "When in doubt, lie."

"I'm just a messenger," I said.

A tumult of objection greeted that.

The senior officer silenced them. "Messenger," and there was sarcasm in his voice, "Jettero Heller disappeared about five days ago tonight. He was due at a party to celebrate the promotion of a classmate just one hour after that evening's game. He never showed up. He is very reliable, in fact he is a combat engineer. An orderly was sent to summon him. A check of all headquarters shows no one sent for him. Ten minutes after he went out the arena door, a parking attendant reported seeing black lorries leave the far end of the grounds."

Wow, I thought to myself, this battleship captain or whatever he was certainly could use some lessons in being an interrogator. He was giving me everything they knew! I was also getting plenty of time to think. Made it as easy as opening up a chank-pop.

"Fleet police have been looking everywhere for him for five days," this uneducated officer went on.

Spiteos was safe. The Apparatus was safe. The mission was safe. What amateurs these spacers were after all!

"Well, they can stop looking," I said. And I was very glad to have found out about it. It was almost worth the beating to be able to turn it off. "Jettero Heller was needed for urgent consultation on a matter of the Grand Council."

It didn't stop them. But it slowed them down. There were some "yah-yahs" of disbelief. Somebody had a smart idea and dived at me and while another held me, my identoplate was taken from my pocket.

"Section 451 of the Apparatus!" It was a yelp of triumph. It was followed with "I-knew-its," "Drunks!" and snarls. And they would have attacked again but I had the situation now.

So what if the mission was confidential. "You don't want that identoplate," I said coolly. "You want the orders in my paper case. It must be over around the counter. Unfortunately, if you open the case, I will have to swear you all to secrecy. But that's all right. Go ahead."

They still didn't believe me. They found the case—pretty badly smashed it was, too. They brought it over for me to unlock. I rattled off the oath of state secrecy and they all said yes. I opened the case and threw them the Grand Council order and the personnel order of Jettero Heller.

The senior officer read them. Some bright spark from Fleet Intelligence held up his hand to halt any further action, took the two orders and went to the switchboard.

He came back, lips curled in disgust. "The first time anything connected with the 'drunks' was ever straight. They're authentic. We'll have to let him go." Thank the Gods I'd gone to Fleet personnel before I came to this den of young lepertiges! The magic of a written order. Regardless of what chicanery lay under it. That was the way they ran their lives.

"I came," I said demurely, "to pick up his baggage."

The (bleeping) fools thought their friend was safe!

Chapter 7

Jettero Heller's room apparently lay at the end of a long passageway on the top floor. The hotel manager had shown up, an old spacer with a totally bald head who, judging from burn scars on his face, was a retired gunner. Behind us trooped several of the young officers, led by the biggest one who had done the most beating: they were coming along "just in case." I really wanted a chance to ransack through his things and find some weaknesses and personal flaws to aid in handling him.

"I think," I said, "that he'll be giving up his room. This mission is going to take a while. I'll be packing up all his possessions."

The manager didn't even glance at me but I could see a reaction. It reminded me I was not wholly out of this place yet. We arrived at the last door and he threw it open. He threw it *wide* open. So I could look.

I'd expected, of course, just a little cubicle, the standard officer's room. What I saw stopped me dead!

It was a suite! *Three* spacious rooms stretched out, and way over at the far end of the last one there were big doors and a garden terrace that overlooked the mountains!

A junior officer's quarters? Oh, no. There was many an admiral who had no such quarters as this!

I went sort of numb. Spacers always tend to bring the look of a ship down to the planet surface. They also have lots of time in space and are given to making things out of whatever is handy: a blastgun breech carved into a wood nymph, a piece of armor shield made into a table, a control seat made into a chair, an acceleration couch converted to a settee, spare porthole casings made into picture frames, that sort of thing. And they were all here, of course, but beautifully done.

One expects the souvenirs from many a planet: the toy muscle-dancing girl that swings her hips as she hands you a bottle opener, the polished shell of a sea animal that glitters but says on it Memories of Bactose, the little boy with six arms who waves flags and spells out Come Home to Erapin, the carved woman that opens an inlaid box and throws you a chank-pop when you say "Kiss me, Serafin!" They were all here along with the banners and wreaths but they were all absolute top of their line: exquisite!

The gleaming metal floors were strewn with rugs from a dozen planets, each one a collector's item.

And the whole place harmonized together with beautiful taste.

Wow! There was many a Lord who would have envied this layout!

I at once thought I had Jettero's fracture point: I doubted he was wealthy in his own right and no Grade X junior officer could ever afford a thousandth of this on

Fleet pay. Jettero must have both hands in the appropriations take, right up to the elbows!

We stepped over to a musical bar in the first room and the old gunner indicated the whole suite with a sweep of his hand. Like a tourist guide, monotonously, he said, "Five years ago the battleship *Menuchenken* crashed a thousand miles inside enemy lines on the planet Flinnup. It was hopeless: the ship's drives were disabled, three thousand officers and crew faced capture and execution. Jettero Heller penetrated the Flinnup defenses with vital spare parts, got the drives operating, pried the *Menuchenken* out of a caldron of fire and brought her out."

He paused. "When the *Menuchenken* crew was released from the hospital, they came here." He moved his hand slowly to indicate the rooms. "They did this while Jettero was out on another mission. As a gift."

He indicated the walls and a few of the fittings. "It has been added to since by others. If his present mission took a hundred years, this would still be here. It's a showplace of the club! And it's Jettero's home."

Oh, well, I thought. So he wasn't a crook. But people have other fracture points. "I better pick up the few things he will need."

"Don't let him touch anything," said the big, tough officer. "We'll do any packing."

They jostled me aside and opened an invisible door, displaying a vast closet of clothes and personal gear. One of the officers lifted a dress uniform off the rack and brought it out.

"No, no," I said. "He'll be under cover. No uniforms. Just personal necessities. He's travelling light."

They shrugged and began to gather those up. But they had dropped the dress uniform close to me and I looked at it. It was red-piped, of course, and had the gold

"Ten" for his grade woven into the stand-up collar. Now most civilians think that the wavy gold, silver and copper lines that ornament the chest of some dress uniforms are just that: ornaments. They wonder sometimes why some junior officer looks like a metal mine on parade and some seniors look so plain. The fact is, those thick, wavy lines of braid are citations; they are sewn in such a way that the top flap can be lifted and under it, in tiny letters, is the citation itself.

Jettero Heller's dress uniform breast had neither silver nor copper braid. It was an almost solid mass of gold!

I lifted some of the flaps: building a bridge under severe enemy fire; mining the orbit of Banfochon III; rebuilding the destroyed control center of Hemmerthon under enemy barrage; recovery of the derelict *Genmaid;* sabotage of the Rollofan transport system; mining the fortress of *Montrail* . . . On and on! I had to look at several more before I even found the battleship *Menuchenken.* Jettero Heller's few years of service had been active ones even for a combat engineer. Behind each one of those brief entries would lie a whole lurid scene of close shaves and violent battle.

I told myself how it must have happened: fellow gets a reputation and they keep drafting him when the odds look hopeless. And in times of perpetual war, there were lots of these. Then my estimate was soured by noting that what they call the "Volunteer Star"—a blaze of diamonds with a ruby center—was tucked with its ribbon inside the jacket. They award that for fifty perilous volunteers. They didn't keep drafting him—he kept volunteering!

I thought I had it then: a glory hound. That was his fracture. If I could play on that . . .

"He has a lot of other citations and awards," said the old gunner-manager. "Some of them are so valuable we keep them in the big vault. He never wears them."

So he wasn't a glory hound. Oh, well, there were other faults he might have that I could exploit. I wandered off to look at the walls.

He had a lot of pictures of people. I don't know why portraitists always insist on cloud-sky backgrounds: when you see one of these three-dimensional color shots against a sky it makes it look like a little bust parked in the heavens; gives it a religious note as though everyone was being made into a Goddess or Godlet. I don't like them; they make the viewer feel like he's in the sky, too, and I don't care for that.

There was an older woman with a gentle smile, evidently his mother. There was a tough old hawk of a man in a shabby business tunic: it was inscribed "To my dear son." And then there was one of . . . I stopped dead. I was looking at the most beautiful female I have ever seen in my life. It was one of these trick portraits where the bust follows you with its eyes and when you lower your head it just looks sweet but when you raise it, the lips smile. Honest, this beauty took your breath away! Wow!

I had it now. This was the handle! I turned toward the gunner-manager.

"That's his sister," said this hope-shattering fiend. "She's a star on the Homeview circuit. You must have seen her."

I hadn't. We are too busy in the Apparatus for self-indulgence like art. I wandered off to an assembled collection of press photos, all in their fake porthole frames. Jettero with classmates; Jettero being carried on the shoulders of some crew; Jettero finishing a bullet ball tournament; Jettero being introduced at a banquet; Jettero pulling a basketload of survivors into a ship. On and on. But before I could conclude I had a publicity freak on my hands, I noticed that the little *other* faces in the pictures were circled and their names written under the circles: they were a gallery of his *friends*, not Jettero. (Bleep), but you can't succeed with just a few tries.

But there *was* one of Jettero alone! It was full color, three-dimensional and gorgeous. He was sitting in the seat of a ship: it was one of these knife-edged racing craft they use in space—the kind that blow up if you just look at them.

"That's the *Chun-chu*," said the gunner-manager. "She broke the Academy interplanetary speed record and it's never been bettered since. Jet loved that ship. It's down in the Fleet museum and Jet's always telling them it will still fly. But you'd have to get an order from the Lord of the Fleet just to move its position on the museum floor. They won't let Jet go near it so he keeps this picture of it."

They had a bag packed. It had taken them time because they'd argued amongst themselves about "Jet would want this" and "not want that."

I was glad to get out of there. For all my prying and hopes, I had really learned nothing useful, nothing that I could use, that is. To handle someone, from an Apparatus viewpoint, you have to have his flaws. And all people have flaws. I told myself I'd keep looking.

We went on downstairs (they call them "ladders" in the club, which is silly because they're twenty feet wide) and I was about to walk out of the lobby when I found my way blocked.

The biggest, ugliest young officer I have ever seen before or since, stood squarely in the middle of the doorway. And he had the toughest, nastiest expression on his face I never want to see again.

" 'Drunk,' " he said. "I just want you to know that if any of this is crooked, if Jet is *not* all right, if anything happens to him, we have your identocopies and we have your photo. And remember what I say," and he spoke in an even, grating voice that leaves the nerves scraped, "we will take you personally ten thousand miles up into cold, empty space; we will remove your clothes; we will push you out the airlock into vacuum. And in seconds you will be a *pale, pink mist!*" The last three words were punctuated with hard, firm taps on my chest.

"Right!" It was a roar! It was behind me! And I turned to find that about two hundred young officers were there in a sullen mob.

I am not all that brave. It scared me.

I got by the brute and ran down the steps with the bag. The airbus was there and I dived in.

With shock I saw my driver, Ske, was soaking wet. They must have thrown him in the nearby fountain.

He took off nearly vertical and fast. His hands were clenched and shaking on the controls. He could see me in his rear screen.

"It looks like they really put you through the grinder," he said. And it's true, I must have looked like quite a mess with cuts clotted up and bruises beginning to swell.

He drove for a bit, guiding us into the diversionary course so we could head, undetected, for Spiteos. Then Ske said, "Officer Gris, how could they possibly have known we was from the Apparatus?"

I didn't answer. Because we're shabby, I thought. Because we're dishonest. Because we're just crooked thugs and never should be permitted to go near decent people. Because we stink. It had been a very trying day.

"Officer Gris," said the driver when he had the airbus scooting above the floor of the Great Desert, "if you had just told me they would know we was from the Apparatus, I could have brung a blasthoser and wiped the (bleepards) out."

Oh, fine, I thought. That was all this mission would need: two or three hundred dead Royal officers and an Apparatus Secondary Executive standing there amongst the charred remains. Maybe I belonged in another Division!

But you don't transfer out of the Apparatus—you leave it feet first, stone-dead.

I had no slightest choice except to carry out this mission to its violent, brutal end! And succeed.

Chapter 8

Lombar, seated in a king's chair looted from some Royal tomb, looked agitated.

We were in his tower office at Spiteos, watching the weekly "freak parade." The whole wall of glass at the office end had refraction index switches: it could be a mirror, it could be a black wall and it could be so set that we could see out but nobody could see in. It was set the last way now. Beyond it, completing the width of the rampart, was a vast, stone-walled room.

Doctor Crobe was showing off the week's production of himself and his assistants and horrible enough it was. They made freaks and the Apparatus got a good price for the products.

Just now was a being that had feet for hands and walked on all fours with a skipping gait. It was comical, really. Especially the way it stamped after each skip. Until recently it had been a normal man. But Doctor Crobe had changed that.

Factually, the doctor was a very skilled cellologist. He had been a member of a government department— Section for Special Adaptions—that specialized in retailoring people for unique duties or habitations: harmless enough, making them see better on dark planets, walk better on heavy gravity planets, breathe under water on planets dominated by sea. But Doctor Crobe had a twist in his own skull and he perverted the technology of cellular alteration to making freaks—real abominations. The government got some protests and a senior, who might very well have been a party to it, blamed it all on Crobe. The doctor vanished from his Domestic Police cell, thanks to Lombar, and was put to work, with a staff, at making freaks for the Apparatus.

The organization, well-connected with the criminal underworld, sold them to circuses, theaters and nightclubs for fantastic prices. They were billed as denizens of newly conquered planets, which, of course, was nonsense, but the publics of the 110 worlds of the Voltarian Confederacy ate it up.

Some, of course, actually were prisoners of war, which made it quasi-legal as such prisoners have no rights and are often slaughtered off. But there never were such beings anywhere except out of the vials and tubes and vats of Doctor Crobe. As some wit in the Apparatus had said, "The evil Gods invented Doctor Crobe to give the Devils some competition."

There must have been some truth in it. These freak parades always made me ill. Here was a woman with her breasts where her buttocks should have been; there was a being whose legs had been interchanged with his arms; then came a female with two heads; following was a thing covered wholly with hair but in half a dozen colors; and then came a monster with eyes in the place of his privates.

While Apparatus guards drove them along with whips, old Doctor Crobe, himself, stood beyond them, looking on, beaming at his handiwork. He was a funny-looking creature himself: too long a nose, too long in the arms and legs, like some weird bird. In my opinion, every cellologist I have met is not only misshapen himself but crazy.

Lombar seemed to be quite agitated. He was fiddling with his stinger, probably to hide the shaking of his hands. He didn't seem to be paying much attention to the freak parade and so I ventured to give him some good news, thinking it would divert him.

"It's all handled now," I said, "but they had the whole Domestic Police out looking for Jettero Heller. I got a line on it and iced it and now they couldn't care less."

He didn't answer but then he never does. But after a little he tapped a silver box beside him and pincers sprang out holding something. He took it.

"I knew you felt bad about losing your post," he said idly. "So I arranged this." He threw it sideways at me.

It was the gold chain and emerald insignia of a Grade Eleven Officer! It bumped me up *three* grades! It made me the equivalent of an Army commander of five thousand troops!

"It's now in the data banks and legal. You'll be drawing the pay as of yesterday."

I started to thank him but he wasn't listening. "That ought to bring some money," he said.

The guards had rolled a cart into the parade. Six children had been cellularly joined together so they made a ring, twisted up into pornographic positions.

The Apparatus got tons of appropriations in secret government channels but its income must be five times that in its criminal sidelines. And true, they would get a lot of money for the six children freak, probably bill it from Blito-P3 or Helvinin-P6, maybe get a hundred thousand credits.

It reminded me I had other news. "We really ought to train this Jettero Heller up in espionage," I said. Lombar sort of twitched at the name but he didn't look at me nor stop me. The "trained act" parade was about to begin but there was a lull while Crobe's staff cleared off and the next lot came on. I took advantage of the time.

"They put a lot of correspondence in his bag," I said. "A letter from his mother, notes from friends, fan mail. He spent the whole evening answering them—it was quite a stack.

"Of course, when he gave them to me to mail for him, I read his answers very carefully. And, Chief, he has no faintest idea of security. He simply spilled his brains all over the paper. Really *stupid!*

"I had to get two forgers and we spent until 2:00 A.M. rewriting his letters.

"He'll *never* make a spy, *never!* He'll put the whole mission at risk!"

Lombar didn't say anything. The one we called Countess Krak was on now behind the glass. She was standing there in thigh-high black boots, a shabby coat and little else, twitching a long electric whip. In a dull and listless way she was bringing on the first performer of her trained act parade. She was actually a very beautiful female, statuesque, young, but she never smiled. She was an enigma even for the Apparatus. Approach her sexually and you could get *killed!* But she could train anything to do anything and *fast*. She was a genius at training. She was rumored to use electric shock and pictures but how she got her results nobody really knew.

Countess Krak had been a perfectly unsuspected government teacher, specializing in adult classes and advanced subjects. But she had a twist. There are some who say it was actually being done by the government and she just got the blame, and maybe that is true, but I think personally she just needed more money.

When the Domestic Police ran her down, she was the center of a ring of children she had recruited from the slums. These children had been taught to crack any safe and get by any alarm system. It was estimated that their total "take" was in the millions. And they might have been going yet except that she also apparently had schooled them in the techniques of silent murder with no weapons and this hallmarked their every job.

The children involved were executed but Countess Krak was simply handed over quietly to the Apparatus for their own uses. And here she had been at Spiteos for almost three years.

Her first act was a juggler who, with his feet, kept twelve objects in the air at once while spitting fire at them. The second act was two females in lepertige costumes who jetted loops of a liquid, that looked like blood, into fancy patterns in the air and appeared to catch them in their mouths. Colorful.

The third act was a fellow who could triple-somersault from a standing position and explode ban-goes at each loop. He had other tricks.

There was no danger that any of these people would ever betray Spiteos. Their tongues had been cut out and they were illiterate. They brought fancy money.

But Lombar was not paying much attention. He turned to me. "Soltan," he said, "I really don't think you actually envision the real scope of this."

He shoved the stinger at some switches and a big screen on the floor in front of us began to roll off views of the hundred and ten planets of Voltar. Near views, far

views. Mobs in streets. Industries. Plains geometric with
farms. Plains teeming with animals.

Lombar, ignoring the remaining acts, hit another
switch. Views of the manors of Lords. Views of Gover-
nors' palaces. Views of the Summer Imperial Residence.
And then a long string of views of Emperors.

"Power," said Lombar. "Authority! The right of life
and death over trillions of peoples." He shut the machine
off. He turned to me. "In not too long a time, Soltan,
all that will be ours. Ours completely and utterly! *These
are big stakes!*

"The present rulers are decadent. Our planning and
timetable cannot fail."

He gestured at me with the stinger. "But there is one
weak point in all this. And that weak point is *Earth.*"

He put his hand on my knee. "That is the key, the
important key to everything. Soltan, when an instant
invasion of Blito-P3 seemed imminent, I almost died. It
would have been the end of everything.

"Soltan, you weren't raised in the slums. You don't
know what a dream of power can be. You don't understand the true necessity of wiping out the riffraff from
the ghettos, purifying the blood of planets, sweeping
away the weak.

"These Emperors do not know what to do with their
power. It takes ambition! Yes! And merciless execution of
plans. They diddle with their wars, they do nothing
about their own homes! Even when they conquer a planet
they do not know what to do with the riffraff in the
population!

"We use evil to fight and sweep away evil! And we
can and *will* prevail!" For a moment his eyes flared.
There was madness in Lombar and sometimes it showed
through.

He patted my knee. "But I am counting on you,

Soltan. There must be no Imperial interference on Blito-P3. We care nothing for the salvage of that planet! But we need it desperately. You *must* keep every Voltarian interest in it nullified! Do you understand?"

He waited for no answer. The trained acts were through. He stabbed the stinger at a console. Flashing call lights went on in the other room. The glass wall turned black.

Doctor Crobe and Countess Krak came hurrying in through the anteroom and stood inside the door. They didn't expect any applause. They never got any.

"Crobe," said Lombar. "I've got a job for you. We have a special agent going to Blito-P3 and I want you to fix him up." Crobe rubbed his hands and rubbed his nose. He liked this.

"Krak," said Lombar, "we have this special agent to train for Blito-P3. Language."

There was something in their attitude, some eagerness or enthusiasm that hit Lombar Hisst in the wrong place. He was suddenly on his feet and across that room like a reptile.

He grabbed Crobe by the coat and snapped his face within an inch of his own. "And (bleep) you, no tricks! No fancy eyes that see through walls! No fingers that become pistols! No telepathic brain receivers!" He had hit Crobe in the leg with each separate order. "Just an average job!" And again he hit Crobe in the leg. He heaved him away.

Lombar turned to Countess Krak. "And as for you, you perverted whore," he snapped her within an inch of him, "off the high tower you go if you teach this agent one single word, one single trick of espionage!"

He slammed her against the wall so hard she bounced.

Then in a perfectly mild voice, Lombar said,

"Officer Gris will tell you what to do. I don't want to hear any more about it. Get out!"

Lombar went back to his chair and took a chank-pop. "Gods, they stink!" he said as he sprayed his face and nose. Then, relieved, he waved a hand to the door.

"Get on with it, Soltan. I don't want to hear another word concerning it or Jettero Heller. He's yours now."

As I left, he was moving toward the chest where he kept the Royal robe.

PART THREE

Chapter 1

At the end of a long, black corridor of Spiteos, going toward my quarters, I thought I heard voices.

I looked quickly about: there should be guardsmen stationed around here. I couldn't see any! The possibility of Heller having escaped shot me full of panic! I could visualize my own body being tossed off the highest tower!

Voices! I paced quickly forward, silently. They got louder. My Gods, they were coming through the closed door of my room!

I halted. I could not make them out. I took a long breath and with a textbook police entrance, I yanked the door open and leaped inside, off to the left, too fast to be shot.

Jettero Heller and the platoon commandant were sitting at the table!

They were eating sweetbuns and drinking sparklewater. Heller was reading the morning newssheet and laughing about some item. There was a new Homeviewer on a wall shelf that had never been there before and a diddleband was playing some goofy tune.

The secret guards that were supposed to be there weren't outside and here sat their commander taking refreshment with his prisoner! What a homey scene!

I knew right then what Lombar was up against trying to work with the Apparatus. Here was a prisoner, supposedly tightly guarded and incommunicado, completely unguarded and provided with the latest news!

The platoon commander must have read it on my face. He sprang back so suddenly his chair went flying! He came to a terrified attention and crossed his arms in an *X* on his breast, eyes straight ahead but glazed with fear.

"Oh, let him finish his sweetbun," said Heller with an easy laugh. "He and I have just had a peace conference and we're celebrating. I let him and his men know where I am at all times and they bring me the necessities of life from the Camp Endurance canteen. Amity prevails."

But the officer knew what he might be facing from me even though he must also understand I would say nothing in front of Heller. He bolted out of the room like a hunted game animal.

Heller tapped the newssheet. "I see that the mysteriously missing Jettero Heller has been found and is now vanished again on a secret mission for the Grand Council." It amused him. And I could see it on the paper, front page, photos of Heller and all. I could read, "FAMED COMBAT ENGINEER . . ." (Bleep) those reporters! Well, we didn't control all the press—not yet!

Heller had tossed the newssheet down and was looking at me brightly. "Hello, hello, hello," he said. "What's this?" He got out of his chair to come over to me. "Been promoted, I see. Grade Eleven no less!"

Suddenly I realized why Lombar had promoted me. It made me one rank higher than Heller, easier to control him.

But if Heller had recognized that I was now his senior, he certainly didn't show it. Grades Ten and Eleven are still relatively low and there is even a saying in the services, "Seniority amongst junior officers is like virtue amongst whores."

He came over and pumped my hands. "Hearty

congratulations. I am sure it was well deserved."
Sarcasm? I looked closely. No, just the expected cliché of
the officer corps.

"This means," said Heller, with mock solemnity,
"that you owe me a dinner in the first nightclub we
encounter!" Ah, yes. Traditions of the Royal services.
When one gets promoted, every other officer he meets
on the first day is owed a dinner in the nearest nightclub
at his expense. It's costly and a lot of fellows just go hide
that first day.

He took the gold chain off me. He went over to the
brightest glowplate and held the emeralds close to his
eye, turning them this way and that. "Uhuh!" he said
interestedly. "You'll be glad to know they are real
emeralds." He kept turning them and looking. "These
three at the top of the number are just faintly off-color.
But," and he tapped it, "this bottom one is a truly valuable stone. It's from the South Vose diggings. The flaw
helps refraction. Lovely green. Remarkable!"

Heller came back over to me and hung the chain
around my neck and pumped my hands again, smiling,
really glad to see me promoted. Then he went back to
the table. "Have some sparklewater? There's plenty more
in your cupboard now."

I finally grasped what had happened. Those
(bleeped) junior officers at the club had put a roll of
money in that bag they had packed for him. I'd glanced
through it but it must have been hidden in an athletic
suit or something. I felt a chill. What more had I missed?

Casually I strolled around the far side of the table.
He was sitting down now. He was wearing a shiny white,
thin flying suit and a pair of ankle-high hull boots. I let
my eyes drift over him without appearing to search.
Then I saw it: a short blastick, the 800-kilovolt type that
would tear a wall apart. They are about six inches long

and he had it shoved just inside the top of his right boot.

I went over to a mirror, pretending to inspect some of my face patches that obscured the damage suffered at the club. I could watch him in the mirror. From the litter of papers and canisters he picked up a short red rod. Another weapon! I planned exactly which way I would dodge, how I would dive at him.

"They put this whizzer in my bag," said Heller, holding it up. "They must have thought I was in trouble. You ever see one of these?" And he tossed it to me!

I fumblingly caught it. "They're quite recent," he continued in an interested voice. "You hold them carefully by the bottom ring and they send up a flare you can see for five thousand miles! Fact. Blow your hand off if you aren't careful."

He was finishing off his canister of sparklewater. "They sent a blastick and a thousand credits: must have taken up a collection. But I've got a lot of money on account at the club and the manager will pay them back."

I felt a surge of contempt. The dumb fool. With a thousand credits he could have literally bought his way out of Spiteos and if he had had any sense he could have *blown* his way out with that blastick. And here he was laying it all in the open. And he hadn't even guessed what was in store for him. On the subject of intrigue he didn't have two brain cells to click together. What a stupid (bleepard)!

Watching him cheerfully sipping sparklewater and idly skimming the sports page, my contempt began to be tinged with pity.

"We've got lots to do today," I said. "You've got two appointments, one with the Countess Krak and the other with Doctor Crobe."

"Hey, look at this!" and his nose was buried in the sports page. "Timbo-chok just beat Laugher Girl in a five lap free-for-all at Mombo Track! Well, well! That Laugher Girl was the fastest car at Mombo. Who'd have thought it possible? Let's see, here, who was driving . . . ?"

Chapter 2

The interior of ancient Spiteos is a labyrinth of windowless, black stone. Above ground level it is mainly a deserted hulk but huge with rooms and vaults and tunnelled passageways. The original inhabitants of the planet believed in fortress security—but it had availed them not at all when our forefathers came.

When we left the room, we were already pressed for time. I had to make a stop at the armory—to get a dummy-loaded, dud blastick to secretly exchange for the one he was now carrying. And Countess Krak was notorious for not wanting to be kept waiting: her reaction to anyone being late could be deadly.

Accordingly, I was not pleased at all when Jettero Heller insisted on walking. I supposed he wanted the exercise—athletes are a trifle loony on the subject—and, obedient to my orders not to arouse his suspicions, I had to acquiesce. So we avoided the first stage of tubes and began a wandering course through the upper reaches of Spiteos, a badly lit stroll through endless mazes of dust.

He was wearing the hull boots. Now, these boots have peculiar soles: they alternate bars of powerful magnets with ridges of a coarse fiber. To walk on a metal wall or deck, the magnet bars are left down—and they are very handy in weightless space and could undoubtedly save your life. But when walking on stone or nonmagnetic surfaces, one simply clicks one's heels together in a certain way and the magnets draw up, leaving one walking on the rough fiber ridges.

But Jettero Heller was walking on stone floors and steps and he had left the magnets *down!* Clickety-clack, clatter, clatter! Loud! He sounded like a tank!

It got on my nerves. All he had to do was click his heels and the magnets would draw up and leave him walking silently.

In espionage one has to cultivate a soft tread. A good agent practices and prides himself on being able to walk with total silence on anything, even gravel. The success of a mission—yes, and even his life—may depend on how silently he can move about.

Heller was not only walking with the subtlety of a tank column, but every ten or fifteen paces he would do a little extra skip, a real loud snap of metal on stone. Deafening!

He seemed much interested in the walls themselves and now and then would rap them with a ring he wore. "These ancients sure could build," he commented many times.

So clickety-clack, clank, we toured the long passages, wandered through huge, deserted halls and banged our way down filthy steps.

The dust was irritating to my nose and I sneezed repeatedly. I was getting a little tired—I am not one to do much exercising. "Look," I said, "we're going to be late and the Countess is going to rip our heads off. Surely you've had enough exercise for the day."

"Oh, I'm sorry," he said. "It's all just so interesting. Did you know these ancients had no metal tools? Nobody knows how they fashioned these chambers or even how they got rid of the rubble. We couldn't do it today unless we used disintegrators. Do you realize there are no seams? No joints. All just hollowed out with no decent tools."

He clatter-clanked on for a while. "I wonder why the Voltarians thought they had to wipe those ancients out. They couldn't have been much of a menace."

Oh, I thought, you and Lombar will never get along. Unless one wipes out the riffraff and excess baggage, one gets an awful lot of problems—problems like we have now. If we let every conquered people live, we would have even more trouble than we've got. Yes, I could imagine an argument between Lombar and Heller. It would end in a dead Heller! I'd better keep them separated if I was ever to get this Heller to Blito-P3!

Praise the Gods, we finally got to the armory. Heller walked on down the passage a ways, examining walls. I stepped up to the armory counterdoor and matched my identoplate to the lock. It swung open.

The old cretin that was custodian of the place came hobbling up to the counter, scowling and hostile. We don't get along. "What are you bothering me for today?" he rasped.

In the Apparatus we have a sign language we do when there's a chance of being overheard. Giving the armory clerk some nonsense cover talk, and with my back to Heller, I signalled for an 800-kilovolt blastick, specifying a dummy load. It was not much trouble for the old cretin—they ship blasticks with a dud cartridge in the chamber to protect the firing electrodes—but you'd thought I was asking for a battleship, the way he frowned and snarled. All he had to do was walk ten feet to a shelf and pick one off it, open it to be sure it had a dummy cartridge in it, hand it over and push my identoplate on the receipt. He did and slammed the upper

door in my face. I had also wanted a stungun but his
action seemed too final.

Heller was feeling the wall from high up to floor
level. "Aha!" he said. "Ground level."

It was my opening. I was about to do something that,
had he been trained in espionage, he would have been
alert to.

"How do you know?" I challenged.

"Half a degree," he said. "Temperature difference.
The outside ground is right about here, just below waist
level."

"Half a degree?" I scoffed. "Nobody can tell half a
degree of temperature with his *hand*."

"Can't you?" he said, seeming much surprised.
"The outside, at this time of day, is in sunlight; these
walls are about three feet thick at this level. But the con-
duction of heat up here," and he reached way up, "is half
a degree above floor level."

I knew he would do it, the fool. He reached for my
hand and made me pat the wall up high and then put
my palm against a point close to the floor. "It's a matter
of training," he said.

Yes, a matter of training. Naturally, I was overbal-
anced by the way he moved my hand; I stumbled against
him. Using my other hand with an expert smoothness,
all in a split second, I eased his blastick out of his boot
top, shook the dud duplicate out of my sleeve and into
the boot. I straightened up and, in doing so, put the live
blastick in my breast pocket. He was now "armed" with
a dud weapon. The pickpockets of the Apparatus are
excellent teachers.

"I couldn't tell the difference," I said, "but then
you're the expert at such things. Come along, we're late.
The Countess will be furious!"

"All right," he said. "But just a moment. Let me finish this."

I had no idea of what he was talking about. He put out his foot and for a moment of heart failure I thought he had detected the weapons switch. But no. He gave the floor a single hard kick. The magnet bars went CLANK! Then he clicked his heels together in the action that makes the metal draw up above the fiber ridges. Praise the Gods, that would be the end of all his clanking.

But we didn't move on. With a gesture that further detained me, he drew out a large sheet of paper and one of those constant-flow engineer pens. He put the paper on a smooth wall spot and began to draw.

His hand was moving so fast it was just a blur. I had never seen an engineer doing a field sketch before; I realized why their pens had to flow such volume. But I was too impatient to be very impressed.

In a few moments, he flipped the paper at me and put the pen away.

I was looking at a complete, fully measured sketch of the above-ground interior of Spiteos! The distances, floor heights and now, even the ground level were marked in! And it was all beautifully done, almost as good as you get from a draftsman after a week of work.

"Give it to your boss," said Heller. "I doubt it's ever been surveyed before. Archeological curiosity."

"Hey," I said, "how can you be so sure of these measurements? You didn't have any tape?"

"Echo-sounding," he said and lifted his foot. "Sound travels at a certain speed. When you make a sound where you are, you can mark the length of time it takes to echo back . . ."

"Nobody can measure fractions of seconds that fast," I protested, annoyed.

"Maybe not, but my watch can."

Then I realized that while he was sketching, his watch had been close to his ear; it must have recorded and converted every one of those louder skip-pops he'd made.

Marvelous enough. Highly skilled. But it annoyed the Devils out of me. He was clever, true, to map the place. He could have used it to sabotage the fortress or escape. But after all that work, he had simply tossed it at me and told me to give it "to the boss," not only giving himself away but also threatening trouble for myself!

He simply did not belong in this game. He understood nothing whatever about internal politics either.

"Just a minute," he said. And he stepped close to me. "One of those false-skin patches has come loose." He reached to my face and adjusted it. "Whoever put you through the grinder did a pretty good job of it. Does that hurt?"

I seethed inwardly. "Nobody put me through the grinder," I lied automatically. "It was an airbus collision."

"First time I ever knew an airbus had knuckles," he laughed. "You ought to enter that vehicle in the planetary fisticuffs tournament." He adjusted another false-skin patch. "Was it your boss?"

I might have felt angry but I didn't. The thought of Lombar being handed this sketch of Spiteos came back. What if this Heller took a notion to survey the *below-*ground levels of this secret fortress? The labyrinth which penetrated a mile deep! The fifty thousand more or less falsely imprisoned souls in their cages, the unburied dead! The torture chambers! He'd seen a tiny portion of what lay below but not . . .

With a wave of apprehension I wondered if Heller had noticed the passageway to the *hangar,* the below-ground parking place that held Lombar's personal warship, specially equipped, illegally armed with enough firepower to blow Voltar's defenses into dust.

Had he seen that some of the rooms we had passed through were fully readied *storerooms?* Ledges cleaned and waiting for their priceless "goods"? Empty enough just now, but within a few months . . .

Oh, if Lombar knew I'd been letting Heller survey this, he would not use knuckles!

The pain of another false-skin patch being moved jolted me out of it. "No!" I yelled, "Lombar didn't hit me!" I shoved Heller violently away from me.

"I'm sorry I hurt you. The patches were coming off with your sweat." And he did look contrite. "It's been a long, hot walk."

But that wasn't what was making me sweat. It was realizing I'd been criminally negligent in not grasping that he had been surveying and knowing what *that* could bring down upon me.

Heller was so stupid, so without guile. I very much began to doubt I'd get him off this planet before he fouled up utterly. He could get us *both* killed!

And thinking of being killed reminded me we had kept the Countess waiting for over an hour. And you weren't late when you had an instruction appointment with the Countess Krak. Not if you wanted to survive, that is.

I pushed him down the passageway toward the training rooms. Being Heller's handler was enough to reduce life expectancy just from worry alone!

Chapter 3

I opened the huge armored door to the training area and started to step inside.

I was hit with a wall of sound!

The first hall is a huge place of platforms and machines, full of shadows and dim recesses.

The hall resounded with a curling, snapping, vicious sound! I tried to back up and get out but Heller was behind me coming in and he closed the door after him.

When sound is too violent, it brings the illusion one is also being blinded and it took a moment to see what lay before me.

An electric whip was making the racket. It was also flashing and leaving its sizzling curls of viciousness imprinted in the air.

Five ugly brutes of the Apparatus, not of Spiteos, dressed in black work uniforms, were twisting and dodging and running this way and that, trying to escape that whip!

Squarely in the middle of the great hall was the Countess Krak! Even as I looked, she brought the roaring whip far back and struck with it again, her jackboot hitting the stone floor like a cannon shot in her forward lunge, her pale hair flying like a thousand lashes.

The whip laid a scorching welt across the face of the nearest. He writhed back. They weren't attacking her, they were trying to escape. They were pleading and blubbering and one of them on the floor was screaming.

It was an odd scene in that the five were not members of her section. They were part of the Apparatus exterior transport teams that brought freight to Spiteos. I looked around in the bad light, trying to understand what was going on. Just inside the escalator ramp, there was an enormous wild animal shipping case. Its front slides were up.

The training areas always stank but I could detect, above the usual smell, the acrid tang of some beast. With a mounting premonition, I looked around hastily. Was there a wild animal in here? Where was it?

I caught a flick of movement not fifteen feet to my right. There in the darkness, beside the instructor's desk, eyes glowed!

It was a lepertige!

Instantly, I tried to get the Hells out of there!

But Heller had closed the door behind us and was standing there, gazing into the room, blocking the way!

I didn't want to show panic. I fingered the blastick I had exchanged. Eight hundred kilovolts might just barely stop a lepertige.

Once my eyes weren't being blinded by the flashing whip, I could see the beast more plainly. It was sitting there, all nine hundred pounds of it, unfettered, perfectly free to demolish everyone in the place. Its black and orange mottled fur was matted. The fangs looked like daggers. There were drops of scarlet blood, *fresh* scarlet blood around its lower jaw. Good Gods, had the Countess just fed somebody to it?

Fascinated with the blood, I eased to the side a trifle, the better to see. Did it have a corpse in front of it? No, no corpse, but there was blood.

It moved and I flinched. But it had only lowered its

head. It was licking its front paws! They were bleeding! Then I knew what had happened.

Once in a long time, they capture a lepertige for exhibit. There had been a very few that had been trained to perform in cage acts, the trainer never going inside, for these lepertiges can tear someone's head off with one swipe of a paw. But as a precaution, every trained one I had ever seen in shows had had its claws pulled out. Somebody in the last few days had yanked its claws.

Yes, there was a trail of blood from the open shipping case to the platform. When it had started to move again, the gaping wounds had bled.

It lifted its head. The eyes, as big as dinner plates, are luminous. Some say they can see in pitch black night. It was, thank the Devils, paying no attention to me. It was looking at the chaos that was going on in the middle of the hall.

The worst of the whipping was that the Countess Krak was showing not one slightest, faintest trace of emotion. That was the most chilling thing about her. She was never angry, never sad, she never smiled. And for all the emotion she showed in whipping these exterior Apparatus brutes, she might just as well have been eating dinner.

There was no way to get away from her. When they sought to hide behind the electric machines or boxes she used the whip to drag them back into the open and struck them anew.

Four were down now. Prostrate. The fifth sought refuge in the animal box. The whip snaked around his legs and he was hauled into the open. The lash sizzled again and struck. I saw then that it must be set at lowest intensity—the most vicious setting that hurts the worst. The fellow screamed and tried to curl into himself on the floor.

They were all down now.

The Countess Krak stood up, straight and tall amongst them. No emotion. She was not even breathing hard.

She kicked the foreman of the transport crew in the side. He cringed, scuttling sideways on the floor.

In a totally emotionless voice she said, "When you get back to base, give this message to your boss: tell him that if he ever again sends me a maimed animal, I will train one to find him and kill him and turn it loose. Understand the message. Never maim an animal and expect I will accept it. You are still alive. Take your crew and get out of here!"

The foreman booted his roustabouts to their feet and without a single glance at her they fled down the escalator, leaving only charred bits of their uniforms behind them.

The Countess Krak took a pocket call disc from her shabby coat and said something into it. Then she threw the electric whip in the general direction of the whip rack on the other side of the room.

With no change of expression whatever, she walked at a normal pace straight at that wild, freshly captured lepertige!

She pointed her finger at it. It sat and looked at her. With one snap it could have taken off her arm. But she just pointed with one hand at its face and then put out her other hand, palm up.

It lifted its maimed paw and laid all thirty or so pounds of it on her extended palm! She looked at the wounds left when the claws had been pulled out by the roots.

Her own crew was pouring out of a side door. They were the usual fortress scum, greasy, filthy, stripped to the waist, a dozen of them. They stayed *way* back. They were not going to go near a lepertige, no indeed.

The Countess Krak put down the paw. Her finger was still pointing at the beast's face and she moved to one side of it. With her other hand she pointed at the box.

With a funny moan, the lepertige stood up on all fours. It was a bit taller than her shoulder. It began to limp across the room. With one finger pointing at it and the other at the case, she went along with the beast. It got into the box.

Instantly her crew was all motion. They slammed the front of the box shut. It was already on a dolly and they were ready to move it but had their eyes fixed on her for instructions.

"Put him in a warm cage," she said in an even voice. "Get one of Crobe's assistants to make a culture and, if possible, regrow those claws. And none of you tease that animal as it will now be even harder to train. Do you understand?"

The mangy crew bobbed their heads emphatically. She snapped her fingers and they sped the shipping case onto the down escalator and were gone.

Chapter 4

The place stank of stale sweat, decayed blood and ozone, the hallmarks of the Apparatus. Coils of smoke from the whip and bits of burning cloth stood in the air. The patches of greenish light held ugly secrets back in the shadows.

The Countess Krak walked sedately to the desk and platform by the door.

Heller moved. His eyes were interestedly gazing at all the vast array of machines in the room, machines made to generate shock and inflict twists and tortures.

The Countess saw me. Her eyes were emotionless. As she stepped up on the nearby platform, she opened her mouth to say something. I knew in advance what it would be. We were more than an hour late for Heller's training appointment. I was about to get my hide taken off, all without emotion, one layer at a time.

But she stopped. Her eyes were on Jettero Heller.

Squinting a trifle to see better, Heller was walking down along the wall, away from us. He was peering at the first machine. It was a squat brute, coated with decay. If a person were put in it, his brains could be fried in varying and precisely calculated degrees. Heller did something to a latch on the side of it and lifted the cover of its circuit section, exposing a dusty array of boards and components. He started poking into its guts and must have disconnected something as he held up a loose wire end and began to examine it.

I chilled like ice. Fooling about with equipment here was not something one did. I looked quickly at the Countess Krak. She was just standing there, watching him. There was no expression on her face at all. There never was. This female was as beautiful as a Goddess on the altar of a church, but every bit as cold as that carved stone. More so. I held my breath. I didn't know what she would do to handle this violation of her area. I suspected the worst.

I really don't think Heller had seen her come to the platform by the door. The light was bad in the place and he seemed fascinated with the machines. Strung out along the walls, they were a brutal display. He went to the next one, a thing of twisted arms and bulky gears: it was a tendon stretcher and, while one might have said it could be used for acrobats or contortionists, it really was a product of torture chambers. He pulled his finger along the seat and gazed at the grime on his hand. He pulled out one of those star-shaped red cloths engineers are always using as cleaning rags and wiped his finger.

The next machine had small fluid tanks all around it and was a tangle of tubes and holding straps. Its purpose was to alternately freeze and roast a body, to deliver temperature shocks and rid it of excess fat, but it too belonged in torture chambers. He opened one of the tanks and looked in. He shook his head and moved on.

Countess Krak's head was turning to follow his progress and, from where I stood, I could no longer see her eyes. I had no faintest idea of what she would do. It had been violently proven three times in the past two years that she could and would kill.

Heller was looking over the next machine. It was a maze of electrodes that could be applied to different parts of a strapped-down body. There was a sort of projector screen. The hapless being strapped to it could be shocked with high voltage and shown pictures at the same time. Heller popped open the cover of the transformers and peered into the circuits. He got out a little pinpoint light and looked deeper. He didn't even bother to replace the cover and walked on.

The Countess Krak stood there, turning slowly, watching.

The next device had huge ear cups that clamped down upon a victim's head. It delivered blasting waves of sound when it was turned on. The sound would go on and off. I knew of it and these other machines because of their counterparts in interrogation rooms. They might be called "training machines" but the agony they could deliver was acute. Heller fiddled with a couple of its switches, shrugged, and then passed on.

There were more machines, one that stabbed with light, another that bathed a whole body in raw electricity, others I did not know. But Heller had lost interest.

The Countess Krak hadn't. She had pivoted until I could only see her back. There was a chair on the platform beside her and she placed her hand on it's tall back. I thought maybe she was going to throw it but she just stood there.

Heller, oblivious of any audience or threat, idled over to the raised exercise platform at the extreme end of the room. His attention had gone off machines but was now on athletics. A big, hundred-pound bag, used by acrobats to practice hefting bodies, lay in his path. He idly picked it up and made it spin rapidly, holding it up on top of one fingertip. He let it drop and looked about.

There were some rings suspended on long ropes that met in the center of the vast hall. One of the rings had been hung on a peg at the extreme end of the room. Heller jumped up and disengaged it and, in the same motion, holding to it, swung from there toward us in a long, graceful arc. He obviously thought it easier than just walking back.

When he was about thirty feet from us, coming fast, he did a body flip, a full spin by one arm. It was perfectly timed.

Ten feet away he let go. He landed gracefully on his toes and halted standing, three feet in front of Countess Krak.

He saw her. He stood up very erect. It was as if somebody had turned on a light inside him.

"Hel*LO!*" he said. "Hello, hello, HELLO! *What* is a *beaut*iful creature like *you* doing in a place like *this?*"

I almost died. Every spacer in every nightclub on every one of a thousand planets has said just that to every

prostitute for thousands of years. It is the corniest cliché
in any tongue. It is an outright sexual pass! And she had
killed men for even reaching toward her. I said to myself,
good-bye Heller, good-bye mission! I gripped the blastick.

For seconds she did not move. Then, abruptly, like
her legs had given way, she sat down in the chair, turned
half away from him.

She just sat there. Her eyes were fixed on a spot a
yard in front of her feet. In a low, strained voice, not looking at him, just looking at that spot, she said, "You
should not talk to me." There was a silence. She seemed
to sink lower in the chair, tense, indrawn. "I am not
worthy of you." It was just a monotonous mutter. "I am
rotten. I am vile. I am not fit for you to talk to."

She took a long painful breath. She sat there rigid
and then she said in a kind of wail, "That is the first
friendly thing anyone has said to me in *three years!*"

And then she began to cry! Heller was plainly very
distressed. He knelt down beside her and reached for her
hand. I thought, oh, no, no, no, don't touch her! She has
killed for less.

But she didn't move. She just sat there, chin sunk on
her chest, *crying!*

Heller just knelt there, holding her hand.

I waited for something else to happen. Nothing did.
After a while I wandered over to the hypnohelmets rack
and fiddled around. These helmets produce a field that
throws the subject into a hypnotic trance; recorded slides
are fed through a slot and the hypnotized person can be
speed-trained in various scholastic subjects. I had
learned English, Italian and Turkish in one.

Heller was still kneeling beside her on the platform.
The tears were making her breast pretty wet, so still holding onto her hand, he used his right to get out his redstar
engineer's rag and put it into her free hand. But she

didn't wipe away any tears with it. She just pushed it against her mouth to muffle the shuddering sobs which were tearing her apart.

This was getting nowhere, I thought. The day was burning up and we were getting nothing done. But I didn't dare go near them.

I got out a communications disc and whispered into it, ordering a couple guards to be posted outside the door. I eased myself out into the passageway and when the guards arrived I told them not to let Heller escape and then took myself down to the cellular labs. I didn't see Crobe around but I didn't want him anyway. I got one of the assistants to handle my face: he bathed the various contusions, put some of the skin cell culture on them from my private bottle—cultures have to be matched to the individual—and then put on new skin patches. I looked better now. With all the sweating I was doing, I hoped this lot would last.

I went back to the training rooms.

Heller was still kneeling beside her on the platform and she was still dabbing her mouth with the redstar engineer's rag. She was still crying!

What a ruined day! Nothing accomplished at all! I knew where the language files were. After all, my old section itself had made the Earth ones. For some reason there are lots of recorded language courses on Blito-P3: they sell them commercially there; all one has to do is duplicate their playing heads with a proper sort of current and then, interspersing the words with Standard Voltarian, copy them onto recording strips. They print lots of children's schoolbooks and so one can also learn to read and write rather quickly. Raht and Terb, the best Voltarian operatives there, had also done some of their own recordings of the accents. We had cubic yards of Earth languages and materials for instruction. It always

amused me that the recordings and books of Blito-P3
bore dire warnings of penalties for copying and promised that some group known as the "FBI" would arrest
any offender! Well, good luck to them. I sorted through
the cabinet labelled *Blito-P3*. There was nothing whatever different about the scene on the platform so I took
my time.

As near as I could make out, the geographic sections
for what we call "zone of operations" would be, in
Heller's case, three locales: Virginia, Washington, D.C.,
and New York City. He would not be spending much
time in Turkey—Gods forbid. I could find a "Virginia
accent" but I could not find any reference to a
"Washington, D.C. accent," so I skipped it. Then I got
all tangled up with the "New York accents" because
there seemed to be a lot of them. I finally found a note.
It said:

> Ivy League accent is that of the upper classes
> of the New England section of the United
> States.

I looked at a map and saw that New York might be on
the fringe of "New England" and guessed it would have
to do. My own English had been learned with
"commercial heterogenic accent" which included the
skill of working out accents. But I didn't think Heller
would have time for that. I chose "Virginia" and "Ivy
League."

The tableau on the platform seemed to be less tense.
They weren't talking. She wasn't crying as much. The
redstar engineer's rag was sopping. I wondered what she
was trying to pull. It crossed my mind that maybe I
ought to alert Lombar in case this female was laying

some deep-seated conspiracy to escape. But I actually couldn't figure out what she *was* up to. If she was conspiring, she would be talking. And she wasn't. It was such common knowledge that the Countess Krak was dangerous that this just might be another facet of it. There's no understanding females anyway.

Finally she spoke. It was in a very low voice. She had stopped sobbing. "I'll be all right now."

And Heller whispered, "Are you sure?"

She nodded her head. She began to dry off her face with the redstar engineer's rag.

Well! I might be able to salvage some of this day after all. I beckoned to Heller and he came over. I knew how to operate these hypnohelmets. If the training section wasn't going to help, I would simply do it all myself. That's common enough in the Apparatus, made up as it is of loonies and crazies and criminals in general.

I slid a recorded slide into the helmet slot and started to put the visored helmet over his head. He looked at it curiously and instead of letting me put it on him, took it out of my hands. I tried to explain to him what it was. He ignored me.

He went over to the cabinet and rummaged around. He put the helmet down and rummaged deeper. And then he found a recorded strip player that was detached from the helmet. He took the first strip marked

Elementary English (Ivy League)

and put it in the player. He carried the lot over to the platform and sat down at the desk.

The Countess Krak was still sitting in the chair. Nobody ever sits at the Countess Krak's desk! She said nothing.

Heller turned the player on. It had a little speaker.

He pushed a button. The strip said,

"My name is George."

Heller said, "Oh, no, no, no."

He pulled a little tool case from his pocket. He opened the back of the player and in a moment had a handful of little gears. Looking up, he said to me, "Call one of your electronic surveillance technicians."

Aha, so he knew Spiteos was really wired! Well, that wasn't a very bright supposition. Everything is, these days. I called on my communications disc.

Heller put on a pair of gloves, the kind that resist all heat and transmit none. He took a little spin-carver from his pocket case and began to work on the player gears. He was cutting down a cogwheel. It glowed red hot in his gloved fingers. It was a job usually done on precision machines. But here he was making what appeared to be a perfect little cogwheel.

The Countess Krak was watching.

The technician arrived. Heller said, "Get me part 435-m-67-d-1."

Well, you know technicians. But at Spiteos they are a particularly scummy lot. He was going to open his mouth to pour out some can't-be-dones. But he didn't get a chance. In the precise language and tone of the Fleet, Heller said, "You undoubtedly have surveillance interceptor converters that absorb outside signals coming in and send them out again as something else. Part 435-m-67-d-1 is the small frequency step-down unit. Get a spare. Step lively."

That technician was gone like a flash.

Heller cooled down his new gear and reassembled the player. A recorded strip takes about an hour to work through from beginning to end. He turned the machine on now and the strip went through, ZIP!, in about thirty seconds. The sound that came out of the speaker was a high-pitched screech, a lot of it above the range of hearing.

The technician came back, handed him the part, gave him a Fleet salute and left. I will admit I felt envy. I had never had anyone around the Apparatus behave like that to me!

Heller took a "hot block" out of his little kit and heated the attachment wires, and with a few deft motions had the new part installed.

He sent the strip through again. This time there was a medium hearing range roar.

"That's better," said Heller. He neated up the area, put his tools away. Then he reinserted the language strip. He looked at the speaker, very composed, hit the starter button and in thirty seconds the hour-recorded strip had roared through the machine.

"Ah," said Heller.

I was just plain incredulous. "Ah" indeed! It took an hour to listen to a strip! I said, "Oh, come off of it. If you are really hearing the words on that strip, you'll be able to tell me the next lines. *My name is George.* . . ."

Heller smiled. "*I have a dog. The dog's name is Rover. Do you like dogs?* . . ." But he was not very interested in playing any game with me. He picked the second strip out of the box and sent it through with a roar. (Bleep)! He could make it out at that speed!

The Countess Krak breathed, "Instant auricular assimilation and retention. At hyperspeed."

I looked at her. "Is that rare?"

"No," she said. She seemed in a daze. "Well . . . yes, at speeds like that, that is." She wasn't talking to me really. "His hearing is trained to differentiate minute time intervals." Her voice sounded so strange. "I've never seen it done that fast." She seemed to become aware of me for a moment. With bright-eyed awe she said, "Isn't he beautiful?"

For a moment I thought she meant the talent was beautiful. But no, she was really looking at his chest and arms. It was true that Jettero Heller was one of the best looking guys around but there was more to this than that. This was all out of my depth. It could be very dangerous.

I had a bright idea. "Well," I said, "if he can speed-learn as fast as that, we'll just take the player and strips to my room and he can study there."

"No!" She shouted it. Then she said, very quietly, "There's a regulation that equipment can't leave here."

That was a lame one. I took stuff in and out of here all the time.

He had done four strips. I stood up and tapped him on the shoulder. "That's all for today," I said. "We've got other appointments. Come on!"

And I dragged him out of there. I don't like things I don't understand.

Chapter 5

We took a tube to the topmost tower of Spiteos. It was after sunset and also because there is a partial roof there we couldn't be seen in case of overflights. The star-pierced desert sky stretched like a jewelled dome from horizon to horizon. The lights of Camp Endurance winked below us. Oh, it is good to get a breath of clean air after a day spent down in the stench of Spiteos!

"Heller," I said, after we had settled ourselves in an embrasure, "I've got to talk to you." I could see the desert wind rumpling his hair, but I could not make out his eyes in the starlight. I seemed to have his attention.

"Mission Earth," I continued, "is of vital importance. I must not take any chances in failing to carry out my orders." Needless to say, I did not tell him those orders involved making him fail. But strangely enough, I had a sort of brotherly feeling for him and what I had to tell him is the sort of thing one junior officer has to tell another whether it is appreciated or not.

"You are new to this espionage special agent game. I am your handler. You know what that means. I am the one that guides your actions."

He seemed to be giving me his attention. So I dropped the bombload on him. "That female you met this afternoon is trouble. Trouble with a capital crash!"

Heller didn't say anything. "Brother officers," I said, "have to tell their brother officers these things every now and then. I know you may not like it but it has to be done.

"It is true she was a Countess once. But that is the only thing true about her. Do you remember the name 'Lissus Moam'? The one that was in the news so much about three years ago?"

He didn't speak, so I went on. "She was arrested and tried and sentenced to death. Forty-three children were also sentenced and executed. It all happened on the Planet Manco. She is a genius at training. And she used her position in the Division of Education to recruit and train youngsters as bank robbers. She taught them to open any vault, to bypass any alarm system. They raked in millions.

"Now, there is some question about the next part as it is said that the Assistant Lord of Education for Manco did it—at least she said so at her trial. But those children were taught to murder and at every job they murdered every guard, some of them pretty horribly.

"The Domestic Police turned her over secretly to the Apparatus: that's how these things work. And she has been here at Spiteos for nearly three years." It was all right to give him details. If I got him to Blito-P3, by the time he returned here everything would be changed anyway. "In those three years, she has murdered three guards. The first simply reached for her hair, probably to stroke it. She had a whip in her hand: she took the butt of it and jammed it straight through his heart.

"A few months later, one of the toughest beasts in Spiteos whispered something in her ear—nobody knows what. She seized him around the back, put her head under his chin and pulled. His back snapped in three places and it took him about four days to die.

"Just two months ago, right down there in the training area, she was teaching one of our toughest special agents a new twist on hand-to-hand combat. Probably in a teasing movement, but not even that, most likely, he made an improper gesture. You know, she wears those thigh boots and jacket but nothing else—factually I don't think she has anything else except some work coveralls she wears to handle big lizards that have scrapey skins. Witnesses say he didn't even touch her and others say he did reach her crotch. Heller, just using the edge of her hand, she broke his arm! Then he called her a stinking whore. They say that, without the faintest trace of emotion, she said, 'I am a virgin and you will apologize' and without waiting for any answer, she broke his jaw. And that isn't the worst of it. She stamped him! She just stamped him on and on. Heller, there wasn't an unbroken bone left in that fellow's body! I didn't see the others, but I did see this fellow afterwards and he looked like red paste!

"The only one that can hit her and get away with it is Lombar Hisst."

Heller showed his first interest. "You mean the Chief Executive of the Apparatus has hit her?"

"We're all terrified of him and with very ample reason. After all, he's . . ." I checked myself. I had almost said "The most powerful official in the Voltarian Confederacy" but that wasn't quite true yet and would give things away. So I said, ". . . too dangerous."

Heller seemed to be very thoughtful now. So I really drove it home. "Jettero—and I can call you Jettero, can't I? I am a brother officer and have a personal feeling, too. I have got to get you off this planet alive. I have got to do my duty with regard to Mission Earth. And listen, Jettero, you go fooling around with the Countess Krak, making remarks like you did today, getting funny ideas about her and, well, I don't care how good you are with hand-to-hand, you will be one very dead Jettero Heller.

"You steer clear of the Countess Krak! There may be others that don't want this mission to succeed, but this afternoon they took the rear seat. The primary danger you're courting right this moment consists of making passes at that female. Now, I know it is lonely in space and that you're just back from a long trip and all that. But the Countess Krak is death incarnate! Stay away!" I laughed a bit to take the sting out of the order. "After all, it will be hard enough to get you off this planet without that! Now we won't say any more about it."

Heller sat there for a while. I could see he was thinking about something very hard. I respected his silence. It was obvious he had a problem now for I could see him gnawing at it.

"There's one thing I can't remember," said Jettero.
I was all attention, inviting his confidence.

He looked at me searchingly. I could see he was deeply troubled, even perplexed. "Would you say her eyes were gray? Or are they pale blue?"

I gave it up in disgust. I got him back to the room. I had other important things to do anyway.

Chapter 6

Lombar always said that when you let an underling get away with something and did not punish him severely, you yourself would shortly be in trouble. I considered this very wise.

I could sense that I myself was walking on a very thin crust and, without any doubt whatever, I was headed for trouble. Therefore, it was obvious that I had not properly handled underlings. Before things got further out of hand, I knew I had to punish that platoon commander. His conduct while "guarding" Heller was unforgivable!

So as soon as I had stuffed down some moldy bread—what passes for food at Spiteos—I headed for Camp Endurance. And when I got through, it would have another reason to be nicknamed "Camp Kill."

The fortress is connected to the camp by an underground tunnel about a mile and a half long. Traffic with the outside world, for Spiteos, had Camp Endurance as its terminal: any overflight of the area or any inspection for that matter, found only the sprawling camp; it's traffic being justified by the "training activities" it conducted.

We tried to keep traffic to a minimum but there was plenty of it just the same. The tunnel traffic was very heavy tonight. The outgoing zipbus I caught was halted for a good twenty minutes in the middle of the dark tunnel, parked on a turnout, letting incoming transports through to Spiteos.

The view I had from the zipbus was restricted, limited to a small diamond window beside the seat; the lights were bad but they flashed upon the sides of the incoming vehicles in a green blur.

Plenty of traffic! I wondered what was up. I caught the flick of high-rank flags. I was battered by the roar of heavy-armored trucks. The air disturbance of escort tanks was like a blastcannon and hurt my ears.

Something was certainly up! I yelled up to the half-naked zipbus driver, "Is there a general alert?" But my voice was drowned in tunnel roars and I had to repeat it louder.

He heard me and yelled back, "Ain't none I know about. That first lot was incoming freight with guard tanks. This stuff now is just staff cars—a bunch of (bleeping) bigwigs. You can't never tell what them (bleepards) is up to."

The driver hadn't turned around until he said the last. He did now and abruptly realized he was talking to an officer. He went white with shock and whipped back, looking rigidly straight.

Riffraff, I thought. Lombar is right. Trash like this driver ought to be exterminated. But I didn't take it up. I was too impatient to get at that platoon commander.

We finally got to the Camp Endurance outlet and went through the heavy security barricade. There had never been an escape from Spiteos but this would be the logical route—all other Spiteos exits were sealed solid with stone.

The black-uniformed barricade guards double-checked my identoplate, holding blasters pointed at me the while. A gray service uniform is suspect always but I was (bleeped) if I would ever don the shabby black of the Apparatus troops.

The platoon commander who had been assigned with his men to guard Heller was named Snelz. He and his platoon were barracked in Camp Endurance but sent their guard details into the fortress for duty watches. As I did not want Snelz alerted, I said I was just going to the camp club. I knew where Snelz had his quarters.

The officers lived in small bunkers, like animal caves, along the north side of the camp, dug into the hill. It was pretty dark along there. Scraps of music and echoes from a brawl seeped up from the camp along with a fetid stink.

I saw the cave number ahead. There was a light leak underneath the closed door so Snelz would be there. A couple of big boulders stood beside the entrance. And I am afraid my attention was so thoroughly on the light leak that I didn't see the sentry.

Apparatus troops may parade and all that but they are not like the Army. Criminals, the worst riffraff of the planets, they tend to hide even on casual duty. It is either a trait they get from the Apparatus or the Apparatus gets from them. They never do anything straightforward.

They also have entirely different regulations. They can be killed by their officers without censure. This places any guard in a quandary. He either tries to do his duty of protecting his superior—and maybe die in that—or he fails to protect his officer and the officer kills him.

This one made a mistake: he played it for his officer. When I was eight feet from that door, expecting nothing, the sentry leaped up and lunged in full attack!

I am pretty fast. Otherwise I would have died in my tracks!

The blastgun barrel was into my stomach with violence!

I hardly even saw the man behind it.

With a roll to the side I made the barrel shoot by. I brought my right hand down on the back of the sentry's neck!

He staggered and it gave me my chance.

As he fell, I snatched the gun barrel and got the weapon out of his hands.

His boots drove at my shins and I reeled with the impact.

A green beam of light from the camp flashed as a distant vehicle turned. I saw clearly for the first time that it was a sentry and not an assassin.

But you can't let someone get away with that! Not an attack on an officer.

I reversed the gun and drove the butt against his skull! There was a dull, crushing sound. I hit again just to make sure. He lay there bleeding. He didn't move.

So far, good. And now for Snelz.

The thick door would have masked the sounds of the fight. I stepped over the sentry's body and approached. The thing to do in such a situation, where one is trying to enforce authority and gain respect is play it very bold.

I simply opened the door and walked in. Such a casual act would make him think it was a friend.

He must have. He was sitting at the table in his shirt sleeves, playing twelve-sided dice with himself. Over in a bunk, sleeping peacefully, was one of the camp prostitutes; her clothes lay all over the floor and she looked exhausted. The place stank of spent passion.

When one is really trained, one can reconstruct a situation in a fraction of a second. Snelz had had money.

The first thing he had done was call in a prostitute. He was practicing with six twelve-sided dice so the next thing he planned to do was call in at what they laughingly called a "club" and try to clean out his fellow guard officers to make up what the prostitute had cost him.

Snelz looked up casually, thinking probably that it was some friend intent on getting a loan. He suddenly registered who it was and went white!

Now, duels between officers are not unknown. But Apparatus officers are such swine, they don't duel. They simply murder. And where a General Services officer is concerned, when it comes to a fight with Apparatus troop commanders, they don't even bother to count the bodies.

My face told him why I was there. He raised his left hand in a defensive position as if it could ward off a shot. He almost screamed: "I can explain. . . ."

"Platoon Commander Snelz," I said, for I might as well make this execution official, "you are guilty of fraternizing with a prisoner you were ordered to guard. Apparatus Regulation 564-B-61 Section D. The penalty, as you well know, is death."

Unlike civilian life or the Fleet or Army, there are no trials in the Apparatus. Ordinarily he would have simply accepted it. But something had gotten into him.

He stabbed a hand toward his belt! I was certain he was going to draw and shoot.

Well, I am not slow. I wouldn't have lived as I have if I could be outdrawn.

My own hand leaped, with no thought from me, to my breast pocket and the blastick was out and levelled at him before he had hardly touched his belt.

The field of fire took in the prostitute on the bunk behind him and 800 kilovolts would kill her, too. But it wasn't any time for niceties.

I pressed the switch-trigger!

The blastick pin made only a faint pop!

No explosion!

I was holding a dud-loaded blastick! It was a very bad moment. I had no other weapon. I could not reach him to strike or kick. I was defenseless!

He was still scrabbling at his belt and my heart almost stopped as he lifted his fingers. I was quite certain I was dead!

But he was holding two ten-credit notes! He had not been drawing out a weapon. He had been trying to get at money!

Had he heard the switch-trigger fall on a dud load? No, he had not!

He was holding out the two ten-credit notes and he moved sideways from the chair and fell on his knees. "Please, Officer Gris. Please! Don't kill me!"

There was a big stungun lying on a bench not three feet from his reach. I am well schooled. I let no sign of my emotions show. I toughed it out.

"I was just following your orders, Officer Gris. I wasn't fraternizing with a prisoner. You said the prisoner mustn't suspect he was being guarded. You said to make it look like he was under protection from outside threat!"

He was bobbing up and down, head lowered, holding out the two ten-credit notes. His hand was shaking like a loose wing on an atmosphere plane.

The prostitute had awakened. She pulled her dirty hair away from her face with a filthy hand. She didn't take it in at all. "Hey, don't give away no money! You can buy another (bleep)!"

Snelz crawled forward, head down. He laid the two ten-credit notes at my feet and scuttled back. He crouched there, all curled in on himself, trying to give a crossed-arm salute while kneeling on the floor.

Ridiculous. All he had to do was reach out and grab the stungun and shoot me. A stupid (bleepard).

I said, "How much money did Heller give you? And for what?"

Snelz whimpered. "He gave me fifty credits for sweetbuns and sparklewater, to buy them at the camp store. Oh, and also for papers. He didn't bribe me to do anything else. He said he might need something later but as for the fifty, I could buy something for my men and keep the change."

He looked up and clasped his hands under his chin. "We haven't been paid for ages. I didn't realize you would want your share. Don't kill me. I won't forget again! Please!"

Any reply I had was interrupted by the prostitute. She scuttled across the floor and made a grab for the twenty credits at my feet. I stamped a boot heel on her hand. The bones snapped!

She gave a scream and went running naked out of the door. Outside she stumbled over something and gave another scream. She came rushing back into the room, completely dazed, not knowing where she was going. "He killed the sentry!" She cowered back in the corner of the cave, gripping her broken hand, too demented to realize all she should have done was run away.

Snelz gave a glance toward the outside darkness. With all this screaming, other officers might well come rushing over. Before he could get up too much hope and realize he had a gun within reach and that I was holding a dud, I thought I'd better finish this.

"Snelz," I said, and had his gaze riveted upon me at once with the tone I used, "you have reminded me that you were in fact executing an order. However, you were doing it in far too friendly a fashion."

He seized upon it. "I did it to get his promise," he

said in a hopeful rush of words. "He gave me his word as a Royal officer, he would let me or my men know where he was at all times. He said he knew I had a tough job and that he'd make it easy for me. I actually persuaded him to fully cooperate. And Officer Gris, that's the word of a *Royal officer,* not like that of Apparatus people."

It was a slur, really. He obviously included me in "Apparatus people." He recognized his mistake. He wailed, "I'll give you your share after this! Please don't kill me!"

I had been edging over toward the stungun. I was now blocking the route to his reaching it.

"I'll execute my orders faithfully!" said Snelz. "I'll keep him cooperating. He won't suspect he's a prisoner and he won't escape. I pledge my life on it." He thought for a moment to see if there was anything else. There was. "I'll give you half whatever I get from him!"

As I now did not have to back down because I was defenseless, I decided to be magnanimous. "All right. If you do that faithfully, you can have your life."

His relief was obvious. "You won't be sorry, Officer Gris. Can I get up now?"

I put the dud blastick back in my pocket. I pulled the charge out of his stungun and threw it back down on the bench. A close one!

He went outside and pulled the sentry back toward the light of the cave. He checked to see if he was dead. "You certainly squashed his skull," said Snelz. "But he isn't dead. Can I have one of those ten-credit notes back? The camp doctors will want six to fix his head and another four to repair the whore's hand."

The nerve of him. The going charge for both would be under five. But I kicked one of the notes over to him and then, as an afterthought, picked up the other one and put it in my pocket.

The whole thing had been so messy, I was gloomy all the way back to Spiteos. I could not for the life of me figure out what had gone wrong with the blastick. Obviously it was the one Heller's friends had sent him in the baggage for I had expertly put the dud armory one in his boot. I couldn't figure why his friends would send him a dud-loaded weapon. Of course, when you get them off the shelf, they have a dummy load in them. And it came to me that he simply, stupidly had not loaded the weapon.

Riding the zipbus back, I was almost at the Spiteos end before I recalled that he had adjusted my face patches. But he was not that clever. And I would have felt the blastick leave my pocket if he had shifted back.

I was all out of sorts. Things were not going right at all. But one thing I knew for sure: I was not going to be left standing, holding a dud weapon in a bluff again. Even coming back, unarmed, through the camp tonight had been a risk I had no right to take, what with Lombar counting on me.

It was very late but I went straight to the armory. The old cretin that runs the place slept inside. I unlocked the top half of the door with my identoplate and yelled into the darkness. After three tries, the lights went on and the old fool came fumbling up to the counter, half-asleep.

"What the Devils do you mean, waking me up?" he snarled.

I was in no mood for this. I reached my hand over the lower part of the door and tripped the latch. I sent the bottom section slamming into his stomach!

I was inside in a second and before he could recover, I hit him with a backhand. He fell and I let him have a boot. "When you are talking to me, show some respect!"

He lay there on the floor. So I picked my way along the shelves. I got down a stungun and holster. I picked up two blasticks and a case of cartridges. Then I saw some Knife Section knives and neck scabbards and took a set.

I booted him again. "Log these out so you can't claim you were robbed!"

He got up. His papers had gone all over the place when the door was slammed back. He gathered them from the floor and began to record the numbers of the weapons I had taken. He held out his hand for my identoplate and then pressed it on the sheet. He said, "Officer Gris, you're getting more like Lombar Hisst every day."

I looked at him. If he had intended a slur, he could have been killed for it. I decided he had not.

"Thank you," I said.

Later I lay in my bed, listening to the even breathing of Jettero Heller, asleep on the other side of the room. Things were not going well at all!

I thought it out very carefully, staring into the dark. As long as we remained on Voltar, my neck was at risk. Here, Jettero Heller was surrounded by a world he knew and could manage. He had subverted the guard— although I had sure slowed that down tonight. He had tons and tons of friends in Government City and the Fleet. He might pull anything. And we were directly under the view of Lombar Hisst. I did not dare foul up. It was an awful position to be in.

I took my resolve right there. Regardless of anything, I would rush through all preparations and leave Voltar fast!

When we got to Blito-P3 it would be a different story. I would have no worries about Heller breaking out. He would have no friends.

I would really push it to get Heller to Earth, for there, he would be completely at my mercy!

The thought of Jettero Heller safely imprisoned in some nice Earth penitentiary was so pleasing, I had trouble getting to sleep, just gloating on it.

Chapter 7

I awoke at dawn, all full of energy and ambition to blast us out of the Voltar Confederacy quick and get safely to Earth with Heller. As I piled into my clothes, I glanced over at him. There he was, sleeping with a half smile on his face as though he hadn't a care or worry in the world. He was very good-looking, even in sleep, which is unusual. He was a very masculine fellow but he was pretty, too. I wished I had more blackmail material on him. Anyone that was that handsome must have had plenty of wild adventures in the sex department. I told myself I wouldn't need the data now. We were going to leave and *fast*.

I gulped down some of his sparklewater and crammed a sweetbun in my mouth, rapidly planning out the day. I would rush down to training and make an appointment for him. I would dash over to Crobe's and schedule any operations. Then I would come back and grab him and within just a couple of days we'd be gone. He could finish his studies and heal up en route to Earth.

As I rushed out of the door, one of the sentries grabbed my arm. "Officer Gris, you're wanted in the Chief Executive's tower office. Very urgent. They told me to tell you about a minute ago but you're awake."

My mouth dried up. A summons from Lombar usually meant trouble. Like a dying person's life flashing past their eyes, such news always brings a review of one's crimes. Had he heard of Heller's survey? Other things?

I put a brave face on it. Whatever it was I would handle it speedily. I hoped. I had my own plans to execute. But one of Lombar's troubles, and he had a few, was telling you that some job was entirely up to you and then, shortly after, barging in again and interfering—one more good reason to blast off from Voltar.

In the tower anteroom, I might have dashed right on through and into Lombar's office. A clerk stopped me. The clerks there don't like me—a sign of obvious envy. "That office is jammed with Apparatus planet heads. A lot more rank than you. Sit right down over there and wait."

Must be all the staff cars I'd seen rushing in last night. Maybe Lombar had been working all night. He was like that, work like mad but *only* when his personal pet projects were involved; at other times he just loafed and did things like reviewing "freak parades." I was annoyed.

The blazing star of Voltar struggled up beyond the distant hills to drown the desert in its daily fire. The administration office buzzed along. Clerks came, clerks went. I waited and began to seethe. I had to get going. Every extra hour I spent on this planet was full of danger to Mission Earth.

The light was practically burning the stone floor back to lava now. From the murmur that came from Lombar's office, there was no sign of end-conference.

I racked my wits as to how I could spend this time gainfully and speed things up. Then I remembered Heller sleeping and my thoughts about the sex department adventures. Ho, ho. Yes, I could spend my time here. There was a big central data bank console right over there in the corner.

The clerks yow-yowed and said no until a sour old criminal snarled, "Let him. Hisst just promoted him so he can do no wrong—yet."

I went over to it, sat down and plugged my identoplate in. When you find yourself with the whole Apparatus data bank available, you make the most of it. This was a master console, not a restricted one like they have in other offices. *Everything* is here, especially blackmail. The only restriction is that your identoplate gets recorded on everything you ask for. I was almost tempted to punch in the Emperor and see what I got. I fought an urge to punch in Lombar Hisst and then I realized it would be just banal or blank. I succumbed to punching in my own name with "Recent Additions." I knew my own file, of course. Anyone high in the Apparatus manages that.

One can actually extract any document and banish it from the file, using a master console. One can add any document to a file, even a flagrant forgery. The trouble is, the identoplate appears in connection with the action. There is a tale of an Apparatus officer that made himself a Fleet Admiral—and so he was, until the next day when they executed him. I hope he found those twenty-four hours worth it!

Disappointment. The only recent addition to my file

was my promotion. I thought it a little strange it did not
record my removal from Section 451 and then I foolishly
rationalized that even though the data banks occupy thirty square miles of buildings, they sometimes fall
behind—the Apparatus is not that free from error.

I looked around. The conference was still in
progress. I had a wide-open line here, the whole Apparatus data bank before me and no fee to pay. Let's see
what else I could find out for free.

I punched in,

> Doctor Crobe.
> Dead,

said the screen. Well, all right, so the Apparatus lied.
That wasn't news. Try again.

> Countess Krak,

I punched. I took off my cap and laid it down.

> No such person,

said the screen. So I punched in her real name,

> Lissus Moam.

The screen said,

> See Countess Krak.

Aha! I was getting somewhere. I punched in,

> Countess Krak.

The machine said,

> Lissus Moam.

So I punched,

> Why are you cross-referencing?

The machine said,

> You have your finger holding down the repeat key.

Oh. My finger wasn't but my cap was. I put the cap
elsewhere and punched in,

> Lissus Moam

again. The screen promptly said,

> See Graves Reference.

So I punched,
>Graves Reference.

The screen said,
>There is no connection to Graves Reference.

I hit *Query* three times. The machine said,
>Please do not argue. The computer is always right.

The criminal clerk said, "Are you sure you know how to operate that machine?"

"Be respectful," I said, and he tottered off sneering.

At least I knew Countess Krak did not exist and that Lissus Moam was recorded as dead: they didn't keep the records of dead people. Technically, she had no criminal record now. Useful data to keep to myself.

But, to business: Jettero Heller! If I could find some juicy bit, I could perhaps blackmail him at need into being more compliant. I punched in the name and the subtitle,
>Sex.

The screen said,
>Male.

That made me cross. These machines are so confounded literal. So I punched in,
>Sex Irregularities.

The screen said,
>None.

(Bleep) the machine, and I sort of slugged it. "You having trouble?" said the old criminal clerk. There was hope in his voice that he could throw me out of there. I ignored him.

The way the Apparatus screen operates, it can summate in single words or it can show a whole document and then zero in, in a flash, upon the required paragraph. I had been asking for summations. I had better get to documents so I pushed the lever for those.
>Affairs with women.

Blank screen.
>   Affairs with fellow officers.

Blank screen.
>   Affairs with underage.

Blank screen.
>   Affairs with prostitutes.

Blank screen. Then I remembered he had a beautiful sister.
>   Incest.

Blank screen.

Annoyed, I looked to see if the machine had gotten turned off. I made a test.
>   Jettero Heller?

The screen said,
>   Yes?

It was operating. I sat there. Suddenly the screen lit up,
>   Warning. Data time is valuable. Please prepare
>   your questions in advance so they can be rapidly
>   handled. Section Chief Data Banks Apparatus.

It would close off in exactly five seconds after such a notice.

Desperate, I punched in,
>   Mental Interviews.

A document! At last! I had saved my console connection.

The document, a smudgy mess scribbled by some doctor in the loony section,
>   Routine Interview before hospital discharge.

I hadn't asked for any portion heading. I punched,
>   Why hospital?

It zeroed in to the top of the sheet.
>   Wounded in rescue of battleship.

I punched,
>   Why mental interview?

The screen zeroed to,
>   Fight in hospital with male homosexual nurse.

Aha! I punched in,

> Conclusion?

The machine zeroed in on,

> Male nurse hospitalized.

I thought no, no, no, you (bleeping) machine. I punched,

> Findings on mental condition subject.

The screen zeroed in on,

> No psychotic nor neurotic signs or symptoms found on the subject of sex. Interview null.

Real disappointment.

Hastily, so as not to lose my machine time, I punched in,

> Disciplinary actions of all kinds and types.

The machine said,

> When?

(Bleep) machine.

> Since baby,

I punched in.

Ah, now we were away! Real documents! Police report when he was seven: arrested for riding speed-wheel on sidewalk; fined one credit. Another report, age twelve: arrested for driving airbus when underage; case dismissed. Another, age fifteen: arrested for illegal skydrop into parade, said done to call attention to new technique in skydropping; case dismissed. Age sixteen: arrested as stowaway on expeditionary space freighter; judge used influence to get subject appointed to Royal Academy. What a talker Heller must have been to get a judge to do something like that! Well, I knew how he'd gotten his appointment anyway. I got mine by my father bribing a Lord's chief clerk.

There didn't seem much hope here. And then a document flashed on,

> Recommendation for Court-martial.

Aha! There it was. I scanned it. Heller isn't the only fast reader around. In his very first posting after leaving the Postgraduate Corps of Engineers school, one Jettero Heller, Grade I, protested his crew being trained by electric shock; he had argued that he had never been so trained, it being frowned on to electric-shock officers for any reason, and he claimed he didn't want "a goofed up, fried-brained crew on a mission dangerous enough without that." He had refused all persuasions and he had slugged the training officer when he started to put the crew into the machines. He had been relieved of command and remanded to custody pending court-martial.

I eagerly watched for the transcript of the court-martial to appear. Instead, an endorsement flashed on:

> The said Jettero Heller being senior by three days date of rank to the training officer, said battering does not constitute a charge of an attack upon a senior. The court-martial recommendation is cancelled. Secretary to Admiral of the 95th Fleet.

That was all. But it was enough! Or was it? It introduced a new puzzle. Why would he go nutty over Countess Krak when he was violently opposed to electric-shock training? Was he playing some deep game?

The file, (bleep) it, was otherwise blank for my uses.

"Are you through tying up our machine now," said the criminal old clerk. "Or do you want us to move your bed up here?"

Ah, well, maybe I could use this information to chill his affair with Countess Krak.

I made one final punch,

> Deletions from file,

and expected a whole series of identoplate numbers to show up. Nobody can be that good. No deletion numbers showed. (Bleep)!

"Will you please get the (bleep) away from our console?" said the old clerk. "The conference is breaking up."

Chapter 8

They exited from Lombar's office, some of the cream of the Apparatus high ranks: gaunt, grayish faces, suspicious eyes, black uniforms, shabby, shabby, shabby. A general in the Army Division looks like a monument lit up for a feast day; a general of the Apparatus looks like a tramp abandoned him in a garbage can as not worth scavenging. They were stuffing papers in their cases, talking to one another out of the corners of their mouths the way felons do. There were fifteen of them. Four were Apparatus heads from other Voltarian planets, eleven were troop commanders. The military arm of the Apparatus—the one they maintain at home, that is— numbers four million guardsmen and while this is minuscule compared to the vast array of the Army Division of Voltar, it is enough to keep other parts of the government at bay. That eleven Apparatus generals had been seeing Lombar meant that something was having to be protected—something secret and sinister in the best Apparatus tradition.

I took my cap in hand, hoped for the best and walked bravely into Lombar's office. He was standing at his desk, scrabbling around, putting some order into the scattered papers of the conference. His hands were shaking. He looked irritable. *Not* good signs!

Lombar looked up and saw me standing there. He scowled. "Who sent for *you?*" he rasped. It was pointless to say that he had. "Shut up!" I hadn't even opened my mouth to speak. Where was the camaraderie he had shown on my last visit? But that was Lombar.

He scrabbled around some more. "Oh, yes," he said, and dredged a file up from the mess. It was one of those his clerks prepare for him to group all related matters of one subject. He snapped a paper out of it. "The invoice. Sign it!"

The paper he hurled at me was a shipping receipt. I studied the form:

The below named officer hereby signs for and acknowledges the safe receipt of SECRET CARGO No. 1, Shipment No. 1 from Blito-P3. All warrantied in good condition and full content.

_____

Signed Officer Soltan Gris, Section Chief, Section 451 (Blito-P3).

So *that* was what all the traffic was last night. The first freighter load in from Earth!

A wave of near nausea hit me. Supposing Jettero Heller had done his survey today instead of yesterday. I shuddered. He would have found this cargo piled up in its ready storeroom!

Somebody, one of the clerks, popped in and told Lombar, "It will be ready in a few minutes." He popped out. What "it" was, I had no idea. But I wasn't registering very well. Pure luck had saved this cargo from being exposed by Heller! (Bleep) him, he was too hard to control here on Voltar.

"Well sign it, sign it!" Lombar yelled at me.

I looked at him in helpless confusion. I didn't dare argue with him. Not Lombar Hisst!

Then he seemed to realize what was wrong. He sat down. "I forgot to tell you. You are still Section Chief of 451." He waved aside the remarks he must have supposed I was making. Talking with Lombar is pretty one-sided. He can imagine you are talking. Eerie. "I know, I know," he went on. But we looked all through the personnel files and we could not find anyone suitable to relieve you as Section Chief of 451. Yes, yes, but the numbers of Academy trained officers in the Apparatus are very few. And due to their silly Codes, they can't be trusted with honestly dishonest crooked business. So that leaves you."

It was a very left-handed sort of compliment at best.

I did manage, emboldened by hope, to get out a remark. "That means I'm relieved as handler of Mission Earth."

"Now you may wonder," said Lombar, "if this relieves you as handler of Mission Earth. It doesn't. You continue to have that, too."

He was getting down to it now. He sat back, fiddling irritably with a pen. "You may wonder how you are going to be on Blito-P3 and handle Section 451 on Voltar. But that is very simple. You have the 451 clerical staff here on Voltar and they'll continue under your chief clerk and they'll simply send anything to be signed to you on Blito-P3. You'll just send it back here, signed.

"Oh, yes, that reminds me. I don't trust the base commander in Turkey so you'll supervise him, too."

I felt like I was being pulled in several directions at once. He wasn't mentioning the key point: Jettero Heller would be operating in what they call "The United States" and I would have to be in Turkey! He was hard enough to control face-to-face. How could anyone control him a third of the way around a planet! This I would have to solve and quick!

"No, no, no," said Lombar as though I had spoken, which I hadn't. "The order for the 'goods' will come from here in blank. You'll sign it. The shipping form, attesting it has been shipped from Blito-P3, will be signed by you down there. And you will include with it a postdated receipt acknowledging the receipt of the shipment here. Very easy and straightforward."

It meant I wrote an order for a shipment as though I was on Voltar, got the order filled on Blito-P3, signed an attestation it had been shipped and then signed and attested it had been received back on Voltar.

"You're the only one whose signature we trust," said Lombar. "So we want only your signature and idento-plate on all this traffic. So sign that receipt you're holding there and you can get back to work."

I hadn't even *seen* the shipment. I only had a hint, from the blur of trucks in the tunnel, that it had arrived.

Lombar seemed to misinterpret my confusion. "Oh, the pay. Well, I'll see that you continue to be paid as Section Chief of 451. Then I'll see that you are paid again as mission handler for Mission Earth." Apparently he thought I was hung up on pay. "And then I can arrange for you to be paid as an inspector of cargos. Three additional paychecks." He looked searchingly at me. My confusion had not lightened one bit. "And then, of course, you'll get your little whack out of various allocations, outfittings, padded accounts and all that. You'll be wealthy. Well, I'm glad we settled all that."

He certainly was jumpy. He barked into a communications box, "Is it ready yet?" and got back, "Shortly."

I was standing there, trying to wrap my wits around these developments. I must have looked like I had been hit with a stungun.

"No, don't go," said Lombar, looking at the ready folder before him. "First sign that invoice."

What could I do? Numbly I signed and put my identoplate to the receipt for the first shipment from Blito-P3. I handed it over to him and he glanced at it, nodded and put it in the folder. It seemed to give him momentary satisfaction.

"Now," said Lombar, fingering a second paper, "there's this matter of a leak."

I went chill. What had he gotten word of now? The survey? What other thing?

"I have a clipping here from the newssheets, (bleep) them. One of these days we will wipe them out. Somebody leaked Mission Earth to the press." He flipped a page and there was the story: *"Famed Combat Engineer,"* the same one I had seen Heller reading. But I did not think it was much of a leak, really, for the orders were on the data circuit and, even if confidential, were available to many.

"I didn't leak it," I blurted.

"So I have ordered a full investigation of potential and existing leaks. Oh, I'll get down to this. You can't have Apparatus business being yelled from the building tops. Somebody, somewhere leaked this to the press!" He threw it aside. "So you don't know anything about it. Well, I didn't think you would."

An investigation? Oh, I better get off this planet!

Investigators turn up facts and they also turn up delusions. Dangerous!

I felt like I had been hit repeatedly with stunguns. I was really standing there paralyzed.

"No, don't go," said Lombar. "There's this letter from the Grand Council."

I read it upside down. Fortunately I have a few skills. One needs them in such a dangerous environment. It was from the Grand Council. It commended the Exterior Division for so wisely choosing an experienced combat engineer like Jettero Heller. It wondered why the Grand Council had had to be informed of this by the press. It said that the Grand Council would appreciate the courtesy of being kept posted on the progress of the mission. Particularly, the Grand Council wanted to be advised the instant said Jettero Heller departed from Voltar so the council could expedite if there were any unseemly delays.

"This means," said Lombar, "that so long as this mission is still on Voltar, the Grand Council will be in a position to stick their noses into our business. If there is delay in getting off, we'll have Crown inspectors all over the place looking into everything.

"Once you have this fellow out of here, we're all right. The Grand Council can be strung along for years. They can get agents into everything on Voltar but they sure can't get any onto Blito-P3.

"Your agent, of course, has to be language trained and prepared and it would make them suspicious if we just launched. But my advice to you is to let no dirt cool under your feet. Crown inspectors running all around could mean your neck, Soltan. Don't delay that launching! Understood? Good."

I was practically in a spin. Crown inspectors! But it was my decision to get away fast anyway. I felt a stab of irritation. Lombar wasn't helping. He'd delayed the mission himself by keeping me waiting half the morning.

I was saved from Lombar's further "help" by the entrance of a creepy looking staff doctor carrying a tray. Lombar looked at him in sudden relief. "Oh, it's here."

When I passed the old criminal clerk in the anteroom, he said, maliciously, "Feel better now that you've had your interview?" I must have looked like a wreck.

PART FOUR

Copy of a letter inserted in the manuscript at the date of this writing:

To My Lord, Chief Justiciary of the Voltar Confederation, Sir!

I, Soltan Gris, late Secondary Executive of the Coordinated Information Apparatus, Exterior Division, Royal Government (Long Live Their Majesties and the Voltar Dominions), in all humbleness and haste do herewith reply to your most urgent letter.

First, thank you for the acknowledgment of the first three parts of my narrative of events in this matter. I am happy to hear that you are satisfied that I am putting down everything I know concerning it, even to the smallest detail. I am aware that it is vital and important.

Second, thank you deeply for the assurance that there remains some chance of leniency for me and I am aware that it hinges upon my truthfulness.

Third, I express my deepest gratitude for your order to the guards, reaffirmed, to keep me supplied with water, food and writing materials. I wish to inform you that daily torture continues suspended and I abase myself in thanks.

And now, as to the underlined portion of your

message: Yes, I am aware that there is an arrest warrant out for one Jettero Heller, ex-Fleet Combat Engineer. No, I am sorry to say that I cannot give the Domestic Police tips or hints as to where he might be hanging out. This is not done from any impulse to protect Jettero Heller— heavens forbid. I have dreams of meeting him again so that I could kill him on sight.

I will, as you order, continue to detail the entire matter. Perhaps from these writings, some scrap can be gleaned as to his habits that would assist the Domestic Police.

All hail Your Lordship and His Court!

Your Most Unworthy Servant,
Soltan Gris

I resume my narrative.

Chapter 1

I had been rushing so hard down the tubes and corridors to get to the training rooms that when I opened the door and jumped in, I thought for an instant I was in the wrong section.

The smell of soap and disinfectant was overpowering! The Apparatus steals its cleaning materials from the Army Division—they are so seldom used it is not worthwhile to buy them properly. And the Army doesn't think anything is clean unless it stinks to the heavens of germ killers. It never occurs to anyone to steal materials from Fleet whose spaceships have to be odorless.

There is no circulating air in Spiteos. And the usual stench of these rooms, soaked as it is into the very stone, was simply being battered down by this gas attack of army cleaning chemicals.

I peered through the fog. Fully forty people, must be Krak's whole training crew, were spotted around the vast hall and nearby rooms. They were stripped to breech clouts and—I couldn't believe my eyes—their personal filth had been washed off! They had buckets and brooms and sprays and mops and they were gouging away at the centuries of litter and dirt. Bins of it were shooting down the escalator, going to only the Gods knew where.

Technicians were finishing the replacement of burned out lights. Another team was bringing in some new chairs and desks. What a turmoil! And too unusual in Spiteos to be readily understood.

But I had my own urgencies. I had to get Heller trained and gone. And fast. I shifted this way and that, looking for the Countess Krak.

And there she was! Over by a far wall. In a half-moon before her stood a group of fortress officers. I stepped toward them, fearful that something was up that would delay Heller's training. It was the deputy commander of Spiteos, the one that handles internal administration, and several of his troop officers, all in their filthy, ragged uniforms. There was some sort of argument in progress.

The Countess Krak was standing there talking to them. She was leaning on a broom. She was garbed in her shapeless work coveralls. The coveralls were wet! They had been *washed!* Through the gape in front was another surprise. She was clean. She had *bathed!* There was an exercise cloth wrapped around her head. Her hair had been *shampooed!* What in all the prayers to Gods was going on?

"I am very sorry," she was saying to the deputy commander. "But you will just have to accept it. In the future, I will train no more people that you have maimed!"

The deputy commander was a harassed-looking fat fellow. "But, Countess," he pleaded, "if we don't cut out their tongues before we send them to you, they will betray Spiteos when we ship them out."

"I have told you before," said the Countess, "but I will repeat it. The people picked up and sent here to be trained don't know where they are when they arrive. They don't find out while they are here. And in any event I can give each one a posthypnotic suggestion that he will become unable to answer the question, if he were ever to be asked where he had been. It is simply senseless and brutal to cut out their tongues. It makes them much harder to train."

The deputy commander sort of moaned.

"So that is how it is now," continued the Countess Krak. "I have tried to get this into effect before but it is final now. If you send me any damaged people, I will not train them. And that will be the end of your trained acts program."

The troops shifted restlessly. They were very nervous, having their eyes on that broom handle she was leaning on. With a savage one-two, she was capable of skewering any one of them with it before they could even flinch.

The deputy commander knew he would be the first to be spitted. He had been very ill at ease talking to her and now, with a sort of relief, capitulated. He lifted his hand in a self-protective gesture. "All right. As you say, so it shall be."

She gave a bright little laugh. My eyes bugged. The Countess Krak laughing?

The deputy commander got himself and his troops out of there. They went, whispering to one another, glancing back over their shoulders at her, just plain scared!

The Countess Krak swept up a pile of debris and dumped it in a box. She pushed the box along toward the escalator. She was humming! No words. Just the tune of some little ballad.

Her crew and workmen seemed to be finishing up for they were working at double, triple speed. Their eyes kept flicking toward her as they sped about polishing the place up. They were terrified at this change in her.

I myself was too frightened to go near her. I supposed her wits had flipped. There was no telling what she would do next! As they say in the high country beyond Kabar, "Lepertiges do not change their fangs."

Frankly, I was too scared to approach her, urgent as my business was. Lombar was clear up in the high tower; the Countess Krak was right here!

Her crew was practically finished. I drew off to one side after a while. The movement must have attracted her attention.

She came waltzing over to me. "Oh, Soltan," she said, "I am so glad to see you!" And she gave me a bright smile.

The Countess Krak *smiling* unnerved me. There was a big padded chair, a fairly new one, close by the wall. It had a new glowplate over it. A low table was in front of it and a matching chair was on the other side. A newly created cozy nook. I stumbled back against the big chair and sat down in it abruptly.

She had turned and was facing the whole room. She

clapped her hands together to attract attention. The more than forty men hastily turned to face her.

"I think," said the Countess Krak, "that this is enough for today. You have done very well. You are all sweaty now, so you should go wash your clothes and take baths. And then, because you have been up since the middle of the night," she paused and smiled brightly, "you can have the rest of the day off!"

You could have created the same effect by levelling a blastcannon at them. It had never happened before in the modern history of Spiteos. They looked at each other. They looked to the door to see if execution squads were waiting. They looked at her. They had worked for years for the Countess Krak. They didn't understand this. She lightly laughed. "Well, run along!" In terror they plunged en masse to the exit ramp and vanished.

She turned around and came walking toward me. Halfway across her smile vanished and her eyes blazed!

I knew it. I knew this change was not there to stay. She was still the Countess Krak! I braced myself for a blow.

She seized my arm and yanked me out of that chair like a cargo hook had grabbed me. She hurled me to one side.

Then she did a very idiotic thing. She took off her headcloth and carefully wiped the seat of the chair where I had been sitting. Just as if I had gotten it dirty!

She looked at me severely. "That is *not* your chair! This," and she swept her hand toward the small ensemble of two chairs and the table, "has been set up for Jettero!"

Then she softened, made some minute arrangements in the position of the table and adjusted some books and a language machine. And then she patted the chair.

She was all mellow again when she walked over to

the area where I was picking myself up. But there was a bit of calculation in her eyes, too.

"I've just remembered, Soltan, that you'll be going back to Blito-P3, too. You're Jettero's handler, aren't you?"

Well, she could figure that out from the language courses I'd laid out and that I was making Heller's appointments. I mumbled something about this being the case.

"And you're in full charge of preparing him and running some mission he is on?"

I nodded.

She smiled. She has very beautiful white teeth. I was very conscious of those teeth. She gently took my arm—ignoring my flinch—and guided me over to a bench and sat me down on it.

"You need a language brushup," she said.

I tried to get up nerve to tell her my English and Italian and Turkish and half a dozen other languages were in perfect shape. But my mouth didn't seem to want to talk. Too dry.

She walked sedately over to the racks and got down a hypnohelmet and came over to me with it. I offered no slightest resistance. After all, I'd spent weeks in these things. She patted my head comfortingly and then slid the helmet over it. From her coverall pocket she took a recorded strip.

"It's just a little accent check," she said, smiling gently.

She slid the strip into the slot and turned the helmet on.

There was the familiar buzz. I was out like a turned off glowplate.

I came to. I was a trifle surprised to see that a half hour had gone by. She was piling some books onto the table and neating up the chair some more. She saw I was out of it. She picked up a book and came over.

When the helmet was unstrapped and off, she patted me on the head again. "Now," she said, "read this and we'll see how your accent is. First, Virginian."

I thought this was pretty silly. There was nothing wrong with my accent in commercial English. She sensed resistance. "Now, Jettero will be talking Virginian. It's a city or something, isn't it? On some planet named 'Earth.' And you must be able to understand him. Read." And she pointed her finger at the page.

I read aloud,

> *Obedience is the mother of success, the wife of safety.*

Then,

> *The fear of some divine and supreme powers keeps men in obedience.*

She clapped her hands like a child. "Oh, that is very good, Soltan. You read it in perfect Virginian." I wondered how in Hells she knew it was perfect "Virginian." Had she been studying English?

She pointed her finger down the page, "Now, Soltan, read this in New England."

I read, speaking a bit nasally,

> *He who takes his orders gladly, escapes the bitterest part of slavery—doing what one does not want to do.*

"Ah, splendid, splendid, Soltan!" She yanked the book away. "Truly perfect New England."

Now, I myself had not been able to notice any real difference. I had imitated what they call "Americans" before and you just speak through your nose. I felt sort of funny.

A slam-bang opening of the main door halted any further conversation. The Countess Krak went flying off in that direction. I got up and went over to see what this was all about.

What? It was one of Snelz's guards with a big package for her. I was in time to catch a flash of the label: something about, "To a dazzling star."

She took the package. She seemed confused. Upset. Embarrassed. "For *me?*" she asked.

"That's what he said, Countess."

In a sort of a daze she put it on her desk and tore it open. Then she just stood there, staring down. At length she said, "Ooooo!" and put her hand to her breast. She was cooing!

I got into a position so I could see what it was. A bomb? So she could break out?

She lifted something up. She ran over to a mirror and held it against her. She said, "Oooo!" and ran back to the package and got something else and then ran to the mirror. . . .

The card slipped off. It was signed "Jet."

Oh, my Gods! He was giving her clothes! Now giving an unmarried woman clothes means just one thing: a pass! Trouble, I thought, you have my address!

The package, when it all got sorted out, contained *three* skintight, elastic cover suits, the very latest fashion. One was shimmering black, one was bright scarlet and one was gleaming silver. Each had a matching pair of elastic ankle boots with small flowers on them and each had a matching headband with flowers to match the boots. Extremely feminine stuff. For the Countess Krak?

I got it. All he had heard of my dissertation on her, possibly, was that she had no clothes!

(Bleep) him. And (bleep) Snelz! The platoon commander must have sent a guardsman all the way to the city at dawn. Heller, sleeping so peacefully when I left, must have been right behind me out that door!

She was waltzing around in the center of the room, holding the silver one against her.

Then she rushed back to the desk and found his card and pressed it to her chest.

I looked at my watch. Ouch, were we overdue for instruction this morning! I started to hurry out.

"No, no!" cried the Countess Krak. "Give me twenty minutes before you bring him down. I have to bathe again and get dressed!"

Right that moment I got a horrible premonition that all this was going to wind up in catastrophe. I do wish now I had learned to obey my hunches. They were right!

Chapter 2

In my room I found Jettero Heller lounging in an easy chair, eyes half-closed, idle beyond belief. The furthest thing from his mind appeared to be Mission Earth. Some supplementary reading I had given him lay in a neglected pile. Soft but plaintive music was coming over the Homeviewer and some female singer was on the screen. Love songs!

Now if there is anything that hurts my sensitive ears it is a high-pitched, echo orchestra and the quavering, sobbing soprano of a love balladess. Furthermore, they paint their faces black for "unrequited love" and by means of tubes beside their eyes they shed red tears— tears of blood. And the melodies are all down scale:

> *And so faded my glow*
> *Into the sorrow*
> *That took me in tow*
> *To the deep pits of woe*
> *And with my last breath*
> *I'll still cry for death*
> *And grave clothes to use*
> *as my trousseau.*

Sickening!

So this was Heller's idea of charging out and getting the job done!

In a flash of insight, I realized what I was up against. Love! There are warnings in the standard espionage texts: they give a lot of biological tables stressing that it is irrational; they go over a lot of examples of how even Royal houses have been destroyed because the practical marriage orders were flouted by young Princes and Princesses who stupidly fell in love with somebody else; they don't tell you how to use it but they warn against pairing a male and female agent. They say there's no way to thwart it short of shooting somebody. Well, the professors might not be able to use it, but I could. I owed my rise in the Apparatus to being cunning.

I was cunning now. In a very sweet voice, I said, "You had better get cleaned up. In . . . ," and I ostentatiously looked at my watch, ". . . twenty minutes you have an appointment in the training rooms with the Countess Krak."

Holy Gods! He came out of that chair like he'd been catapult-launched.

He had washed his white exercise suit the night before but in this airless cubicle it wasn't dry and he frantically rigged a heat fan. He rushed about, showered, dried and combed his hair and dressed and all in about eight minutes. Then, of course, we had to wait three or four minutes and he sat there fidgeting. I turned off the Homeview: I couldn't take any more echo orchestra and down scale love ballads—they came through to me more like funeral dirges and if I didn't get Heller off this planet, there was going to be one more—mine.

Still a minute early, we arrived outside the training rooms. He went through the door.

I was about to follow him when a hand stopped me. It was the Countess Krak's training assistant, a very ugly brute. "Message just came, Officer Gris. You're wanted at the central guard office at Camp Endurance."

What now? In some alarm I made sure two guardsmen were posted outside the door and went tearing off.

It always takes time to get through the tunnel and it was almost an hour later when I arrived at the Camp Endurance guard office.

The filthy Apparatus duty officer looked over his sheets in some mystery. "Oh, yes. There was a general call for you . . . wait. It is logged as just before dawn. Good Devils, Officer Gris! Didn't they find you this morning? I am sorry, Officer Gris, but it's for the fortress internally and we didn't get more than the general recording of it. . . ."

I cut him off. "I answered that call hours ago! Cancel it."

"But we're not sending it out!" he said. "It was for the internal . . ."

In brand-new alarm, I realized I had been fooled!

The Countess Krak! She had wanted me out of the way. What were they planning? A breakout?

Real terror gripped me at the thought of what Lombar would do to me if Heller got loose! I grabbed a tunnel zipbus that didn't zip fast enough to satisfy me. I raced through the fortress and back to the training rooms. Gods knew what I would find!

I burst in.

It was the most peaceful scene you ever saw. Heller was sitting in the chair she'd gotten for him; the recorded strip player was on the table running, putting out quiet roars; the Countess Krak was sitting in the other chair. She was dressed in the silver elastic suit; her hair was tied with the silver ribbon with flowers on it; her feet, relaxed, were cased in the silver ankle boots: I will say she looked heart-stoppingly beautiful. She had her elbows on the other side of the table and her chin was cupped in her palms. She was looking at him adoringly.

I sidled over, pretty mad, really. "That was a cute trick you pulled," I hissed, too low for Heller to hear.

She turned her face to me. Her eyes were a smoky blue and shining. She had a half-smile on her lips. Utterly relaxed, she whispered back, "Isn't he beautiful?"

I was disgusted. But then, I thought, even a female lepertige probably falls in love from time to time. I went out in the passageway: I really couldn't stand to look at them. To me, the situation was too dangerous.

Using my communications disc, I got an underground line to the Section 451 office in Government City. My chief clerk there—an old criminal named Bawtch—didn't sound very happy that I had been retained as Chief of the Section. He told me they had been shuffling papers perfectly all right and hoped I didn't have any orders: he said they didn't need any disorders right now. It wasn't really insolent; that's just the way Bawtch is. He soured on life some seconds after he was born and has made a profession of deteriorating ever since.

I did find out that some new texts and paperbacks had come in on the just arrived freighter from Earth as well as recent issues of the *New York Times* and *Wall Street Journal,* a couple of newssheets they print on that planet. I told him to put the lot on the Spiteos shuttle and he sighed and hoped I wouldn't be calling again soon.

I dawdled around, made some notes on what I was supposed to get going. Then I went back in to see how the language lessons were progressing.

What? They were no longer at the table! I stepped further inside and there they were in the middle of a big training platform.

She was teaching him unarmed combat? My orders were that no espionage tactics . . . Then I checked myself. They weren't doing unarmed combat. Heller was showing her the latest dance routines! The "Shatter" had been popular in the last few months. The male lunges out and the female flips away; the female lunges and the male rolls away: back and forth, somewhat athletic but kind of monotonous. They had a timing ticker, used to coordinate acrobats, and it was going to a dance beat. Heller was showing her the foot positions and the arm reaches.

She had killed a guard just reaching toward her. And here it was happening. In sort of like the frozen state where you watch an inevitable accident about to occur, I stood there and watched this. Sooner or later he was going to touch her on a reach. . . .

He did! I expected sudden death.

"Oh," she said, "I have been here so long I am all out of date. Let's see: when you lunge, I am supposed to roll, not just stand there like a ninny and get hit!"

He lunged again and once more she didn't roll and his hand touched her shoulder. The Countess Krak being clumsy? Hard to teach? Never!

And he finished the lunge by taking her in his arms and holding her close to him. And they just stood there.

And then he kissed her!

I expected fireworks. But the only fireworks was a sort of invisible glow that I could practically feel clear over where I was. She dropped her head back and looked up at him. "Oh, Jet," she whispered.

I came out of my daze. This would never, never do. I clapped my hands together three times sharply. I had to do it again, louder, before they took any notice of me.

They finally walked over, holding hands, looking at each other like a couple of kids sharing some secret.

"We're due," I said severely, "for our appointment with Doctor Crobe. Come along right now, Heller!"

Chapter 3

The biological section occupied a complex series of old stone vaults and rooms about a hundred feet below ground level. Unlike the rest of the fortress and despite the black stone, the place was glaringly lit. I never have been all the way through that section: it is too repulsive; but it consists of libraries, operating rooms, freeze banks and vast compartments of vials, vials, vials and tanks, tanks, tanks. If Spiteos smells bad, it is nothing compared to the biological section: they have a habit of spilling cultures which putrefy and leaving around discarded flesh and body parts that rot. It is about as sanitary as a sewer.

In the first library an old crone was pottering about, shifting files and noisily snuffling back the snot which trickled onto her upper lip. I waved one hand at an upper shelf, the other at Heller and yelled at her, "Blito-P3." She is quite deaf, being over a century and a half old, but she heard me. She moved to get a rickety ladder and so I left Heller standing there while I went off to find the chief cellologist.

Doctor Crobe was in a rear operating room. The moment I entered he held up a filthy hand not to be disturbed. I had to stop and watch.

He had a poor wretch strapped down on an operating table and was finishing up some work. The man, who had probably been a perfectly normal person a few weeks ago, was getting the last touches needed to make a circus freak.

By means of reorganizing and grafting cells, Crobe had replaced the poor (bleepard's) arms and legs with big tentacles from some sea creature. Bone had been grafted above the eyes to make a protrusion over each one. Crobe was checking the growth and rooting of a "tongue" taken from some insect-eating animal, a tongue that could be flicked out half a yard, as though the new monstrosity lived on flying bugs.

Crobe's twist was making freaks but he never realized, I am sure, that with his overlong arms and legs and beaked nose he himself was a freak. As he worked he had an eerie, ecstatic look on his face: a real, dedicated scientist! He would give anyone the creeps. Crobe really believed in what he was doing!

I caught a glimpse of the new freak's own eyes. From their expression it was obvious that the poor (bleeper) had gone insane. Oh, well, Crobe's freaks didn't live too long: when the old ones died, the circuses just bought new ones. The public got tired of them anyway: good for business all around.

"There," said Crobe, standing up and getting the crick out of his back. "The one and only specimen of life from the unconquered Planet of Matacherferstoltzian!"

I knew my astrography. "There is no such planet," I said.

"Well, maybe not," said Crobe. "But here's a specimen of life from it anyway!"

"Come on out," I said. "I have a special agent for you to fix up."

Instantly, a pain hit me in the stomach! I looked around. Maybe it was the smell that was making me feel sick. Very peculiar. I've been on many planets and eaten lots of strange food; I had been in the Apparatus for years with all that entailed. And I had never before had a pain in the stomach!

Crobe's assistants took over and I got the old loony out of there.

In the library, Heller had found a stool. He was looking through some books the old crone had gotten him. He nodded briefly when I introduced Crobe.

"I never got down on the planet's surface," said Heller. "All this is very interesting. It's a beautiful planet, you know." He had found some pictures of Earth people and was suddenly very thoughtful, looking up and then back at the pictures.

A couple of Crobe's assistants had followed us in. One was carrying a portable table, the other had a tray of things.

Crobe sat down, "What planet you going to?"

"Blito-P3. Earth," I said.

"Ah," said Crobe, and one of the assistants started opening some file drawers and piling things on his desk. Crobe looked at one of the references. "Blito-P3. Humanoid. Gravity . . . er . . . hmm . . . atmosphere . . . Styp, hand me that table of bone densities." And the assistant did. "Ah," said Crobe.

"The agent," I said, "must be undetectable by Blito-P3 planetary standards."

"Yes, yes," said Crobe, brushing me aside. "Styp, no scales." And Styp rushed out and returned rolling a dolly loaded with equipment.

"Strip," said Crobe, gesturing at Heller. For some reason, I felt a twinge of nausea and pain. What was wrong with me?

Heller, his attention more on the bookshelves than on Crobe, stripped. He seemed to be looking for some title up there. But he stepped on the scales and, although a bit distractedly, did what he was told. The assistants punched and measured and recorded away with occasional grunts from Crobe.

Styp had forgotten to bring in a bone densimeter so he went out to get one. Crobe didn't run a very organized show. Shortly after Styp's return with the bone densimeter I heard some little mutters and commotions at the door.

There were about five staff females standing there, peering in, whispering to one another. I do not know what they were saying but their eyes were getting sort of round and they were excited and stirred up.

I looked back and saw they had their attention on Heller. An assistant was making him bend and flex so as to measure potential foot-pounds of muscle power. Yes, he was quite a figure. He looked like some big woods God with a lot of little dirt Devils capering around. He was as out of place here as a temple sculpture in a cesspool. Come to think of it, he resembled that statue in the Voltar Gallery, the famous one done by Dawvaug called *The God of Dawn.* Hey! I thought, what the Devils is the matter with me, I'm no man-lover: and when Crobe gets through with him . . . I was instantly sick at the pit of my stomach. I had to sit down quickly on a stool to keep from doubling over.

They had finally finished. Crobe had a thick sheaf of notes. *"You,"* said Crobe to Heller, like it was an indictment, "are from the Planet Manco. Weight, height, densities . . . yes, Manco."

Well, Hells, anybody would know Heller was from Manco just glancing at him. It's not that Voltarians from Manco are so different: any one of its five races has a special look; but that's also true of any planet's population. Then I had a sudden realization. The Countess Krak was from Manco! They were of the same race exactly!

Crobe was rattling through his reference books on Blito-P3. He hummed and hawed and scrubbed his jaw. Then he said, "The weight difference between Manco and Blito-P3 is not that extreme: Blito-P3 is about one-sixth less gravity. That means you'll have to practice walking and running before you go out in public.

"Hmmm. Oh, yes. Atmosphere. The atmosphere is less dense and so you will have to remember to aerate yourself regularly—about once a day. Just breathe more heavily. And oxygenate yourself well before any strenuous exercise. Otherwise you will feel tired after a while.

"What's the local name of this planet. Earth? Oh, yes. Well, your bone density is greater than theirs, due to the gravity difference.

"Now as to nutrition, you'll have no real trouble. Their water and food is digestible by you. Hmm. But there is something here on nutrition you must pay attention to. For some reason, their food doesn't meet normal nutrition standards and especially not for you. Now, what I would advise is that you eat more often and don't let yourself go hungry. Hmm. Yes. They have a food called 'hamburgers.' You can eat most anything you please but hamburgers provide a balanced ration for you.

"Drinks. Hm. Water, all right. Ah, yes, alcohol. They heavily imbibe alcohol. Don't touch any drinks called 'strong spirits.' They disorganize the cerebral orientation. Hmm. Beer. They have something called 'beer.' You can drink that without trouble but not 'strong liquors,' whatever they are."

Crobe pulled his notes together and I was feeling better. "So," he said, "you be sure to exercise every day. Otherwise, in that low gravity, your muscles and tendons will get flabby. And oxygenate yourself. And eat hamburgers and drink beer and you'll be fine."

I felt a surge of relief for some reason.

Then suddenly Crobe's voice was very sharp. "Are you listening to me?"

Heller was still abstracted, glancing now and then at the shelves. But why should he listen? Crobe, whether he knew it or not, was talking to a spacer who had to do all these things anyway—except the hamburger and beer.

"I go to all this work," snapped Crobe, "and you don't even listen!"

"Oh, I heard you," said Heller. "Learn to walk, oxygen, exercise, water, nutrition, hamburger and beer. I appreciate it." He bent over and picked up a book that had big color plates, pictures of people, the races of Earth. He tapped them with the back of his hand. "I was just struck by the appearances of these races on Earth. You wouldn't happen to have here the book *In the Mists of Time*, would you?"

That really annoyed Crobe. "No, of course not! This

is the anthropology library!" I got sick at my stomach again.

The old crone held up her hand in a gesture to wait and snuffled off. She came back carrying a scuffed-up volume about two feet thick. "It was in the history library," she said with a toothless smile at Heller.

He put it down on the table. Crobe was gathering up his papers with some hostility.

The volume cover tabs said,

> Abridged Edition. In the Mists of Time, Legends of the Original Planets of the Voltarian Confederacy, Compiled by the Lore Section, Interior Division.

I wondered what the unabridged editions must be if the abridged was this huge tome.

"Fables," Crobe was muttering to himself.

Heller had found what he wanted. He had turned to the *Manco Section*. His finger was poised at *Folk Legend 894M*.

"Got it," he said. "Haven't seen it since nursery school." He read:

> Folk Legend 894: And it is said that some thousands of years ago, during the Great Rebellion on Manco, that Prince Caucalsia, finding his cause irretrievably lost, did flee Manco with the remnants of his fleet, taking with him numerous followers and their families and did depart the Manco System. And it is further related, nine years having passed by, that two transports did return to Manco, landing at the Fortress City of Dar. They were treacherously betrayed, it is said, by a

woman named Nepogat and apprehended in
the night. The crews were interrogated by the
Apparatus and it was later claimed that they
revealed a landing by Prince Caucalsia upon
the Planet Blito-P3 after his escape from
Manco. And it is further said that the Prince
had founded a colony named Atalanta with
all his numerous followers and they did pros-
per there. But failing all but little fuel and
lacking some supplies, two freighters had
been sent in hope of peaceful return and
even engagement in trade. But it was decreed
that mercy be given not. Blito-P3 coloniza-
tion was deemed illegal at that time and in violation of the Holy Invasion Timetables of
Voltar. At the insistence of the woman Nepogat the freighter crews were put to death.
The turmoil of the times foreswore any further campaign to punish Prince Caucalsia,
the Fortress City of Dar was burned in the
Great Overthrow of the succeeding year and
all records that could substantiate the legend
have vanished from view. This folk legend
forms the background of the child fairy tale:
Nepogat the Damnable and is found in the
Manco child's song "Bold Prince Caucalsia."

"Rubbish!" said Crobe. "I will have you know, whatever your name is, that the moment fable enters the
world of solid science, we are lost!"

Crobe was almost frothing. "You are overlooking
one important fact!" he told Heller. "Humanoid forms
are the commonest sentient forms in the universe! They
comprise 93.7 percent of all populations discovered to

date. The humanoid form is inevitable from the basic sur-
vival demands of any reasonable carbon-oxygen planet: if
sentient life is to appear and succeed, the adeptness of
hands, the articulation of feet, the symmetrical right-left
body construction and flexible skin are needed."

Why you old fraud! I thought. You know all that and
yet you make freaks and pretend they are other populations!

"The facts are built into the structure of cells!"
harangued Crobe. "But every sentient population of a
planet evolved there. And *that's* the scientific fact. Forget
your religions and fables! Oh, of course," he said, mod-
ifying his view, "the blood cells are different, humanoid
race to humanoid race, and these are the one channel by
which you can identify crossbreeding between planets."

Heller said mildly, "I was just interested in the similarity between the facial bone structures of the races on
Earth, some of them, and the races on Manco."

"I'll show you!" snapped Crobe as though Heller
had been arguing with him. The cellologist rushed out.
I had an idea where he was going: the deep freeze body
vats. And sure enough I shortly heard from there the
chunk of an axe.

Crobe rushed back in. He was carrying a frozen
human hand chopped off at the wrist. He dug into the
dirty litter on a cart and came up with an instant-thawer
and in a moment the severed hand started to bleed.
Leave it to Crobe to hack off a hand when all he wanted
was a little blood. I began to feel ill, very ill.
"Earthman!" said Crobe, dripping some blood into a
culture.

Heller looked a bit startled. "Soltan, do you kidnap
Earth people?"

Yes, indeed, Royal Officer Heller. "No," I said. "We

picked up some bodies years ago from vehicle accidents and they're here in deep freeze for study."

Crobe shot me an odd glance, as well he might. He threw the hand on the floor where it landed with a plop and gave his attention to lining up the culture vial in a microscope.

Then the doctor took a filthy, sharp probe and, before I could stop him, seized Heller's hand and punctured his thumb. I almost threw up. I couldn't account for my reaction.

But Crobe didn't do any more to Heller. He took the blood sample and put it in another vial and set it up in a second microscope. "Now take a look at that!" he challenged Heller. "And once and for all you see there is no crossbreeding between Manco and Blito-P3! Anything human on Earth generated on Earth. That's scientific fact!"

Heller looked at both. "They're similar," he said.

"Ha!" said Crobe. "Unqualified observer!" He gave Heller a shove off to one side and looked himself. He straightened up. "Officer Gris, was that one of your Earth agents? Go in that vault and look. No." He changed his mind and picked up the hand and threw it into a bone densimeter. "Well, it *was* an Earthman."

Crobe gathered up his notes and bawled at an assistant to collect up the dolly and table. He pointed to a stool and said to Heller, "Go ahead and sit there and dream up your fables." And Heller smiled faintly and picked up the book of color plates again.

The doctor went to the door and beckoned to me urgently and I followed him into an even more filthy office. I was afraid to sit down for fear I'd find a piece of a corpse under me. But I was feeling poorly and I got on a stool.

Crobe sat down and indicated his notes. He leaned

forward like a conspirator. What else? "Officer Gris, we've got problems with this agent. We're in trouble."

He hadn't sounded like that before. My stomach felt worse.

"Officer Gris, we'll have to work over that agent." He looked at his notes. "The weight is all right. He weighs about 239 pounds here and he'll weigh about 199 pounds on Earth. That will pass unnoticed. It is his age." He thumped some tables. "Now according to this, possibly due to nutrition or some malfunction inherent in their organ evolution, Earthmen do not live out a proper life span. Any self-respecting mammal on any self-respecting planet that has any self-respecting cellular structure normally lives six times as long as its growth period."

Well, I knew that. What of it?

"On Blito-P3," said Crobe, consulting his tables, "they are reported to mature and achieve full growth by the age of twenty. That may be too fast for them. But, whatever, they should live to about one hundred and twenty years of age. They don't. They usually kick off at seventy or before."

"Crobe . . . ," I began to say that he wouldn't be there that long and then I definitely realized he would! But so what?

"To compound this problem," continued Crobe, "the growth period of a humanoid on Manco is thirty-two years. And they *do* live their factor of six. Now, unless something else gets to him first, this special agent of yours will live to be about one hundred and ninety-two."

I couldn't see what all this had to do with it.

"That special agent in there is about twenty-eight years of age. He is right this moment six feet two inches tall. Growth in the last years is small but by the time he is thirty-two, he will be six feet five inches!"

I was feeling sick and apprehensive. I knew something was coming.

"The average height," said Crobe, consulting his table, "for a race on Earth that has his skin color—white? more like bronze—is only five feet eight and a half inches." He threw down his papers and looked at me. "He is too tall! He is going to stand out like a lighthouse!"

I started to pooh-pooh it. Crobe said, "Wait. He will also look too young to them." He peered at his tables. "Yes. He will look to them like a boy of about nineteen, even eighteen." Crobe held up some age photos he had. "See?" Then he smiled. "But all is not lost. We can save it."

He leaned over toward me, very close. He got that crazy look on his face he gets on the subject of freaks. He said, "We can subsection his legs and arms. We can take out some pieces of bone from each. We can also shrink his skull . . . Officer Gris! What is the matter?"

I was doubled up. I was holding my stomach with both hands. I have never before felt such pain in my life! I started to vomit. I vomited all over my legs, all over the floor. I threw up everything I had eaten for a week. And then went into agonizing, dry retches.

It must have made a horrible commotion. Noisy! The next thing I knew, Heller was standing there, holding my head.

One of Crobe's assistants got a tube and tried to get some fluid down my throat. I threw it up violently! Another fanned a vapor bottle in front of my face but it just made it worse.

Heller was barking some orders to someone. The two platoon guards came in. Heller took a redstar engineer's rag from his pocket and wiped off the worst of it from my face. Then he got a stretcher from an assistant and put me on it very gently. The two guards got on either end and we left that place.

Chapter 4

In my room, Heller got my clothes off me and put me in the bath and when he had the mess washed away he got me into my bed. He was amazingly solicitous. He turned a drying lamp to put heat onto my stomach area, hoping that would help.

I lay there in dull misery. I had never felt so ill in my whole life, even worse than talking to Lombar.

Heller picked up some of my clothes from where they had fallen. "These are ruined," he said.

I went rigid with alarm: he was emptying the pockets! I couldn't think of any way to stop him. When one is not going regularly to a place of work, he tends to make himself into a sort of walking office; there were notebooks, old envelopes, messages, you name it. If he were to comb through them, the double cross of Mission Earth might be exposed!

But he was just putting them aside in a pile. He was not even looking at them. Sick as I was, I felt a slight edge of contempt for his total ignorance of the espionage game. He was a child!

He put the numerous weapons in a second pile and then he took the whole uniform, cap, boots and everything, verified it was empty and dumped it in the waste disposer. Well, it had been pretty dirty and stinky even before the "accident" today.

One of the guards had remained inside the room, ready to help him. Heller fished my identoplate from the pile of papers and handed it to the guard.

"No!" I pleaded weakly.

"Go down to the camp," Heller told him, "and get a complete new General Services uniform from their supply."

The guard gave him a crossed-arm Fleet salute—they never saluted me—and vanished with my identoplate.

"Heller," I wailed. "With that plate he'll just buy half the prostitutes in Camp Kill! You've bankrupted me."

"Oh, I don't think so. Soltan, you'll just have to learn to trust people."

Trust riffraff and criminals like these? "Oh, I am too ill for a conduct lesson! Don't moralize at me."

He adjusted the heat on my stomach and put a cool wet cloth on my head. "Feeling better?"

I wasn't. Heller cleaned up the mess the clothes had transferred to the floor. These Fleet spacers are amazingly neat. He undressed and took a shower himself. He washed out his redstar engineer's rag and then his exercise suit. He neated the whole place up and then put on a one-piece casual evening suit. He combed his hair and then, looking like something that just stepped out of a tailor's window, he turned on the Homeview and sat down.

My heart almost stopped. He was leaning forward and reaching toward the two piles from the suit. I thought he was going to go through my papers!

But he didn't. He reached toward the weapons pile and picked up a blastick. "Quite an arsenal you've got here." He opened the blastick load chamber and checked the power cartridge. "You have to be careful of these things. They ship them with a dummy load—looks just like the real thing. Well, this one is okay."

I expected him to, any moment, start pawing through the papers. But he picked up the stungun and verified its load. He reached again and once more I held my breath. But he picked up the ten-inch Knife Section blade. He looked at it curiously. They certainly aren't common. If you know them, there is a certain way you can flick at the tip and make them sing. He flicked the tip and made it sing. "Good alloy," he said.

His hand moved up and before I could even see what he was going to do, it left his hand with such velocity it hissed. I flinched. Was it coming at me?

There was a melon on a shelf and the knife hit it dead center and went through it with a thunk! He went over and removed it with a sort of double flip of his wrist and stood there offering me a neat slice of melon. "Want some?" he said. The thought of it made me go green inside again. "Sorry," said Heller, "but sometimes a melon can cool one down."

He replaced the piece of cut melon and returned to the chair but he still didn't reach for any papers. He cleaned up the knife and its scabbard.

The guardsman came back with a package of uniforms. He returned the identoplate. Heller handed him a credit note and the guard said, "Will that be all, sir?" They never said "sir" to me. But then, I thought nastily, you can buy a lot of things with a credit note.

But that wasn't the end of it. The fellow leaned over and whispered something in Heller's ear and Heller smiled and whispered back. They both grinned. What were they planning? A breakout?

The guard stepped back and was about to salute when Heller pointed at the floor. "You dropped the money."

"So I did," said the guard and picked it up and put it in his pocket. Then he gave Heller a salute and left. So the guard wasn't only interested in money, I told myself. They *were* up to something.

Heller got a textbook about Earth and began to read. He still ignored my papers. What a fool! He wouldn't last ten days on Earth.

Somehow this made me feel worse and I began to worry about myself. I had never before had any stomach trouble. I didn't seem to have a fever.

What could it be?

If I were to go down to Doctor Crobe, he would tell me that he would put in a new stomach. I thought about Crobe. I would never, never, never permit myself to go unconscious around that loony: you could wake up with a cow's head!

That suggestion he had made about Heller's legs . . . !

I was sick all over again! There was nothing left to throw up. I just hung off the side of the bed, retching.

Heller got a pan but it wasn't needed. He dampened a cloth and put it on my forehead. But I didn't pay much attention. I was desperate. I could not go on being sick like this. I'd not just be sick if I didn't run this mission. I'd be dead!

I lay there. Heller had gone back to the textbook. I made myself think calmly and rationally. When had this illness begun?

With careful concentration I thought it over. It had started when I went into Crobe's area. There was something totally poisonous about Crobe!

Yes, each time I concentrated on him, I felt sick!

Ha! It was obvious! I must never go near Crobe again! Never, never, never!

Abruptly, I was totally well! One instant I was feeling horrible. The next instant I was feeling great! There was not the tiniest suggestion of pain or nausea!

I sat up in happy relief.

"Feeling better?" said Heller. I nodded vigorously.

"Well, sometimes these things pass away pretty quick. After all, you're young and healthy. Some fast bug, no doubt. I'm glad you're better."

I got up, washed my face again and put on my new uniform. I stuffed my telltale papers in my pockets and rearmed myself.

Life looked absolutely wonderful!

Chapter 5

But as the priests of Voltar say, "Never get too fond of happiness or the Gods will take it away." And so it was that evening.

Heller pottered about, neating things up, cleaning things, polishing up the table, straightening up the room. I ignored his spacer passion for bright, good order. I didn't even mind the echo orchestra he had playing on the Homeview. I occupied my time neating up my pocket papers.

There was a knock on the door and I opened it. Two of the guardsmen were standing there with a big box on a low, wheeler dolly. "For you," said one.

It was an awfully big box. I couldn't remember ordering anything of the sort. "For me?"

"For you all right," said the guardsmen. "See?"

It was too dark in the passageway to read the label so they pushed it on into the room and closed the door behind them.

Sure enough, a big sign on top of the box read,

URGENT. OFFICER GRIS ONLY!

The solemnity of their expressions, the way Heller was watching, should have alerted me. But I had been feeling too good.

I put out my hand, grasped the handle on top and opened the lid. What I expected to see I don't know. But what I did see was pure horror!

The head of a zitab! The wide-open, gaping fangs of the most venomous reptile on Voltar! A murder plot!

The lid flopped open!

I went backwards from that box as though catapulted!

I literally sailed through the air. I hit into the shower compartment! My scrambling hands pulled the curtain down! The perched lotion and soap bottles fell and hit my head in a cannonade! I was still trying to go backwards through the wall!

The zitab rose in the air, all five lethal feet of him! I felt that in the next second it was going to strike straight through the air and clear across the room. How was it suddenly stationary in midair?

And then, oh, my Gods, even worse, the Countess Krak, dressed in flaming red, stood up out of that box!

They all went into shrieks of laughter! The guards, Heller and the Countess Krak, that is!

She was holding that zitab just behind its head with one hand. She had held it under the lid and lifted it up as though to strike. But right now, with her other hand, she was holding her stomach she was laughing so hard!

And they went right on laughing. They doubled up. A guard collapsed on the floor, absolutely dying with guffaws! Heller was laughing so hard he had to support himself on the back of a chair and tears were rolling out of his eyes.

It felt like it went on for ten minutes at least!

I wasn't taking it very well. Oh, my Gods! A fortress prisoner up here in the upper works, totally out of bounds: somebody could be shot! It was a terribly dangerous game they were playing. And they were *laughing!*

After a bit, I looked at the zitab she was holding. For a moment I had supposed it must be stuffed. And then I got another shock: it was writhing about! It didn't even have its fangs drawn! One bite and you're dead. And there she was reeling around in laughter!

Gradually the din died down. The Countess Krak stepped out. She turned the zitab's head to face her and pointed a finger at its nose. It closed its mouth. She put it down in the bottom of the box and wagged a finger at it with a "you be good now" gesture. She closed the lid.

They had stopped laughing now and Heller went over and they held hands, just standing, looking at each other.

The guards got their breath back and with a cheery wave at Heller, wheeled the big box out into the passage and closed the door.

I was still lying in the wreckage of the shower and I made a noise trying to get up. It somehow attracted Heller's attention and he reluctantly disengaged his hands and came over to me.

"That was sort of rough on you, Soltan. But you'll have to admit, it was an awfully good joke." He helped me to my feet and then straightened the shower disarray.

I didn't admit it was a good joke. These stupid idiots were playing with bombs to bring her up here.

"So this is where you live?" said the Countess Krak. "I often wondered what else was in the top of the castle." She went around touching some things. "Except for Hisst's parades, I haven't been out of those dungeons in three years! But no window." She seemed puzzled for a moment, then, "This is Soltan's room, isn't it?" I wondered how she knew: Heller had cleaned it up.

Heller went over and got some soft music on the Homeview. Then he bustled back, the good host, and sat her down at the table. He opened the cupboard and I saw with amazement that it was stuffed with nice drinkables and edibles. He put a canister of pink sparklewater before her like she was Royalty and then, as an afterthought, tossed down two more at the other table places. He got out four varieties of sweetcake and heaped up a plate for her. He sat down beside her. Then as a distinct afterthought he waved at the chair on the other side of the table. "Draw up, Soltan. Don't be bashful." But he had turned back to her before he finished speaking.

They just sat and looked at each other, pleased so hard they glowed!

I sat on my chair and sipped cautiously at the pink sparklewater. It is pretty expensive; it has a lot of minerals and protein in it and its bubbles jump up about six inches above the canister top and make tiny, glowing explosions. Because it instantly assimilates, one can get a trifle high on it.

Without looking at me, Heller pushed some sweetcake my way. They were just gazing at each other, eyes happy, smiling. The soft music played. They didn't eat or drink. They just sat there, so pleased to be sitting there, so fed with each other's company that they didn't even touch their food or drink.

After a long time, Heller reached over and put a

piece of sweetcake in her mouth and then lifted his canister to her lips. She gave him a drink from hers.

I sure was extra, unnecessary company here!

Finally they got around to eating their supper but I knew that, under the table, their feet were tangled up.

When they had finished the meal, Heller finally sat back. At length, he said, "Oh, yes. There was something I wanted to show you." He reached over to a side table and picked up a pack of race-recognition practice cards he had evidently brought from the library. They have faces on the front and the correct names are on the back.

He showed her a card. "Who does this look like?" he asked.

I could see the back. It said,

Girl, English
Blito-P3 (Earth, Europe).

She looked very interested. But I felt she would have been interested in anything he showed her, even had it been a blank sheet of paper.

She said, "That looks like a farm girl from the highlands of Atalanta province, Manco. My people come from that area, you know. They had some estates there a few hundred years ago—until they lost them, that is."

"That's wonderful," said Heller. "I was born in Atalanta province. In the capital, you know: Tapour."

And they got into one of these "Did you know Jem Vis?" and "Do you remember the old lady Blice?" and "Is the courthouse still there?" interspersed with "You do?" and "What do you knows?" and "It's a small universe" that went on and on. They were fellow denizens of Manco, all right! Old Manco Reunion Week! It went on and on.

Finally they ran out of that, at least for the moment,

and Heller got back to his picture cards. He held up one
that said on the back,

Old Man, Polynesian
Blito-P3 (Earth, Oceania).

"One of the boat people from the harbor of Dar?"
she said.

"Now this one," said Heller. The back said,

Film Star, Female
American, Blito-P3
(Earth, Americas).

"That isn't your sister," said the Countess. Heller
showed her another. The back said,

Male, Caucasian
Blito-P3 (Earth).

"Is this some member of your family? It looks
dimly like an uncle I had." She pretended, only
pretended, to be severe. "What is this, Jettero Heller?
Are you trying to tell me you've just been to Manco? But
those pictures are not three-dimensional and their color
is poor. Oh, I place them now. They're anthropology recognition cards. Give them to me!" She playfully
snatched them out of his hand and looked at their backs.

She examined them a bit, turning them back and
forth. "Blito-P3?"

"You remember an old fable?" said Heller. And with
no prompting, he rattled off Folk Legend 894M, word
for word in its entirety.

"Wait," said the Countess. She was thinking hard.
Then she picked up her canister and began to swing it
back and forth to get a rhythm time. Then she started

singing in a rather throaty but pleasant voice. But she did manage to give it a childish pronunciation:

> *If ever from life you need fly,*
> *Or a king has said loved ones must die,*
> *Take a trip*
> *In a ship*
> *That will bob, dive and dip,*
> *And find a new home in the sky.*

Heller joined in:

> *Bold Prince Caucalsia,*
> *There you are on high.*
> *We see you wink,*
> *And we see you blink,*
> *Far, far, far above the Mo-o-o-o-n!*

They both laughed, pleased with their duet of the nursery song. They must have learned it as children.

The Countess Krak said, "What star really was it that we used to point to and call 'Prince Caucalsia'?"

"Blito," said Heller.

"You mean he really got there?" said the Countess, delighted.

Now, in my opinion, an engineer trying to get into historical anthropology, a subject far out of his line, can be awfully wide of the mark.

Heller turned to me. "Why do they call this race type Caucasian?" and he threw down the card. "You

know the planet. Is there some continent called
Caucasian?"

"I think it's just a general race type," I said. I
thought. Then I remembered. Heller does not have a
monopoly on memory and I had had to really grind
about Blito-P3. "There's a *Caucasus* district in southern
Russia. That's just north of Turkey. It's a sort of border
between the two continents, Asia and Europe. But I
don't think that's what type the name means. Maybe the
people came from there and maybe not, but there is a
Caucasoid race that migrated around and spread out pretty far. You find them all over the place now. The type
has minimal skin pigmentation, straight or curly hair,
high bridged, narrow noses. They have a high frequency
of what they call Rh-negative blood type and the
presence of a special blood element: I think you must
have been looking at it today."

"All right," said Heller. "Is there an 'Atalanta'? A
country or something?"

I thought about it. I had to go over and get a reference book out of the pile, a thing they call an
"encyclopedia." I read it aloud.

> "Atlantis, also called Atalantis and
> Atalantica, legendary island in the Atlantic
> Ocean beyond the Straits of Gibraltar. Its civ-
> ilization was thought to be very advanced. It
> was supposed to have been overwhelmed by
> the seas."

"Aha," said Heller. "Whatever Prince Caucalsia
founded got destroyed and the people had to migrate
elsewhere."

"Heller," I said patiently, "an engineer is *not* an
anthropologist!"

"Oh, but they are!" said the Countess. "They work out the whole geological cycle of a planet and to do that they have to know fossils and bones!" She was very prim about it. I realized that a certain person had been studying like mad!

"Well, maybe so," I said. And it might be true. "But a couple of names don't make a historical fact. Just coincidence! There are humanoids all over the place. There is no reason to believe that your Prince Caucalsia, or whatever his name was, put some races down on Blito-P3. I can show you fifteen planets where there are inhabitants that look like you or her or me."

"The poles shifted," said Heller, "probably got relocated in sea areas, the ice caps melted and it drowned the colony out. Poor Prince Caucalsia."

"The poor fellow," said the Countess.

"So that's what must have happened," said Heller. *"Well!* We better make awful sure it doesn't happen again and drown his descendants, too!"

"That would be a shame," said the Countess.

I should have had my wits examined. Here they were agreeing on the mission! And such was my dogged devotion to fact—except where it concerns affairs of the Apparatus, of course—that I just couldn't stand this much stupid sentimentality based on total illogics. "But Heller, we don't have any data, not real solid data, that Prince Caucalsia of Atalanta, Manco, colonized an island on Earth and called it Atlantis! Countrymen of yours weren't part of that migration!"

Heller was looking at me with his eyes slightly closed. "It's more poetic that way," he said.

Oh, my Gods! Was this an engineer? A hard-minded, rock and metal and explosives engineer?

"Besides," said Heller, piling illogic upon illogic, "she likes it."

The Countess Krak nodded very emphatically.

Conversation had ceased. I thought at first it was because I had put my foot wrong with them. They were just sitting there looking at me. Gradually I got the feeling that I was an unnecessary part of the scenery.

"Are there any empty cubicles along the passageway where you could sleep?" Heller said to me.

A shock ran through my head. If one of the sporadic guard patrols did a room check tonight, three heads would roll, including mine.

There weren't any other rooms cleaned or made up, though almost all of them were empty.

They continued to stare at me. In fact, they almost pushed me out with their eyeballs. I closed the door behind me and stood in the dim passageway.

The two guards were sitting to the right and left of the entrance, hunkered down against the floor, smoking puffsticks. I could tell by the smell they were an expensive brand. Money had been passed out and I wondered if Snelz would remember my cut.

I leaned against the wall and after a while absent-mindedly sat down. There was no moral indignation involved in my reaction: as you know, it is customary with many of the Voltarian Confederacy races for a male and female to live together two or three years before they get married. No, it was the danger of the thing. They say there is a very narrow line between a brave man and a fool. In my estimation, their daring had entered the world of (bleep) foolishness.

It was at that moment I realized that I had had them both agreeing in principle that the mission should be done and I recognized I had taken no advantage of it. Was it the pink sparklewater?

I heard some very small sounds coming from that room behind the closed door. Whispers? My eyes had grown accustomed to the gloom of the passageway and I looked toward the two guards. I would have expected to have found lascivious expressions on their faces, the look soldiers get when they hear about sex. But no, these two guards looked more like the relatives of the bride and groom, serious, hopeful. They sure had their ears glued to that door. They were communicating with each other by looks.

Inside, chairs scraped, plainly heard above the soft music. Then a long silence. A buckle clinked on the floor.

In espionage there are four types of operation: overt, clandestine, covert and secret. Those two in there apparently had no inkling of even common sense. They were engaged in something secret and they had it graded overt! They hadn't even turned up the music to muffle the sounds.

My imagination was running amok on what they were doing. The guards, from their looks, had some idea of the progress being made in there: they were sort of reassuring each other.

There was a creak of the bed. Then some more creaks. The soft music played on. Knowing what the Countess had done to that special agent that had touched her, it would not have surprised me to have had to rush in there with a stungun to save the last of Heller if I could. I felt there was no predicting the Countess.

Then her voice, plainly heard, "You will have to be careful with me, darling. I have never had a man before."

A reassuring murmur from Heller. Who was he to reassure? By his record, he had never had a female before! But races do continue and babies do get born. I stiffened in alarm. What if he made her pregnant! But I relaxed, we would be long gone by then.

There were rhythmic creakings then. They went on and on and on.

Then the Countess's voice, "Oh, Jet." She repeated it. She said it faster and faster, "Oh, Jet, oh Jet, oh JetohJet. Oh JET!" And there was a shuddering moan from Heller.

The two guards instantly leaped to their feet, totally silent! They shot their arms above their heads the way people do in a bullet ball game after a winning hit. They beat their fists together and jumped up and down. They had ecstatic expressions on their faces. They turned to each other and enthusiastically shook hands. And all without the tiniest sound! My, they were pleased!

At length the guards sat down and lit new puffsticks. The soft music flowed on inside.

Once more the bed began to creak in rhythm. It went on and on. Then the same shout and groans inside. The same performance from the guards.

Quiet once more. It came to me that those two in there were young and very strong and very much in love and that this was quite likely going to go on most of the night.

Another thumping distracted me. It seemed to be right under me. I looked down. Good Gods, I was sitting on the dolly box and the Zitab snake had come to life!

I leaped clear across the passageway!

The guards snickered.

I went into another cubicle. I lit the lights. It was dirty and a mess. It didn't even have a bed. Wearily, I closed the door, turned off the glowplates and with my cap for a pillow, lay down on the floor to get some sleep.

Some writer has said that all the planet loves lovers. It might include the guards, but it sure did not include one Soltan Gris.

What was going to become of Mission Earth?

Chapter 6

If the "rescue of Prince Caucalsia's colony" was so important, Jettero Heller and the Countess Krak certainly showed no signs of it. It wasn't that they, like me, considered the possibility that there had ever been a Prince Caucalsia to be farfetched and even preposterous. They had other things on their minds. And following more or less the same routine—daytime study in the training hall but nights in my room—they let one day follow another, beautifully happy in a world of their own.

My urgency to get Heller off Voltar was growing. And there were things to get done that weren't getting done. One of them consisted of getting him operated on to install a "body bug": unless I could keep track of his every minute on Earth, I would be unable to control him; that required that a device be put into him that he would not suspect; and *that* required that he be gotten onto a cellular surgery table. But as soon as I started planning this step, I got ill again: not violent all the time but very nagging and very uncomfortable. I was miserable.

If I could get him moved into town, I might be able to find a cellologist and get to work on him. But get him out of this fortress and away from the Countess Krak? All systems stop!

Five days went by. The shadow of Lombar seemed to loom closer and closer. Yet I had not yet come up with a single idea.

One afternoon I heard that Lombar was going to spend the next couple days at Endow's palatial country

estate. He would be secretly absent. The next morning
I used the fact to pretend I had to see him in his office.
Of course, he wouldn't be there and of course the clerks
would not be allowed to tell me so: I could use the pretended wait to get a crack at the master console.

The old criminal clerk would have suspected his
mother of high treason had she even ventured to say
"hello" to him. So when I sat down at the button board,
he went into his usual flap. But, as he did not dare say
when Lombar was expected and I pretended to believe
Lombar would be back any moment, the old clerk was
blocked.

I wanted to know if I had really been appointed. So
I slid my identoplate into the slot and fed in my own
name and punched,

> Present posts?

And the screen rattled off:

> Section Chief Section 451 on Voltar; Handler for
> Special Agent/agents of Mission Earth; In charge,
> Mission Earth; Inspector General Overlord all Oper-
> ations and Actions of Blito-P3 for the Exterior Divi-
> sion and Coordinated Information Apparatus.

The screen might be blinking but I really blinked!
Four paychecks! Lombar really was doing me up
beautifully. And as he said, there would be all the kickbacks and commissions and rake-offs. I could see myself
coming out of this quite well-off: maybe a cottage in the
Vaux Mountains, maybe even a hunting preserve!

Then the computer rapidly added a string of letters
saying,

> All appointments made at the insistence of said Offi-
> cer Soltan Gris; routinely ratified by the clerical
> section.

It puzzled me for a bit and I sat there staring at it. It sort of meant that neither Endow nor Lombar Hisst had forwarded or ratified the appointments. But it made me totally responsible personally for everything that went on anywhere concerning Blito-P3. A little overwhelming. But I brightened: I was, in effect, in total charge of Earth!

The screen had begun to blink a warning that I was about to be cut off due to delay in use.

"You going to pay for the chairs you wear out?" snarled the old clerk.

I hastily pushed the *"Deliver copy"* button and *"10"* to keep the machine busy for a moment and also to have the sheet to use as authority pending the routine delivery of the appointments on other channels.

What could I do with this thing to help my dilemma? Maybe if I fed Heller data about Blito-P3 he would get more interested.

As soon as the printer had finished spitting out ten copies of the appointments, I punched in,

Blito-P3 Prince Caucalsia.

The screen promptly said,

In the Mists of Time, Folk Legend 894M.

Well, (bleep), I knew *that*.

"Console time," said the old criminal clerk, "is charged double to idiots."

I hastily tried to think of something else. Ah! I punched in,

Royal Successions. Pretenders.

The machine said,

Really? You really want 125,000 years of threats to throne?

I hastily punched in,

Fortress of Dar, Manco and Atalanta, Manco.

The screen started to roll up lists so fast I couldn't follow them. Good Gods, had there been that many revolts and pretenders in just one area of one planet? I remembered the poet's quote, "Shot full of holes is the head that wears a crown." I couldn't track with the speed frames. I pushed *"Deliver copy."* The machine promptly began to spit out paper. Yards of it.

That gave me time to think of something else. So when it finally halted, I pushed,

Nepogat.

The screen said,

In the Mists of Time, Folk Legend 894M.

(Bleep). Right back where I started.

I quickly punched,

Apparatus records, Fortress of Dar, relating to interrogation of crews of two freighters returned from Blito-P3.

It said,

In the Mists of Time, Folk Legend 894M.

I quickly punched,

Fortress of Dar, Manco.

The computer said,

If you are so interested in fables we suggest you consult a competent poet.

One way of saying it wasn't going to flash In the Mists of Time any more for this operator! And that also meant it was going to go off!

I had to get *something* that might interest Heller. I punched,

All surveys and surveillances Blito-P3 prior to one hundred years ago.

Ah, a speeding roll! They *had* been surveying it for a long, long time! With a sigh of relief, I punched *"Deliver copy."* Promptly a series of papers started to spit out. And they spit out and they spit out! I hastily started to corral them before they inundated the whole console. It went on for minutes!

"You there!" screeched the old clerk. "You're going

to run us out of paper! Quit it!" He stood over me positively squeaking! But there is no way of shutting the contraption off once it starts: computers can do no wrong.

I was busy baling up the spit-outs. Gods, I would need a dolly!

Finally it quit. I thought the old clerk was going to hit me. But it had given me time to think. It's all very well to tell operators that they should know what they were going to ask before they begin to work a console. That doesn't allow for inspiration. And I had one!

It was *money* that made it possible for Heller to delay leaving. So long as he could buy guards, he had me at bay. If there was some way to run him out of money . . .

I held the old clerk off with one hand. I punched in,

Jettero Heller. Financial standing and credit.

The screen promptly flashed,

Fleet officer pay. Engineer pay. Combat danger pay. See tables.

Ow, I thought. I don't need any tables. Heller, by just those items, received ten times my old General Service pay.

The machine said:

Money disposition: does not spend much as usually on combat missions. Sends half his pay to mother and father for their support but they are moderately well-off and mother puts it in trust account for him: mother does same with money sent by his very wealthy sister Hightee Heller the Homeview star; rooms at Officers' Club gratis.

Ow, ow, I thought. Lots of money, far beyond the average junior officer.

Credit: very honorable about paying bills. No known debts. Totally trustworthy.

Ow, ow, ow, ow! I thought. Bad show for me.

And then the computer said something astonishing.

> Credit rating: zero! Do not extend advances or credit to this officer.

I was really startled. The machine looked like it wasn't going to say any more so I pushed *"Query."*

It said:

> Zero. Hazardous life. Combat engineers have average professional life expectancy of two years service: subject has exceeded this by triple; statistical demise grossly overdue; Fleet pays only terminal pay for symbolic funeral.

Well, that didn't leave me much option. I couldn't kill him here. And it didn't solve my problem as he *was* still alive and he *did* have money.

Ho, ho! Big thought. If I could get the money he had away from him he would be broke.

The old clerk had sort of gone into apathy and wasn't struggling so much so I punched in,

> Any bad financial habits?

I wasn't very hopeful due to what the computer had already said. The machine flashed:

> Gambles on occasion. Dice and other games. Common to officers in danger categories. Not listed as a negative because by tax records he usually wins games of chance.

I had it! Right there! Heller gambled! Aha!

Some guards had come in by that time to see what the commotion had been all about. I gave them a masterly handling. I said, "I'm leaving at once!"

Chapter 7

I was utterly elated. I was sure I had found Heller's fracture! Gambling!

If I could get all of his money away from him, he wouldn't be able to bribe the guards, the Countess would no longer be brought to my room, he would simply leave for the mission in disgust. No threat from Crown inspectors, no further danger from Lombar. Perfect!

I broke all records getting to my town office. I went tearing through my desk and there it was, in the bottom under the secret panel.

Two months before, one of the Section 451 clerks had been killed in a gambling row. He was trying to bet with counterfeit money but in going through his effects I had found a little dice bag. I had almost passed it by but, knowing the clerk, I examined them.

The six twelve-sided dice appeared perfectly normal. But they were hollow. A densimeter showed that the hollow was lined with a sticky substance and contained a lead pellet. By turning upward the number you wanted and giving the die a slight jolt, the lead pellet was momentarily stuck in the goo. When you threw the die, of course the weight would make the chosen number come up.

Old Bawtch, the chief clerk, wanted to know what I was doing there. I gave him a copy of my new appointments and instead of congratulating me, he shook his head sadly. He said, "Now I know everything is going to Hells." Nobody can get along with Bawtch.

The roaring heat of the Great Desert scorched my airbus but I did not even mind. I landed in an explosion of dust at Camp Kill. I sprinted to Snelz's cave. I was running so fast his door sentry hardly had time to leap up. But it was daylight and he let me by.

Snelz was lying back on his bed, hands folded behind his head. A not too bad-looking prostitute was putting some food on the table: she had on a new dress and looked like she was a permanent fixture. Food, his own woman; Snelz was doing all right for himself!

They both flinched when they saw who it was.

I pointed at the prostitute. "Get outside and don't listen at the door."

"Don't break my hand!" she said. But it was more a sneer than terror. The camp riffraff never learn. She spat on the floor in front of me and left. Maybe the other whore had been a friend of hers. Funny people, whores.

"Snelz," I said, "you are doing all right now, but you are going to be wealthy."

He was instantly on his guard.

"How much money does Heller have left?"

"Oh, no," he said. "He's a nice guy. Don't seek my help in robbing him."

"No, no. Just tell me."

He figured for a bit. "He hasn't spent much really. A credit goes a long way here. He's only spent about two hundred credits."

"Means he must have eight hundred left," I said. "And *you* are going to win it off him." As an afterthought, I said, "And split with me, of course."

Snelz has a very suspicious mind. I got out the bag of dice. I arranged them in my palm so the 12s were all up. I gave my knuckles a rap on the table and threw them. They all came up twelve.

Snelz said, "Weighted dice! And what happens to my head after he knocks it off? That guy can *fight!* Also, if you have a set of dice weighted to always come up 12s, you have to do an under-the-table switch with another set and I'm not that good at palming."

"Snelz," I said, "this is a modern world. Science advances. Don't you trust me?"

"No."

I picked up the six dice, cupped my palms over

them and shook them and then threw again. The lead pellets inside had let loose, of course. I threw. The dice came up with random numbers.

The platoon commander looked at them in confusion. He thought I must have palmed in another set. So he did it. He put them, all twelve up in his palm, knocked the back of his knuckles, threw and got all 12s. Then he shook them and threw and got random numbers.

"Good, fine," I said at his rounded eyes. "Science, as you see, has triumphed again. Do it some more."

He arranged them in different combinations, knocked his knuckles and got what he arranged every time. He shook them without knocking and they were random.

The usual dice game is just two throws, one by each player and the one that gets the highest count of points in his throw wins.

"Now," I said, "as you know, the maximum number of points is 72. Half of 72 is 36. So if you always arrange the dice so as to total more than 40, in the long run you will win. The other player, using these very dice, will get random. But the different combinations you arrange, if always above 40, will let you win all the other fellow's money. And he will never suspect."

"I'm not going to do it," said Snelz. "Aside from fraternizing with prisoners" (was there a sneer at me here?), "I like Heller. I was an officer in the Fleet marines until I was cashiered. Even amongst Fleet officers, he would be tops. I'm not going to do it and lose a friend."

"You're going to do it or lose your head," I said.

He looked at my hand on a blastick and sighed. Beaten. Then he bristled a bit. "But I won't use my own money. You can't order me to do that. You'll have to fund me."

This was a new twist. I thought it over. But then, I

realized, it was a good investment. I started to reach for my wallet but Snelz held up his hand.

"I doubt," said Snelz, "that you're carrying enough. You have miscalculated how much Heller has got. I am absolutely certain they shipped him at least five thousand credits. I see him handle his money more than you do."

Ow! If we started with too little, the odds could make us lose. It would take a lot of throws to do it or Heller would become suspicious.

"To be convincing in a deal like this," said Snelz, "you have to be able to lose before you win it back. I'm an expert at this. I was cashiered from the marines for cheating. So what you have to do is go draw some money. Match his bankroll. Five thousand credits to be safe. Otherwise we'll never get started."

It was very painful. And then I realized how many paychecks I was drawing. Being General Service pay and not hazard I could get an advance easily. I even had the certified orders on me.

So, after a lot more persuasion by Snelz, we went to the finance office and bribed the clerk to do his routine duty and my identoplate got us a five-thousand-credit advance. That was nearly a year's pay. But soon, I was confident, I would be several thousand credits richer. And I would be in no danger afterwards from the stalled mission.

My stomach was acting up again but I was very hopeful.

I gave Snelz the money and the dice and left him practicing. Heller would shortly be headed for Earth!

Chapter 8

Jettero Heller sat in my room, idly watching Homeview. Each day there had been three sagging hours between the time he came back from training and the moment the Countess was smuggled up for supper and the night.

Apparently the Countess had to put in some time late in the day to teach her assistants to train and, femalelike, there was some nonsense about bathing and getting dressed before her nightly date.

Heller had glanced over the four-foot pile of old Blito-P3 surveys, more to identify them than get any data out of them. He had smiled to see the lists of revolts and pretenders in that one province of Manco but he had also laid it aside. He was doing just one thing—waiting for the Countess. He glanced at his watch: nearly all of the three hours had yet to run. He sighed, bored.

I sat in a chair over by the wall, pretending to study some entries in my notebooks—actually I was looking at blank pages. Tonight would be different!

A knock on the door. Snelz entered. He took off his cap to indicate it was social. He said to me, "Officer Gris is it all right with you if I talk to Officer Heller for a bit?"

It was all rehearsed. "Go ahead, go ahead," I said.

Heller looked up languidly. He pointed to a chair.

Snelz said, sitting down, "Jettero, I need some help. As you know, we play a lot of dice down at Camp Endurance and there are some very sharp fellows there. I once heard in the Fleet, before they cashiered me, that you were really an expert at dice. As a personal favor, could you teach me something about it?"

Heller looked at him a bit oddly, I thought. I held my breath. Was this going to work?

But Heller laughed. "I shouldn't think there could be much about dice that a Fleet marine officer didn't know."

"Oh, come along," pleaded Snelz in a very convincing protest. "There's lots to know about it. I've just come into a bit of money and I don't want to be smarted out of it. What I don't understand is probabilities and second bets."

In the most popular version of dice then in vogue, there was always a second side bet between the players. The original bet was made and then there was a throw and then a second bet was made based on odds for or against the other player winning. The one who threw would then chant something like, "Ten credits to one you can't beat that." Then the other would throw and if he had beaten the first player's throw, he won both bets.

"Oh?" said Heller. For a bit it looked like he wasn't going to help. Then he shrugged and took a sheet of paper from his kit. He rapidly wrote, from left to right, across the bottom of the page, the numbers 6 to 72. "With six dice, each one with 12 points, the total you can shoot will add up to anything from 6 to 72."

"Yes, yes," said Snelz, pretending great interest.

Heller wrote a series of numbers up the left side of the sheet vertically. "These are the number of combinations of dice that produce the total score. As you can see, it is a high number."

"Interesting," said Snelz, gazing intently, just as if he weren't a past master at it, which he was.

"Now," said Heller, "when we draw a curve, using

these two factors, we get a bell curve." And he drew it: it did look like a bell, bulged very high in the middle.

"Fascinating," said Snelz, who must have worked out the same curve a hundred times.

Patiently, Heller drew a vertical line roughly up from the 28 and the 50 at the bottom so they crossed the bell shape. "Now the odds against your making anything below 28 or above 50 are very high. The odds in favor of shooting anything *between* 28 and 50 are pretty good. So on the second bet, you keep that in mind. There's more to this but that's a starter. You sure you don't know all this?"

"Oh, I really appreciate it," said Snelz who probably learned it at the age of five. He turned to me. "Officer Gris, would you mind terribly if Jettero and I had a little game?" He turned to Heller. "I surely would like to try this out. Just for modest stakes, of course."

"You sure?" said Heller. "I don't want to be accused of taking advantage of a beginner."

"No, no, no," said Snelz. "This is all fair and square. Anything you win, you win. Anything I lose, I lose. All right? I just happen to have a set of dice on me."

They sat down on either side of the table and Heller took the dice Snelz held out.

"I always like to do something," said Heller. "I don't want to be accused of switching dice during play. So we'll just mark these." He reached for his little tool kit, took out a tiny ink bottle and in the upper corner of the 1 on each die, made a microscopically small dot. "That ink fades after a few hours. It just makes sure we're playing with the same dice all the time. No offense. Just a precaution."

I mentally rubbed my hands together. If they played with those same dice the whole game, I was going to wind up a much richer officer. I began to calculate how

much I would give Snelz: a hundred credits? Fifty? Even
forty-five would be a fortune for an Apparatus officer.

They began with a modest half-credit bet. Snelz
threw 20. Heller declined to make a second bet that he
could beat it. He threw 51. He won. Ah, well. Good
strategy. Heller was to win for a while.

"Let's bet one credit," said Snelz. "I feel lucky."

Heller took the dice. Now dice players have a routine all their own, all unnecessary. They take the six dice
in their cupped palms; they shake them on the right side
of their head; they shake them on the left side of their
head; then they tap one set of knuckles or the other on
the table and send the dice bouncing onto the board with
a sort of shovel motion. And they sing to the dice as they
do it. Heller did all this. But he had two wrinkles of his
own. He blew onto the palmed dice first and then shook
them and he shook them longer and harder than I have
seen dice shaken before. His hands sort of blurred in the
shake—very, very fast!

Heller threw a 62. Against his own advice, he said,
"One credit to a hundred says you can't beat that. I frankly advise you to decline."

"No, I'll take it," said Snelz. He placed the dice carefully in his palm. When he shook them, he didn't permit
them to roll about. He banged his knuckles on the table.

I thought, hey, this is early to start winning. The
bang on the table, of course, settled the lead pellets into
the goo in the hollow. The dice rolled out a 10!

Oh, I thought. Clever boy. He's carrying out the
strategy.

"Ouch," said Snelz. "Looks like I better up my
stakes to recover my loss. Two hundred credits all right
with you for this next bet?"

Of course it was really Heller's turn, as he didn't
have the first throw, to set the stake for the first bet. But

he shrugged, overlooking the irregularity, looking as tolerant as you would look at an amateur who didn't quite know the rules.

Snelz threw. It was a 50. Any dice player can add up the points at a glance if he is expert and I thought Snelz made an error by calling "Fifty!" instantly in a loud voice. I guessed Snelz was too excited to mask his expertise. "Fifty credits to fifty credits says you can't top it."

Heller was in the swing of it now. He blew upon the dice. He shook to the right and shook to the left and as he did it, he sang:

> *Money for my honey,*
> *Booze for my cruise,*
> *Fly them over fifty*
> *And don't let this spacer lose.*

He threw and cried, "Fifty-five!" after the dice stopped rolling. He picked up the money with an easy sweep.

Snelz said, "You certainly are lucky. I know I am just a beginner at this, but I am afraid I will have to double my bet again. Four hundred credits all right with you?

"Actually," said Heller, "doubling is a Devil's game. I advise against it."

"I'm afraid I'll have to insist," said Snelz.

Heller shrugged. He picked up the dice. He blew on them quite a long time. Then he sang:

> *Don't reimburse the purse,*
> *Of the loser we won't nurse.*
> *Fly a winning number*
> *And win the universe.*

His shake had been extremely hard. The roll was
expert with a back spin. "Forty! Try and beat it. Ten
credits to three hundred and seventy-five says you won't."

Snelz put the dice very carefully in his palm, blew
on them, pretended to shake them. He sang:

> *Dicies balm and calm,*
> *Don't cramp the champ.*
> *Better up the forty*
> *And put money in my camp!*

He threw. "Thirty-five!" Heller raked in the money.

Good. Snelz was following the strategy. Any
moment now, he would turn the game around and start
to win. And that would be the end of Officer Heller's
ability to buy favors, and off to Earth we'd go.

There was a knock on the door. A guard tiptoed in
and whispered to me: "Doctor Crobe just sent up word
that if you didn't see him at once, you'd be real sorry."

Well, I should have expected it. I was supposed to
take Heller back to him, and what was it now, seven
days? and we hadn't gone near him. I didn't want to
leave this game. But Snelz would bring it off. How could
he lose with those dice? I left.

But the second I started to go down the tube, I also
started to get sick at my stomach. A bad feeling of pain
with a bit of nausea.

I found Crobe in his foul office. He left off scraping
some cells from a severed foot. He raised his head and
levelled his scummy eyes down his beak nose.

"You," he said, "are up to something. You have not
brought that special agent back here for bugging."

I felt very ill. "I've been busy."

"I have a direct order from Lombar Hisst to fix up

this special agent. You have not brought him back. You are up to something."

I had to sit down. I really was feeling ill. Maybe it was that severed foot. It looked green in the green glowplates. It was putrefying.

"Officer Gris," said Crobe, "do you know of any way to prevent me from reporting this to Lombar Hisst?"

My stomach gave a new turn. I could hardly lift my head. But in my field of view, there lay his filthy hand, palm up. It was unmistakable.

Feebly I reached into my tunic and got out my wallet. I only had about thirty-five credits in it. I pulled out a ten.

Crobe took the ten, then reached over and took the rest of the money out of the wallet. "Thirty-five credits," he counted. "Won't do." He threw them aside.

It was a lot of money. For the dungeons of Spiteos. They never had any money down here. But I realized that I would shortly have thousands. "Make it a hundred. I'll pay the rest later."

Crobe picked up his gummy scraping knife and pointed it at me. "You're really up to something, Officer Gris. Do you realize the danger to me personally if I don't follow out Lombar Hisst's orders?"

I was too sick to think straight. The pains were like dagger stabs!

"Two hundred," said Crobe.

Oh, no! But I was about to be rich. I hurt. I wanted out. I nodded numbly.

Crobe picked up the thirty-five credits and counted them again. "Then you'll owe me a hundred and sixty-five and you'll pay me tomorrow or up to Hisst I go!"

I managed to say, "All right," and then I got out of there. When I got into the tube and started going up I suddenly felt completely well! Mysterious. What was this odd illness?

Reasoning that my recovery was probably an anticipation of Snelz's winnings, I got back into the room.

Heller was just finishing a song. He threw the dice expertly. "Sixty-five!" And he scooped up the bet money.

It took me a moment to register the scene. Snelz was sitting there tense. Beads of sweat were standing out on his forehead. The pile of money in front of Heller was huge!

I glared at Snelz. He was carrying this losing streak too far! He had better turn this tide around and quick!

Snelz said, "I bet a thousand!"

Heller put the dice in his palm, cupped his hands, blew into them long and hard. He sang:

> *Conserve your nerve,*
> *You made the parade,*
> *Roll a high number*
> *And complete the ambuscade!*

He was shaking those dice so hard I couldn't really find any shape in his hands. He knocked his knuckles on the table. "Seventy!"

Snelz looked stunned. He stammered, "I decline to make a second bet."

"Wise boy," said Heller.

Snelz picked up the dice for his throw. Who could beat 70? He looked at each die very carefully. He was looking for the spots.

"You don't think I switched dice on you, do you?" said Heller.

"No," said Snelz in a little tiny voice. "These are the same dice."

Heller laughed. He said, "I'm so glad. Duels can get

so final and as an ex-marine, you're probably a good shot."

Snelz looked like somebody in torment. The joke Heller had made was far too near home for him. He probably couldn't win a duel with Heller if he had the odds of a blastcannon. Snelz placed the dice very carefully in his palm. I knew what he was doing. He was taking an awful chance but he was covertly arranging the dice to shoot a 72! All 12s! With a shock, I saw that his money was very low. His money? *My* money. Snelz sang:

> *Don't bust through the crust,*
> *Put a flag on the crag,*
> *Please, please, a high number!*
> *And bring home the swag!*

He threw. The dice stopped. He looked at them like he was seeing a zitab snake. "Sixteen," he whispered.

Heller raked in the credits. "I shouldn't tell you to stop playing as I'm the winner. But you ought to think about it. I had no intention of trying to clean you out."

Snelz was in a total spin. From the looks of him, he couldn't figure what had gone wrong. He was in desperation. "I've got just twelve hundred credits left," he said. "I'm going to bet all of it."

"Oh, no," groaned Heller.

"Oh, yes!" cried Snelz. And he pushed out the last of my money, the last of *five thousand credits!*

He put the dice in his palm with great care. He blew on them prayerfully. He began to shake them lightly. He sang:

> *Don't bruise with bad news,*
> *I'll cry if I die,*
> *Give me a HIGH number,*
> *A total in the SKY!*

He tossed them ever so gently, hoping not to disturb the lead pellets in them. They came to a stop. He didn't even call the number. It was *8!* Almost anything could beat it.

Heller said, "No second bet possible, as you're out of money. So I'll just roll."

He hardly bothered to shake them. He didn't even sing. He just tossed them on the table. "I'm awfully sorry," he said. "Forty-nine." He picked up the money, cleaning the board. "I really shouldn't take your money. I could be accused of laundering a beginner."

I anxiously awaited Snelz's "I'll take it back." But he didn't. Factually, by the codes, he couldn't. Heller was just being very polite. "I started the game," said Snelz, trying not to look at me.

"There's an awful lot of money here," said Heller, mounding it up. And indeed there was: you could have bought every officer in Spiteos with it and a hunting preserve as well! He didn't count it. He wadded up all five thousand and held it out to Snelz. "You better take it back."

I silently screamed, take it, take it, you idiot!

Snelz was collapsed into himself. Then he put the expected bright face on it. "Fast gotten, fast gone," he said. He collected the dice. He picked up his cap. He said the polite thing, "Thank you for a nice game, Officer Heller." He got out of there.

Heller shrugged. He dropped the money into his kit bag. There was too much of it and he had to stuff it in. He yawned and picked up some of the papers from the console. Perfectly relaxed, he began to read.

Maybe it was the yawn. It meant so little to him. And the horror of this evening's misadventure hit me.

I was in debt almost a year's pay. No! With Crobe's hundred and sixty-five it topped a year's pay. You can't draw more than a year's pay in advance. I was not only broke. I was in debt! I couldn't even buy a chank-pop!

And then a second wave hit me. I was drawing four paychecks. That year's pay was for all four. If I lost the additional three it would take me five years of no money to get square with the boards. If I were to be taken off Mission Earth, losing those extra checks, I could get cashiered for debt! I couldn't move. I felt paralyzed.

A half an hour later, the Countess Krak was smuggled in. She and Heller embraced shamelessly. She was quite bright, wearing silver. She filled the whole place with a radiance. She was extremely beautiful. I hated her! Heller could and would hang around forever now! I was sunk!

Chapter 9

In midafternoon of the following day, I stood on the high ramparts of Spiteos. Before me stretched the Great Desert, a panorama of awesome if grim beauty. Once it had been a garden land, a verdant productive area of the ancients, splendid with trees and fields and flowers, vibrant with life. Robbed of humus and soil, devoid of life and even hope, it had become a naked, vast expanse of yellow sands, minerals and white salt, more of a tomb than a living land.

And yet, for all that, there was a sort of noble majesty in it; it stretched two hundred scorching miles to mountains which, in the afternoon's blistering sun, barriered the stretches of death from the civilized world of Voltar.

Sun-dancers, two-hundred-foot pillars of dust, rose with lazy grace in the blistering thermal currents of the desert floor to be twisted by the flame-tongued wind. The dust contained bright flecks of sparkling mica, flashes of feldspar and the poisonous green salts of copper. Six of them were going now, their tops almost stationary, their desert-connected bottoms moving this way and that, sometimes toward each other, sometimes away: they simulated a chorus line, dancing gracefully in a parody of a glittering review, or more like the writhing of grief-torn mourners singing a song of death.

A fitting funeral scene: Crobe had just told me he was going to turn me in. I was contemplating throwing myself off the tower to plunge down thousands of feet into the chasm which held the bones of ancients and the more recent smashed remains of luckless Apparatus personnel who had erred.

When one is deep in the throes of the self-pity that goes with contemplated suicide, one does not enjoy being interrupted.

"Oh, there you are," came Snelz's voice behind me. "I was searching everywhere." Too bright a voice, inadequately solemn for my mood and the deathly desert scene.

He came within range of the corner of my eye. He was wearing brand-new black gloves. He was wearing a brand-new black uniform. He was carrying a couple of small boxes in one hand and he had a tattered old book in the other.

"You look *down*," he said. "Can't have that." And he took a chank-pop from a box of them. I noticed the label on the box: it was from one of the most expensive shops in Commercial City. He didn't pop it: it would have been a silly thing to do in this wind anyway. "No?" he said. "Then have a puffstick." And he opened the lid of the other box: they were the fourteen-inch puffsticks, the kind affected only by the rich. Equally silly to try to use one in this blistering wind.

I contemplated how I would go about throwing him off the rampart. It didn't even lighten my gloom. I thought, can't you just go away and let someone be quietly miserable?

He shoved the boxes into the wide grenade pockets of his tunic. He took the tattered book from under his arm. "I know," he said, opening the book, "that you are just dying to find what must have happened."

I hadn't slept trying to figure it out. But I wouldn't give him that satisfaction. If I gave him a slice-blow on the back of the neck while putting out my foot, I could probably spin him off the rampart and into the depths.

"After I left last night," said Snelz cheerfully, "I went all over Camp Kill looking for a specialist in crooked dice. I finally found one. Unfortunately I had to pay him some of your cut of Heller's purchases today to find out. I knew you would be dying to know. He gave me this book."

You're going to die telling me, I thought. Just as soon as I find enough energy in this heat to deliver the slice-blow and put out my foot.

"It says here," said Snelz, "that those are known as 'thudder dice.' Because if you shake them real hard and listen real close you can hear the lead pellets in them thud." He took the dice out of his pocket and shook them near my ear. "Hear the thud?"

Like the thud you are going to make when you hit bottom down there, I thought.

"My friend told me that a lot of people have been killed trying to use thudder dice. So we were lucky!"

Five-thousand-credits-owed lucky, I thought. I might as well hear him out. *Then* kill him.

"It seems they have a goo in them that momentarily positions the lead pellet. But it says here in this paragraph, *Warning: Do not use these dice more than a few throws.* It seems that the goo in them warms up and melts when you blow on the dice too much. And when they are shaken very vigorously for a prolonged period, the lead pellet in them also develops friction heat in moving rapidly. The insides of the dice get quite hot and the lead pellet won't stick in one place anymore. So they just behave like regular dice all the time."

He put the book up so I could see the reference. I didn't bother to read it. "So Heller," continued Snelz, "just thought it was a regular dice game and he didn't have any suspicions. So he won't be after our hides. Isn't that nice? He's just a good dice player and kind of lucky. So he won't be pestering me and I won't have to tell him whose dice they are or how you tried to set him up."

You won't tell anybody anything after you hit the bottom down there, I thought. I tensed to make my move.

Something was flashing in front of my eyes. Snelz was flipping some gold-colored credit notes in front of my face. I steadied his hand.

That morning I had drawn the hundred and fifty-five credits I still had left in a year's pay advance. I had given it to Crobe. He had snarled that I was still ten credits short and he would now go to Lombar anyway if I didn't come through by nightfall. But there was another hitch. I had gotten sick down there again and I couldn't stand to go near him even once more.

And here were ten credits!

"Heller sent a man out to buy a lot of things this morning," said Snelz. "It was Timyjo that went and he is a great thief. He stole most of it, so your cut is big. It was eleven credits but this book cost one credit. Hey, what's the matter?"

I had sat down weakly on a ledge. After a little, I said, "Snelz, I happen to owe Crobe ten credits. Take it down and give it to him."

"Oh? Right!"

"Wait," I said, reviving a bit. "Give me those dice."

"Indeed, yes! I wouldn't use them again for anything!"

I took the six dice, gave them a blasphemous funeral prayer and threw them off the rampart and into the depths below. Let the ghosts of the ancients and the executed Apparatus offenders get in trouble with them way down there in their black chasm and let the living live!

PART FIVE

Chapter 1

A half an hour later, I was in the training hall, sitting by the desk. I was about to get one of the worst shocks in my life. At the moment my worries consisted only of a dull nausea in my stomach and the realization that if I were taken off the mission, I would find myself hopelessly overdrawn on pay, bankrupt and cashiered. I was sitting there, hoping to get some idea of how to pry Heller out of Spiteos, observing the scene before me to find any inspiration.

The vast hall was a patchwork of independent projects. Four assistant trainers, in four different places, were trying to get four different acts into shape. One was a wrestling act, one was a juggler and the other two were in such early stages I could not make them out, consisting as they were of just some minor exercises.

The Countess Krak was far back on the right side of the room, quite distant. She was instructing one of her trainers to teach a juggler: the objects were six medium sized lizards, the kind with razor-sharp spines; it would be a good act when perfected but the juggler was afraid of cutting his hands and the assistant trainer needed coaching on how to get his student to overcome this fear with confidence. I couldn't hear what the Countess was saying to him but now and then she would herself flip a couple of lizards into the air and grasp them correctly and then pass them to the assistant so he could show the juggler. I didn't envy the assistant: you could lose a finger on a spiny lizard; but the Countess was being very patient and reassuring. She seemed to have on new clothes and I hoped she wouldn't be fool enough to wear them on a trained act parade: Lombar would be investigating like a swooping bird of prey.

I hadn't paid much attention to Heller when I came in beyond making sure he was there as stated by the guards at the door. But now my attention shifted to him.

Heller was through with his studies for the day. Clear over at the opposite corner of the hall from Krak, he was simply going through some ring exercises to keep in shape.

He was doing what is called a "startler"—so labelled because it always brings a shock of indrawn breath from an audience which, of course, supposes the gymnast has lost his grip and is falling.

Performed with a single, hanging ring about ten feet from the floor, the gymnast does a single handstand on the ring, his body rising upward, parallel to the rope. It is difficult enough to do one of those handstands on a ring—I never could. But the rest of the stunt is why it is called a startler.

Heller's hand would slip off the bottom of the ring and his body would start to plummet downward vertically. But his heels would flick forward and, tight together, would catch the rounded top of the ring, one on either side of the rope, and abruptly stop the fall. It is difficult to make heels hold on the rounded top of an iron ring but, even after a drop, he was having no trouble with it. Then he'd reach up for the ring with the other hand and do the startler using that one.

He was having no trouble at all. He was very graceful. To him it was just casual exercise. He was doing it over and over, right hand, then left hand. It really looked like he was thinking of something else—and probably he was: the evening and night with the Countess Krak.

My attention shifted to the wrestling act. It was going on a short distance to the side of Heller's ring. The assistant trainer there apparently had his hands full—full of trouble. The assistant was a tall, muscular fellow in the usual loincloth. The two he was trying to train were not cooperating: one was a primate, a shaggy beast covered with hair, captured in the jungle of some wild planet; the other was a yellow-man, probably from the Deepst Mountains, one of the race you often see in circuses doing "strong acts"—you know, the kind with no body hair, huge muscles, given to a lot of roaring and posturing. Both primate and yellow-man were about six foot eight inches tall and weighed maybe three hundred pounds. Big.

I got interested in the act. Apparently the primate and the yellow-man were supposed to be having a fight over a big, red, piece of fake fruit. It was really a comedy-acrobatic wrestling act, all rehearsed and precisely timed. But to an audience it would look like a funny fight. It was supposed to begin with the primate hunched down eating the fruit. Then the yellow-man was supposed to jump on the primate to take the fruit away and they would leap and spin and so on for a time and finally the primate would solve it by splitting the fruit in half and they'd both sit down to eat it, the funniest part being that it was the primate, an ape, really, that solved it.

The assistant trainer wasn't having any trouble with the primate. Like any big ape, it could spin and somersault with great agility. The trouble was with the yellow-man. And I must say that I would not have liked to meet him in an alley. He was so motivated by brute force that he was really punishing the primate and it was making the ape a bit sullen to be side-punched and kicked when it wasn't part of the scenario.

At one point of the act, the yellow-man was supposed to get a strangle armlock on the primate. The ape was then supposed to front somersault out of it. Apparently the yellow-man wouldn't let go enough so the primate could flip. The yellow-man, hate in his eyes, was trying to finish the grip and really strangle the ape.

I heard the assistant trainer's voice dimly in the din and clatter of the hall. He said to the yellow-man, "Look. I'll take the place of the ape and you put the grip on me and I will show you exactly where to clamp so the ape can get out of it and do his somersault." I thought, trainer, I wouldn't do that if I were you, that yellow-man is kill-crazy.

The primate had turned a bit sullen and, rubbing its throat, shuffled off to one side out of the way. The assistant trainer stood in its place and indicated that the yellow-man should begin.

Well, I've seen some looks of savage anticipation in my time but the look that came over that yellow-man beat them all. They had probably found him in some Domestic Police cell charged with murder or he wouldn't be here at Spiteos. He had probably suffered what he thought was injustice and bad treatment—rightly so at Spiteos. And *here* was his chance!

He sprang on that assistant trainer like a ferocious beast!

With an animal snarl he slammed his arm around the trainer's neck. Gripping his own wrist with his other hand, he began to apply the pressure!

There was murder in the yellow-man's eyes, hate in the roars which went past his bared teeth. I expected at any instant to hear the trainer's neck snap. He could not cry out.

The racket in the place was such that no one else seemed to be paying any attention. Maybe this sort of thing was too usual in these acts. I was certain the yellow-man was going to chalk up a new murder right that instant. My eye caught a movement to the side of them.

Heller had not caught the ring with his heels. He front-flipped to land on his feet.

In a flash of motion, Heller was close by the fight!

He reached down, almost unconcerned, and with a thumb and forefinger put a clamp on the giant's elbow! It is an ordinary release defense action, it produces considerable pain and paralysis, though how Heller knew what points to touch on a yellow-man—who is made differently—I do not know.

The roar of the giant turned to a screech!

He let go of the trainer like the trainer had gone red hot. He whirled to rear up against Heller!

Heller quietly kicked the giant in the back of the head with his toe. It was not a lethal kick. The yellow-man flopped forward, out cold.

The trainer was struggling up. Heller gave him a hand. The fellow couldn't talk yet but thanks was on his face.

I couldn't hear what Heller was saying but he was being solicitous about the trainer's neck and was rubbing it for him. The primate then got up and came over to them and—it made both the trainer and Heller laugh—solemnly shook Heller's hand. Actually it was very funny for one doesn't expect apes to know much. I laughed myself—and it was the last laugh I had that day!

The trainer went over and got an electric whip. The

giant was still out cold. Heller saw that it was under control and apparently decided that was all the exercise he was going to do today. He picked up his exercise suit top and slipped into it. Then he trotted across the room, threw a kiss to the Countess Krak and left the hall.

Knowing the guards outside would be hard on Heller's heels and that he was just going up to bathe and dress anyway, I lingered on a bit, my eyes on the Countess. *There* was my enemy, *there* was the one stalling this mission.

She had had some minor success training the trainer but it was almost as if she had been waiting for Heller to leave. And, if I had been about to follow, I would have stopped because here she came, walking through the noisy hall toward me.

Well, I must say the guard Timyjo exercised good taste in his stealing. Or maybe Heller had specified it. But the Countess Krak was certainly gorgeous in her new turnout.

She was wearing brand-new, hip-length shimmering boots, black with gleaming brass heels. She had on flesh-colored tights and wore a tight, waist-length jacket of black leather and spangles. On her head, as a crown to her neck-length yellow hair, she wore a little visored hat, smaller at the top than around her head: it was glittering with black discs and it had a little plume upright at the center front. It was a costume patterned on the clothes she used to wear but oh what a new and expensive difference!

And she was beautiful. There is no arguing with that. She was fabulously, magnificently beautiful. My enemy. She sat down in a big chair across from me, her back to the room. She turned her perfectly formed face toward me.

"Soltan," she said, "you've got to help me!" And there were tears trembling in her eyes!

A little alarm bell started going off in my head. Was this the cold, emotionless Countess Krak? What new ploy was this? I have never trusted women and I certainly tripled that for the Countess Krak.

"Soltan," she continued, "Jettero has done the English. He has the New England and Virginia accents down perfectly. I even went off into slang and mannerisms and he has those. I have gotten him through Earth geography and geology. He has a grasp of political structures and demography for the planet. He has reviewed the peculiarities of the Solar System. . . ."

One tear fell and coursed down her smooth cheek. Almost a wail came out of her. "Soltan, I have run out of things to teach him!"

Oho and aha! I thought. And you're running out of ways to stall his departure!

"Soltan, can't you get me permission to teach him espionage? He will be in danger if he does not know that. And I don't think he has the basics of it."

Lady, I thought, that is the understatement of all time.

"Countess," I said, hoping I didn't sound as smug and lofty as I felt, "Lombar gave very definite instructions about that."

"But why, Soltan, why? He'll be in danger if he doesn't understand a key subject like that!" And another tear spilled out.

"Lombar has his reasons," I said. For some reason I suddenly felt sick. "And Lombar's reasons are always good ones. I think he simply wants Heller to be more natural. You know how real special agents act: darting about, peering under garbage can lids, sure to draw attention to themselves. Right now Lombar could kill us both for what I'm permitting. It's really a very simple mission, just introducing a little technology onto the planet. . . ."

My attention was suddenly drawn to something happening behind her.

The giant had recovered. The assistant trainer was not to be seen. But the yellow-man was walking toward us. He was rubbing his elbow. He looked very annoyed. I felt a surge of fear.

The Countess was trying to think of some way to persuade me. She did not alert to the fact that I was staring at the giant. Maybe I was not being obvious. Maybe there was a tiny trace of hope that this murdering brute of a yellow-man now walking up behind her would kill her and solve all my problems. She was unarmed. I studiously kept my hands away from any of my own weapons.

She was sitting down. She was out of position. There was even a chair arm in her way if she tried to rise swiftly. The giant came on, rubbing his elbow, aggrieved, unnoticed by anyone but me. He stopped right behind her. From the look of him he was going to kill her. My hopes rose.

She was about to speak to me again, a pleading look on her face.

The yellow-man let go of his elbow and cuffed her shoulder hard!

He roared at her, "You keep that (bleepard) Heller away from me or I'll break his (bleeping) neck!"

She swivelled in the chair and looked up at his towering height.

She snapped, "Don't you dare talk about Jettero that way!"

There was a hiss of indrawn breath from fifty people. The hall went tomb-silent instantly.

The giant slowly raised his arms to seize and strangle her. His voice was grating and every word held death. "I'll say anything about him I please! He's just a Devils (bleeped) Royal officer! A snotty, rotten, stuck-up (bleep)!" The arms came down.

Her face had gone white.

Her hand flashed to the back of her chair and it went spinning away!

She was over to his right!

There was a sound like a shot. I hadn't even seen her hand move but his left wrist was broken, dangling!

And then began a Devil's dance I shall not want to watch again.

This was no emotionless statue. This was a live ball of raging fury!

She hit him in the face with the backhand swing of her left.

She turned. Her right arm came swinging in in a wide sweep toward his face. Just before it hit, her right foot hit the floor, the brass heel cracked like a shot. It seemed to give the back of her hand a whiplike propulsion. The blow against his face was the crunch of breaking bones!

It had spun her to the right. Her left arm began a sweep back. Her left foot exploded on the floor. The back of her open hand impelled into his cheek and more bones broke!

This had carried her to the left. Her right arm went out. She turned back. The boot stamped! The hand crashed into his jaw!

The back of her left hand, the back of her right hand, one after the other like a remorseless machine, she drove him backwards.

The yellow-man had sixty feet of hall behind him. Step by punished step he was being driven backwards!

Blood was cascading down his chest. He was howling like a trapped animal!

Step by step, strike by strike she drove him back. A ghastly, precisely timed ballet of blood and punishment. Only those sounds, the stamp of a boot, the crash of the hand, the raging howl of the giant echoed in the room.

Fifty of the sixty feet he went, dying all the way.

And then he tried to counterattack!

He kicked at her! Had it connected it would have smashed her chest. But with perfect timing she seized the heel! Using his own momentum against him, she pulled the heel up until he lay horizontal in the air. Her foot lashed out at what remained of the giant's jaw.

Like a huge arrow he shot backwards. The electric shock machines were there. His head slammed into a machine arm. The sound was like an exploding melon! He crashed downward to the floor.

The Countess Krak was no cold killer now. She was a blazing fury. She followed up and stamped upon his chest, his arms, his face!

She drew off, panting, still angry. "You!" she pointed at the paralyzed cluster that was her crew. "Take him to the dispensary and get him patched up!"

An assistant trainer crept to the yellow-man's side and felt in the mess for a heartbeat. The assistant trainer looked up. "He's dead."

The Countess Krak was adjusting the chin strap of her cap which had been knocked askew. She said, "That'll teach him not to threaten Jettero!"

Until that moment I had been only paralyzed. But when she said that, standing there fussing with her cap, standing there in the blood which now stained her new boots, a jolt of pure terror went through me.

I do not know how I got out of there. I was simply in the tubes flashing away from her.

I halted before I turned a corner to my room corridor. I tried to calm myself. I was trying to throw up and trying not to throw up. My hands were shaking. I tried to get out a chank-pop but my fingers were fluttering so I couldn't get the top off and it fell to the floor.

Only one thought was dominating me. Somehow, someway I had to get Heller out of there. If I remained a day longer I was absolutely convinced I would be dead. If the Countess Krak had any inkling of what was planned for Heller, what she had just done to the giant would be mild for me.

I had to coax myself out of the thought that I was already dead. They say that in total fear of one's life one can get very brilliant. I had to and I did.

Tugging at my tunic to straighten myself up, breathing as naturally as I could, I walked by the room guards and entered.

Heller had bathed and he was now lounging in a chair, feet on another one, listening to music on the Homeview.

I threw my cap on the bed and then sat down at the table. I didn't dare open a canister or he would see my shaking hands. I can control my voice: one is thoroughly trained to do that in the Apparatus.

"Jettero," I said, "has it occurred to you that this is a very dirty place?"

He looked at me, languidly, still listening to the music. Then he smiled. "You say that to a Fleet spacer?"

"It is not a good place to be in. You are used to the finer surroundings of life."

He thought that over, I had his attention now: he was no longer just listening to the music.

Would this work? A desperate prayer was running off in the back of my head and I hoped it was going to the Gods.

"You factually have completed all your studies," I said, my voice carefully matter-of-fact and calm. "There is no real reason to remain."

Heller looked around the room. It was as though he was seeing it for the first time. The black floor, the shabby fixtures, the scarred black walls.

He looked at me. "Soltan, you are right! This fortress is *uncomfortable!*"

He suddenly leaped up out of his chair. He took three steps one way, turned and took three steps back, steadying himself on the bed ends the way spacers will even when groundside.

His quick action startled me. I could not quite grasp the thought processes of his decision about something. I foolishly thought I had magically gotten the mission going!

He didn't say another thing about it all that evening. He just smiled and hummed and grinned to himself and was charming.

He even coaxed the Countess out of a bit of a cross mood she was in when the guards brought her. She felt she had made a spectacle of herself, not saying how or why. And she confessed she had ruined the new boots he had given her.

Heller simply told her there were plenty of boots where those came from and told some funny stories about spaceboots. I took it that his mind had now turned to travel. A good portent.

There was even a brighter sign. He got out the "revolts and pretenders" list covering Manco history and they soon had their heads together, canisters of green sparklewater in hand, and, while the music played on, went over the material.

I was so happy at the possibility of seeing the last of Countess Krak that I almost enjoyed Manco's history!

"See?" said the Countess Krak, a beautiful finger on a line. "There *was* a Nepogat! Right here:"

> And the handmaiden Nepogat who had forsooth suborned the princely morals was banished from the Fortress of Dar and forbidden ever to return.

"Oho!" said Heller. "It doesn't say what princeling but do you suppose it could have been Prince Caucalsia?"

"Oh, it must have been," said the Countess Krak. "A woman spurned can do some very nasty things."

I didn't follow it. They were inventing their own history.

After a while, Heller said, "Here's a whole list of Princes condemned without giving a single name. Do you suppose one of them could have been Prince Caucalsia?"

"I'm sure it was!" said the Countess Krak. "Isn't that the right period?"

"Indeed it is," said Heller. "So that proves it!" And they both laughed with delight.

I snickered to myself. Some engineer. I hoped I didn't have to walk on any of his bridges if he couldn't think any better than that.

I left them to it. I went and lay down in the filthy, cluttered closet I used for sleep, idiotically hopeful that I would shortly be out of the reach of the Countess Krak!

Chapter 2

A light shined in my face. "Officer Gris! Time to get going."

I groaned and stirred in the stinking litter of the cubicle. I looked at my watch. A half hour before dawn?

"Time to get going," the guard insisted.

I dug around and found my cap under some old food scraps. I stumbled after him back to my room.

The place was a jumble of sound and motion! It was full of cartons and noise! The platoon usually split itself into two watches of twelve hours each, meaning seven guards on duty at a time: but there seemed to be more than that here.

Snelz was astraddle a backwards chair. He was holding a canister of hot jolt and using it to point directions to his men. They were packing the place up! They were all laughing and talking.

Heller was tying up a bundle. He was dressed in a race driver's suit, white with red slashes. He had a red visored cap on the back of his head, the kind they wear under their helmets. He looked fresh and clean and vital: how could he manage that this early?

He saw me and picked up a canister of hot jolt from the heat pad and came over and handed it to me. He was laughing. At my bedraggled appearance?

In thick, Virginia accented English he said, "Mah name is Rovah. Ah have a George named dawg."

He had it wrong.

Patiently I corrected him. "It's 'My name is George.' It is the *dog* that is named *Rover*."

For some reason it sent him into a gale of laughter. Far too early to laugh that heartily.

Snelz said to me, "You keeping this room? If not, we'll pack up for you."

Was I keeping this room? I always kept a few personal things here at Spiteos just in case. Hardly more than a ready bagful. But then it hit me. I wouldn't need this room for ages. In fact, I never wanted to see Spiteos again! "I'm moving, too!"

"Pack him up," said Snelz to his men.

It was amazing how much stuff had been accumulated in this short stay. The food lockers had been filled. Covers had been gotten for the beds, bath towels . . .

Heller was unhooking the Homeviewer. A guard took it toward a carton. "Pack 'em up, move 'em out!" said Heller. The guards all laughed and kept busy. I couldn't understand why they were laughing until I realized Heller's words were the first words of a song, "Spaceward Ho!"

For the first time since awakening, the joyous possibility hit me. Were we really on our way? I finished the last drops of hot jolt and then paused. Wait. Why was he packing up a Homeviewer? It was no good on Earth. Had he just tamely told the Countess bye-bye kid? I didn't think so. Why should the guards laugh at the first words of that old song of the spacers? Did they know something I didn't know? Was there something secretively amusing in Heller's attitude? Long service in the Apparatus teaches one to note the signs in scenes carefully. There was something wrong here.

But they now had the place all packed up. They put the cartons on dollies and shortly we were boarding a tunnel zipbus, baggage and all.

The only attention anyone was paying to me came
at the various barricades where the alert guards demanded satisfaction for all the commotion. Heller, each time,
just jerked a thumb at me and I presented my orders and
identoplate. And well the sentries might be curious:
somebody in a racing suit was not an ordinary sight at
Spiteos or Camp Endurance. Heller had *no* security
sense: if trained, he would have worn something old and
shabby, more fitting to the scene. He wouldn't be standing out like an emergency beacon! And he made it even
worse by handing the sentries puffsticks and shaking
their hands and telling them good-bye. They were not
very good sentries, either: they laughed and made jokes
with him. In espionage you don't get yourself remembered! This guy wouldn't last two minutes on this
mission—if he was really going, which I sourly doubted.

We finally got to my airbus in the Camp Endurance
departure zone. My driver had evidently been alerted
and he greeted our guards like old friends. He gave Heller a grinning crossed-arm salute. Dawn was hardly
breaking. What was there to grin about? My suspicion
that these people were up to something deepened.

Although the driver opened the back for Heller, the
engineer stepped aside. The dollies rolled up and the
guards pitched the cartons and baggage into the back
seat. They almost filled it!

"In you go," said Heller and the driver scrambled in
on top of the baggage!

Heller climbed into the driver's bucket and gestured
for me to run around and get into the guard's seat up
front.

He was going to drive!

No guards were getting in. There wouldn't have
been room for them anyway. They showed no signs of
going off to get another airbus. I didn't want to expose

to Snelz that I didn't know what in blast was going on. In a sort of rattled way I thought I might come back and give him further orders when *I* knew. "I'll see you later," I yelled at Snelz.

"I know," he said.

I wondered if I was participating in a jailbreak for Heller. But I was well armed. Heller was gunning the drives—rohw, rohw, rohw. I scrambled into the guard's bucket beside him.

The rest of Snelz's people were all standing around grinning. They didn't say good-bye. The airbus vaulted straight up and the group below were pinpoints in the half-light of desert dawn. The red sunlight flashed blindingly in our faces as we ourselves, with altitude, made it rise.

You don't drive airbuses this way. At least sane people don't. Apparatus vehicles are not all that well maintained. But Heller was draped back in the seat, only one hand on the wheelstick, only one toe on the bars. "You comfortable back there?" he shot over his shoulder at my driver.

The pilot had settled himself in a nest in the boxes, only his feet were visible. Then a canister of hot jolt rose in a happy hand. Where had he gotten that? "First-rate, Officer Heller, sir." Heller certainly broke down discipline, I thought sourly.

Heller turned to me. Now it was my chance to gain some control over this crazy departure. I said, "The Apparatus freighter terminal is just to the southwest of Government City. You've got lots of time. There isn't one leaving until midafternoon."

He looked like I had said a dirty word. "Freighter?"

I opened my mouth to say of course, freighter; they leave once a week on a regular run for Earth. And then I clamped my mouth shut. It was too early in the morning. My wits were not about me. I mustn't tell Heller or anybody else who didn't need to know that Earth had a scheduled Apparatus freight service to it. If that got out, questions would hit the Apparatus like balls of fire! From all over the government and Grand Council.

Heller had the airbus at about twenty thousand feet. He was holding it there. Dangerous. The things slide off-balance if you're not an expert. They crash. It made me nervous.

"Well?" he prompted. "You said 'freighter.'" And then he must have seen that I didn't have any more to say so he did the saying. "Soltan, are you telling me the mission ship is a *freighter?* But that's silly, Soltan. A freighter would take six weeks or more to crawl along to Blito-P3. And we don't have anything to carry. Besides . . ."

I plunged, "We don't have a mission ship."

"Ah," said Heller. He was thinking. He perched the cap a little further back on his head. He had the airbus hanging there like a ball balanced precariously on a finger. Didn't he know these things crashed? The desert, getting lighter now, stretched out from Camp Endurance. Government traffic control detectors would be asking shortly what the Hells we thought we were doing. We shouldn't be attracting attention this way. He shot over his shoulder, "You all right back there?"

A curl of puffstick smoke rose out of the nest. "First-rate, Officer Heller, sir."

"You do have some craft in the Apparatus hangar, though," said Heller. And he must have taken it that I had nodded. "Good. We'll go there and look at them."

With a blasting roar it was never made to endure, the airbus catapulted across the sky. Heller, flying with one hand and one toe, picked up the traffic control communicator. "Airbus *469-98BRY* heading for Apparatus hangars from Camp Endurance." He had read the numbers on the communicator disc. He thrust it at me. I fumbled for my identoplate and pressed it on the disc; and I had a horrible feeling that that was going to be my sole function the rest of today: presenting my identoplate! Fronting for whatever mad scheme Heller might have in mind. At least we were away from the Countess Krak!

The desert fled below us. Spiteos got smaller behind us. Way over on the horizon the place where Palace City should be seen and wasn't, loomed as only a snow-capped mountain. Commercial City spread as a smudge, still in night, way off in the opposite direction. Government City rolled up toward us as we passed the desert-fringing mountain range.

"You ought to get this thing fixed," said Heller. "I can't get it above five hundred miles an hour. You ought to get this thing fixed," he yelled back.

"Yah, I keep telling Officer Gris," came from the languid spiral of smoke.

They were both idiots. An airbus's safe top speed is only four hundred. It was shaking like it had palsy—and maybe it did, it was old enough. I closed my eyes. It was a trifle cruel to die just when I might possibly be getting Heller off this planet, me out of danger and him into it. The bottom fell out!

I stared down to see where my grave would be. But it was just the landing target of the Apparatus hangar field. Heller slammed us down dead center on the *X*.

Before us loomed the huge hangars of the Apparatus Space Section. It is a pygmy compared to Fleet hangars but it is big enough. It rises about five hundred feet, a huge, rickety structure covering a square mile. Gantries and tractor platforms lay about in various states of decay and disarray.

Black-uniformed sentries with blastguns at port came racing up. This Apparatus area is extremely secret and well guarded.

"Officer Gris and party," shouted Heller. With a finger he indicated I should push my identoplate at the board a sergeant held aloft. "You stay here," he yelled back at my driver. "We may not be long. Come on," he said to me.

We piled out. The guards, disinterested now, slouched off. Odder things than a race driver came and went in this place. All in all, despite savage orders for top alertness, the Apparatus space hangar and area is glum, apathetic and shabby.

Heller was trotting briskly toward the hangar. I followed him not so briskly. I felt all this was out of my control someway. I was just an animated identoplate.

We got inside. Spaceships just arrived, spaceships waiting to go, spaceships being repaired, spaceships that wouldn't ever go anywhere again, stood far and wide, shadowy monsters full of secrets, half-operational machinery and old bloodstains. I groaned at the idea of having to walk endlessly amongst these assorted craft. It made my feet already begin to hurt.

But Heller was looking around alertly. And this was odd because you couldn't see much past the first three ships. He spotted something. I didn't understand his interest. It was a gigantic crane hoist used to lift heavy machinery.

The operator was in his cab way up in the air, sitting in bored idleness.

Heller called to him. Now, in the Fleet, officers accustomed to serving in the gigantic barnlike spaceships develop a type of voice. It is high-pitched and cuts across the rumble of drives with startling loudness. He was using that voice. "Hello the hoist! Stand by to lift!"

Ordinarily an Apparatus man in this hangar wouldn't take orders from his own foreman. And I was somewhat startled to see the operator, almost a speck in his high cab, give a wave back.

Heller took a pair of gloves from his pocket and handed me one of them, putting his own on.

The hoist hook was resting on the floor. I went into shock as I understood. Heller put his foot on it and took hold of a handle on the upper plate. It was a huge hook. There was plenty of room to put more than one foot on it. He expected *me* to step onto that hook!

I had seen high riggers do it on gantries. But never in my days had it ever occurred to me to ride a hook!

Heller was gesturing at me, his attention elsewhere. It was nothing to him to ride a hook. Life around a combat engineer, I groaned to myself. I put on the glove, put my foot near his, seized a hand bar and closed my eyes tight.

"Take her to the top!" shouted Heller in that peculiar ear-splitting voice.

Up we went! I left my stomach on the hangar floor. With nothing under us or around us but one steel hook, with nothing above us but screaming cables, we were zipped to the top of the hangar. We stopped suddenly, the spring of the cables making us bounce.

I cautiously opened one eye and closed it again. Heller had one foot over empty space. I grabbed the hand ring with my other hand.

"Look over there," said Heller. And then he must have seen that I wasn't looking. "Hey, open your eyes. It's only five hundred feet down."

They say never look down. I couldn't help it. I was

horrified at the amount of empty space and the hardness of that concrete far below.

"We've got to find a mission ship," said Heller. "Look them over."

I cursed the security which forbade me to tell him we should just be going by regular freighter.

"How big a ship will the hangars take on Blito-P3?" said Heller, nonchalantly swinging in the air.

I blurted the answer, "Five freighters, a couple combat ships."

"Then it will take a big ship," said Heller. He was looking down upon the whole expanse of the Apparatus space vessels now groundside. From this vantage point, a few were still hidden beyond others.

"Take her to the right!" shouted Heller to the cab that was just behind us now.

The hook swooped horrifyingly to the right. Heller could now see between several of the ships that had formerly blocked his view.

"Freighters. Transports. Some old model war vessels." He turned to me. "Where'd the Apparatus get these ships? Some temple rummage sale?"

"We're not the Fleet," I managed to get out.

"*That*," said Heller, "you definitely are not! I've got to think this over."

Can't you think it over down on the ground? I silently pleaded. The hook was still swinging. He seemed to be determined to hang way up here in thin air and think. I got desperate. "We're supposed to take a freighter."

"Oh, no, no, no," said Heller. "Six weeks or more on the way. And no mission operating ship there. I've got to change your mind."

You've changed it, I silently said. Anything, but get me back on the ground. He was still hanging there, thinking. "This stuff is all a pile of scrap," he said. "It just won't do. And a freighter won't do either. You certainly agree that we should have a proper mission ship."

My hand was so sweaty it was slipping inside the engineer glove. My other one had already slipped! I screamed, "Yes. Yes! We need a proper ship! I agreeeeeee!"

Heller turned and waved a hand at the crane operator just behind us. Then he signalled, palm down.

We plummeted! The cables screamed! We dropped five hundred feet so fast my foot came off the hook!

The steel heel banged into the hangar floor. Heller had stepped off just before it hit and stood there very composed. I reeled away and sat down on the concrete. I couldn't make my legs function.

Heller didn't seem to notice. He was sort of surveying the hangar floor around us, looking at a big empty space. "Aha!" he said.

His voice went racketing up to the crane cab. "Thank you and very well done, crane master!" The operator waved back.

"Come on," said Heller, trotting away.

Where the Hells was he going now? I gathered myself up and gazed after him. What was he up to? I desperately tried to think of some way to get this back under control. My neck was out a mile and a half. My prisoner was running around like a celebrity, without a single guard to back me up. He might take it into his head to go anywhere! But I had no ideas. I couldn't get even an inkling of what was really in his mind. If Lombar got wind of any of this . . .

Helplessly and hopelessly, I followed Heller back to the airbus.

Chapter 3

We took off again. It was still very early and the inter-city air traffic had not even gotten thick yet. The sun was still so low that the shadows on the ground were like long black fingers. I had no slightest idea where we were headed.

"This thing well fuelled?" Heller called back to my driver.

"For any place but the Royal Officers' Club," said the driver. I shook my head at him. Heller mustn't know about that. He sure did break down discipline around him: my driver had opened up a canister of sparklewater and was sipping it, admiring the view.

"Give me back my glove," said Heller. I handed it over. He was about to put it in his pocket when he felt that the cuff was damp.

We were at about twenty thousand feet and he was flying at about five hundred miles an hour. There was even some light traffic up this high now. But he took his hand off the wheelstick and began to fly with his knee! He rolled back the glove cuff, blew into it to turn it wrong side out, took out his redstar engineer's rag and wiped the glove dry. "You must have been nervous," he said consolingly. "I keep forgetting you might not be used to certain things."

Heller turned the cuff back, blew the glove right side out and put it and the rag in his pocket. "Well, don't you worry, Soltan. We'll get something nice and safe to travel in." Not very reassuring when the pilot is flying with one toe, one knee and, while admittedly very relaxed, is paying no slightest attention to whizzing traffic at his flight level. The overdriven airbus felt like it was about to shatter!

We were to the north of the main Fleet base. Below us an isolated plateau rolled up. The airbus was shaking so hard my vision was jittered and I couldn't see what it was.

"Here we are," said Heller and made what would be ranked in any book as a crash landing.

The dust settled. We were sitting before a low administration building, white and decorated with antique blastguns. It was very quiet. Nobody seemed to be around. Behind the building was a huge and seemingly endless fence. On it was a gigantic sign,

EMERGENCY FLEET RESERVE

Heller bounced out and I followed him up the building steps. There was a hall, a lot of empty desks, some unposted bulletin boards and plenty of echoes.

Apparently knowing where he was going, Heller trotted to the end of the hall and, without knocking, burst into a tomblike room.

A grizzled old space officer was sitting in a gravity chair, working on some lists, nursing a canister of hot jolt with his left hand. The unlighted sign on the front of the desk said,

Commander Crup

He looked up, a thundercloud scowl on his face. And then he burst into pure radiance. "Jettero!" He leaped up. They came together like colliding spaceships, pounding each other on the back. They laughed. The commander backed off, "Let me look at you! I haven't seen you for a year!"

Suddenly he caught sight of me. His scowl came back. "A 'drunk'!" How do they always know?

Heller whipped out the orders: the Grand Council authorization and his own. He handed them to the commander. That worthy looked hard at me. "He's all right," said Heller. "Commander Crup, meet Officer Gris." But Crup didn't offer to shake hands. He read the orders. He relaxed a bit.

"Well, what can we do for you, Jet?"

"Just on a shopping tour," said Heller. "Can I have permission to overfly the place?"

"Better than that," said Crup. "I'll come along with you." He gathered his cap and a case full of papers and outside we went.

The scene which had been so lonely before was now a bit populated. Six tough, scowling Fleet marines were standing around the airbus, fingering their electric daggers. My driver was sitting a bit white-faced and alert in back.

"It's all right, sergeant," said Crup. "This is Jettero Heller."

The biggest Fleet marine relaxed and smiled. He gave the single-arm salute of marines casually. "What you doing in 'drunk' company?"

I held my breath.

If Heller were to tell these tough brutes he had been held prisoner and was in actual fact under guard, I am sure they would have slaughtered me and the driver.

"I'm in disguise," said Heller with a perfectly straight face.

For some reason they thought this extremely funny.

"Sergeant," said Crup, as we piled into the front seat, "call perimeter defense and tell them this airbus has permission to overfly."

Heller took off, jumped the fence and, very low and slow, began to fly along. I had seen this place from high altitude and had often wondered what it was. What must be fifty square miles of black-hulled spaceships, sitting on their tails, stretched before us, the long morning shadows making it appear they were even more numerous. They were tall, they were short, they were broad, they were thin. What an assemblage!

I promptly destroyed what little tolerance I had gained from Commander Crup. "Emergency Fleet Reserve," I said. "This looks more like a boneyard!"

Crup withered me. He wasn't going to answer at first and then pride got the better of him. "These ships are *not* scrap! They have the status of 'suspended activation.' When vessels are still serviceable but have been outmoded they are added to the Emergency Fleet Reserve!"

"But I don't see any men, no crews," I said.

"There are retired officers and superannuated spacemen aplenty that could be summoned up to man these ships," said Crup. "And believe me, in time of planetary emergency, the Fleet would be thankful to have them."

Heller changed the subject. "Hey, there's the old *Juba!* I didn't know they had retired the five thousand spacer class, any of them!"

I looked in that direction. It was a huge black monster, covered with dust. It looked like a Commercial City office building. But I didn't get any time to admire it as Heller barely flicked its antennas with our undercarriage.

Rows and rows of ships, thousands and thousands of

them. We cruised along, Heller looking. I wished he'd put more of his attention on flying.

"If you could tell me what you want," said Crup, "maybe I could help. What kind of a mission is it?"

Untrained as he was, I thought Heller would blurt it out. But he said, "Kind of a peculiar one. I'll just keep on looking."

We had gotten to the far perimeter. "See that old baby over in the corner there, Soltan?"

It was a monster's monster. It was built of cubes apparently added on at random until they were mountain high. A more dilapidated spaceship I have never seen.

"That," said Heller, "is the *Upward Strike*. You are looking at the last of the original intergalactic battleships. She was part of the force which attacked Voltar, an immigration ship. A hundred and twenty-five thousand years old. She must be sunk into the ground thirty feet by now."

"I thought you said all these ships were operational," I quipped.

Crup sneered at me. "She is equipped with the original time drives that made immigration possible between galaxies. Academy cadets studying engines are brought here to see her."

"It was my weak subject," I said lamely. I did recall now there had been such tours. I had always been on punishment drill.

I was jolted out of it by a yell from Heller. "There she is! There she is! There she is! Oh, you baby!"

"What?" said Crup. "Where?"

"There! There!" cried Heller, pointing and diving us down toward a landing.

"Oh, no!" said Commander Crup. "Jettero! As I love you, boy, you don't want that!"

I finally credited that what they were looking at was what they were looking at.

It was a pygmy amongst these monsters. It was the ugliest, dustiest thing I ever hope to see. It was standing on its tail. It looked like a headless old woman with two arms outstretched, her black dress reaching the ground. It was only about a hundred and ten feet tall. It was fat beyond belief. All around it were graceful, swept-curve cruisers and patrol craft, any one of them preferable to this horrible looking little blob.

Heller was out and literally stroking its side in ecstasy. "Oh, you darling," he was saying. "Oh, you wonderful beauty!" Then he was eagerly beckoning to Crup to bring the keyplates to open the entry lock.

Crup was shaking his head sadly.

I arrived by Heller and looked up at this mess. "What is it?" I said.

"Oh, don't you see?" said Heller. "It's *Tug One!* It was the Flagship of the Tug Section!" He was vibrating like a kid that has just gotten his most heartfelt birthday present. He must have read my face correctly. "Soltan, it's all engines! It's nothing but engines! Like any tug, it has the engines of the biggest battleship in space. It's the fastest thing in this universe!"

Oh, here we go, I thought. Speed. I've got your fracture now, race champion Heller. It's *speed.*

He still thought I didn't understand. "You know those motor locomotives on the highways, the kind that pulls half a dozen trailers after them? Well, if you detached the motor locomotive and ran it with no trailers, it would be the fastest vehicle they've got. Well, it's the same way with a tug! It's just battleship engines with a skin around them. Fast! Open the spacelock, Commander! Let him see!"

"I think there's a watchman in this sector that you know, Jet," said Crup. He took out a little board and pressed some buttons, giving our sector location. And then he got a ladder and clambered way up to open the door.

Dust! Dust and darkness. But Heller was up that tall ladder and into her in a flash, dragging me along. First he went down. I dimly perceived a large stateroom and lots of knobs and rails: they were all black-crusted, horrible looking. There were several cabins. We climbed upward on the crisscross ladders that work when the vessel is vertical or horizontal. Dust! We got to a flight deck that was crammed with controls, all coated with filth.

Heller had finally gotten out a light; there was apparently no current in the ship. He opened a door and we entered a small engine room crammed with ordinary drives. "These are her auxiliaries. You use them for atmosphere maneuvering and speeds less than light." He was checking boxes and panels rapidly. "They seem to be set up all right."

We dropped down and he opened a door into a second engine compartment and as he flashed his light around, I found myself looking at the most monstrous engines I have ever seen. Actually, I had never connected with anything like them. They certainly were battleship-sized drives but other than that, I couldn't classify them.

Heller seemed happier and happier. He swarmed down a catwalk and opened a door at the back of the main engine room. I was looking at very strange, huge metal drums.

"These are her tractor beam generators!" he said. "They are some of the most powerful ever built! These are what she fastens onto things with and pulls."

We went out a side door. He shined his light again

into the large cabin. Aside from everything being black-stained I couldn't see much. What a dirty ship!

We went back outside. An old, old spacer was just creakily getting off a triwheeler. The watchman Crup had called. He saw Jet drop off the tall entrance ladder and peered carefully. Then he said, "Oh, my Gods!"

He and Heller flew together and pounded each other. "Atty!" Jet was saying.

Finally, the old man—he must have been a hundred and seventy if he was a day—drew back. He wiped a tear from his eye with the back of his hand. "Oh, Jet, lad. It's good to know you're still alive!" Jet introduced me and the old fellow said, "I was Jet's engine repair chief when he made the record run at the Academy."

Crup said, "Jet's thinking of taking out *Tug One*."

Old Atty went rigid. "Jettero Heller, you know as well as I do why she's a-lying here to rot."

"I know I used her sister ship with success. And she did just fine!" said Heller defensively.

"Ah, yes. The speed," said old Atty sadly. "Jet, you know why *Tug One* is lying here?"

"She couldn't have been here more than three years," said Heller.

"Two," said Crup.

"I was aboard her three and a half years ago. Right after Admiral Wince fixed her up as his flagship."

"Oh, yes," said Crup. "He fixed her up all right." He glanced at a sheet he was holding, "He spent two million credits on a special refit. I recall he said that every other flotilla admiral had a fancy flagship and he didn't see why he shouldn't. Of course, he never used her much. He wouldn't listen any more than you're listening now."

My hair was beginning to rise a bit on the back of my neck. Heller had a stubborn look on his face. What was he letting us in for? "What's the matter with this ship?" I blurted out.

Crup said, "She's dangerous!"

Atty turned to me. "She doesn't have the usual warp drives. She is equipped with Will-be Was main drives."

I thought it was some maker's name.

"*Time* drives," said Crup. "The type designed for intergalactic travel where distances are truly enormous and they have to work directly with time. When you run these engines inside a galaxy without a heavy load behind them, they pick up more energy than can be wasted. They work all right in a battleship with all its auxiliaries to burn the excess energy but not in a tug. And Jet knows it."

I'm no expert on drives. Somebody would have to explain this to me someday. The only thing I got out of it was that this (bleeped) tug had engines that were *dangerous!*

But it was Atty that caved me in. "When old Admiral Wince was told *Tug One*'s sister ship had blown up with all hands lost while running flat-out with no tow, he instantly ordered this ship straight to Emergency Fleet Reserve and she's been here ever since."

"That settles it," I said. "No *Tug One!*"

"Good," said Heller. "Make out the papers."

Chapter 4

I frantically tried to think of some way to stop this madman. But my wits just didn't seem to work! His direct counter to my decision had robbed me of my usual smooth ability to exert my will. The contradiction had been done so coolly and his cancellation of my authority seemed so final that I felt just like he had pulled a gun and shot me.

I could muster no real arguments. So I simply drew in my breath and prepared to shout "NO!"

He must have heard the breath intake. Before the word I was forming could come out, he said, "Soltan, you know and I know that we must not put secrets of the Apparatus before unauthorized personnel."

It was a stripped, naked, totally unclothed threat. We were on Fleet territory. He was amongst friends. With a shock I realized he knew one tightly guarded Apparatus secret—the existence of Spiteos. He undoubtedly knew nothing else but that was enough! Something inside me seemed to break. I really *had* lost control. But just for now, Heller, I said to myself, just for now; when we're back in Apparatus territory, and certainly when I get you off this planet, watch out; you're going to pay for this!

I closed my mouth.

Seemingly oblivious of this byplay, Commander Crup and Atty were muttering together in a kind of huddle.

Commander Crup looked at Heller sadly. "Jet, I'm too fond of you to let you have this ship."

My hopes soared!

"Jet, my boy," continued the old commander, tapping the Grand Council order, "you know and we know that you'll not be pulling any heavy loads: you'll be running any ship you get as just a mission ship. You certainly won't be going to some other galaxy. You'll be working in this one. And *Tug One* will develop more energy than you can use or waste and *boom!*, there you'll go just like

Tug Two did. So don't waste any time in pleading. We know you."

Heller smiled a disarming smile, "And what would you say if I told you I had invented a way to bleed off the excess energy?"

My hopes fell.

"You mean," said Crup, "that you'd undertake to remodel the vessel before you left?"

"I would certainly promise to remodel it," said Heller.

Wait, wait, wait, I cried silently. This would take time!

Crup looked at old Atty. Then they both shrugged.

"But there is another hitch," said Crup.

My hopes rocketed up.

"Ordinarily," the commander continued, but this time looking at me, "if Jet wanted this ship he could simply sign for it and fly it away. In this case, he can't."

I was eager to hear his next words.

"For some reason or other," said Crup, tapping the Grand Council orders, "the directive that the mission be undertaken assigns it to the Exterior Division. I can't imagine how the Exterior Division also got a Fleet man. . . ."

"They probably didn't have nobody who knew how to run a spaceship," sneered old Atty. "Certainly nobody like Jet."

" . . . but in any event," continued Crup, "I cannot transfer a unit of the Emergency Fleet Reserve to the Exterior Division, much less its 'drunks.' Their Lordships in the Fleet would have my head."

Relief! I had been rescued!

"However . . ." said Crup, getting some papers out of his case.

My hopes faltered.

He found what he was looking for. ". . . we quite routinely sell supernumerary spaceships to commercial companies engaging in peaceful interplanetary traffic. We simply strip out their guns and sensitive equipment and transfer ownership. Any transaction that can be done with commercial companies can be done with the Exterior Division. *Tug One* has no guns or sensitive battle equipment so . . ." He had a list. "The price of constructing *Tug One* was four million credits . . . the refit done on her by Admiral Wince was about two million credits . . . that's six million in round figures."

My hopes rose. We only had an allocation of three million total. Six was way, way out of our price range.

Crup was pulling a finger down a column of figures. "But, of course, a resale figure wouldn't be that high."

I held my breath. Please, please and please now give a figure in excess of three million.

"Ah," said Crup. "Here's a note about *Tug One:*

> Due to the Fleet having in excess of two
> thousand service tugs of the normal type, and
> if any purchaser will undertake upon the sales
> papers not to hold the Fleet responsible if
> this vessel blows up, the resale price is hereby
> fixed at a half a million credits.

My hopes crashed with a loss of all hands.

"Perfectly agreeable," said Heller.

"You sure you will remodel?" said Crup.

"Absolutely," said Heller.

"Good," said Crup and he began to scribble and copy numbers and add conditions to a fatal paper that would transfer *Tug One* from the Fleet to the Exterior Division. But just before he asked for my identoplate he spoke again. "I don't think you can take it today. You don't have any engineer for her."

There was not even a flicker of life in the dead ashes of my hopes.

And sure enough, old Atty said, "But he'll just need somebody to run the auxiliaries. They're simple! If you'll give me the rest of the day off, Commander, I'm his man!" He cackled. "Just so long as he don't ask me to turn on the Will-be Was main engines and just sticks to the planetary drives, I'll chief engineer for him! Today only."

I am extremely well trained at hiding my feelings. I was certain that I had permitted no slightest trace of my reactions to show on my face. So I could not account for the possible malice in old Atty's voice as he turned to me and said, "I got a wife, kids, grandchildren and great-grandchildren but I'm a lot too young to die at the throttles of time drives!" An idiot remark. It seemed to amuse him out of all proportion. He went tearing off to steal some spare fuel rods from a nearby ship.

Crup had to joggle me twice. He was holding out the completed documents.

With a feeling I was putting my own seal on my own death warrant, I pushed my identoplate against the paper.

Tug One had just become the mission ship for Mission Earth! And there was nothing I could do about it. Nothing. Not right here anyway.

Chapter 5

Heller was over by my airbus. My driver appeared to have breakfasted well on supplies in back. He was looking at Heller with a keen eagerness while the combat engineer gave him some very exact instructions. What was Heller telling him? Apparently there was something not entirely clear for Heller whipped out a notebook and wrote something very rapidly on it, tore out the sheet and handed it over. I was about to interrupt what might be a violation of security but before I reached them, Heller handed him some money. My driver, without even asking permission from me, took off. Oh, well. I'd grill him later.

The Commander had gotten on the old watchman's triwheeler. Heller went over and they shook hands and I heard the tail end of Crup's farewell. ". . . if you know what you're doing. Remember you promised to fix her up. Well, if I never see you again, good luck anyway." I shuddered. Crup backed the triwheeler to a safe distance and sat there to watch our departure.

Heller sort of hazed me into the ship the way they do animals that have gotten out of the pasture. He got me up the ladders and into the flight deck. There was still only his own beamlight and the dust motes made it look like muddy water. I could hear old Atty banging and swearing in the auxiliary engine room just below us. He seemed to be having a lot of trouble and must be using a sledgehammer to fix it.

There were two gravity flight chairs; Heller pressed

me gently down into one of them. The dust clouds absolutely geysered. "Now this is the star navigator's seat you're in and we won't be going to any stars just yet. I'll be sitting right over there in the local maneuvering seat. We don't have time to unseal the ports and all the viewscreens are around the other seat, but don't worry just because you can't see anything."

He was buckling clasp-straps around me. The dust was horrible. I began to cough and tried to sit up to cough better but he just shoved me back. "Now this is a tug," he said when he had finished. "A tug is the quickest maneuvering ship ever built. Don't lift your head out of those pads or you could snap your neck. A tug can move sideways, up, down, back and forward in the flash of an eye. They have to be able to, so as to position themselves around battleships. So *don't* lift your head! Even on auxiliary drives, these things can be deadly fast. Understand?"

All I understood was that I was choking to death on dust.

If he was so careful to tuck me in, how come he simply went over and perched on the edge of the local maneuvering chair?

The banging still went on in the nearest engine room. Then old Atty yelled, "You got power there yet?"

Heller took his finger and ran it along a huge line of switches like a musician makes a run up the keyboard of an instrument. "Everything on. No lights!"

More swearing from the engine room. Then, "(Bleep) it, Jet, we'll just have to run her on emergency lighting!"

A feeble glow came on. The dust flying around made it look like green soup.

"I got the (bleeped) rods in," shouted Atty. Two more huge bangs. "I think the throttles will move now.

Let me get strapped down here where I can reach 'em."
A long spell of coughing: must be dusty down there, too!

Jet said, "Let me see. Been three years since I
touched a tug's controls." He was perched on the edge of
the chair looking at what must be two thousand switches.
He yelled, "You all set, Atty?"

"Set as I'll ever be."

"Give me power and local control."

There was a shudder throughout the tug as Atty
engaged the engines.

Heller looked thoughtfully over the array. "Hey, the
viewscreens came on. What do you know." He hit a
switch.

My hair rose. The inference was that he had been
about to fly this blind!

But for all my fears, *Tug One* rose smoothly into the
sky. I felt Heller fumbling at my tunic pocket. He was
fishing out my identoplate. He cleared us for the Apparatus base and transmitted my identoplate and I felt him
putting it back in my pocket.

I should have known he was up to something else
but at the time, frankly, I was too scared of this tug and
too choked with dust. Later I would realize that all he
had to do at this moment was to fly to a Fleet base, turn
me in and expose the whole Apparatus. But it wasn't
until much later in that day that I found out he had his
own personal plans.

The tug's communication system worked and he had
a mild argument with the Apparatus base concerning the
readiness of a trundle dolly to land on. Once more he
had out my identoplate and he got his way.

We got there so quickly that he had to skyhang a
couple minutes until they had the trundle dolly in
position. Then I felt us plummeting down. We must
have been quite high. It made me feel queasy. It sent dust

up in clouds! I began to choke. And then I thought, oh, wait until I get you on the ground in Apparatus territory: you'll certainly hear about this day's work, Jettero Heller. And I had no more than thought that than I became painfully sick at my stomach. I wasn't throwing up but almost.

We were down!

Heller unbuckled me. He swung down the ladder and out. I followed him slowly and painfully. I emerged into the midmorning sunlight. We were at the Apparatus base all right. There loomed *Tug One* on the trundle dolly in all its awful ugliness.

Heller had the ear of the landing master and the signal sticks began to wag. The trundle dolly rolled ponderously back through the door of the hangar, going under cover. *Tug One*'s weight was so great it made the dolly sag.

I was still coughing and wheezing and trying not to actually vomit. I didn't follow closely what was going on for a while. I just leaned up against the window of the inside hangar office and tried to get myself back together. If this was a sample of *Tug One* travel, I wondered sadly how we would ever get to Earth—with me still alive, that is!

But Heller was all bounce. You would have thought he had just been presented with a feudal dukedom. He got the trundle dolly under the crane and then got the crane master to engage his hook just right into the big steel loops on *Tug One*'s back and with Heller's careful supervision, lifted the ship into the air. What a strong crane!

They got the trundle dolly out from under it and Heller showed them where to put some steadying chocks to make a cradle. And then with a swoop the crane laid *Tug One* on its belly into the chocks. She was now in normal flight position, horizontal, a common enough practice. The crane disengaged.

The hangar chief went over to Heller. Like all Apparatus personnel he was not a very pleasant fellow— mostly scars and bluster. "You're taking up one of the best places in the hangar," he said.

"I want a cleaning team," said Heller. "A very big one, all the men you've got."

"A what?" roared the hangar chief. Believe me, the last thing they had in the Apparatus was a cleaning team.

"I want it finished by midafternoon," said Heller.

The hangar chief looked like he was going to slug Heller. It was obvious that he was thinking, who the blazes is this bird in a racing suit, giving me my orders, me! here in my own hangar.

Heller said, "What did you say your name was?"

The hangar chief roared, "Stipe, that's who! And I . . ."

Heller reached out to shake his hand.

The hangar chief took it, probably intending to do an arm-pull-hit routine. He suddenly froze. As he let go of Heller's hand he looked down and I caught a flash of gold paper.

The strangest look came over Stipe's face. Then he turned his palm to see the denomination. He looked up and if I have ever seen a person beam, he beamed!

"Say, you'll want your water and sewage and power hoses, won't you. A cleaning team, you say. Well, fellow, we never ain't had one before but we're going to have one now!" And he rushed off bawling for foremen and work gangs.

My driver staggered in, carrying some bundles and cans. "Here they are Officer Heller. Fleet cleaning supplies. I'll go get the rags!" He dumped his load and ran back to the airbus.

Old Atty had been standing around, watching the
sudden scurry, so unlike the Apparatus. He went over to
Heller and Heller thanked him and they embraced.

The old spacer came over to me. "I get the idea
you're going off some place with Jet. There's something
you ought to know. Jet's a dear boy. Everybody loves
him. But he's really quite mad, you know. Speed. It's like
food and drink to him. I think of him every now and
then—you've not much to do as a watchman—and while
there's a lot of smiles in remembering things he has
done, there's always a bit of a worry, too. I'm getting old.
I got a feeling I'll never see Jet alive again. *Tug One* is
a killer."

He fixed me with his swimming old eyes and punctuated every word with a piercing flash. "You hold him
down. You make him keep that throttle just a little bit
shut. You make sure *Tug One* don't kill him. Because,
Officer Gris—yes, I saw your name on those orders and
saw also you're a 'drunk'—if anything happens to Jettero
Heller that can be laid to your account, there's a lot of
us will find and kill you, Officer Gris."

It was so illogical! It was so unjust! It was *I* who had
tried to prevent Heller from getting that ship! The old
spacer might be in his dotage and his wits might be
adrift but there was no mistaking the menace in his
voice. In some intuitive way, did he sense I was Heller's
enemy?

Hastily, I got Atty into an airbus and told a driver
to return him to the Emergency Fleet Reserve. I certainly hoped he would never find out or guess what was
intended to happen to Heller. I watched them leave.

I was sick all over again.

Chapter 6

I should have been more suspicious. My only excuse is that I was a bit confused and dazed with the events of the first half of the morning. I remember looking at my watch and being amazed that it was still so early.

But Heller wasn't dazed. He was moving with fast, determined movements, putting speed and control into this scene.

I saw him go over to the hangar security guard captain. There was a money handshake and a sudden look of awe from the captain. "Yes, *sir!*" the security chief said, pushing golden paper into his tunic, "Post guards and make absolutely certain nothing is stolen from that ship. Good as done, sir!" And he rushed off to post his guards.

A motley mob of mechanics, cargo handlers and odds and ends of personnel had been gathered up by the bustling hangar chief to act as cleaning crews. My driver was standing beside a stack of cans and boxes and was handing out rags and cleaning materials to the workmen who then began crowding into the ship.

Heller and a mechanic were rigging vacuum hoses and passing them into the open airlocks and ports of *Tug One*. Another crew was fastening water, sewage and power lines for groundside utilities.

There were so many bodies rushing about doing so many things, it made me quite dizzy.

Then, to cap it, a big lorry suddenly roared into the

hangar. My driver rushed over to its cab and some workmen spilled out and began to unload it.

A commercial lorry? Big signs on it:

Drink Tup for a Terrific Treat!

Tup? It was the mild, brewed concoction workers are supposed to rave about.

The truck workers found a long sheet of hull shielding and put it on a couple of supports, making a kind
of bar. Then they unloaded some cases of canisters and
stacked them along the shielding. This tup company, I'd
seen in ads, provided "everything you need for a picnic
party." And sure enough, they unloaded some expendable portable stands with banners on them in garish colors and strewed them about the bar and spotted them on
the floor. Then they all jumped back on the lorry and it
roared away.

Heller let loose a piercing whistle, the way they do
on battleships. All work ceased abruptly within and outside the ship. In that distance-defying Fleet officer voice
he said, "Attention all. If this ship passes a Fleet-type
inspection, totally clean, by four o'clock this afternoon,
you will all have a tup party!"

Heads, incredulous, poked out of openings in the
ship. People turned and stared. And there was the makeshift bar and there flowed the bright banners and there
in cases was the tup!

A concerted yell of enthusiasm went up from all over
the place. And if there had been action before, there was
a blur now! Nothing like this had ever happened before
in *this* hangar.

The voice of the hangar chief rumbled behind me
and I turned, half-expecting to be attacked. But he
wasn't looking at me. He was looking with awe at the

busy Heller. "Who is that guy? He's a Royal officer, I can tell that. But I got the feeling I've seen his face before."

Without thinking—I wasn't being very bright that day—I said, "Jettero Heller."

"No!" said the battered old hangar chief. "Jettero Heller the famous race driver! Oh, wait until I tell my wife and kids I've actually met *the* Jettero Heller."

Oh, my Gods! If this got to the Grand Council we hadn't left . . . I had an impulse to seize him by the tunic and drag him close and snarl. But he was too tough. Instead, I said, "He is on a mission that is totally secret. No word that he is here is to be spread around!" I had a vision of Crown inspectors swarming in to find out why we were still here and not on Earth! "You'll forget his name! That's an order!"

I might as well not have opened my mouth for all the attention he gave me. He was still looking at Heller. "My, but he's a grand fellow! So efficient, so friendly." And then and only then did his eyes shift to me. He looked me up and down. "Wish we had some in the Apparatus like that!" And walked off.

It didn't help my morale. But looking at *Tug One* further depressed it. I slumped down on an old fuel rod case and looked at her. Lying on her belly as she was now, she was about forty feet high and about sixty feet wide, all out of proportion for her hundred and ten feet of length. And the massive arms that stuck out on either side of her bow looked silly.

The trundle dolly operator was preparing to move the machine: he was nearby, lifting the chock levers. I said to him, "What are those arms sticking out from her bow?"

He looked at her. "Those are to butt with. That's a space tug. They butt into the sides of battleships and things and if they didn't have those wide arms, they'd buckle the hull plates of what they were trying to move. Her stern is big enough to use, too. They butt and bump and push things around. I never seen that exact type before, she looks more powerful than the usual run; and that's saying a lot, fellow. Even the auxiliary drives on those tugs are the same as they put in battleships today. Gods know what her main power is. And she'd have traction beam towing, too. You have to be careful of traction beam towing: one careless yank and it'd pull a battleship in half. A tug is all engines. I heard a few years ago one blew up: lost everybody aboard. Awful thing: you wouldn't catch me serving on no tug. What are we doing with that thing in here anyway?"

I wished I knew! But one thing I did know: it was the ugliest spacevessel I had ever laid eyes on.

Heller seemed to have everything organized and going now. I saw him entering the hangar administration offices over on the other side. Even at that distance I could see he had some notebook out, consulting it as he walked. In a surge of fear, I realized he was heading for the communication control cubicle: he was about to personally place outside calls! With his in security, he could blow us apart! I raced after him.

There he stood, red racing cap on the back of his head, blond hair escaping around it, a totally composed look on his face. He was regarding the usual lengthy list of civilian contractors they place in hangar offices; in this case it was a smudgy, tattered list, augmented by little cards the contractors themselves stick on and around it to advertise their names. He was already reaching for the brush levers to register a call number when I stayed his hand.

"That's an out-security action you're doing," I said. He looked at me a bit languidly, his mind on his open notebook, "You know as well as I do that any of these contractors is totally secure. They handle all sorts of sensitive installations. And they well know that one leak from one of them would cause an instant cancellation of all future business." He freed his hand and reached toward the brush levers again.

But I had gotten a glimpse of the lengthy list of items he had jotted down. "We've only got three million credits. We've already spent half a million for that tug. If we run over allocation . . ."

"This list total is under half a million," he said.

But I had gotten a further look at the list. "I don't see any note here to do something to shed the excess energy that makes these things blow up."

"Oh, that," he said. "I haven't gotten around to inventing how to do it yet. It's never been possible, you know." He freed his hand once more and hit the brush lever plate.

He got his connection. "Hello, hello. Alpy? Hey, old boy, this is me, Jet. . . . Glad to hear your voice, too. How's your father? . . . I got *Tug One* here! . . . No, I'm not kidding. She's beautiful! . . . Now, Alpy, I want you to bring a design and estimation group down here tomorrow morning. . . . No, it's just a job on the controls. . . . Will be good to see you, too." He brushed off.

I tried to find some other objection. Heller was looking at the list on the wall. More brush levers. "Hello, hello. Let me talk to Petalv. . . . Enii? That you? . . . Yes, you're right: Jet here. Enii, could you bring a design and estimation group down to the Apparatus spacebase hangar one? . . . Tomorrow morning . . . Ha, ha. No, I didn't lose my wits and transfer to the Apparatus. . . . Just a general engine-maintenance checkup . . . Good. Will look forward to it."

Another call. And another call. All first name, old pal calls. Gyro specialists. Cable renewals. Viewscreen refurbishing. Gravity coil reintensifying. Antisurveillance hull work. On and on and on. He was almost exhausting the contractor list.

Finally, between calls, I could stand it no longer. "Heller!" I wailed, "you're planning work that will take months!"

"Weeks, unfortunately."

The specter of Lombar began to loom over me. "Heller," I said in desperation, "we've got to get out of here! We've got to get started on this mission!"

He looked at me in surprise. "I know! You were going to take a freighter. It takes a freighter weeks and weeks and weeks to get to Blito-P3. If we started right this minute on a freighter or if we started weeks from now in *Tug One*, we'd still get to Earth faster my way. I'm saving us time!"

And threatening us with being blown up, I snarled to myself. Oh, I thought, I could wring your neck! And instantly I was too sick at my stomach to stay in there.

I went and found a corner out of everybody's way and wrapped myself in solid gloom.

After a while, I saw the irony of it. He was actually perfectly safe here, in reach of friends. Danger for him began when we hit Earth. But I certainly could not tell him *that*. Somehow, some way, I had to get him off this planet. And I couldn't even understand why just thinking about it made me feel so ill.

Maybe it was that (bleeped), ugly abomination of a tug!

Chapter 7

The day rushed itself forward into the afternoon. And at four o'clock Heller inspected the ship. All eyes were on him expectantly as he came out.

He cried, "A beautiful job! It passes! The party is on!"

About two hundred people let out a whoop that made the hangar ring. In a mad, happy mob they converged upon the makeshift bar and the tup canisters began to pop. There were buns there, too, and funny hats and streamers. And for the next two hours, the place was a bedlam of cries and songs and toasts to Heller and *Tug One* and anything else anyone could think of, except the Apparatus.

The hangar security guards were still at their posts but they had canisters of tup. The guard captain, a bit unsteady on his feet and his mouth full of sweetbun, tried to put his arm around my shoulder. "What a wunnerful bird that Heller is!"

I shook him off.

Heller was no place to be seen. A short time before I had seen him and my driver carrying the baggage from the airbus into the tug along with some new boxes. Heller must now be inside the ship.

My driver—blast, might as well call him Heller's driver now—had had a busy day. He must have made a dozen trips to town. He had even been the one handing out the tup at the party start. He was apparently finished now. He had gotten himself a canister of tup and was sucking it down. He came over to me, grinning and happy like an idiot. "You got any orders for me?"

"No," I said coldly.

"Then I'll just go back to the old airbus and have me a little nap." From a slight slur of speech, I realized that wasn't his first tup today. Heller certainly could crash discipline. The driver hadn't even asked permission or saluted or said "Officer Gris!"

How much of Heller's money had today cost? Certainly not less than three hundred and fifty credits. Heller's money? *My* money! And all on a stinking piece of ugly scrap metal!

The party finally died down. The Apparatus people had drifted off with happy, stupid grins on their faces. It was nearing sunset. At least, I thought, it's all over. I was wrong!

I heard a "Hup, yo, hup, hup, yo!" cadence counting coming nearer! For an instant I thought it must be Fleet marines come to rescue Heller. Only Fleet marines counted cadence that way!

Slam, trap, slam, trap, slam, trap of military boots. And in through the hangar door came Snelz and half his platoon, eight men. They sounded like a regiment, their heavy combat boots banging on the hangar floor, shattering the echoes!

I remembered that Snelz was an ex-Fleet marine. He had an officer's baton—really a long blastick—and he was twirling it in blurring spins the way they do. What a precision picture of the perfect military drillmaster.

And his half-platoon . . . Hey, they were in riot helmets and they carried blastrifles! They were a perfect example of crack elite troops. All eight of them.

The hangar guard captain had been lounging against the tug, half-finished canister of tup in his hand, the only one left on guard. He straightened up in amazement, particularly when he saw they were Apparatus troops.

"Scuh-wahd, halt!" cried Snelz. "Grough-und, har-rums, hup!"

With the whirring spin and strap-slapping perfection of marines, the squad flipped their blastrifles off their shoulders, spun them down and over their arms, whizzed them around their backs, spun them again with an expert twist of wrist and brought them, all as one, to a uniform crash, butt beside their right boot. I hadn't seen it since the marine's fancy parades at the Academy.

"Reh-yust, heasy, hup!" barked Snelz.

Each blastrifle jutted forward, each left boot moved a half-yard to the left and came down with an ear-shattering slam.

To the goggle-eyed hangar captain, Snelz said, "We-yuh ahh hear-uh to re-LEAVE the gah-yard, SUH!" And he saluted smartly with his baton.

Despite this amazing display of eight usually mangy, drunken, criminal Apparatus riffraff from Camp Kill, I was a bit glad to see them. This was the squad that would take the night duty. They would be relieved at dawn by the other squad of the platoon. They would shuttle back and forth each day. They undoubtedly had an air transport outside. At least this was running well. Heller would be thoroughly guarded. I did wonder dimly at the riot helmets and also at the extreme, well-drilled precision of these eight men.

Eight? There should be only seven left in this squad after I had bashed in the skull of one of them. A skilled Apparatus officer always notes things like that. I peered at them but the riot helmet visors made it hard to make out the faces. Oh, well, Snelz had simply gotten a replacement.

The disbelieving captain of the hangar guards had

returned the salute with his tup canister. "The gah-yard is yuh-ores, suh," he said, mimicking marine custom.

Snelz turned. His baton did a spinning, expert twirl. He held it aloft, "Attention all! Poh-stings!" The baton spun again and came to point at a figure toward the center of the squad. "Gy-yardsman Ip! Your posting is within the ship. Hup!"

The one designated as Guardsman Ip did a precise back yank of the blastrifle, heels popping together at the same time. With the incredibly complex reverse swing of the heavy weapon—around the back, a spin around the other arm—the indicated figure shouldered the weapon, gave a precise, slapping salute and with firm, military marching steps, pivoting on exact right-angle turns, marched to the door of the airlock, stepped into the tug and slammed the door.

With a suddenness that startled me, a strange thing happened. All the remaining members of that squad and Snelz let out an exultant yell! Their military discipline was gone in a breath! They leaped into the air and slapped their hands; their blastrifles they flung upward! Then they grabbed one another by the shoulders and did a kind of crazy dance, yelling all the while.

Not one shred of military discipline remained. Even Snelz. He was laughing and doing a private waltz.

Then the guard captain, who had walked over to the makeshift bar, called to them, "There's still some tup left over here." And the whole group streamed, still laughing, toward the drinks.

It was not until that very moment that I suspected what this day really had been all about.

I rushed to the airlock. I yanked it open and dashed in. The door slammed behind me. I got open the second door. I stopped.

Standing in the passageway was Heller. A groomed, freshly bathed Heller in a powder blue lounge suit.

In front of him stood "the guardsman" taking off the riot helmet. A mass of silky hair tumbled out from under the helmet and there she was revealed: a laughing Countess Krak!

Chapter 8

They hugged like they hadn't seen each other for years! They hugged and rehugged.

Finally, Heller drew back from a long kiss. "Wait," he said, "there's lots of night left." He stilled his mounting excitement; for a moment it had looked like they would get no further than the couch behind him tonight.

"Darling," said Heller, still panting a bit, "I've got to show you this beautiful ship!"

For an instant, I thought he must be being sarcastic. I had had my eyes on them. I looked around. It was clean. But it seemed like the usual officers' or crew quarters of any Fleet vessel.

"Up here," and he led the way forward, "is the control deck." It was shiny now and, although nothing was activated, it was well lit. Fancier than most flight decks, more controls, but, after all, just a flight deck.

He spent no time at all on that. The Countess Krak looked not quite as bright as she had. She was still beautiful even in her Apparatus black uniform but she seemed to see the control deck as something that would carry him from her—I could almost read her mind.

Heller pushed open a door just forward of the

airlock. "This is the officers' and crew's eating salon."
It was quite small, only room enough for about eight. He
saw her puzzlement. "Oh, this ship takes a very small
crew. A captain, two astropilots and two machinery
engineers. That leaves three extra places! I see you are
thinking in terms of five-thousand-crew battleships."

He guided her aft and opened a door between the
passageway and the skin. "This is the captain's cabin."
It was quite tiny, really, but well appointed. "There's one
just this size on the opposite side of the ship that's a little
crew library and reference room."

She was standing there, swinging her riot helmet by
its strap, looking interested for his sake. Perhaps she was,
femalewise, trying to understand the suppressed enthusiasm he had for this ship. Maybe a rival to her?

Heller went a few feet aft and opened another door.
"And this is the crew's food-making area. It's so tiny and
still it has all the essential machines. Isn't it cute?"

She allowed that it was cute.

"There's another compartment this size on the other
side of the ship. It's a laundry and sewing room."

Why don't you tell her, I thought, that that bulkhead
just behind you hides the deadly main drives—the drives
that blow up when run by crazy people like yourself.

"And these next three doors," said Heller, opening
one, "are crew cabins." They were very small, just a
three hundred and sixty degree swivel gravity bed and a
locker and a hidden shower and toilet. "There are three
more just like this on the other side of the ship. *Lots* of
crew room."

I could see she was wondering how anyone could
ever get dressed in a space that small.

"Now, under our feet and over our heads are storerooms and lockers, entered by shifting these plates. It's

the same on the other side. *Tons* of storage space! Isn't she cute?"

The Countess Krak allowed it was. She was looking a trifle restless.

We had progressed aft and we were now up against a big, airtight door. "Now we have seen the officer and crew area," said Heller. "Close your eyes."

She did, obediently. I didn't. Heller gave a big manual wheel a spin and the passageway lock slid smoothly open.

For an instant I thought the current had surged, everything went so bright. What the Hells? I was looking at glitter so bright it hurt!

"Open your eyes," Heller said.

The Countess Krak did. And she said, "Oooooooooooo!"

It was just more passageway but it had changed! The lock wheels on doors, the handholds, the rails were gleaming white metal. The inset lights were flooding down upon a gorgeous inset pattern of blue and black.

"What is that metal?" I said, hardly daring to ask. "I was along here this morning and it was all blackish."

"Silver," said Heller. "That's all solid silver. When they put her in suspended activation, somebody neglected to paint her fittings with anti-tarnish. A few good coats of anti-tarnish tomorrow and they'll never go black again."

"Solid silver?" said the Countess Krak, staring down the passageway.

"Yes, indeed," said Heller. "They don't care about weight in a tug. In fact, they don't have enough of it. From this part of the ship back, every fitting is solid silver."

She knelt and felt the tile. "I can't believe it. Isn't this Astobol tile, the famous imperishable woven rock like in the Emperor's palace?" She petted the floor and side walls.

"Right," said Heller. "It won't burn or chip or conduct current and it won't reflect sound at all. No echoes from the drives. The whole rear half of the ship is totally sound insulated." And it was true. When the door swung shut behind us, the noises of the hangar outside vanished.

"That's how the admiral coped with the noise the main engines make. But I better tell you about this ship." And he gave her a swift resumé of Admiral Wince and his Flagship tug, totally omitting any mention of Will-be Was drives or the fate of *Tug One*'s sister ship.

"I didn't know she was even over in Emergency Fleet Reserve," said Heller. "I was hoping to find a flagship of a patrol flotilla, as they're pretty fancy sometimes. And here sat *Tug One!* What luck. Oh, but you haven't seen anything yet. Wince spent two million on her and she's only about ten years old and hardly ever spaceward. Come along."

He was not touching things now. At the next door, he simply said, "Open." And it opened. "Food makers," he said. "There's a uniform maker and reprocessor on the other side of the hull." He went to the next door. He said, "Open." And it opened. "Equipment storage. The one on the other side contains data banks."

We had come to another airtight door. It had been open when we had clambered about earlier and I had seen just a dark, dusty, black-metalled cavern. Heller said, "Close your eyes."

She did. I didn't. "Open," said Heller.

The wheels silently spun, the door swung back. I couldn't believe it. "Open your eyes," said Heller.

And if the Countess Krak had said "Oooooo!" before, she certainly shouted it now. For before us lay a large, spacious eating room. It had gyrotables and chairs and couch, swivel bookcases and what must be food warmers and servers. It was all done in fantastic taste. But that wasn't what was astonishing. The plates and canisters, the vases, even the corners of the table and chairs were gold. "Gold?" I said.

"Solid gold," said Heller. "Now you can see why I posted guards today. All her service plate was in her lockers and they could have been opened then."

Heller said a word, "Reflect!"

I hadn't seen the mirrors. They instantly lit up and crisscross reflected the whole room so that it seemed to go on forever. Then Heller said, "Lights!" And immediately color music in changing patterns began to flow in the mirrors.

"Oooooo!" said the Countess Krak.

"Oh, you haven't seen it all yet," said Heller. "This rear section is built around the traction beam generators and they don't take up near the space of the main drives. So the admiral built here what is called in architecture a 'circle of boxes.' You'll see in each one of these rooms what will appear to be a step which goes up or over to the next room. That covers the return cables to the generators. He used all this space. Wasn't that clever of him? Come on!"

We walked along the wall and stepped down into another spacious room. It was a very ornate gold and silver bedroom with a large gravity bed. It had wood nymph scenes on the walls. It had new sheets all turned back.

Heller and the Countess looked at each other knowingly. "But come on," said Heller. "The night has long to go."

We stepped up on a ledge and we were in a gymnasium! It wasn't very big and you'd crack your head if you jumped too high but it was certainly a gym.

"Exercise!" barked Heller.

Smoothly out from the bulkheads slid some bars and exercise machines. "Sunlight!" said Heller. A table unfolded that could be lain upon and sunlight glowed from the ceiling. "Massage," said Heller. And a massage machine slid out and approached the table, already vibrating. "Fight!" said Heller. The machine and table folded back.

I don't know what I expected to happen but it was not what happened. A cupboard popped open and what seemed to be a real live duellist leaped out. I felt the Countess instinctively go into combat posture. The thing looked vicious enough. Heller reached out and gave it a fast, expert chop and it dodged aside!

Then I saw what it was: a three-dimensional illusion. I could see other parts of the room through it. It was just a complex light pattern and now I could see little beams glowing in the ceiling. I had heard of these before. They were used for duelling practice.

Heller gave an expert kick. There was a small flash. The thing seemed to fall down on the floor and a voice from somewhere—it?—said, "Spare me, Oh master!"

"Enough!" barked Heller. The illusion vanished. "It duels with electric daggers, swords, bludgeons and just bare hands. I never saw one before that fell down. They usually just flash when you hit a vital spot. Now, you may wonder why that massage table wasn't on gimbals. Well, all this afterpart of the ship," he patted the bulkhead behind us, tapped the floor and pointed at the ceiling, "has automatic adjusting gravity-simulation coils. They usually take so much power that they don't install them but *Tug One* has power to spare."

And if you don't burn it—and more, I thought sourly, it also blows you up!

"So she's quite safe to exercise and move around in,"

said Heller to the Countess. "The enormous gravity surges you get with tugs get cancelled out. You don't ever have 'space float' back here. You don't bump your head."

"That's good," said the Countess.

I wondered what she'd do if she knew he were telling her a one-tenth truth. Then I realized she would use every bit of her influence with him to get him off this dangerous ship. I vowed fervidly she was not going to find out this was a deathtrap for her darling.

Heller whispered to us, "I don't dare say the next word aloud. That entrance closes and the place becomes a steam bath!" He led us up on the next level.

It was an ornate bathroom. He lifted a towel off the rack and simulated multicolored fish began to swim in three dimensions around all the walls and ceilings. It was like being at the bottom of the sea. It certainly would change a spacer's mind about where he was! Heller put the towel back and the fish vanished.

We went up a little stair. We were up in what must be the top of the stern.

And once again the Countess said, "Oooooo!" And well she might. For it was a huge room! It was exquisitely carpeted in dark flowing patterns. It was furnished in some glowing black wood. It had what must be a desk on black gimbals and a chair to match. But the place was not an office. It had black leather settees. Leather? Yes, real leather! And every wall was just a big black expanse that looked like shining glass.

"Sit down," said Heller. "*Now* you are going to see something!"

I wondered what in the Heavens there could be left to see? The Countess sat down in a chair, expectant, her riot helmet dangling from her hand.

Like a master of ceremonies, Heller raised his hand. "Autumn forest!" he said.

Instantly, on every wall around us, in brilliant three-dimensional color, totally real to the eye, there appeared a landscape in the brilliant hues of autumn. The trees were even moving. There was a gentle sigh of wind. Good Heavens, there was even the scent of fields. It looked so *real!*

"Oooooo!" said the Countess, delighted.

"Now watch," said Heller. "Winter!" And a totally different landscape appeared, majestic mountain peaks, snowy fields, stark trees. And the low moan of a winter wind. It made me feel so cold, suddenly, that I had to verify that the salon temperature had not changed.

"Spring!" said Heller. And the whole area seemed to become a blossoming of color: orchards, a young animal frisking in a field. The smell of fresh earth and buds.

"Summer!" said Heller. There was a burst of birdsong, the sweet fragrance of flowers, the sigh of a gentle zephyr. Leaved trees shaded the ground. A pair of lovers went hand in hand down a path.

"Oh, I like those," said the Countess.

"There are lots more seasons on lots more planets. I just chose Manco for tonight to please you."

"Oh, it does. It does!" But she looked like she was going to cry and Heller comforted her quickly, all contrite. "No, no," she said, dabbing at her eyes. "It's just that aside from today's trip, I haven't seen the sky or fields for three years!" She cried a little and then she dried her eyes. "I'm spoiling your show."

He made certain she was all right now. Then he said, "Space!"

I jumped slightly. I do not really care for space. I do not look out spaceports even when they're available. The vast, brutal violence of elemental force, the unimaginable distances, the cruel, lonely black of it, when you're in it, inspires worse than awe. To me, it is overpowering.

All around us was *space*. Studded with stars and nebulae, a near planet and moon of some system, it felt exactly like a real look at space while sitting on a suspended floor. Only the furniture made me keep my composure.

I said aloud, using the same voice volume Heller did, "Autumn!" I thought it would change back. It was only a voice-activated projector. Nothing happened. "Winter!" I said. Nothing happened. Space still gaped around us as though hungry for our lives. Cruel, pitiless space. I looked at Heller. "Why doesn't it change?"

"The whole rear section of this ship, cupboards, everything," said Heller, "is keyed only to my voice frequencies and harmonics. No two voices are alike, ever." He turned to the Countess. "There is a capacity to key it all to two or more tones. I'll put yours into the bank."

"What about me?" I said. "You'll have to show me how to set and change the voice keys. I'll be on this ship, too!"

He just looked at me. He never showed me or anyone else where or how to change the voice response keys on that ship. And I never was able to open or close or operate a single thing in the rear of that ship. I think he changed the process so that not even a technician from Fleet could do it. But at that moment I felt a surge of anger. When I got him off this planet . . . I felt sick at my stomach. It must be this cursed scene which suspended me in space, supported only by a rug.

"Now," said Heller to the Countess gently, "I have a little surprise for you. This was something that was popular about fifty years ago but the driver managed to find a strip of it." He removed a little rod from his pocket and reached down to the underedge of the settee he was sitting on and slid it in. At least I knew where the projector feed was!

Space vanished! What a relief!

In its place, all about us, appeared a theater as though we were just spectators along with a couple hundred others. The people seemed live.

Directly before us was the stage. It was a woods scene, totally artificial. There were trees like cardboard cutout trees and a path. There were footlights.

Music started up. An actor in an animal suit, a lepertige, came out of the wings. He had spats on and a hat and was carrying a cane. He pretended he was peeking into the woods. Then, in a little dance, still looking about him into the woods, he began to sing and as he sang the trees all began to wave in rhythm to the music.

Down on a path in the forest today,
I saw a sight that took my breath away,
The charms I beheld, that were on such display,
Made my poor empty paws just itch to stray.
Oh, Lepertige Lady,
Come out and play,
Come out and play,
Come out and play!
Oh, Lepertige Lady,
Come out and play!
We'll dance our whole lives away!
Oh, Lepertige Lady,
Do not depart,
Do not depart,
Do not depart.
Oh, Lepertige Lady,
Do not depart!
For you've stolen my heart today!

And then, amongst the trees, an enormous pair of phosphorescent eyes showed, blinked twice and a coquettish voice said, like an animal purr, "Why not?"

The stage curtains snapped shut. The audience roared with applause.

The Countess was laughing so hard she kept falling against Heller. It took her a while to catch her breath. Then she flung her arms around Heller's neck and said, "Oh, you darling!"

Then she held him off and in imitation of the last line, said, "Why not?" And they fell together and laughed again.

"There's tons of those," Heller finally said. "And a lot of games. But you haven't seen it all yet. I have a surprise for you."

Was there no end to these surprises? I thought the song had been silly. Maybe he was calling up the first time he had met her and she had put a real lepertige in its cage. Yes, that must be it. And a really suitable name for this absolutely deadly Countess Krak! A real lepertige lady indeed!

We were down a little stair and back on the same side of the ship where we had started. It was a small shower and it was pictured in a lake with ducks swimming about when Heller lifted a towel.

Heller guided the Countess over a ledge into the next level but, before he let her step down, he put a hand over her eyes.

"Now look," and he lifted his hand.

And the Countess really did say "Ooooooo!" It was a second dressing room, a gyrobed and wardrobes. And on the bed lay two absolutely gorgeous garments. One was a filmy night robe, done in intricate silver lace. The other was a golden ball gown!

The Countess clutched them to her and started to cry again. After a bit she kissed Heller. "I've never had any clothes like these in my whole life."

Heller petted her. After a bit, he said, "The admiral had a wife who used to cruise with him. It's all yours now, darling." He gave her another kiss.

He took me by the arm. "Well, we've been the full cycle now. Let's step down to the dining salon here and let the lady get out of her military fashion, shower and dress."

"I won't be long!" cried the Countess, looking adoringly after Heller.

"Take all the time you want," he called back. "Time is something we have lots of!"

We were in the salon with its gold dishes. Time, I thought sourly. Yes, you think you have time. You pulled a total swindle on me! You didn't have any idea of starting out! You were just looking for a fancy ship!

"I think," I said, somewhat stiffly, "that you have your nerve! You have been fooling me all day!"

Heller shrugged and gave me a mild smile. "Well, Soltan, you did say that Spiteos was too uncomfortable."

He started to offer me a gold canister filled with pink sparklewater. But I knew they didn't want me around. I said, "I'll see you tomorrow," and stalked out.

I knew I wouldn't be able to get Heller off this planet now with a whole bag of blasting charge. I was for it!

PART SIX

Chapter 1

It was a foolish thing to do, to walk out like that. But somehow I just couldn't stand to be that close to the Countess Krak. Inside the ship I had had pains in my stomach. Outside now, standing in the darkened hangar, the pains were gone. I felt hungry.

Things were quiet now: the excitement was over. The tup lorry must have come back for the decorations and empty canisters. There wasn't even the crumb of a sweetbun left on the makeshift bar.

Abruptly, the full extent of my foolishness came home to me. I was *broke*. Not only did I have not a single credit in my pockets but also my identoplate would be out-of-bounds: if I tried to use it for money or purchases of any kind, I would overdraw into next year's pay and even maybe get cashiered for debt.

Being an officer has its good points: one gets an identoplate, one gets paid; and in the ranks below, the finance officers routinely pay no pay at all. But being an officer also has its bad points: one has to pay for his own food and lodging and clothes, not only while on base duty but also on campaign.

If I could not lay my hands on a credit or two, I would not eat tonight! Or tomorrow either.

Over where the makeshift bar had been, I saw somebody sitting in a discarded gravity chair. In the dim light, I saw it was Snelz. Aha! A plan formed. I would scare some money out of Snelz!

When I came up, he remained slouching there, idly twirling his baton, humming quietly to himself, a song called "The Girls All Have Four (Boomps) in Old Kiboo," a favorite of the Fleet marines.

The calm mien of the man, well tupped and suppered, raised a vicious streak in me.

"Snelz," I said, in a very nasty voice, "do you realize that you have not only set loose a Spiteos prisoner but have also armed one with a blastrifle?"

"Oh, oh," he said mildly. "The lightning bolts of authority have been unleashed."

It was possible that he was being brave because he was twirling a baton that was really a blastick. Ignoring his slur, I plowed on. "It is quite obvious that you must have had money to bribe the tunnel barrier guards. Otherwise you never could have gotten Krak out and could never hope to get her back in."

"Money?" said Snelz, tossing the baton aside and lighting a puffstick. "It would be far too dangerous to try to bribe those fellows: Hisst would hear about it for sure." He looked at me through the smoke. He saw I didn't believe him. His face is not unhandsome in a sort of Devils-take-you mold: he didn't look afraid the way I'd made him look before. I didn't think it was the blastick. He had put it down. What was I looking at here? Some renewed pride? Was his association with Heller pulling him back out of the depths? He wasn't cringing!

In a patient tone of voice, he said, "Oh, I see. You don't understand how we are operating to get her in and out. Well, I suppose you should know, if it will ease your mind. There was this transvestite . . ."

"Snelz," I threatened. "You had better not be spinning me some long string of lies!"

He barked a small laugh. "Imagine that coming from you. Anyway, you know of course that Camp Endurance, aside from being a cover for Spiteos traffic, is there to dispose of Apparatus personnel who are designated as 'unsuitable'—though I might comment that it seems impossible to get lower than the low. How could anything be unsuitable for the Apparatus. I'm in it. You are too."

I put my hand on my beltgun. He just laughed and blew a cloud of smoke. "So, as you in your lofty position may or may not know, they send in drafts from other Apparatus units, on or off this planet, for 'special training' at Camp Endurance: the 'special training' teaches them only how to die fast and fall, as a dead body, into the chasm."

"Oh come off it, Snelz. I know that. That's why it's nicknamed 'Camp Kill.'"

"Well, I'm glad you do know something," said Snelz. "I was beginning to wonder." It crossed my mind that association with Heller absolutely ruined personnel! "So, anyway," he continued languidly, "when I realized that this operation might be coming up, I told my platoon to keep their eyes open. And sure enough, there in an incoming draft of kill-bait, they spotted just what we wanted."

He took another puff, blew it out and went on. "He was a fellow named Tweek. There he was standing in what they call an 'incoming garbage truck.' According to the records Timyjo managed to get a peek at, this Tweek had said 'no' when he should have said 'yes' to some horny senior and so, as you can't let *that* sort of thing happen and still have discipline—and warm bed companions—he was shipped to Camp Kill.

"What we were looking for was someone that was the height and build of the Countess Krak. And that was Tweek. He was blond, similar eye color and even a little pretty, though of course," and he let out an adoring sigh, "no real comparison to the Countess who is one of the most beautiful women I have ever seen. *Or* anybody else has seen."

"Get on with this," I snapped. A twinge of pain had hit my stomach at the mention of her qualities.

"So we just kept track of the truckload. When they stood them up on the chasm rim, one guy didn't get killed: Tweek!"

"That cost money to bribe the execution squad!" I snapped, remembering why I was talking to him at all.

"Well, no, it didn't," said Snelz. "They execute them in the evening so the action isn't spotted by chance overflights and it just happened that, courtesy of Timyjo, Tweek had a safety line on him. When the execution guards had gone, we simply pulled up Tweek, hand over hand. As instructed, he had fallen early before the stutterguns went off and aside from a minor bruise or two, he was fine.

"We fed him up—you'd be amazed how they starve those garbage cargos—and by the time we needed him, I had him able to walk. His hair had grown pretty long both from his own habits and his long trip from the planet Flisten and, for a transvestite, he looked good.

"So what we did this afternoon was march a detachment of four men through the tunnels and Tweek was one of them. When we got to the cubicle of Countess Krak, we stripped Tweek and then the Countess Krak dressed herself in his uniform. Tweek got into her bed and there he is, snoring peacefully right this minute."

"Aha!" I felt I had him there. "You had to give this Tweek freak *money* to get him to do that!"

"Money?" said Snelz. "I'm afraid we gave him something a lot more valuable than that. We gave him his life. And when we're through with this operation, we'll find a dead one in the recruitment drafts for Camp Endurance—they sometimes fight between the prisons where they get them and the outfit to which they're assigned—and give those papers to Tweek and simply put him in the platoon. We're short several men, including the one whose skull you cracked. He's getting well, by the way. I'll have to teach you to hit harder one of these days. Ah, well, where was I before you started carping about money?

"Oh, yes. At dawn," Snelz continued, "when we're relieved here, we'll fly her back, march her in through the tunnels. She and Tweek will change clothes and out will march Tweek. And we'll just keep on doing that, day after day, from here onward. The Countess Krak will be visible all day long, right in her own training room, and at night nobody ever dares go near the cubicle of the Countess Krak. She has a reputation, you know."

"Fine, fine," I said. "But how did she get so well trained so fast to do a Fleet marine manual of arms! *And* march drill!"

"Oh, didn't you see me down there training her one afternoon? Oh, I remember—we stayed back of a couple of the big shock machines and you weren't much around. She learns awful fast—must come from being such a good trainer herself. But it was mostly me: I'm a pretty good drillmaster. Don't you think I did a fine job? It sure had you fooled today!"

That made me savage. "(Bleep) you, you'd still need money to bribe your way in and out through the tunnel. Troops can't go in there without authorization!"

"Oh, we have a reason. We're taking out some training equipment for evening use and returning it each morning because the training department says it needs it in the day."

"Even that would require money to buy a pass! You can't move in and out of Spiteos without a stamped pass!"

"Oh, don't you remember? You put your identoplate on a permanent pass for my platoon." He looked at me with a bit of mischief in his eye. "And in case that expires, you put your identoplate on a permanent equipment demand."

"I did no such thing!"

"Oh, yes, you did. This morning. Just before you woke up!"

I was stunned. The guard that had awakened me! The dirty thief had picked my pocket of my identoplate and put it back in before he woke me up!

It made me furious. "Don't tell me Heller isn't paying you handsomely to do this, Snelz!"

He looked at me wonderingly. "Well, I suppose he will one of these days. Gris, what is all this (bleep) about money-money-money? Do you think I'd take all this risk for just money? You've got a peculiar idea of life, Gris. One doesn't do everything just for money. Sometimes, like today, one does it just for fun. Try it."

I turned on my heel and left him. I was desperate. I didn't need his advice. I was hungry and I was broke!

Chapter 2

My driver was sleeping peacefully in the airbus. I looked at him. He had been eating and drinking the whole (bleeping) day!

Abruptly, I had an idea. Heller had been shovelling money at him to buy things. This driver had once been a commercial shuttle pilot: he had murdered a flight attendant and had fled to another planet where he joined a smuggling ring; he had stolen stolen goods from them once too often and had been convicted; the Apparatus had taken him from prison, given him false identity papers, thinking to use him as part of their Theft Section. He hadn't been good enough and they had given him to me as a driver. With his criminal background, he would have stolen Heller blind!

I opened the door and hit him. It was not dangerous to do. He is a small fellow. Without giving him time to collect his wits, in a savage voice, I said, "Give me my share of the money you tore off from Heller today!"

He sat up. He had had too much tup. Without even thinking, he said, "Oh, certainly I will, Officer Gris."

I was saved! "All right," I snapped. "Hand it over!"

"Well, Gods, I'm sorry, Officer Gris. There ain't any left." He was trying to wake up. I helped him with a rough shake.

"Gods, Officer Gris. Don't do that. I got a headache. . . . The money? . . . the money? Oh, the money!"

"Don't stall! Give it to me straight! Now!"

He was fumbling in his tunic. He had some pieces of paper. "Oh, yeah. I remember now. I got all the receipts. Gods, Officer Gris, you got no idea how much things cost! Do you know he spent three hundred and two credits through me today? The Fleet gave him the cleaning supplies for nothing—he has a pal in supply there and all it took was a note." He was fumbling with the receipts. "The tup truck cost a hundred and seventy-five credits. Oh, yes! It was the dresses!

"Officer Gris, I ain't ever going to get married. You

won't believe it, but them dresses cost one hundred credits! Oh, that was embarrassing. I'd spent twenty-five credits for some other things. . . ."

I shook him again, "Come to the point and stop stalling!"

"I'm trying to tell you," he wailed. "Where was I? You got me all mixed up and I lost a paper to boot. Ah, there it is. It was such a fancy store and they looked on me like dirt. I had the dresses all picked out and I only had ninety-eight credits of his money left and I knew he was really counting on me. I myself had two credits of my own so I put that with the ninety-eight and I got out of there with the dresses. I got it now. He owes me two credits."

He thought for a moment. "I'll give him his receipts tomorrow and he'll sure pay me back my two credits. But that ain't important." A note of admiration crept into his voice. "Ain't he a really great guy, Officer Gris!"

Such insolence! I hit him and I hit him hard.

The blood started trickling down the side of his mouth. He gathered up the receipts quietly. Without a word, he got into the driver's seat. That's how you have to treat this riffraff. It's all they understand. Lombar was right. They should be exterminated for the good of the Confederation.

I got in back. "Take me to my town hotel," I ordered. At least I had a place to sleep.

We flew through the early evening traffic toward the north end of Government City. The area has long been a sort of slum. That's why the Apparatus has its offices there. The offices themselves are on a cliff where the River Wiel takes a bend. But well inward from the cliff and down the hill, there is a sort of stew where Apparatus clerks gloom away their off-time and just a little further up is where some Apparatus officers live. The area stinks, not just from the dirty river but also from the dilapidated buildings themselves.

My "hotel" was not strictly speaking a hotel. It had been some notable's residence long ago and clapboard shacks had been added on and these were lorded over by a female who called herself Meeley. I had a small room there.

The airbus stopped at the side entrance, setting down in what had once been a small yard but was now a garbage dump. The driver usually sleeps there in the airbus so I left him and went up the crooked stairs to my room.

It was locked. Not just locked but barred.

I stamped over to a stairwell and yelled down for Meeley. I was gratified to hear a rush of feet. She was practically beating the stairs apart she was coming up so fast. For a moment I was gratified to get such quick response.

The light was dim and I did not anticipate anything. I could not see the expression on her ancient and cut-up face—she has several knife scars.

"Where's my money?" she demanded.

"Why, Meeley! You know I always pay you!"

"Always means never!" she shrieked. She has never liked me. "You been gone for days and days without no word. I thought we'd had the good luck you'd been killed like you deserve! You Apparatus scum is all alike. (Bleep) you!"

She hit me!

"Open my room door!" I said, prudently stepping back.

She found a keyplate and dropped the bar. She flung the door open. She flashed on the lights!

Without another word, working like fury, she began grabbing up my things. She blasted past me and rushed to the balcony above the side yard. She pitched the whole armload down toward the airbus.

"Driver!" I yelled.

Meeley came rushing out of the room again with another armload. She hurled it into the night!

She returned and came out with an old pair of boots and my one bedcover and pitched those after the rest!

"Now get out!" she screamed. "I'm going to tell every lodging keeper in this whole area that you haven't paid a particle of rent for a year! GET OUT!"

I thought I ought to look in the room to see if she had gotten everything. But I changed my mind. There are times to fight and times to run. She had always had a dislike for me for some reason.

My driver and I picked my things out of the garbage in the side yard, cleaned them off as best we could and bundled them into the airbus.

"Where to?" said the driver.

I couldn't think of anyplace.

"How about your office?" said the driver.

"Old Bawtch doesn't like that," I said.

"It's the only place you got," said the driver. "If you want my opinion, a desk is better than a gutter anytime. There really ain't room for two to sleep comfortable in this airbus. I'll take you to your office."

There were cabins on that tug. But the very thought of it brought heavy pains into my stomach.

(Bleep) this mission. And (bleep) Heller! I ought to kill him!

And then I really got sick. A little later, the driver even had to help me to get up and stretch out on the hard desk.

It had been an *awful* day!

Chapter 3

I woke up as I hit the floor in a shattering crash. It was daylight. Somebody had pulled me off the desk.

"You know you're not supposed to sleep in here," said old Bawtch, peevishly.

"Whose office is it, if it isn't mine?" I muttered from the floor under his big feet.

"Now get away from the side of the desk," he said. "I've got to stand there to put these papers down." And it was true. He was standing there with about a yard-high stack of documents and forms. I understood the situation then. He had needed the top of the desk to put this massive stack of papers on it.

I scrambled sideways out of the road and got to my feet. "That's an awful lot of papers," I said.

He had gotten the load down and was stacking it by categories. "You might drop by once in a while to validate forms. I can do all the rest of your work. But *not* push your identoplate. You do remember how to push it onto a piece of paper, don't you?" I detected a sneer.

Bawtch, for some reason, has never liked me. He stands—I had better say stoops—about six feet tall. He has two wild tufts of gray wool that stand out on either side above his ears; his nose is so sharp you could cut paper with it; he wears black blinders to keep light from side-striking his protruding black eyes. He doesn't talk, really: he bites. I think about eighty years ago he had ambitions to be an officer. The highest he ever made was chief clerk of Section 451. I worked it all out once. He is just jealous.

He was standing there threateningly to ensure I sat down and started stamping. "You might at least bring me some of the clerk's hot jolt," I said.

"The office funds are totally depleted. We heard a rumor you had been transferred elsewhere and we had a party. Then we heard you had been left on post and we had a wake. There is no jolt, hot or otherwise."

I sat down, got out my identoplate and started to stamp. I was hungry and wondered if paper were edible. If it were, there was sure a feast here. The Apparatus rides, walks and sleeps on forms, forms, forms, nearly all of them lies.

Manifests for supplies that were personally stolen, certifications of payrolls that were never paid, sums scheduled for informers that went into the pockets of agents instead, personnel lists which falsely attested twice the number, "customer expenses" from the base chief in Turkey that were really fees of local prostitutes for himself: tons of made-out forms, the usual fare of the Apparatus.

I reduced the pile about half in half an hour. I was just about to bang my identoplate down on the next one when my attention was drawn to it simply by all the numerous currency symbols on it. I was broke. Here were all these people getting fat but not me. I stared at it: *Renovations, C764.9* it said at the bottom of the figure column.

"This is local," I said. "Renovations? For this place?"

Bawtch muttered to himself something about my having the memory of an insect. Aloud, he said, "That's the repairs on the roof last year. *This* roof. The rain was coming down on our papers. The work was done. You even complained about the noise. The bill has been presented several times. You always find something else to do before you get that far down in the pile. The contractor has been on the phone twice a day for his money. Stamp it."

"What's this *'Unused Allocation'* down here at the bottom?" I said. *"C231."*

"I was nice enough to think, when I made the official request for funds, that you might like to get your office redone. You never said what you wanted done so it's unused."

I looked around. There was a little paint peeling off the walls and a water stain over only half the ceiling. "I never could see anything wrong with it."

A cunning thought had hit me, as yet only a proton moving out of the nucleus of an idea. Contractors kicked back when it was demanded. "Get me the original authorization," I ordered sternly. "Oh, I'll keep stamping the rest," I added hurriedly and only then did he move off.

I had finished the rest of the pile by the time he came back. He was wiping hot jolt off his mouth. But I had other things in mind. He had the additional, unused two-hundred-and-thirty-one credit slip. I took it. "I'll handle this now."

He carted away the tall stack of forms and I sat there looking at the two sheets. Now, first, let's see if I could get a kickback from the contractor who had done the work. He was pretty anxious to get paid, it being so overdue.

I got him on the communicator box. "You want this roof job paid fast?" I said and gave him the number.

"Who is this?"

"Officer Gris."

He hung up. Well, that was a dead end. Bawtch had obviously been saying things behind my back.

I sat and thought. Redecorating this place was a

waste of time. Who cared about pretty walls? Something more in keeping with my profession.

I had to go to the toilet. Now, one of the privileges of being head of the section was a private toilet opening off the office. While I was in there, I looked around. It was pretty messed up with paper scraps and all. When I finished, I chanced to look out the window. And it was then that the proton moved all the way out and went bang!

The toilet window of my office is right above a five-hundred-foot straight drop down the cliff into the River Wiel. Standing on tiptoe I could even see the river edge.

I went right back and put a call through to a building contractor we had never used. And to prove we had never used him, he was over there inside of fifteen minutes.

"I am an influential executive," I told him.

He looked around. "Oh, I can see that," he said.

"I have an unused allocation for two hundred and thirty-one credits."

"So little," he said. But I knew he was just trying to act like a big contractor. They are hungry these guys. I was, too.

"Come with me," I said. I took him into the toilet. "Now you see this wall?" And I tapped it. "I want it to be brought forward a bit and a secret undetectable door put in it. Then behind it, I want a ladder and a hatchway to the roof."

He inspected it and shrugged. It looked easy enough to do.

"Now you see this window?" I tapped it. "I want the glass changed to a type called silent-break."

"Well, I can do all that. But why?"

"People are sometimes after me," I said.

"Ah, you're part of the Apparatus. I understand."

FREE

Send in this card and receive a FREE GIFT.

Send in this card and you'll receive a free MISSION EARTH POSTER while supplies last. No order required for this Special Offer! Mail your card today!

☐ Please send me a FREE Mission Earth Poster
☐ Please send me information about other books by L. Ron Hubbard.

ORDERS SHIPPED WITHIN 24 HRS OF RECEIPT!

PLEASE SEND ME THE FOLLOWING:

___ The Invaders Plan Sound Editions	$14.95	_____
___ MISSION EARTH hardback volumes		
(specify #s:_____)	$18.95	_____
___ MISSION EARTH set (10 vols)	$142.12	_____
___ Battlefield Earth paperback	$4.95	_____
___ Writers of The Future Volume I	$3.95	_____
___ Writers of The Future Volume II	$3.95	_____
___ Writers of The Future Volume III	$4.50	_____
___ Writers of The Future Volume IV	$4.95	_____
___ Buckskin Brigades	$3.95	_____

SUB-TOTAL: _____

CHECK AS APPLICABLE:
❑ Check/Money Order enclosed
 (Use an envelope please).
❑ American Express ❑ VISA ❑ MasterCard

SHIPPING*: _____

TAX**: _____

TOTAL: _____

Card #: _____

Exp. Date: _____ Signature: _____

NAME: _____

ADDRESS: _____

CITY: _____ STATE:____ ZIP: _____

Call Toll-Free 1-800-722-1733 (1-800-843-7389 in CA)

BUSINESS REPLY MAIL
FIRST CLASS   PERMIT NO. 62688   LOS ANGELES, CA

POSTAGE WILL BE PAID BY ADDRESSEE

BRIDGE PUBLICATIONS, INC.
4751 Fountain Avenue
Los Angeles, CA 90029

But he hesitated. "I still don't get what you mean to do."

"There's no back door to my office," I said. "If I were chased in here, there would be no way out. But if this job I'm asking for gets done, I can rush into the toilet, smash the window, duck through the secret door, climb the ladder and get out on the roof."

He still looked a bit puzzled.

"If the glass is silent-break type, it gives me time to get into the secret door and out."

He got up on the toilet bowl and looked down. "That's a drop of five hundred feet and into a wild river!"

"Exactly," I said. "They'll think I made an impossible attempt. No bodies are ever recovered from that river as we in the Apparatus very well know. They won't even look for me! But I'll be on the roof. Now don't bother your head about spy tradecraft. That's my department. Can you build it?"

He said he could although the allocation would be a little tight.

"Good," I said, "then hand me over twenty credits and you've got the job."

Well, that began quite an argument. They love to haggle. But I am not too bad at that. We finally settled for ten credits kickback.

I held out my hand. He said, "Oh, kickbacks can't be paid until the finance office pays the bill. There's rumors about you people." He smiled, still friendly. "I'll get on the job right away and in six months you'll have your ten credits."

I couldn't cancel the order. It would have been too obviously just a chance to gouge some money.

He left.

Somewhat bitterly, I sat back down at my desk and out of spite wouldn't stamp the original bill from the other contractor. That would show them! An officer has to have *some* pride. Even in the Apparatus.

Chapter 4

Several times I half made up my mind to go down to the hangar to see what was going on with Heller. Each time I got a pain in my stomach.

But pain or no pain, I was hungry and one of those times I made it out to my airbus.

I was amazed to see the driver had everything out and was cleaning the vehicle up. Unheard of. He had never done it before. He had also spread my gear around on the parking plot to air and get the garbage smell out. Until he saw me, he was whistling away.

"You going down to see Heller?" he said.

The pain hit me. After a moment I shook my head. It occurred to me that I could send him down. But Heller had already undoubtedly overpaid him and he had just been lying about the two credits. There was no relief to be found there. I was in no shape for a fight.

I forbade him to go near the hangar. Heller had sent him on an errand to Fleet for cleaning supplies. Who knows what other messages Heller would send to Fleet? I had a feeling I really ought to die and get it over with for it was only a matter of time before the sky fell in on me. They'd catch Krak. Or Lombar would realize we weren't gone. Or the Crown inspectors would show up. There wasn't a thing I could do about any of it. To Hells with the ladder to the roof. I ought to just dive out the toilet window and get it over with.

I went back inside. There are quite a few rooms to Section 451, what with all the files. I never found out how many personnel it really had due to the padded list and Bawtch's and other high-up rake-offs. But in this main room there were forty-one clerks shuffling papers. I knew some of them and knew about others. But I didn't speak to them and they never speak to me. I wandered back into my own office.

My stomach hurt. I gloomed.

Maybe it was because I was hungry and thirsty. I had had only one sip of hot jolt the dawn before, and now that I thought of it, I had not eaten or drunk anything the day before that. Forty-eight hours, really. My stomach hurt too much. I began to have an odd sort of hallucination. I actually commenced to believe I was sitting in the caves of the offices in Turkey on Blito-P3. I had my own desk. Some of the personnel were there, smiling, friendly. I was stamping manifests of freighter cargo and every time my identoplate went down on one, the clerks would all applaud and say how great that was. Everything was going well. I was far, far away from Voltar. A beautiful Turkish girl, a dancer, came in through the door and began to dance slowly and suggestively toward me, her lips and eyes inviting. She also had her hands full, money in one and FOOD, delicious Turkish *baklava*, in the other.

I opened my mouth to speak to her in Turkish. And then, with a shock, I came to my senses. I had actually *seen* the girl! I had heard the coins clink! I had smelled the food!

I knew I was going crazy.

How I knew this was very simple. But I had better explain it. While I didn't do well in the Royal Academy, when I went to the Apparatus schools I was a whiz, especially in languages.

Of course, they have very good teachers there. They have to. They must teach about four hundred languages just to cover the 110 planets of the Voltar Confederacy. Although Voltarian, imported from the home galaxy, is standard in the schools everywhere, the work of the Apparatus takes one too often into the back country where Standard Voltarian is unknown. And then there are at least ten thousand languages of enemy planets or planets marked for invasion.

They have a cunning system of gradual approach. It graduates upwards from child's blocks to primers and then higher. In the case of Blito-P3, the route for English is blocks, "kindergarten primers," comic books, technical books.

The comic book I chose was one called *Bugs Bunny*. Actually, I recall with a smile the first error I made. I thought the actor named Bugs Bunny was the true shape and behavior of the people of Earth where I had not yet been. How my professor laughed! He pointed out that the true shape and behavior of Earth people was to be found in the same comic book. He was called "Elmer Fudd."

But Bugs Bunny, I must say, has a way with him. Bugs is cunning. And he certainly can handle people. So it was obvious to me that they knew how to handle people on Earth. And when some of the scientists around the school told me there was not much difference between Earth's comic books and their technical books, I took the hint. One can choose his own technical subjects for reading so I chose a subject they call, down there, "psychology."

It is a government monopoly but it is taught in their universities. They claim everybody is evil. They say sentient beings are animals and have no soul. And while this last is unique to Earth and is not believed on any other planet anywhere, I so often fervently hope that I will never live another life anywhere that I was eager to accept it. And naturally, like Lombar, I believed everybody was evil.

So here I had a real gold mine. I read and read those textbooks. Like Bugs Bunny does, the psychologist teaches you how to get around *everybody*.

It is really due to this extensive study that I owe my remarkable ability to handle people.

I was diffident about writing this down in this work for two reasons: people will think I am a nut; and it is really the trade secret on which I operate in the Apparatus on Voltar. Even primitives have secret wisdoms.

So when I saw that Turkish girl, I knew exactly what had happened: I was experiencing "psychogenic hallucination based on fulfillment-denial."

From this, I naturally understood that I wanted to get the Hells out of here. It came as a flash.

However, although I now had the proper label and understood it completely, I still sat there thinking from time to time I was at the Turkish base on Earth and even reached out a time or two to take some of the cakes the girl had put on the desk.

This got me to wondering how I would cope with all the paper stamping I would have to do when I was on Earth. And this led me to wonder how the bales of forms would get to Earth and back. I couldn't imagine them coming as heavily abused freight. Bawtch would have a fit if the corners were wrinkled.

Then, as the day crept on and I got hungrier and thirstier and any hopes of eating seemed postponed at least a year until I could draw pay again—unless I lost my paychecks, which would make it five years and maybe never—I got more and more worried.

On Blito-P3, I would be cut off absolutely. I would

not be able to snoop around. I would have no master console to steal time at. My fantasy of being on Earth in
peaceful plenty began to have a dark core of not knowing
what the Hells was going on on Voltar.

I considered what Bugs Bunny would have done in
a similar circumstance. He would have approved of the
caper of the toilet escape route I had just ordered. But,
although my memory is superb, I could not remember a
single strip that solved this uninformed situation except
one where he takes a telescope on a platform he has gotten onto and, by means of many curves and levers, looks
in on somebody who was chasing him in a police car. I
obviously had no telescope that long.

Surmounting my hunger, I made a supreme effort
and, being well endowed with wits, suddenly solved it.

Endow was the crossroads of information between
the Apparatus and the Grand Council. Lombar had to
take up everything with Endow. Endow had a weakness:
pretty boys!

I got out my blackmail folders, local office.

I pushed buzzers. I got one to work and very shortly
I had two of the Section 451 clerks in there looking slightly amused and tolerant.

These two boys were nicknamed "Too-Too" and
"Oh Dear." Their real names are Twolah and Odur.
They were from Endow's home planet, Mistin. They
were promising children, doted upon by their separate
mothers, spoiled rotten and totally dominated. They had
entered the University of Mistin with high marks and
had proceeded upon brilliant scholastic careers. They
were excellent students. They fell in love, one with an
elderly male professor of cellology, the other with the
dean of males. They were caught. They were expelled.
They were ruined. They were eminently fitted for my

purpose: they were very pretty. I would shortly wipe the amusement from their girlish faces.

"You, Twolah, and you, Odur, have just been promoted."

They liked that but were wary.

"By the powers vested in me as Section Chief, you two are appointed alternate couriers to Blito-P3. At intervals comparable to the time it takes to make a round trip to Blito-P3, you will relieve each other. One of you will bring me all the paper I have to sign and return. Then the other will do so."

They looked uneasy. I have something of a reputation in the office. They knew this was not all. Three months of travel, followed by three months layoff, even though space travel in a freighter is not that comfortable, was a bit of a plum.

"On your off-time at home," I said, "you will take messages to Endow personally. Any kind of a message from here you can dream up. And you will hang around for answers. And you will pretty yourselves up and display yourselves so that each one of you, by turns, becomes his beloved. And you will pump him for all current news about Blito-P3 and bring it to me."

Too-Too minced coyly, "And what if Lord Endow refuses to slip into the trap?"

"I don't think he will refuse. Because you are each of you going to make sure that he doesn't. Have you ever heard of a magic mailing?"

It is tradecraft. They were trained as spies but not in the higher levels of the art. "I will explain," I said.

"I am sure you will," lisped Oh Dear.

"A magic mailing is a message or order which is held in place in a postal chute. It sticks there in the chute for a determined time, in this case three months. A separate card with a frequency stamped on it has to be mailed past it before the stick expires. If it is, the magic mail stays unmailed another three months. But if at any time the renewing card isn't mailed, the magic mail drops into the post and gets delivered."

They were getting white. Pretty. But white.

"Each time you deliver a batch of forms to me on Blito-P3, you will also deliver *all* the news there is on the subject from the Apparatus, the Grand Council, Endow and Lombar Hisst. IF I consider you are not making it up, that you are really diligent in doing your espionage job in your off-period here, I will give you a receipt with a frequency and you can mail it. It will hold up the magic mail."

They were whiter and not prettier.

"Who is the magic mail to be addressed to?" said Too-Too.

"Whom does it concern?" faltered Oh Dear.

"The magic mail will be addressed to the Commander of the Knife Section on Mistin. You understand that it won't ever be delivered if you thoroughly do your jobs."

They got that, so I plowed on. Psychology is a wonderful thing. "You both love your mothers, don't you?"

I knew this because there are exact states and phases in all boys and males. It says so right in the Earth textbooks. First they are oral passive, then they are oral erotic, then they are anal passive after which they become anal erotic. This is followed by what is called "latency" and finally, genitalia is arrived at. So these two boys were fixated in the development stage of anal erotic. Mothers change diapers. So, of course, it follows as day and night that they loved their mothers.

"You wouldn't order our mothers *murdered?*" said Too-Too, incredulous.

I flipped the Knife Section knife from its sheaf behind my neck and threw it into the floor between their feet where it stuck, quivering. This, I knew by the texts, added the phallic symbol. They fell into each other's arms and wept.

I called Bawtch and had him shoo them out. They were both crying so hard that even Bawtch was impressed. He stood for a full minute in the door just looking at me. I can tell when people are impressed.

Later, I was much braced up. Psychology is a wonderful thing. No wonder the governments on Earth will use nothing else!

Well, one thing had gone right today.

I reached for some of the food the dancing girl had left on the desk but it wasn't there again.

Chapter 5

At midnight, lying on my desk in the darkened office, I was rudely awakened by the noisy entrance of a visitor. It was a Manco Devil. I knew right away he was from Manco because, over there, their Devils are not the ordinary woods Devils so common to other planets. Manco Devils have horns and long tails which end in a spike and they are a dark, flaming red.

I wondered for a moment why it was that Bawtch had let him in without formal announcement, but a glance at my watch showed that it was midnight and, of course, Bawtch was not there.

I told him not to make so much noise: he would bring the "bluebottles"—the Domestic Police—or, much worse, a Crown inspector down upon us. But he did not pay much attention, so I composed myself as courteously as possible to give him the attention due to a caller.

He had a form in one hand and a pen in the other and he seated himself in the interview chair and with those little shrugs and hitches one makes to get comfortable, began his interrogation.

"Name?" he asked. And when I told him, he, of course, wrote it down on the top of his form.

I was, however, curious. "What form is that?"

"Form 345-678-M," he said.

I told him I was not familiar with that form. He crossed his legs and leaned back. His voice was tolerant. "It's the form one makes out to see if you know."

"About what?" I asked, for I myself am very skilled in interviewing.

"That is the thing we are to establish," said the Manco Devil. He seemed a bit annoyed at my denseness.

I took umbrage at this. "Then how can I answer unless I know about what it is that I don't know?"

This did not phase him in the slightest. He twitched his long, spiked tail and somehow this was a signal for the toilet door to open and in came the whole crew of Patrol Craft B-44-A-539-G, the one that had taken Heller to Blito-P3 on the original mission. I was a trifle amazed for I had supposed they were safely down in the bowels of Spiteos. But then I realized Snelz had gotten them a pass so it was all right. There were twenty of them, but of course they had come in through the secret doortrap I would have cut tomorrow so that ceased to bother me.

They stood around my office in a ring and then, at a signal from their craftleader, they sat down very smartly at attention.

The Manco Devil said to them, "He claims he doesn't know what he is not supposed to know."

The craftleader looked at me critically and then back at the Devil. "Very good. Then we shan't tell him."

The crew got up then and ate the baklava the dancing girl had left on the desk, took out electric whips and began to beat me.

I cowered back, stung, and looked for succor to the Devil. But the Devil had changed to Lombar Hisst!

So I had no alternative. I tried to draw my stungun. Then I was horrified. I couldn't get it out of the holster!

The electric whips were sizzling. I looked frantically toward Lombar but it was now Crobe! I wished the occupant of the interview chair wouldn't keep changing. How could I be expected to answer questions if the interrogator kept shifting?

The crew had now finished the baklava. So they turned to the chair for orders. Old Atty was sitting there now.

"He doesn't know that he doesn't know," said old Atty.

The craftleader drew himself up and gave old Atty a Fleet salute, which I thought was very nice of him and showed respect for Atty's age. "Sir," said the craftleader, "we absolutely will not tell him unless we are very generously bribed."

That satisfied old Atty but he was now the Devil again. The Devil said, "Now, in the matter of your employment as handler for the King of the underworld on his secret mission, we come to the matter of pay."

The patrol craft crew had vanished.

I said, "I will need more pay than that as I am deeply in debt, have drawn all my pay for the next five years, in fact. After they relieved me from this mission I was penniless and couldn't borrow a cent from my driver. When I received the notice that I had been cashiered, Meeley turned me over to the bluebottles."

The Devil said, "Actually, that's why I am here. To collect the bill for this interview."

I tried to tell him his addition was faulty, that he had added a lorry load of tup onto it, but he would have nothing of that. He leaped to his feet and his pen turned into a torch.

The wall was directly behind me. I could back up no further! He rammed the flaming torch straight into my stomach and it was agony!

I started to run but the faster I ran the more I was in one place. The Manco Devil got around in front of me and jammed the flaming torch into my stomach again.

With a tremendous effort I tried to draw my gun and shoot him but I could not get it out of the holster.

I leaped up on the desk. But *Tug One* came screaming through the room, pulled me off the desk and exploded in midspace with the loss of all hands.

"That's your fault," said Commander Crup. "I wash my hands of the whole affair."

Then the Devil was there again. He had two lepertiges, one on each side of him. He was barely able to hold them back. He yelled at me, "If you find out, I will turn these animals loose and they will rip your guts out!"

This intimidated me. I screamed at him, "I'll pay your bill!"

I rushed over to a filing cabinet and I got out huge handfuls of counterfeit credit notes and began to throw them at him.

Abruptly the room was empty!

With a groan, I lay back down on the desk. After I had recovered a bit, I looked down and was interested that the flame had not scorched the secret papers I was carrying for the Emperor.

Thankfully, I dropped into a troubled sleep.

Chapter 6

I hit the floor with a crash. It was midmorning.

From a long way off, Bawtch was saying, "You only stamped half of them yesterday. I was taking it easy on you. But there's months of accumulated work undone."

I got my eyes open. Bawtch was standing there with a yard-high stack, trying to step over me and get them on the desk.

I struggled to get up. Then I must have fainted. For when I came around again, there were two more clerks in the office. Bawtch was saying to them, "But if he dies on us, we won't ever get these forms stamped."

Probably I fainted again. When I came around, I had been dragged over against the wall and there were four clerks in the office.

"I think he's sick," said one of the clerks. "His forehead is hot."

"Be just like him to get one of these new fevers and infect the lot of us," said Bawtch.

"I think we ought to call in a doctor," said another clerk.

"Yeah, you can't have him just dying in here," said another clerk. "It would stink the place up and it's bad enough already."

After what may have been hours later, I came around again. I was being laid out flat on my back. There was a doctor there—I recognized him; he was what they call a "medical doctor" because they push out medicine; this was one the prostitutes of the district used; he gave them pills which caused abortions when they got pregnant. He was unpacking a bag on my desk.

He bent over me and pushed a strap down on my forehead and I tried to worm away, thinking he was about to give me a shock. He might not heed the penalty for shocking an officer. These medical doctors are pretty criminal.

The strap turned out to be a temperature gauge. "He's got a fever," this medical doctor said.

"Probably infect all of us," said Bawtch.

The doctor said, "Open your mouth!" and he forced it open. "Aha! Swollen tongue!" He stood up, evidently talking to Bawtch. "It's an obvious case of *diploduckus infernam*," he said learnedly. "The new disease that came in from Flisten," he added learnedly. "He will break out in black spots in a couple days and then they will suppurate."

"Is it infectious?" said a clerk.

"Very," said the doctor.

The clerks hastily got out of there.

"How am I going to get these papers stamped?" said Bawtch.

That was out of his field so the doctor said, "I am going to make out a list of pills, powders and wonder drugs. They don't work but he will feel more comfortable."

"We can't buy those," said Bawtch. "He doesn't have any money on him. I looked."

"What?" roared the doctor. "You mean you got me all the way over here . . ." Oh, he was angry!

He tore up his list, threw his things back in his bag and stamped out. He slammed the outer door.

"Now you see what you've gotten me into," said Bawtch. He left. And *he* slammed the door.

I lay there waiting for the black spots to break out and then suppurate.

I was probably unconscious for a long time and when I woke again it was quite late in the day. The patrol craft crew had left the toilet door open and the afternoon sun was slanting in.

My driver was kneeling there. He had been shaking my shoulder. He turned into a Crown inspector and then back into my driver.

"I know you told me I mustn't go there. But this noon when I finally heard you were sick, I thought I'd better go down to the Apparatus hangar and tell them."

I must have passed out again. He shook me awake. "When I told Heller he said he was very sorry to hear it and to tell you he hoped you got better real soon and he asked if there was anything he could do to help."

Probably I passed out again. He was shaking me. He turned into the Turkish dancing girl. She put her arm under my shoulders and was lifting me up a bit.

"Heller sent this up," she said. "A whole case of canisters and ten pounds of sweetbuns. Here, put your mouth around this space canister tube. It's green sparklewater. Now draw in. That's the way."

It tasted just like *boza,* a drink they make in Turkey from fermented wheat. It proved she was, in fact, real and that she *was* a Turkish dancing girl. I was afraid it was all an illusion.

I must have passed out for it seemed to be some time later. My driver had an arm under my shoulders and was making me take some more sips.

He must have spent an hour or two at this for the sun was way down when he said, "Now that's the end of that canister." And laid me back.

My tongue wasn't so swollen. "What happened to

the dancing girl?" I whispered. "Did she leave when I couldn't pay her?"

The room was quite dark the next time I awoke. My head felt much clearer. My tongue wasn't swollen at all. My driver was holding me up again. "This is one of the sweetbuns Heller sent. We have lots and lots of them. Take a small bite and chew and don't choke on the crumbs."

I got some of it down. My head seemed clearer shortly. But I now had a pain in my stomach.

"I can't pay the doctor for the pills," I told my driver frankly.

"Doctor?" said my driver, quite surprised. "Oh, you mean that medical doctor. We were thinking back and you know, we don't think you had anything to eat or drink for three days. Two days without water can make anybody crazy. Run a fever, too. Heller said so. He told me what to do. Snelz told him it would upset you if he left the hangar, it being a secret mission and all. So he couldn't come himself and that's why he had to tell me what to do."

My driver was fumbling in his tunic. He got something out. "Look, he paid me the two credits I spent and he gave me twenty credits for all the work I did running about and all. So here's yours."

He was holding a five-credit note in front of my nose.

I decided instantly not to kill Heller today.

The pain in my stomach vanished!

Chapter 7

For two days Bawtch waited for me to break out in black spots which would then suppurate. He must have had a hole in the door he could look through, for he was his old, very assured, nasty self when he came in.

I had had no more hallucinations, only a few nightmares. I had slept most of the time. And I sure had soaked up sparklewater and gorged sweetbuns.

Bawtch put the tall stack on the desk. "I am certainly glad we can get this work stamped," he said. "The whole section labors like mad making up papers and it is very bad for morale when they don't get stamped in the end."

I was feeling pretty good so I just stamped away. The whole pile was finished in an hour.

"There isn't any more work for you," said Bawtch with some hostility. "So when are you going to get out of here?" He must have seen I was thinking of something else. He really bored in. "Your driver took five credits over to Meeley and you've got your room back."

I hastily looked into my pockets. Sure enough, the (bleeped) driver had not given me the five credits but had given them to Meeley! That meant I would have to move out of this office: I would be about and visible!

The cheer I had been feeling evaporated. The specter of Lombar seemed to loom outside the building.

"This is *not* your living quarters!" said Bawtch getting almost savage. He had said it so hard his sideblinders flapped.

I decided to take a hard line with him. I realized that I had, in effect, been hiding here. As I was never in my office, no one would ever look for me here. I said, "I have some strategic decisions to make. This *is*, after all, my office! I have a perfect right to sit here and think!"

The only answer he had was a sort of "Hmph." He flapped out.

I found out almost immediately why Bawtch had wanted me out of the office. The contractor people! They bustled in with a few glares at me, probably thinking I had wasted part of their day, and began measuring and pounding in the toilet.

Oh, well. Nothing that minor could drive me out into the threatening daylight.

The escape plan the contractors were doing reminded me of dear Bugs Bunny. I wondered what *he* would do in circumstances similar to mine. I couldn't remember any comparable strip and thinking about it unfortunately brought my thoughts to Heller and the mission.

It was not that I *could* do anything about any situation I was in, it was just that I really ought to be thinking about something. I am not happy with my mind idle. It threatens to dive in the direction of terror if I just let it drift.

Little scraps of the euphoric feeling of being safe on Earth had continued to touch me from time to time. This very morning I had enjoyed such a period and had completed all the administrative details of the magic mailing. Bawtch would not tamper with the orders for it would unbalance his despatch tally slips. If I ever got to Earth, I was assured of regular couriers and intimate news and no complaints from Bawtch if the corners of his forms got wrinkled.

Feeling at a loss for occupation, I recalled the midnight dream I had had. I flinched from it a bit and then knew why. I had not done a dream analysis on it!

At first I had to resolve whether it was a dream or a hallucination. Because there is no way to do a dream analysis on a hallucination, I decided it was a dream. I got to work.

While I worked, I made marks on a piece of paper. It is a trick I picked up from a professor of primitive ethnology. It is called "doodling." It had nothing to do with the dream analysis.

The Devil was, of course, a father figure. This was quite visible. The whips of the patrol craft crew were phallic symbols. Ah, now I was getting somewhere. The torch the father figure had wielded was caused by (bleep) envy. It followed logically that I wanted sexual intercourse with my mother and so hated my father. There! I was done. That dream would never bother me again.

Unfortunately, even with doodles, this dream analysis had occupied no time at all. My command of psychology is too certain and swift. My mind again began to drift into my problems.

Suddenly, I was gripped by a premonition of horror to come! The patrol craft! I had been back and forth across the Great Desert several times and I had not noticed any wreck! With near terror, I wondered what had happened to the crew. If those spacers got loose, if the Fleet got word of their kidnap, the duress I had undergone at the officers' club would be nothing!

I hit buzzers. Even though he was sullen, a clerk found me recent newssheet files and I tore through them. No faintest mention of a wrecked patrol craft!

What had happened? Had the Commander of the 2nd Death Battalion, whose men had been placed aboard, sold the ship and crew to smugglers? The Fleet guarded planets against smuggling. What if they intercepted their own ship? It would be enough to start a civil war and I would be in the middle of it!

I made myself fight down the surging horror. Psychology teaches you how to do that. You count slowly. That always works. But by the time I got to twenty, I leaped up and started pacing. I bumped into a workman who, in his powder blue cover suit, looked like the craftleader in the dream.

Shaking, I sat down so as to not call attention to myself and so I could press my hands on the desk top and mask their shaking.

I forced myself to go back over the dream again. The craftleader in it had said, "Sir, we absolutely will not tell him unless we are very generously bribed." Aha! The operative word was "bribed." More clues. The Devil had gone away only when given counterfeit money! Bribed!

Then, with deep probing insight, gritting my teeth so as not to flinch, I realized that all those people in that dream thought I knew something I did not know. What was it?

I also knew they wanted to be bribed.

I went over it again. In a flash, I realized that the patrol crew knew something about Heller. Why not? They had spent fifteen weeks with him!

Bribed?

Yes, but I did not know if they had ever really reached Spiteos.

And furthermore I had no money to do any bribing!

I held my hands so tightly together the knuckles were bone white. That was one way to steady my nerves. I had to think!

Death Battalion. That rang a bell somewhere.

Then I remembered the part in the dream about bribing the Devil with *counterfeit* money.

Suddenly I laughed. My subconscious mind had

been repressed by my censor. Deep in the primordial reptile brain which every sentient person has, I had worked it all out already! Because of a normal fear of erotic self-gratification, I had just not let myself know about it.

Although I had been afraid to go out, I was now more afraid to stay in.

I worked out an elaborate charade to account for my trip. I would tell Bawtch I was going hunting. This is my one extravagance: hunting trips. I like to kill small songbirds. One is likely to go anywhere to do that and nobody could trace me.

I got my hunting gear out of my office closet and with great nonchalance, sauntered out of the office, the game bag and needle blastrifle prominently displayed.

"Tell anybody who calls that I've gone hunting to recover my health," I said loudly to Bawtch as I passed his cubicle.

"Good riddance," I heard him mutter. And I knew my ruse had worked.

PART SEVEN

Chapter 1

The airbus was all cleaned out and polished up—Fleet cleaning materials. The driver had on a new uniform—he had even bathed. Heller's influence, (bleep) him. I felt a twinge in my stomach.

"Glad you're better," said the driver.

I know sneers when I hear them. I said, in a cold voice, "Provocation Section!"

He closed the door and off we flew. No one had been hanging around outside. I am well trained on such things. We were not being tailed. I was not in instant danger. I sat back in some relief.

I was not without resources. By a lucky fluke six months before, I had been snooping about a brawl some high Apparatus officers were having. They are infrequent as they can get pretty vulgar and scandals have to be hushed up. It had been held in an old ramshackle hotel out in the country, one that had long gone to seed. It was surrounded by acres of dead shrubs and decayed trees. I was wearing one of those tiny lapel cameras. At the time, I had been disappointed in being passed over in rank promotion and I had been shopping around to see if I couldn't get some embarrassing blackmail that might help my career.

With an attentive eye, I had seen a furtive figure slipping off into the shrubs and I followed. And what luck! A female was waiting on a hidden bench. The furtive figure slipped behind her. I had not been able to

make it out at first. But from the squabble which
followed, unheard above the din of the main party, the
female had been waiting for some high officer and the
furtive figure wasn't him! She threatened to report the
intruder. This may have terrified him or he may just
have been awfully drunk. But he proceeded to rape her.
I got several shots from a nearby bush. And then, the
beauty of it, he took out a knife and cut her throat and
silenced her once and for all. And I got several pictures
of that.

There were some other possibles that evening. I ran
off the whole batch myself in a lab. The camera used was
very light sensitive and the pictures were quite good.

Then ensued the laborious process of sorting out
who the principals were. Apparatus face files are a little
hard to come by but, after a time, I got the pictures all
connected up with names.

And wonder of wonders, I identified the woman as
the mistress of the Commander of the Death Battalion!
The male in the rape-murder shot turned out to be the
Chief of the Provocation Section!

I first established that the Commander of the Death
Battalion had not himself arranged it to get rid of
an unwanted female. He actually was making covert
inquiries. The matter never came out in the newssheets:
the Apparatus frowns on that. But he had even gone as
far as the bluebottles—Domestic Police—to get a list of
confirmed rape-murderers.

Accordingly, one day when I was idle, I had drifted
down to the Provocation Section office. The chief's
name was Raza Torr. He had been tagged several times
by the bluebottles of Flisten on suspicion of rape-murder
but there was no proof. He had finally been recruited to
the Apparatus and had risen to the post of Chief of

Provocation. I got him alone, gave him copies of the pictures—I had many others in a secret place—and told him, "You're perfectly safe. In the course of duty I killed the fellow who took these and have the originals. They were not entered in the master data banks. I do not want any money"—I knew he was heavily in debt and couldn't pay and would kill if he had to—"but I only want to be your friend. And as a friendly act, I wanted you to know I have safeguarded your reputation." He hastily shredded the pictures. As a result, I practically own the Provocation Section. Nothing else I had shot would lead to promotion and this one wouldn't either. So I had to settle for what I could get.

This section specializes in framing. When the government decides it wants to get somebody, it hands it over to the Provocation Section. They infiltrate gangs and encourage them to do ridiculously foolhardy crimes for which they can be arrested and executed. They get prostitutes to compromise fellows who might be dangerous and feed the scandal to the newssheets and destroy their lives. In other words, pretty standard police work. The bluebottles also do this kind of thing but not on the scale of the Apparatus which is mostly political.

Down on the River Wiel, where it spreads out onto mud banks, there is a sprawling, dilapidated expanse of warehouses. Some say they used to be fish warehouses when the river still had fish in it. Some are used by large businesses. And the public does not know that right in the middle of that muddle lies the Provocation Section, very masked.

My airbus flew along the turbulent, brown river and then ducked into the tunnel leading to the section. I debarked and ran up the rickety stairs to the chief's office.

He saw who it was and looked a bit hunted. I had used his services a time or two. He would not feel

threatened. "I see you been promoted," said Raza Torr,
a bit sourly. He was a very slithery sort of fellow, keeps
one hand hidden in a drawer when he talks to you.

And yes, I was wearing my promotion. My driver
had suggested I sell it or get false stones put in it and sell
the real ones but Lombar would have noticed, the way
he sometimes yanks you close to him. It is far better to
starve than to attract unwanted attention from Lombar
Hisst. Starvation is less painful!

I greeted him quite affably. "Been meeting any nice
girls lately?" It was a friendly thing to say. Anything to
put him at his ease.

But, actually, he's not a very friendly fellow. His
hand went deeper in the drawer. "What do you want?"

"Oh, just the run of the place for a bit."

Sourly he buzzed for a clerk. "Give him what he
wants," said Raza Torr.

I followed the clerk. Behind me I heard the drawer
slam. Raza Torr said, "(Bleep)!" He must have hurt his
finger.

I knew exactly what I wanted. One of the favorite
ploys of the Provocation Section consists of planting
counterfeit money on people. It is a pretty good counterfeit. The casual public would never detect it. But a
trained store clerk and every cashier with a detection
machine can spot it at once. They usually just say to wait
a moment while they get some change, step on a floor button connected to the Finance Police and in a couple minutes the passer is picked up, taken to the Finance Prisons
and after some torture and a brief trial, is executed. It
is really a nice, smooth operation and the State is rid of
some malcontent or critic or rival. There is real power
in those counterfeit bills!

We walked through the endless rows of costumes of
every type and size, past the boot department and past

many another accumulation of riches. They mostly get them from morgues, accidents and battlefields. They seldom clean them up and the stench is a bit strong even in the Apparatus. We went by the Personal Effects Drawers, thousands of square yards of them containing every imaginable item from every imaginable place, mostly taken from the dead, all vital to make a Provocation Section agent seem authentic. I peeked in the wallet drawers as sometimes real money is left in them but some clerk had been there before me.

We walked two hundred yards through the weapons area where every criminal kind of crazy weapon conceivable can be found. They use them to equip "revolutionary forces" that will then attempt some crazy coup. Most of the weapons explode and that's that. Quite clever, really. Only the knives can be trusted and even then you better look in the handles to make sure there is no explosive charge that triggers when the knife touches flesh.

Finally and at last we came to their "Bait Office." It contains safes full of fakes: fake stones that will get somebody arrested, fake gold, fake identoplates that trigger a police alarm when used, even fake certificates that are sometimes handed out to real graduating students who might cause upset somewhere. All highly intelligent material.

And money! I stood right in front of the vast vault and gestured to the Bait Office clerk to open it. My escort said, "Give him what he wants." And they opened it.

Truly, the stuff looks beautiful. "Toilet paper" is the Apparatus slang term for it. And looking into that vast vault and at those piles and piles of lovely golden notes, one can get quite euphoric even if he knows it's all counterfeit.

Actually, I was so money-starved I sort of overdid it. I picked up quarter-notes and then threw them down as too petty. I picked up ones. Safe enough as who looks hard at a one. But not too thick a pack as I had just so much room in my pockets. I grabbed some packs of fives, then tens, then twenties, fifties and hundreds. I ran out of pocket room.

"You must be trying to get a whole platoon killed off," my escort said.

I thought that was a good idea, too.

Finally, I tried to seal my pockets. I couldn't. So I got rid of most of the ones.

The Bait Office clerk was presenting his board for my identoplate. I waved him off. "Very secret operation."

"It'll start an investigation done on that scale," said the Bait Office clerk.

"The chief said to give him what he wants. Must be somebody in disguise. Right?" The escort was backing up Raza Torr. Wise fellow.

I couldn't resist overwhelming them. "Emperor," I whispered.

"Well, he's got enough rivals," said the Bait Office clerk. "I hear Prince Mortiiy is making real headway over on Calabar. You using this to tag some of his lot?"

I frowned. It was the best ploy. It made him think he had come too close. He nodded wisely. But he said, "Don't plant too many of those hundreds. They're the ones that even bluebottles can spot. Mortiiy's agents themselves could detect them and knock *you* off."

"I'll be careful," I promised. "Not a word of this to anyone, no records."

"Right! We got to get rid of lice like that Mortiiy. Did you know he promised to abolish the Apparatus?"

My escort said, "Silly (bleepard). How can anyone run a government without an Apparatus?"

"Maybe you've guessed too far," I said.

That put him in his place. But he was now anxious to please. "That uniform looks awfully chewed up. There were some General Services officers killed in a gas leak they were investigating last week. Didn't hurt their uniforms a bit. Maybe we've got your size."

They did have! It only smelled a little bit like gas. I changed. And while I was changing, I noticed a luggage item on a shelf. Being well trained, I knew what it was. It's called a "magic bottom." When an inspector opens it the interior rotates in such a way that he never detects he is always searching the same side.

"Take it along," said my escort, quite friendly now.

I stuffed the counterfeit money in it and then, lacking something to make the rotation work—something to inspect—I took some cans of food off a shelf marked *Poisoned Food* and put them in. The Apparatus thinks of everything.

"Don't offer me none of those counterfeits as a tip," said the escort. "I'm a lot too young to die!"

I guffawed over it. A really good joke. It wasn't until afterwards that I realized he had been hinting for a tip in real money. That accounted for the sour way he let me out.

But then, I had other things on my mind. *If* that patrol craft crew was in Spiteos, they would soon be unable to testify to anyone. They would have given me the data I needed about Heller and they would soon thereafter be dead, if not from poisoned food, then from trying to pass counterfeit money to the guards.

One has to be thorough. One has to be neat in the Apparatus.

Chapter 2

We set off on our mission of mercy; and indeed, anyone would be better off dead than held in the dungeons of Spiteos. So it was no criminal act, I fully realized. It was even a friendly thing to do.

Besides, Heller would kill me if he knew that a Fleet crew had been kidnapped the same night he had been. Dead crews don't blab, as my favorite Apparatus school instructor used to say.

Beyond all this, however, was the possibility that this crew *knew* something about Heller's habits that would make it possible for me to get back in control of things. The craftleader had said so in the dream and, as psychology teaches you, dreams never lie.

My driver said, "I smell gas!" He was looking around, sniffing. He rolled a window down despite the heavy slipstream and smelled outside. He decided the smell was inside. "Oh, it's *you*," he said. "Smells like sewer gas and cadavers all mixed up. And I just cleaned up the car, too."

I ignored him. We were just passing over the last edges of Government City and had not yet gone over the barrier mountains to the Great Desert. I wanted to get this magic bag fixed. I dumped it all out on the airbus floor.

Even though it was deadly counterfeit, the money sure was beautiful. Stacks of it! I piled it around in the airbus back, admiring that lovely gold paper.

"My Gods!" said my driver. "Did you hold up a Finance Office all by yourself?"

There had been awe and sudden respect in his voice, usually so absent. I was sorry I had to crush it. But it was necessary in case he got ideas of larceny himself. "You better leave this money alone," I said. "Every credit of it is totally counterfeit." I passed him a bill.

"Looks real," he said, handing it back quickly, like it was poison. "Who you planning to kill off? The whole of Camp Endurance?"

That was none of his business and he knew it. So I began to arrange the money in stacks. But the more I looked at it, the less willing I was to simply give it away. Thriftiness is a trait.

I decided I had better not be going around with a wallet looking so empty. So I took a couple hundreds, a few fifties, a couple twenties, some fives and quite a few ones. My wallet looked nice and fat. Good for show, even though I could get killed for passing it. I put the wallet in my tunic where it felt very comfortable.

Then I studied the problem of buying information from the crew. I was just plain unwilling to part with very much of this money. It looked so *real*.

There is a toolbox compartment in the rear floor of an airbus. My driver, of course, had long since sold the tools and the hole was pretty big. Lifting the cover, I studied things out.

I made a firm decision. I removed the remaining ones and fives from the mass and put them in the magic bag. And then I put all the rest of that lovely looking, deadly money in the tool compartment and locked it. I had fought the battle of giving it away or keeping it and giving it away had lost! I put the thin stack of ones and fives in the hidden compartment of the magic bag. Then, with sudden inspiration, also hid the poisoned food in it. I had just decided on a new course of bribery.

We were past the mountains now and I spent my time looking down. According to Lombar's orders, there should be the burned-out wreck of a patrol craft in the Great Desert. The whitish expanses were white. The sun-dancers danced but not over any trace of a wreck. Never mind, I would first see if the crew had ever arrived at Spiteos and after that I could search for the wreck. Maybe the newssheets hadn't heard of it: after all, they are just newssheets, mostly trash.

We landed at Camp Kill. The driver ground-wheeled along the cluttered streets of the slummy place and, at my direction, stopped at the brothel control office. I went in, carrying the magic bag.

The commandant of Camp Endurance might make a fortune out of the place but actually the superannuated females who run it don't much care whether it runs or not. Sloppy. There was garbage lying all over the floors and the bulletin boards hadn't been posted for years. The female in charge didn't even have a desk.

She may have once been beautiful, now she looked like an executive. Four hundred pounds of fat slumped over the edges of a half-recline chair, wearing a dirty towel, she didn't even look up until I stamped my foot.

"I want a mute for fortress bribery," I said. They often take hill girls from other planets and cut out their larynx: they can't speak Voltarian anyway. Only a prostitute that is mute can be passed through the tunnel. Others at Camp Kill might suspect what was in Spiteos but none must be able to talk about it. It was common enough to entice a prisoner with a woman if it was thought he would not talk under torture. A lot of riffraff will do anything in return for a female.

She looked at me with contempt. Then she put out a filthy hand. Her attitude was such that I decided she would be better off executed anyway. I got out my wallet and put a counterfeit fifty in her palm with a great show of reluctance.

Really, it was like shooting a blaster into a jelly bowl, the way she shattered. She reassembled the globs into an ingratiating smile. She crooned over the fifty. She was no trained cashier!

"I may need her for some time," I said.

That had no bearing on it. She screeched in the direction of a hall and shortly a couple other old hags dragged out a young girl. Dirty, bedraggled, she was nevertheless fairly pretty. I checked the larynx: it had been removed. She stood there, beaten, dejected. From the back country of Flisten, I guessed, kidnapped on some government raid into the primitive country. She certainly did not look able to arouse anyone, pretty or not.

"And some tricks," I demanded. They have a lot of erotic gadgets that vibrate and do other things.

No trouble with that. Another screech and another crone came out with hands full of tricks. I dumped them into the visible compartment of the magic bag.

The girl only had a loincloth on, a dirty one. But clothes were no point. Then I thought of something. "There's a lot of men involved. She may get pretty used up."

The fat old bat said, "We got 'em by the hundreds." She kissed the fifty. "Kill her. Who cares?"

One of the other old hags looked at me archly and pulled back her loincloth. "You want something for yourself, dearie?"

Not a Camp Kill prostitute! I got out of there.

I gave the girl the bag to carry. It was a very cunning move. If any counterfeits were traced, they would be traced to her.

At the tunnel barricade, I told the guards, "Bribe

meat. I'd appreciate it if you would search her for weapons and all that. She's too dirty."

A guardsman grinned, put on a pair of gloves, took her aside and had himself some nice feels. He and the barricade officer were so engrossed, I had to tell them to search the bag. Of course they would find only the erotic tricks.

When they had, I said, "Note the search on the pass."

"For how long?" said the barricade officer.

"Mark it indefinite," I said. "They might not talk just on the promise of one go."

The guard officer laughed. "Wish I had a secret good enough for this." He let me put my identoplate on the pass and then handed it over.

The girl looked more beaten down. I had been surprised to see her blush at the guard's handling of certain places. Prostitutes are very cold meat usually. Riffraff.

Riding the zipbus, she began to look terrified. Maybe she had never ridden a zipbus before. It was true that now and then a prostitute taken into the fortress never came out again, got overworked and died at it or was simply murdered for kicks. But how would she know? She didn't understand Voltarian and couldn't talk either.

When we got off at the Spiteos end, she didn't want to get off the bus! I had to hit her, drag her off and then had trouble making her stand up. I kicked her and forced the bag into her hands. I actively had to keep thrusting at her back to keep her walking ahead.

It dawned on me that I had been swindled. This was one of those noncompliant, *won't* types the customers reject. They had given me this girl because she was useless to them! Ah, well, I had my revenge already. The brothel executive would be no more if she tried to pass that fifty. It amused me. Trouble for trouble, fair exchange!

But one trouble seems to breed another. In the roster office, the half-naked, yellow-man clerk spent a long time over the records. Spiteos records are pretty bad—nobody ever gets out. But to have no trace at all of an entrance is pretty unusual.

I gave him the probable date and hour. No, nothing. I was just beginning to believe they had never arrived when the yellow-man said, "Military? Did you say military? Well, you should have given me that data. They would be in the military section."

With considerable directions, taking some more tubes, finding out I had gone too deep and coming back—and all the while enduring the trouble of thrusting this girl ahead of me—I wound up in another section of Spiteos with an office even closer to the entrance than I had first visited. Spiteos is quite a snarl.

I found myself in a guardroom. There were about twenty-four actual guards, uniformed and in riot helmets, sprawled about, some of them shaking dice, others snoring.

The officer was a shabby type—what else in the Apparatus. His contingent was evidently a daily guard from the camp. These were not the usual wardens.

He had no interest in the girl—boys were probably his twist. He had no interest in anything, apparently, but getting his twelve-hour shift over with, getting back to camp and his own vices.

It turned out that there had been a riot amongst military rank and file prisoners a century ago and so captures of nonofficer prisoners of possible future value were slammed into the military section. He explained all this to me, yawning.

I gave him the number of men, date and time they must have been entered. He looked at his watch as though I was using up valuable time. But he said, "Two

more hours to go in this stinking place." He searched
around and finally found the rosters under some abandoned equipment. He sat down at a mess table and began
to go through them.

He shook his head. And just when I had decided
they'd never arrived, he put his finger down on a page
and traced it along.

"Your date is wrong," he said peevishly. "Forty-
eight hours off. Here they are, but it's two days later than
you said. You ought to keep better administration!" As
though I had charge of their records! "They're in Block
Five. You understand, I can't give you any other data
than that. It isn't that it's secret, it just isn't here.
'Twenty men,' it says, 'military, potentially dangerous.
Hold until further orders.' No other orders noted so
they're still there. Jeemp!" he said to a lolling subofficer,
"show this guy where's Block Five."

I noted none of them gave the prostitute a passing
glance. They were obviously daily back and forth from
the camp. All the better. This crew in here would have
no easy time of it as they would have buying from the
usual wardens. The money, even counterfeit, would be
nearly worthless to them and would be detected sooner
as counterfeit. These tough mugs would kill them if they
tried to pass it. Riot helmets. I was encouraged.

I thrust the prostitute along after Jeemp. We went
through some old black tunnels and he finally stopped
and pointed. "It's down there someplace." He left.

The area made me nervous. I loosened the stungun
in its holster, checked the knife behind my neck and the
blasticks in my pockets. Most of the glowplates had
blown out. Water was trickling somewhere. Some large
type of vermin leaped out of a sagging cell door. It
scared me.

All these black walled cells and rooms were empty

save for some bones. It was all quite different than the
area they had put Heller in.

The military section wasn't very military! It was a
good thing I was taking care of this. Dead crews don't
blab.

Chapter 3

I looked through a grate at the very end. And there
they were, twenty men. Their clothes had been stolen, of
course, and they were naked. They were draped about on
stone ledges. But they didn't look in too bad a shape. I
saw why, then: there was a pile of vermin bones in the
middle of the floor and a very active stream of water, an
underground seepage, trickled blackly down a blacker
wall.

I pushed the prostitute into a nearby empty cell. I
would save her for a surprise.

I decided to be brisk. I shouted through the grate,
"Who's in charge here?"

A tall, husky guy got off the bench, he came over to
the grate. "And who the Hells are you?" he said.

Not very beaten down! Well, they'd had vermin to
eat and there was water coming down the wall they could
catch. They probably didn't see a guard more than once
a day and yet here was somebody being spunky.

I decided to be military, "The number of your
patrol craft, please."

"So you know we're a Fleet crew," he said. "And
what happens when Fleet finally finds out what was
done with us?"

"Come, come," I said. "I am here to help you. Do not take that tone with me, my man. Give your craft number, name and rank."

Somebody amongst the rest said, "No harm. He knows it anyway."

The one at the door shrugged. "Craftleader Soams, Fleet Patrol Craft *B-44-A-539-G.* Who are you and where are we?"

Ah, they didn't know where they were. Excellent.

Now, there are two approaches one can use. The first is to be friendly, the second is to extort. Being friendly takes time.

"In return for certain information, I can give you certain things. They will make your life easier. Don't bargain. I haven't got much time."

The others were stirring around now, they formed a half circle behind him.

I went back and got some of the counterfeit out of the bag. I left the girl hidden. I returned and waved the notes.

"If you will tell me everything you know about one Jettero Heller, a combat engineer, who accompanied you on your last patrol, this is yours."

He went back and they put their heads together. They whispered for quite a while. I could see their various ranks from their conduct. A Fleet patrol craft does not have Royal officers—there are too many patrol craft. The "captain" is called a "craftleader." He has two sub-officer pilots, a subofficer engineer and odds and ends of specialists who attend to things like finance and food and then a few common spacers. You could see who was who in the deference paid to whispers. They sort of consulted by chain of command. But awfully democratic. They're different than the Army, it is said, because of living so tight together and at such long times in space.

They seemed to be resistant so I said, "With this you can bribe food."

Soams came back to the grate and looked at the money I still held. "It isn't enough," he said.

I went back in the other cell and got a few more bills. It appeared to be enough. Aha, I thought. Heller's charm isn't enough to prevent singing birds.

They made a drill of it. That's sort of the way Fleet is. A man would step up, speak his piece, then step back and another would step ahead and speak up.

And of all the sickening drivel I have ever listened to in my whole life, that period in Spiteos talking with that crew topped it.

Heller was a tall, very handsome officer. Heller knew exactly what he was doing. Heller was brave and afraid of nothing. Heller had an excellent singing voice. Heller did thoughtful things, illustrated by bandaging up the medical rating when an airlock slammed on him. Heller was amusing in that he told jokes when things looked grim—examples included.

Absolutely, utterly sickening!

Finally they stood back and Soams reached out and took the money. I had meant to snatch it back but he was too quick.

I looked them over. According to the dream—and it was amazing how closely they resembled themselves in the dream—they had said they knew more than that. I was sure they did.

I went back and got some more money. Imagine paying for such useless trivia! But I had no choice. I would trick them in the end.

Now began parade number two: Heller was very athletic. He held a racing record. He scared them to death once walking with magnetic shoes up to the top of the hull just to get a measurement of waves the interior of the ship was cancelling: he hadn't been able to find a safety line aboard that was long enough and so, four hundred miles above Blito-P3, he went walking on the top of the ship carrying some meter, and no safety line. Stuff like that. Sheer drivel.

They were done. Soams reached through the bars and took the money. But I could sense they were holding something back. A couple looked at each other secretively.

I went and got the food. I was mad enough by then to take a real satisfaction in it. They would soon be dead!

Instead of being impressed by these gaudy cans—they would look and taste just like the real thing and death would follow in minutes—this nut Soams said, "Where you getting all this stuff? You couldn't carry it in your arms."

I went back and got the magic bag to show them. I didn't show them it was a magic bag.

And then, catastrophe! That (bleeping) girl, curious about where I was disappearing to, or maybe looking for a possible way to escape, peeked out of that cell!

Soams saw her! (Bleep) her. She deserves everything that must have come to her.

"A girl?" said Soams.

"A girl?" chorused the rest of the idiots. They crowded up to the grate, peeking one after the other.

Oh, well, I knew I had them then. They went back and put their heads together and whispered by chain of command and ship department. And then Soams came back to the grate.

"You want to know something about Heller, don't you?" he said. And seeing my eagerness, he continued. "Well, we know something about Heller that it is vital *you* should know. In fact, knowing it could save your life!"

That was what I wanted.

"Down here," and he kicked the bottom of the door, "there is a food slot. They seldom put anything through it but it is big enough to slide that girl through. She looks small. And it is big enough to slide that bag you're holding through."

"All right," I said. "You tell me and I'll slide them through."

"Oh, no," said Soams. "You'd just walk off. After all, you're armed. You could open the door and take them out again if you didn't like it."

What could I do? I slid in the bag. Then, with more hope than effect, I tried to wrestle the girl down and shove her through. She had the long nails they cultivate in the Flisten back country to show they never work. I did *not* want to get scratched.

Then one of the spacers came to the grate and he said something in one of those outlandish tongues nobody can talk and the girl instantly went dead still. I thought to myself that spacers really got around. She went through the tight slot without another protest.

Soams took the food cans. He looked at the money. He looked at the bag. He looked at the bundle of sexual tricks. He looked at the girl, lying very quietly now inside the big cell. I held my breath. Ah, he nodded.

The craftleader came up very close to the bars. He said, "And here is your information. Heed it and it will benefit you."

I was all ears.

"When Heller," said the craftleader, "gets word of what has happened to us, he will kill you with his bare hands! Run like mad and maybe it will save your life!"

Of course my immediate impulse was to smash the door open and snatch those things back. I even could have shot through the bars. But I couldn't see all the walls in there and they looked dangerous.

The Hells with them.

I stalked up the passageway, ignoring their catcalls and cries of "drunk!" I should stick to orthodox psychology. My original dream analysis had been correct. Only thirst had caused me to act otherwise. The real reason was a censored desire for sexual intercourse with my mother.

I told the guard officer I was through. I even tossed down the pass for the girl. But she wouldn't need it. They would all soon be dead as she'd eat some of that food as well! I was confident I had handled that scene perfectly.

Chapter 4

With one less worry on my mind, I addressed my attention to the crash of the patrol craft. Actually, it was sort of like the Apparatus not to follow through on a project and I didn't want Lombar coming down on me suddenly with a "Why didn't you take care of that?" as he had in the original kidnapping.

So, much to the consternation of my driver, instead of going back to Government City, I directed him to fly along a little-used traffic route toward the Blike Mountains. He had lots of fuel. We had lots of food and sweetbuns, thanks to Heller. I had my needle blastrifle and game bag. But I told myself that this was duty, pure duty. And thus it was that we flew and flew.

There was no sign of any crashed spacecraft. I worked it all out. If the crew had arrived at Spiteos forty-eight hours late, then it was a forty-eight hour circle by lorry that we were looking at. You can't run at random in the Great Desert even in sand lorries; if it wasn't between Government City and Camp Endurance, then it was on a seldom followed track forty-eight hours *beyond* Camp Endurance. Simple logic. But if it wasn't there, either, then they had sold the patrol craft to smugglers and returned to Camp Endurance by airbus and Gods only knew where the patrol craft would be: while that was a sort of nervous idea, I would do my duty so far as looking for the crash was concerned. If I found it, I might leak it to the newssheets.

The driver was helpful once he got out of me what we were doing. He spotted something and we landed. But it was a crash so old it was almost gone into the ground. While examining this, I spotted a songbird, a type they call a "thriller"—found in the desert—and brought him down. He was only a few feet away and sitting but it was a good shot. I put him in the game bag.

Further toward the Blike Mountains, I pretended to find another crash which turned out to be a rock, but I got two more thrillers.

The Blike Mountains were beginning to rise higher and higher. They are icy peaks and while not the tallest on Voltar, their thirty-eight thousand feet will do. You can't walk over them. The air at their summits is too thin. Even in their passes it is too thin.

After two more false sightings, during which we got six more thrillers, my driver said, "Officer Gris, are we looking for wrecks or are we going hunting?"

For the first time I realized I really was going hunting. The more distance and the more time I could put between me and Heller and *Tug One*, the better it would be!

Of course I didn't answer the driver. He would have interpreted it that I was running away!

We got very cold crossing the first ridge of the Blike Mountains but we came down very fast into the valleys beyond it. This country is all hunting preserve areas, under the domination of the Lords, patrolled and guarded. But it is so vast, there are so many plateaus and gorges, that you can get lost in it utterly and no one would ever find you if you didn't want it to happen. It is full of all manner of game, some of it even brought in from other planets.

"Somebody followed us over that first range," said my driver.

I looked. I saw nothing behind us in the sky. An airbus has no detectors. I was nervous.

"I don't see him now," said the driver.

I told myself sternly that it was just my nerves: after all, I had had a trying time lately. It was proof I needed a hunting trip!

Amazingly, dusk was falling. Perhaps it was just dropping lower behind the first range of the Blikes, but it seemed awfully dark. It's not a country to land in, in the dark!

I quickly chose a landing spot. It was a little plateau. Grassy, a few scrub trees. It was right on the edge of a three-thousand-foot drop down to a white running river. But there was a line of rock at the edge that jutted up.

"Land!" I ordered.

He did. He shut off the drives. What beautiful quiet! Just the hiss of wind through the scrub trees and the mutter of water far below in that gorge. I relaxed. Delightful. After a bit I got out and walked over to the piles of rocks that rose at the edge of the cliff. I climbed up. There was an animal path on the other side, a couple of caves and way, way below, the water. My, it was black down there: already you could see no more than some white foam.

The driver had gotten some sticks together. I put a little firepowder on them and when the air soaked into it, the blaze crackled happily. It was cool and it was getting very dark.

The driver ripped the feathers off the thrillers and we put them on sticks and began to roast them. After half an hour of fond attention, they were done.

I was sitting on a boulder, eating a thriller. The fire was bright. Beyond it sat the driver eating another bird. I had just reached back for another stick.

WHAP!

The blastshot was right where my head had been!

The heavy concussion blew the fire out totally!

Believe me, I scrambled!

The driver heard me going and he followed. I got over the mound of rocks at the cliff edge and got to the other side. If my driver hadn't plowed into me, almost knocking *me* loose, he would have gone three thousand feet down!

I crouched down on the animal trail on the cliff. I was not going to peer over the top of those rocks. Not yet!

"I was right," said the driver. "Somebody followed us!"

"Get up there and peek over," I said.

He scrambled a bit. A rock came loose and started a small avalanche. That sound was what did it!

A spray of blastfire roared over the top of the rocks. The concussion was awful! Whoever it was was using a fangun! It is a weapon that puts out electric fire in a forty-degree front arc! No hunting weapon that! No gamekeeper weapon! That was military! My Gods, who was after us? The Army?

"Maybe they made a mistake," said the driver. And before I could stop him, he yelled, "Hey! This is just us!"

Another fangun blast! This time it actually took

some of the tops off the protective wall rocks. Splinters, melted rock, spattered us.

But the enemy, whoever it was, had made a mistake. He or they had given me light to see by. We were crouched on an animal path. About ten feet to our left was a cave. Three thousand feet down was the river, unseen now. It was black night!

"It's robbers," said the driver. It is true that people were often robbed in these mountains. But it wasn't true that he had ever learned much working with the contrabandists.

ROOOOOOOOAR!

They or whoever it was were shooting at his voice!

But I am up to such things. I whispered to the driver, "Can you do a dwindling scream?"

"No," he said.

"Well, you just better imitate what I do. As soon as I do it, I will dive for that cave and as soon as I do it, you do it and dive for that cave. Understand?"

"I don't know how!" he whispered. The idiot. It is right in the training manuals.

I shouted, "Go away!"

ROOOOOAR!

I shouted a dwindling scream. When you do it right it sounds like it is declining in the distance. Whoever it was would think they'd made a hit and knocked me off the edge.

I was diving for the cave.

My driver, prompted by necessity and probably on the verge of screaming anyway, imitated it for all he was worth. He spoiled it a little bit because when he hit his knee landing in the cave beside me he said, "(Bleep)!"

We crouched there. After a few minutes a light played down over the path where we had been. We hugged back out of sight in the cave.

The light went off.

Then, mysteriously, a couple of minor shots sounded. Then a crackle of flames.

Finally, in the distance, there was a screech of a vehicle's drives starting up and then a roar as it went away. The sound racketed around the mountains and died out.

I became brave. I sent the driver up to look.

"My Gods!" he said at the top.

He was still standing there and hadn't been shot so I went up.

"We're stranded in the Blike Mountains!" said the driver.

The airbus was burning.

"Good," I said.

"But we can't cross those mountains! Even in the passes the air is too thin."

I suddenly remembered that my driver had a name. I never used it. Now was the time. "Ske, have you ever dreamed of the sylvan life, the woods, the trees, the streams? Living off nature? With no cares?"

It had no appeal, apparently. He started cursing like fury and ran down and started throwing sand on the wreck. I didn't help him at all. It was just the engine burning. Whoever it was had fired a shot into the fuel capacitors and another one into the generator converter. That engine would never run again.

I hummed happily. I found my needle blastrifle in the brush. I found my game bag and the ammunition. I pulled somewhat toasted sweetbuns out of the back and somewhat boiled sparklewater from under the driver's seat. And while I was doing this, I suddenly beheld that the toolbox lid was open and the toolbox was empty.

I sat down and began to laugh. I laughed and laughed. It was the first time I had laughed for a long while. The driver, who had gotten the engine fire down to a flicker, looked at me a little scared. Well, maybe I did sound a bit hysterical.

"What's so funny?" he demanded.

"The money! It's gone!" And I went off into another spasm. "They followed us in to rob us. They cut their engines way back and coasted in. They crept up carefully. They thought they killed us. And . . ." It was so rich I had to laugh and laugh again. The driver got me by the shoulders to steady me or shake me or something. I didn't mind. I sat down and laughed some more. Finally, I could talk again.

"They did it all to rob us of counterfeit money! Spreading that much around they will start a major investigation. And they'll be executed out of hand!"

Ske didn't think it was funny. "All I know is, we're completely off all traffic lines, we don't have any communication at all, we can't walk out of here and we're surrounded by deep canyons and a country full of savage beasts."

"That's the nice part of it," I said.

I watched him build up the cooking fire again— whoever it was would just think the airbus was still burning if they looked back and saw a pinpoint of light. He located some of the game birds and began to pick the dust and rocks off them. I sat there grinning.

Gone was *Tug One*. Gone was Heller. Far away was the Countess Krak. If found, I could even explain to Lombar we were looking for the patrol craft he had ordered burned and we crashed.

I was looking ahead to happy years in this wilderness full of game. All my problems were solved.

Looking back, I wish it had been so. How wrong I was to feel happy that night!

Chapter 5

At the end of three weeks, my "idyll of primitive atavism" came to an abrupt end.

I awoke from a dreamless, lovely sleep to find a hunting blastgun prodding my chin.

These valleys between the ranges were the heavens themselves: grassy plateaus, stately forests, picturesque rock formations, streams which rippled or roared in an interesting complexity, surrounded all about by majestic snow-crowned peaks!

Songbirds and an infinite variety of game abounded and fed the stomach and the eyes and ears alike.

Day after day we had wandered, from one enticing campsite to the next, each one seemingly more charming than the last.

I had a bit of trouble with my driver, Ske. Because one has to have the identification impress on the vehicle frame, or one can't get a replacement, he had insisted, at great labor—since he had no tools—in hammering that section off, using rocks, using twists to heat the metal so it would break. It had taken him hours and hours. The result was that he was left carrying a twenty-foot piece of vehicle frame, quite heavy and cumbersome, always getting in the road when he scrambled down cliffs or tried to go through dense trees.

He also had to carry the toasted sweetbuns and the remains of sparklewater in its warped containers as well as some singed upholstery I was using for blankets. When you added to this the weight of recent kills, one could imagine that it was a burden. And as I wandered along, pausing to admire the view, savor the redolent perfume of the air or take a shot at some songbird, I was nevertheless aware of his critical stares at my back when he thought I was not looking.

One day, as I sauntered up a steep path, and after he had fallen back down three times, tripped by the vehicle frame's propensity for gouging into the dirt, I heard him muttering. And so, while he stood teetering on the unfirm path, I took the time to try to put him right. I sat down on a boulder and began to explain to him what this was all about.

I told him that every being had in him a throwback, an atavism, to the primitive; I went into considerable technical details, all in the best traditions of Earth psychology. I even analyzed him as having an atavism deficiency. And all the thanks I got was him falling down the path again and this time swearing!

But, undaunted, I essayed another approach. When he got back up to me again, I explained how every sentient being of our type had yet retained, left over from evolution, a reptile brain below and between the lobes. This brain was what prompted blind leadership. I even drew him a picture of it in the slanted dirt. And then I diagnosed his trouble as a reptile brain deficiency that made him blind to the necessity of blindly following where I led. But once more all the thanks I got was him falling down to the bottom once more.

However, I did not permit this problem to blunt the acute pleasure I was taking in my stroll across this vast land. Not only did it have no *Tug One* in it, it had neither Heller nor Krak and only the faintest shadow of Lombar Hisst.

As days proceeded onward, I must have shot at least five hundred songbirds. Some of them, when they fell, were hard to get to or only wounded and my driver often had trouble recovering them, burdened as he was.

But he was making his own trouble. I told him to throw away the identoframe: we would never again have need of an airbus, so why carry the frame you have to turn in to get a replacement? I just couldn't seem to get through to him about this.

He couldn't be taught in other ways as well. Each time we would make a camp, instead of locating dry wood, he would start a fire with the greenest bark to hand and for the last half hour of daylight, huge columns of white smoke would rise like pillars into the air, absolutely towering into the sky. I tried and tried but I couldn't break him of it. I decided he was simply atavism deficient!

Thus, when the cold muzzle of the gun awoke me that dawn, I was not too surprised to hear my driver talking in a rather high, urgent voice when any atavistic impulse would have been to shut up!

" . . . And so we almost had the contrabandists and they up and shot us down!" Ske was saying. "But true to our duty, we have been following them day after day, scouting on their trail. They left fantastic amounts of evidence behind. You just look at that game bag! We found it just last night and it's full of fancy feathers!"

One always studies the enemy. The two fellows who had us were dressed in the green of game wardens. They had the emblem of some Lord sewn on their chests. They looked very ugly. They were heavily armed. I heard a twig snap back under the trees and knew there was a third one back there, covering us.

"And," Ske was saying, his voice pitched even higher, "to prove that we flushed them and that they fled afraid of us, look at that needle blastgun they left behind!"

"Ah," said a three-hundred-pound brute, the other one that wasn't holding the gun on my chin. He picked up my needlegun. "We'll just confiscate this. Nice gun."

"Evidence of the Crown," I said hastily. "You must not tamper with legal evidence!"

"This," said the three-hundred-pounder impressively, "is Lord Mok's preserve. All half-million acres of it. And anything found in it is Lord Mok's!"

For "Lord Mok's," I thought, substitute "game warden's."

The gun muzzle bruised my chin with a poke. "Get up. We're taking you in!"

I noticed for the first time that they had a rope around Ske's neck. The "you" didn't seem to include Ske as the three-hundred-pounder seemed to be looking about for a limb to hang him from. Oh, well, I thought. One can always get a replacement driver.

Ske did not seem to take to the idea of being hanged. But instead of grovelling, he grabbed the rope to slacken it and drew himself up tall. Not very tall as he isn't very big.

"That!" said Ske pointing dramatically at me, "is Officer Gris of the Apparatus! He is on a secret mission for the Emperor!" His voice could be heard for a mile!

It produced an interesting effect. *Three* men emerged from the trees and came forward at a run with levelled guns! It looked like there was going to be a double hanging right now!

Ske had freed himself for an instant. He dived to my side. He yanked open the flap of a pocket, grabbed out my communication disc and screamed into it, "For the sake of the Gods, don't fire! Officer Gris will be in your range!" It was a pretty silly thing to do as we were about ten times the distance that that communication disc could reach.

Ske whispered to me frantically, "Tell them they're all under arrest!"

I blinked. The yokels had all hauled up. They were suspended, looking up and around anxiously. Yokels, indeed. Lord Mok didn't hire smart men for game wardens.

I got up. "You're all under arrest," I said.

"For posing as game wardens!" shouted Ske.

This hanging or battle or whatever it had been about to become, disintegrated into, "We've got credentials!" and "How do we know you are an Officer Gris?" and that sort of thing.

Everybody showed everybody their badges. Ske ran around pushing my identoplate into people's faces.

They finally told me that they'd have to keep the needlegun and game bag as "evidence" we'd actually been following poachers. And they said they had a supply plane leaving their preserve headquarters the next morning for Government City and we could hitch a ride on it.

Ske seemed very elated and almost cheering.

I wasn't. It seemed like the sky had fallen in. I was very certain that catastrophe awaited me. The very thought of going back made my stomach hurt!

Chapter 6

Dispiritedly, I sat and watched the Transport Issue Clerk.

The wardens had dropped us off at the Apparatus Vehicle Center in Government City, not even thanking me for the needlegun and game bag.

Ske had lugged in the frame from the wreck and the Transport Issue Clerk, instead of giving Ske a blast, had practically cooed over it. Ske had written out a report—*Crash in Line of Duty*—and had then made out the application for another vehicle.

"Uuuuuu! It's been promoted!" cried the Transport Issue Clerk. "It's a Grade Eleven now!" He slapped Ske's wrist: "You naughty boy. You didn't have to *wreck* the other to get a new one. You just could have brought it in. What unnecessary paper work you drivers make!"

And then he was onto his communications link with the commercial suppliers—Zippety-Zip Manufacturing Outlet—in Commercial City. "Uuuuu, Chalber, dear," he said musically to whomever was on the other end. "We've had a pro*mot*ion. And it will need a Model 794-86 right away." He muted the disc and turned to Ske. "They've only one with purple upholstery and green tassels. Will that do?" Apparently Ske thought it would, for the clerk got "Dear Chalber" to rush right over with it himself.

"Oh, you are so lucky," said the clerk to Ske. "The Model 794-86 is absolutely a*dor*able! It has the circular seat in back that makes down into a bed."

"Hot Saints!" exclaimed Ske, and well he might for he had to sleep in my vehicle most of the time.

"Oh, yes," cooed the clerk. "And it has window blinders and the cutest bar. You and me will just have to take a ride in it," wink, wink, "won't we?"

I decided there were things I didn't know about Ske.

Shortly "Dear Chalber" arrived and there was a hurried and furtive interchange between him and the clerk and I saw the golden flash of money changing hands. Aha! So that was why the Apparatus had so many strange vehicle wrecks!

The clerk gave "Dear Chalber" a kiss and when a following vehicle had flown him off, the clerk turned to Ske and there was a furtive interchange there and I distinctly saw another, smaller golden flash.

The new airbus was quite elegant: purple light spinners and green landing wheels with a bright red band all around it. Hardly the thing for undercover work! The interior was so *clean* it was disgusting. I got in wearily.

"Have some more wrecks, dear," I heard the happy clerk tell Ske.

I was wrong about Ske. He was wiping the clerk's kiss off very vigorously as he eased in under the wheelstick. We took off for my office.

"I think you owe me something," I said. I had to repeat it in a louder voice even though the new bus was much quieter.

"Oh, you mean the money," said my driver. "That was just one credit he owed me."

He protested he would need it for food but he knew how firm I could be. He finally threw it over his head at me. And even though I was quite certain he had had to peel it off a roll of bills, the airbus was diving about in traffic so I decided to be satisfied. The back windows were down and I hadn't fastened my belt. The note had almost sailed out! A close one!

At my office, when I walked in, the two boys Too-Too and Oh Dear instantly, with just one glance at me, fell into each other's arms and began to cry. The rest of the clerks in the front office left and it wasn't even lunch hour. It was quite late in the day. Must be early quitting time, I thought.

Bawtch came stooping out of his office and saw me. "Oh, it's you!" he said. "Why do you have to keep coming in here and upsetting everything?"

I tried to point out that I had been *missing* for three weeks. And he just kept raving on about me always being underfoot!

Defensively I went back into my office. I looked on the desk, half-expecting to see a warrant-for-my-arrest notice. Nothing. Same dust.

The contractors had finished their work. I went in and checked and sure enough, when you pressed the wall just so, it revolved and there was a ladder to a hatch in the roof. The silent-break glass was innocently in place. The river roiled along five hundred feet below.

When I came out, Bawtch, a very inconsistent type, had piled some forms on my desk. "As long as you're here, you can stamp these forms. You never stamped the first contractor and now there are *two* to stamp. I have a new payroll and the expenses allocation that Twolah and Odur will require. And another shipment came in from Blito-P3 that must be stamped as received in good order. Office expenses have also gone up." He was shoving me at my desk now. "I can't understand why it is if you're always bursting in here why you can't at least do your work!"

I began to stamp. I got even with him. I didn't even read the stuff. Maintain a lofty attitude is always the best way! Puts the riffraff in their place!

I found out suddenly I was stamping blank forms! That would never do. They have to be written on first! I got brave. "Bawtch, you're getting soft in the head. You forgot to make these forms out before you brought them in! Old age, Bawtch. Dotage!"

He snatched the pile away in considerable anger. He stalked out. I could see I had reached him. You have to be very firm with such riffraff. Lombar was right when he had said that there were very few Academy officers about: those of us there were had to really slave to make the Apparatus run as well as it did!

I got up and walked into the main office. It promptly cleared again of clerks. I was aware suddenly that some people were behind me and to my left. It was Too-Too and Oh Dear. My position had them trapped: they couldn't leave without running close to me. They were standing there in frozen horror.

Behind them was a third, it was a training operator from the Apparatus Training Command. And, what do you know, he was sitting at a brand-new master data console!

How out of place it looked, all bright, shining, new plates and keyboards and glittering screens amongst the dirt and decayed furniture of the outer office.

And then I grasped the situation. Bawtch had come up. I spoke very severely, "What is this master console doing here?"

Bawtch, who is silly about some things like keeping security from other parts of the Apparatus, ordered the training operator out and, when he had gone, turned to me. "You stamped the order for it three weeks ago. You are entitled to it with your increase in rank, though why they promoted you, I don't dare imagine!"

I knew that wasn't the reason. That was just his eighty-year-old failure to become an officer talking. "You got this in here so that these two boys could use it!"

Bawtch blew up. "You brute! You didn't expect them to get their data from a dirty old Lord, did you?"

"I certainly did! The kind of data you can get on these machines does not include what Endow knows. They better make up time getting into Endow's bed or I'll include any sisters!"

The two boys had already fallen into each other's

arms. At this last, they went out in a dead faint.

Bawtch left, spinning chairs out of the way and slamming them to the floor. He banged his door shut. He seemed upset.

I stepped over the boys and sat down at the console. Well, well. A master console of my own! I threw it out of training mode and into activation. I took out Bawtch's chief clerk identoplate and was about to insert my own when I changed my mind and left his in. In his agitation he had forgotten it.

I punched in my own name and designation: actually this takes a moment or two as there are twenty-two thousand, six hundred and eighty-one Soltan Grises in the tens of millions of Voltarian officers of all branches and I didn't want the wrong one.

Warrants?

I punched.

Not yet,

said the machine.

Pay status?

I punched in. The machine promptly pulsated red flashes.

Alert, alert, alert! Through clerical error, this officer was advanced one credit in excess of a year's advance pay. All further pay uncollectible until refund occurs.

I had thought I would now have three weeks pay I could draw on. But not so! But what luck! I did have one credit and I could send it in. But as I was reaching for it, the machine went on talking.

Warning, warning, warning. If said officer loses any one of his four paychecks for any reason or suffers demotion or fine, communicate at once to the Finance Department Courts-martial Unit.

I went cold. What if I did lose Mission Earth?

The mountains had their game wardens, Government City had its Finance Department. There was no place to hide!

It was not unknown to me, but the threat of becoming a gutter bum in some slum city, living on garbage, if that, so unnerved me that the five-second warning flash had begun before I realized I had not remedied being broke right now.

I hastily tapped,

Item en route

and scribbled my name and designations on a scrap of paper and wadded it and the one-credit note into a capsule. I slammed it hastily into the slot and punched,

Finance Adjustments

and off it went with a whoosh.

Shortly, the screen flashed,

Adjustment received.

I hastily punched,

Pay status?

and the machine said,

I am sorry but it takes two months to adjust pay errors.

And before I could even protest, the machine again said,

Warning, warning, warning. If said officer loses any one of his four paychecks . . .

I slammed the keys and shut it off. (Bleep) them! I should have paid it with a counterfeit note! That would show them.

I was so angry and so upset that I forgot I had two fainted bodies behind me and I stumbled on them as I left.

Outside I took a deep breath to steady myself. The sour smell of the Apparatus sector and the stink of the River Wiel did not compare with the Blike Mountains.

"Officer Gris," said Ske, startling me in the shadows

of the building. "Don't you think we better go down to the Apparatus hangars while we got some day left?"

While I had some paychecks left, I thought. I climbed hastily into the airbus. I had to get this mission going even if it killed me, which it probably would.

Chapter 7

We hovered in the sky above the Apparatus hangars, waiting for the landing circle to clear. Such was my urgency and determination that I became impatient. It was all very well to hang there in the soft afternoon sunlight, sitting on the gaudy seat of the new airbus, but that didn't keep me out of gutter hollow! Way, way over to the west I could see Ardaucus, the fancy name they give Slum City. It even looked smudgy and dirty at this distance. Lombar was right: it ought to be annihilated! But not with me in it!

"What is holding us?" I at length demanded.

Ske shrugged. "It's that Fleet freight skyhauler."

Alarm shot through me. I had been careful about keeping Heller away from Fleet anything! And sure enough, down there on the landing circle below, a Fleet skyhauler was hovering, bobbing up and down, giving the final adjustments to something huge and brass colored—a sort of cylinder. It was getting it finally onto a trundle dolly.

Even as I looked, the Fleet pilot tripped his let-go and the cables began to reel up. Without waiting for this to be completed, the blue freight carrier zipped up into the sky.

The trundle dolly was moving into the hangar now

and my driver plummeted the airbus down to the target area.

I was actually quite alarmed to see Fleet touching even the fringes of the mission. The thought of the Fleet patrol crew, probably long dead now in Spiteos, and the words of Soams were almost enough to make me withdraw from the area.

But the computer threat was fresh in my mind. I jumped out and ran up alongside the trundle dolly. It was inside the hangar now. The crane hook was coming down to engage the rings on the cylinder.

And there was Heller, riding the crane hook over. I drew back a bit.

Tug One had had some upper hullplates removed. Right in the middle of her back.

Heller was giving hand motions to the crane master way above. He dropped off onto the top of the brass-colored cylinder and then guided the hook to engage a huge ring. Heller locked the hook blades in place with a gloved hand and, with him signalling, was hauled high in the air, riding the cylinder as it rose.

I caught a sign on the cylinder. It said:

HIGHLY DANGEROUS
HIGHLY EXPLOSIVE
DO NOT OPEN

My Gods, I mourned to myself. She isn't enough of a bomb already?

The trundle dolly operator was clambering down. His job finished, he was lighting a puffstick.

"Have any other Fleet units been around here lately?" I asked him.

"What's the matter? Haven't you seen them?" He

hadn't noticed I'd been missing for three weeks.

"Well, have they?" I insisted.

"Naw, this is the first in a couple days. There ain't been anything else, yesterday or today."

"What's been coming?" I persisted.

"That's a funny (bleeped) thing," he said, looking up at the swaying cylinder. "They can't change a time-converter in flight. Taking an extra one means they must be going to some well-equipped repair base. I was a drive operator once, you know. Before space started giving me the creeps."

Heller had guided the huge brass cylinder down through the place that had been opened in the top of the hull.

"He wouldn't let anybody else guide it in," said the trundle dolly operator. "Or maybe they refused to. Those (bleeping) Will-be Was engines! They're danger-ous even in a battleship. That's what they were designed for, you know, not for no (bleeped) tug. But I wonder what he's doing with a spare time-converter."

Heller was directing the final lowering. He looked like a speck from where I was standing. The huge cyl-inder was spinning back and forth with him standing on it.

"I'll give you some advice," said the trundle dolly operator. "Don't never open one of them time-converters up. Believe what it says on the labels. You could lose your hand! I could even give you some better advice. Don't never go no place in that (bleeped) tug!"

He was uncomfortable to be around. I walked deep-er into the hangar. The day half-platoon was lounging about. They didn't even glance at me. I approached the subofficer.

"Have a bunch of things been coming in from Fleet?" I asked him.

He glanced around. "Most of the contractor crews seem to have gone home."

That certainly answered no question. "What do the things look like?" I insisted.

"How does any long box look?" he said irritably.

"Where are they putting them?" I demanded.

"In the lower hold, of course. Say," and he focused on me very sharply, "can't you see, or something?" It was obvious he had not noticed I had been missing.

The hook was now rising out of the open gap in the hull, the cylinder seemingly having been gotten into its storage space.

Heller was riding the hook. It came down like a bomb. He jumped off and it hit the pavement with a crash.

"Oh, say, Soltan," he said, for all the world like he was rebeginning a conversation interrupted a half hour earlier, "like I was telling you, all the cultural notes and observations are missing from all those earlier Blito-P3 surveys. See if you can get hold of them, will you?" And he yelled back up to the high cab, "Very well done and thank you, crane master!" and with a friendly hand wave to him, he trotted over to the tug and went in through the airlock.

The day's work was over. People were drifting off. The sun was gone.

And then here it came, "Hup, yo, hup, yo, hup, yo!" The cadence counting of the Fleet marines, totally foreign to Apparatus areas. The slamming bootbeats of the marching squad. In they came and gave the day suboff-icer a salute. Then, "Pohstings! Guardsman Ip, yuoah post is in the ship!"

And the Countess Krak, in perfect evolution, boot-slammed in through the airlock.

The rest of the squad gave a jump and cheer and

then dispersed. All just as before!

Snelz wandered over to the old gravity chair and sat down. I approached him.

He was lighting a puffstick. "Bit of wind on the desert today. Have a puffstick?" he added as an afterthought.

"I think you owe me more than that," I said threateningly.

"Oh?" He felt in his tunic side pocket and pulled out a five-credit note. "I thought I gave it to you a couple days ago. Well, here it is."

He probably owed me more than that. But realizing he didn't even know I'd been gone sort of took the heart out of me. I put the five-credit note in my pocket and walked slowly away.

I had five credits. It made me brave enough to go "home."

I mounted the side steps, avoiding the broken boards. I heard somebody walking in the hall. It was dark. As quietly as I could I slid along the wall to my room. I knew my way. I had done it very often. I am a master at silent approach.

There were no bars on my door. I slid it open. A low glowplate was burning in there and by its light I saw, standing not three feet from me, Meeley.

She looked like she was going to go through my pockets. I hastily flipped out the five-credit note and handed it over.

She did not even say thank you. She did not even say I still owed her money for last year. She said, "I wish you would sweep that floor up occasionally! The stench is awful!" And she walked away.

Later I lay in the broken bed, staring into the dark. I had been gone three weeks. I could have been dead for all they knew. And not once this whole day had anybody said, "Where have you been?"

Chapter 8

But if I thought I would continue to be unnoticed and that things would just go on forever in this way, I was *very* mistaken. I did not have any forecast at all that, today, Heller's crazy, irresponsible actions would pull the pin and accidentally begin the landslide of events which were to lead us all into catastrophe.

I awoke, well before dawn, ravenously hungry. I became panic-stricken at the thought of starving and thirsting myself to a point where I would have another Manco Devil's dream: my poverty had prevented me from eating the entire previous day. I didn't want to be interviewed again for a job as handler of the King of the underworld.

Accordingly, I piled out and dressed and, down in the side courtyard, booted my driver awake and bade him fly at once, like mad, dark though it still might be, to my office.

My hope was to get there before Bawtch and raid the clerks' supply of hot jolt! It was a cunning plan: I had it all sketched out, complete with the excuse that I had to use the master console. I even embellished the plan with a fancy tale that I had worked like a slave all night, but I didn't think Bawtch would buy that so I deleted it.

In the office, I turned on a low light and worked with a ring of magnetic frequency plates, picking the lock of their jolt cupboard. I am very well trained as a lock picker, the tradecraft name for it, and in hardly any time at all I not only had a canister of hot jolt but also a thin, dry, bun crust somebody had abandoned.

I drank it very quickly, scalding my mouth, and rushed over to the master console, trying not to break my teeth on the bun crust. So far, so good: I had beaten everybody else to the office, I had not been observed. My superb training was standing me in good stead.

I sat down at the console. In my planning, I had neglected to decide what I was going to ask it. Bawtch had removed his identoplate so I had to use my own. I put it in and the console lit up and then it almost went off again while I tried to think of something to punch in to it. It was terribly early to do any thinking, hot jolt or no hot jolt!

Then I remembered Heller's remark of yesterday and I quickly punched in,

> Blito-P3, all cultural, ethnological survey appendages, all surveys prior to one hundred years ago.

The screens seemed undecided. Then they blinked and the master said,

> SORree. The material requested has been deleted from the data banks.

What's this? I thought. I could understand a delete of recent material but not prior to a hundred years. Heller had specifically requested such material. I had to give him *something* that would show I was working these days. I punched in,

> Correction: All such material up to twenty years ago.

The computer said,

> SORree. Deleted.

It provoked me. One can get pretty cross with computers, especially early in the morning. I got incautious. I punched in,

> Correction: All such material from present time all the way back.

The computer said,

> SORree. Comparing question to the identoplate of the interrogator, you know very well it isn't available. Very deleted.

(Bleep)! That really put me up against it. There was nothing I could show Heller that demonstrated my helpfulness. Aha! I punched in,

> Please give me copies of the deletions.

This sort of caused the screen to fog up. Then it said,

> How can you give a nothing to show a nothing is?

(Bleep) computers. They are so illogical. Can't think.

I furrowed my own brow. Then I had it.

> Please give me the number and identity of the person who ordered those deletions.

The computer thought it over. And then, amazingly, it gave it!

> Lombar Hisst.

There was his name, designation and identoplate facsimile! Imagine the great Lombar Hisst leaving his name in the machine!

Hastily, I punched *"Deliver copy."*

And the paper promptly rolled out. It was a certified copy and it said,

---

All cultural, ethnological, political and related material regarding Blito-P3, was ordered perpetually and additively deleted from the data banks on below date now twenty-five years past, by Lombar Hisst, Chief Executive of the Coordinated Information Apparatus, Exterior Division, Voltarian Confederation. Said identoplate facsimile hereby affixed below.

I finally had something that would prove to Heller that I *did* work and was around. I folded the copy up and put it in my pocket.

I was in the act of shutting off the machine when I heard voices coming from a side office.

"But I don't want to go!" It was Too-Too's voice.

"You poor thing, I know how you feel." It was Bawtch's voice. "But that brute is quite capable of carrying out the most insane actions." I couldn't imagine who he was referring to.

There was the sound of blubbering.

"Now hold still." It was Bawtch again. "Blow your nose into this handkerchief. You're getting your face powder all smeared and gummed up." The sound of blowing.

"Here," came Bawtch's voice, "is a packet of trash information. The same material will go to Hisst by regular routing. But you take this packet—here, I'll put it in this secrecy-case—straight to Lord Endow's office. Don't show it to the receptionist or secretary. Insist that you present it to Lord Endow himself, in private. They will search you for weapons—don't flinch—and then pass you in. Lord Endow will open the secrecy-case. He will see at once that it is trash and he will ask you why. And you will say you saw him riding in the last parade and were stricken with love."

Blubbering. More blowing. Finally Too-Too said, "But I hear he is too big!"

"Yes, I know, you poor thing. Here is some grease. Now run along before that unspeakable (bleepard) thinks up something even worse!"

I was frankly shocked. Bawtch could get imprisoned for referring to a Lord as an "unspeakable (bleepard)." But there was a good side to this. Bawtch was pushing the project right along. I got up. I was even thinking of telling him I was glad he had had a change of heart when I heard a violent howl of cursing.

Honestly, it was worse than a spacer pirate! And it finished with, ". . . will call Internal Investigations to find out what happened to this jolt bar!"

Ulp. I had forgotten to shut it. I wondered if this was the time to use the escape route. But I was fortified by the hot jolt and the crust and I braved it out. I walked past the open bar. "How about a canister of jolt?" I said.

He just stood there, glaring at me. I walked on out. I think he suspected.

I woke up my driver again and directed him to fly to the Apparatus hangar. I was on my way, without knowing it, to keep a very grim appointment with the wood Gods of awful fates.

Time had run out on me. Completely.

PART EIGHT

Chapter 1

At the hangar, everything was in a bustle.

We had arrived just as the contractors were coming on the job for the day and there were work crews, work crews, work crews. They were in the differently colored cover suit uniforms of their companies and as they scrambled and rushed about they made a scene of spattered hues and industry, quite foreign to an Apparatus hangar.

I did not see Heller. The day half-platoon was on duty, so Krak had gone.

After I got bumped and jostled a few ways and just after a rushing dolly with a load almost knocked me flat, I withdrew over to the side. I found a pile of old Apparatus debris and sat down, sort of fortified against this rush and clamor. It was absolutely exhausting to watch.

There was a contractor crew inside the main engine room, apparently fastening the spare time-converter in place and their foreman kept popping out, swearing at the lack of room for it in there.

Heller showed up. He had apparently been on the communications switchboard in the office. He looked very calm and efficient. He had his red racing cap on the back of his head and was stuffing a list in his pocket. I was about to go over to him to give him the deletion notice when he spotted the agitated foreman and trotted over to him.

"It wasn't meant to be carried in there!" the foreman wailed. "There's no place else on the ship for that big a spare but it sure won't go in there."

"I think if we move the booster panel about two feet," said Heller, "we can squeeze it in. Get those Willbe Was specialists over there to follow us. Shifting a booster panel can be tricky, but we can do it."

"Tricky!" said the foreman. "You get one wire wrong and it ain't tricky. It's bang! Oh well, it's your neck, Officer Heller." And he rushed off to get the Willbe Was foreman.

It depressed me. Not content with having dangerous engines, we now were going to unstabilize one of the panels! I slumped down.

The engine contractor crews converged on the main drive room and they banged and cursed and showered sparks in there. And after an hour or so there was a concerted cheer. Heller came out with the two foremen and they were all laughing. Whatever they had done had been a success.

Another crew was given a signal and they clambered up on the hull and began to replace the plates that had been removed to gain access to the main drive room. They looked like tiny dolls up there. *Tug One* was not big but a forty-foot fall can make a bad squash when one hits. I looked away. I don't like heights.

It looked awfully busy. From cover suit colors there must be eighteen contractor crews working on that ship. But Heller wasn't fooling me. He was just stalling. I knew you could overhaul a spaceship on and on and on. You could even undo today what was done yesterday! Heller, I decided, had no slightest intention of ever leaving on the mission. Why should he? He had beautiful quarters even though the area was under refit. He had Krak. Why should he go anywhere?

And then I saw something that unsettled me. A Fleet lorry came roaring up outside the hangar and about six Fleet spacers piled out. They had a near fight with the hangar guards but Heller appeared and calmed it down.

The spacers picked up the box. It was long and quite heavy. With a loose-kneed trot they carried it through the tug's airlock and into the ship. After a while they came out. One of the hangar Apparatus foremen jeered at them and the lead spacer detoured about two feet and knocked the foreman flat!

Amidst a bunch of shouts of "drunks!" and "blue-jackets!"—which is what the Apparatus calls the Fleet, a bluejacket being a kind of insect—there was a near second riot.

Heller got it untangled and the spacers went off and Heller picked up the Apparatus foreman who was saying, "I didn't mean you, Officer Heller," and things calmed down again.

But I was *very* interested in that box! I sidled very inconspicuously into the tug. The flight deck was a bit torn up—they seemed to be installing gravity simulator coils in the walls—and a lot of control wires were unhooked. But I had no interest in that.

The floor plates of the passageway were unlocked and up, displaying the shallow underhold below and on the bottomside of the main drives. I quickly lowered myself down.

There were six such boxes. They had letters on them, *Box A, Box B,* and so on. They were heavily fastened. And I could not lift a corner of one by myself. What the Devils did he have here? What menace did *this* pose to a mission that must fail?

I couldn't make it out. Afraid to be caught down there, I scrambled back up.

I ran straight into Heller! He was kneeling there on the passageway crossbars, looking at me curiously. I thought, well, here's where I blew it.

Heller reached down and gave me a hand and in a moment I was standing again in the passageway, teetering because all there was to stand on was the cross-supports of the missing plates. I waited for his blast.

Heller looked at me searchingly. It didn't make it any easier for me that he seemed to be having no trouble standing on the thin threads of nothing whereas I was sure I'd slip and fall back into the hold and break a leg.

"Soltan," he said in a soft voice, "I've got the feeling you've been avoiding me lately."

Avoiding you, I thought. You unobservant idiot! I haven't even been here for three weeks!

Heller looked a little sad. "When you ran off that night, I must have said or done something that offended you. If so, I'm very sorry for it."

He saw I was having trouble standing on the thin braces and he guided me over to more solid footing. "Soltan, whether we like it or not, we're pitched in together on this mission. I personally want to make a go of it."

That really flustered me. That was the one thing he wasn't supposed to do! I did not like the way this conversation was trending. He must not suspect how this mission would be sabotaged.

"Oh, I do, too," I lied hastily. I snatched the flap off my pocket and got out the delete notice the machine had given me. "I was up before dawn to carry out your request. This proves it." I gave him the slip.

He looked at it curiously. He turned it over and looked on the back. Then he shrugged and put it in his pocket.

"I'm sure you're trying to help all you can. And thank you for doing things like this." He seemed to think it over. Then he said, "Soltan, remember the old Academy saying 'All drive and no drink makes disasters'? I think maybe you have been working too hard."

A lot he knew. I hadn't been doing anything! Not to help. Never, never, never!

He snapped his fingers. "I've got it! You owe me a dinner!" I must have looked blank. "You remember! I was the first officer you met the day you were promoted. Did you meet any other officers that day?"

I shook my head, more to clear the sudden shock out of it than to say no.

"Capital!" said Heller. "So I'm calling in the debt. Right now and tonight!" He laughed cheerfully and slapped me on the shoulder.

I knew what was coming next. Such a dinner includes the girls of the other officers and one's own girl if there are any around.

"So you," he said, "just have your airbus out there an hour after dark and we'll all fly away to some fine nightclub and you'll buy us a dinner! *That* will make peace and cheer you up!"

Hastily I said, "Wait. I can't go in uniform." I looked down at myself. Three weeks in the woods and a smelly uniform to begin with and I was a real wreck.

"Oh, think nothing of it!" said Heller. "Right at sunset, you come in here," and he pointed to an officer's cubicle, "and have yourself a nice bath and I'll have a civilian dinner suit all laid out for you."

He swatted me on the back. Very happy. "It's a date! I'm glad we can become friends again! See you at sunset!" And he walked off in good spirits.

The spirits I had were going into a power dive! I

didn't have a credit to my name. My identoplate was worthless on any check. If I tried to pass these counterfeits, I'd be promptly arrested and executed. He supposed I would be solvent as most officers would be—money is not that important to them. But he could have done nothing worse to my morale.

I had a thought. There were silver rails and latches, there were even gold vases and plates behind the airtight door at the passage end.

I tiptoed down and said, "Open" in every voice pitch I could manage.

It stayed shut! "OPen! ohPEN! open! OPEN, (BLEEP) IT!"

A workman up in the flight deck yelled down, "Are you calling me?"

I got out of there.

Maybe I could arrange a convincing air crash before tonight. Maybe from ten thousand feet free fall! That was all I could possibly afford.

Chapter 2

At nine o'clock that fatal night, the Countess Krak was smuggled out of the tug in a riot helmet and gas cape while Snelz and his guardsmen studiously paid attention only to their dice game in a corner of the darkened hangar.

The windows of the airbus were darkened. My driver was nowhere to be seen.

Heller stopped by the dice game and said something

to Snelz and then came sauntering over to the vehicle and slid back of the wheelstick.

I sat there in back, unaccustomed to being so clean and outright uncomfortable in the sparkling one-piece dinner suit. I was trying to look calm but actually I was quite terrified to be sitting so near the Countess Krak.

The airbus vaulted into the night, speeding up to try to match the way Heller drives.

The Countess got out of her riot helmet and cape and straightened her hair. And indeed she looked very lovely: her face perfection itself, her tresses like a halo, her dinner gown a pale, pale orange, the kind with the ripple lights that pulsate to the cadence of the female's speech. Her eyes were sparkling, as innocent as a child's. How looks can deceive—I hoped I could get through this without her killing me for some fault in grammar or table manners. Gods knew what might happen when she found I couldn't pay the bill.

"Oh, Soltan!" she said. "You've got a new skyjumper! And all polished up!" She leaned back luxuriously on the circular settee, her gorgeous body stretching like a cat's. She twitched her pale, pale gold boots. "You like my new boots?"

As she spoke the boots pulsated light. I edged away. I knew her footwork. Deadly!

Heller had unblinded the windows and the last twinkling panorama of Voltar's specialist cities spread out beneath the stars. The streaks of early evening traffic made intricate patterns below. I was caught off base for a moment. It was a glorious night.

And then I saw we were headed in the wrong direction! Had I been decoyed into an escape? We were not heading for Joy City! We were heading for Pausch Hills!

"Aren't you on a wrong course?" I said to Heller up in front. "There aren't any nightclubs in Pausch. There's only the filthy rich!"

Heller laughed, not even looking back. He had the airbus up to five hundred. Thank heavens the new one didn't shake. Maybe, hopefully, it was rated for five hundred. "We're going to pick you up a dinner companion!" he said. "Can't have a solitary male sitting about spoiling the party even if he is the host!"

Oh, my Gods. I couldn't pay for the three of us, much less four. And any female that resided in Pausch Hills would be the extremely expensive kind. The forecast of the evening's bill suddenly soared.

The skyscrapers of Pausch are set amongst artificial streams and lakes, pumped at vast expense up the hills. It is a fascinating panorama at night. The more expensive homes are, however, on top of the skyscrapers. And in renewed alarm, I saw we were not landing at any front door, we were heading for a domed home which had two acres of grounds of its own right on top of the tallest structure. From it one could see vast views or just pretend the gardens limited it to its own solitary world. Expensive!

What kind of a female would live there? One that could spend a junior officer's whole year's pay on a box of sparklepowder! My estimate of the bill to come soared again!

Heller said a code word into a microphone. The lights of the home and gardens went out. What an absence of security and espionage sense. The sudden vanishment of those lights would call attention to the place from miles around.

He landed lightly on the garden flight target.

A hooded and cloaked figure sped out from under a darkened tree and sprang into the airbus.

The door slammed. We zipped into the night sky.

The new passenger laughed a beautiful laugh. "What fun!" She threw off the hood and cloak.

My Gods, it was Hightee Heller! His sister! The most known face on all Voltar. And although my spirits drooped at this new incautious development, her beauty was enough to turn a stone statue into quivering desire. She was wearing a dark blue shimmergown, a contrast with her pale skin and hair but almost matching her lovely eyes. One glance at such as Hightee Heller and any male swallowed convulsively several times.

I had enough courage to warn both Heller and the Countess Krak that they must not use her name to anyone. We hit upon her mother's name, Lindus. I hoped Heller would have brains enough to remember it during introductions.

"Hightee," he called back, "that is your dinner companion, Officer Soltan Gris. And this is *the* girl! We will call her 'Lindus' for now."

Hightee was settling herself on the settee. She gave me a nod, probably used to Heller's numerous friends. Then she looked searchingly at the Countess Krak. Heller, (bleep) him, even turned up the interior lights so she could.

"Jettie," said his sister. "*You* have the finest taste in all the world!"

The Countess Krak beamed!

The girls lightly touched hands.

"My, my!" said Hightee, still impressed.

Devils and Gods, I groaned to myself. This woman you are talking to and complimenting your brother about is a condemned murderess, released illegally only for a brief time, from the dungeons of Spiteos! Hightee, you might be the most beautiful woman on Voltar but you are a complete fool!

"You look like a Manco lady," said Hightee.

"She is," Heller called back. "Her people once owned property in Atalanta."

"Do I know your family?" asked Hightee pleasantly.

"I don't think so," said the Countess Krak. "They lost their property centuries ago. Like so many, they kept their title and don't even have the square yard of land to erect a tombstone."

The girls laughed over this. It was apparently some local Manco joke.

"From your accent, I'd say the family kept their nobility quite well!" said Hightee. I wondered what she was doing. She sounded like a marriage contractor. And then it dawned on me that Heller must have been on the communication lines to his sister and from her type of interest he must have told her—oh, my Gods—that he wanted her to meet the girl he was going to marry! The difficulties this presented almost spun my wits.

"Not really," sighed the Countess. "My mother had considerable skill in training animals. Her family estates were forest estates and the skill runs in the blood. My father really fell from grace. He became a stage magician. They toured all over Manco and even on some other planets." She laughed. "I'm afraid I share your stage background, Hightee. My first appearance was at the age of six months when I was part of an act where I was supposed to be eaten by a *savabeast,* only to magically reappear riding him at the act's end."

Hightee laughed with delight. Then she seemed to be thinking of something, trying to remember. Oh my Gods, I thought. Show people are show people. They remember everything! The Countess had messed it all up!

Hightee suddenly smacked her hands together. "The Crystals! The Crystals!"

The Countess was stupid. She laughed and bobbed

her head in assent. "The same! That was their act's name."

"Then your father was Count Krak!" crowed Hightee. "And your mother was Ailaena! Why, she was the greatest wild beast trainer of all time! Absolutely fearless!"

I expected Hightee to say something about remembering there was a daughter, a daughter called Lissus Moam, a daughter that went to the university and became part of the Education Division and taught children to rob banks and murder.

But Hightee said, "Oh, that was a great act! I am so pleased to know you. It keeps the talent in the family!" This last completely spun me. In what family? Then I knew for sure that Heller intended to marry the Countess Krak! Impossible!

But Hightee had settled it all. She patted the Countess's hand affectionately and then called out to Heller, "Where are you taking us at such speed?" But without waiting for an answer, she said, in an aside to the Countess, "Jettie just knows two speeds: wide-open throttle and wide-open throttle. You'll have to get used to it, dear. He *is* a darling."

Heller laughed at her aside. "Listen to the little girl who used to egg me on to go faster! We're going to the Artistic Club!"

"Oh, dear!" said Hightee. "Isn't that right on Club Row? Right at the end of a whole square of clubs? There are always reporters hanging about there, hoping some celebrity will drop in. I was wishing for some quiet nook."

My sentiments exactly. I warmed to her.

"Soltan chose the Artistic Club," said Heller. Then he laughed before I could protest. "Actually it was chosen because everyone wears party masks there. You can't possibly be recognized. The masks should be right there in a box."

So they were. I pulled them over. There were four masks. They were the kind that are sheet-backed: the type you just press onto your face, pull the heater string and the paint transfers over onto the skin. The easiest type of mask there is, the paint rinses right off. I inspected them. My driver must have chosen them. They were lettered *S.G.*, *J.H.*, *H.H.* and *C.K.* Not much choosing to do so I passed them out.

Much to my surprise, the new airbus had mirrors above the settee and the girls started arranging their hair out of the way.

There is a small picture on the back of what the mask looks like and all of a sudden, Hightee said to me, "Oh, why did you have to choose the sexy wood nymph for me! I know I have been playing the lewd female in my last three pictures. In fact I've had to learn so many sexy songs, I hardly know any other current ones than those. But I should have thought you would have chosen the sweet nymph mask all the same."

(Bleep) my driver.

She put it in place and pulled the heater cord. She discarded the backing into the box and then looked back at herself and laughed. "I'm really no male-eater. But I sure look like one now!" The eyes were languorous looking, the mouth was pursed in a huge kiss, the cheeks were blue, symbolizing longing. It made her look even prettier. Nothing could disguise the beauty of Hightee Heller. I felt uneasy. It was not much of a recognition preventer!

The Countess had hers on now. The huge, luminous eyes, way too big, a black and orange fur. The lepertige lady! As if she needed any hint of her actual dangerousness! But at least it was a good disguise. And it went with her pale orange dress and boots.

Heller, flying with one knee and one toe, put his on. I recognized it in the glass reflection of the windscreen. It was a character known in plays as the steelman: just two huge steel stars, one over each eye. Hardly any disguise at all. His pictures had been in the papers a lot. I was nervous.

They pushed at me to put on my own mask. Yes, my driver must have chosen it. It was the standard character known as the bucktoothed Demon! Frightfully ugly! Ske has no taste at all.

They laughed at each other's masks and at mine and then Hightee and the Countess began to chat amiably about the stage and Manco. It was obvious to see they were immediate fast friends.

The glitter and writhing coils of searchlight beams were ahead. Even in Joy City, this block of clubs stood out. I cringed a bit. This sure was public! Lombar's shadow seemed to loom over the scene. What was I getting into? Had I had any sense at all, I would have sabotaged that airbus while I still had time! Too late now. I was going down the chute into the pit of bad luck.

Chapter 3

Heller zipped the airbus down like he rode a crane hook. I was blinded by the writhing lights and don't know how he did it but the airbus landed as soft as the falling feather of a songbird squarely in the center of the club's vehicle escalator. The girls danced out and I would have followed them in but saw that Heller was still standing there on the ramp. He was watching the air-bus and kept on watching it until he saw exactly where the escalator side arm thrust it. He took note of the position and then turned to the door.

The Artistic Club front was much like the other club fronts facing the square—all rippling lights and letters that threw colored sparks.

The girls had fled off to the ladies room to recheck their masks the way girls will. Right in the entrance stood some club floorman in a white evening suit. He had his hand slightly out. I knew what was required. He wanted a five-credit note to escort us to one of the better tables! And, completely aside from a five-credit note, I had no notes at all other than these counterfeits! I stopped walking forward right there!

Heller said, "I'm going to the men's room to adjust my mask." And there I stood facing the wild animal—which I conceived this floorman to be—barehanded!

It was not the first hair-raiser of that evening!

Then, for some reason I did not understand, another floorman—the manager?—was beckoning to me from deeper within the club and I hastened on by the itching palm.

Heller was there in a moment and presently the girls came out and the manager? led us into the main club.

The evening was just beginning but most of the tables were already full. Masks, masks, masks, all types and shapes and kinds, a blur of hidden identities.

A blare of loud music!

Boots, boots, boots. Every color of boot anyone ever heard of and the underfloor circulating lights rippled and splashed upon them.

Tables, tables, tables. The manager led us to one, slightly raised, against a wall. I quickly checked. It was also near an emergency exit.

We sat down and looked across the club. There was a bandstand and stage over there. And to the right was an open dance floor flanked at the back by drop curtains.

A balladess, not a very good one, was standing in front of the band, black-faced, red-teared and wailing her heart out.

I wondered where the club prices were posted. Even though I couldn't pay them, I still would like to know. Then I saw that they were under the table-face. One pushed a button to light the table-face up but even with the button unpushed one could see the letters and figures. I got an impression of five- and ten-credit items! Columns of them! Nothing less than five or ten credits a person an item in this place? Ow!

The balladess was finished and there was a spattering of applause. She went back to her table and party.

A man stood up and marched out onto the dance floor. He took some hoops out of his evening suit, appeared to light them and then began to juggle them. One would have thought he would have burned his hands but it was just simulated fire.

"This is why they call it the Artistic Club," Heller was telling the Countess. "Everybody who comes here must do an act. It goes on all night."

"Don't some of them get stage fright?" I said.

"The management thought of that," said Heller. "They keep count and if any single person at a table backs out, the bill for the whole table is doubled!"

"What a funny idea," said the Countess. And she was laughing. I wasn't! Even though I couldn't pay the bill in the first place, the thought of doubling horrified me.

"I'm hungry," said Hightee.

And as host I had to ask politely, "What would you like?"

Heller beckoned over a yellow-man waiter. He pushed the table button and the tabletop lit up, amazingly with the menu vertical and straight before each guest.

I felt like I was dying when I saw all those five- and ten-credit items! I made my throat behave. "Order away," I said gaily. It sounded more like a funeral dirge.

They all decided to have mountain springers—the small game animal imported from Chimpton, a whole planet away. Prohibitive! Ten credits a plate!

After solemn deliberation, they elected to have red bubblebrew. At ten credits the canister!

Then they decided on flaming icecake for dessert! At fifteen credits each!

My lightning fast ability to calculate put it at one hundred and five credits!

The management threw in toasted drybuns for nothing. How nice of them! They must be the most expensive club on Voltar!

I let them order me the same. I might as well be cashiered or executed on a full stomach. For my choice was either to use my identoplate and be court-martialled or use the counterfeit money I carried and be executed!

The mountain springer came and I picked at it, expecting perhaps to find diamonds imbedded in it.

Heller whispered to me, "Don't look so worried. It'll be all right. Have a good time. Don't spoil it for the girls."

A lot *he* knew! This (bleeping) party of mine was going to ruin me. But then I remembered that a lot of other officers, faced with promotion parties, had had to starve a month or two. I drank my canister of red bubblebrew. But none of that made me feel any better.

They chattered and joked and seemed to enjoy the dinner immensely. I did eat. I was hungry.

When the last flicker of icecake fire had disappeared

down their throats, Heller signalled a hovering yellow-man and ordered another round of red bubblebrew! That made it one hundred and eighty credits!

They drank to clear skies and bright stars. They drank to success and more promotions. They drank to a not-thinly-veiled "mission." They drank to Hightee's next play.

Heller ordered another round of red bubblebrew! Two hundred and twenty credits!

They all sat back now, watching the other guests perform. Some were good, some were bad, some got a little applause, some got quite a bit.

I had just settled into a kind of stupor. The inevitability of my two choices weighed me down. It couldn't be any worse.

And then it was!

A light was flash-flash-flashing at our table. Hightee poked me in the shoulder. "You're first from this table."

"Me?"

"Of course," said Hightee with a smile. "And you'd better put on a good act!" She laughed. "If you don't perform, they double the bill!"

The whole table thought this screamingly funny. It must have been the red bubblebrew! To me it was sheer tragedy.

I nervously rose to my feet to go out and be slaughtered by the mob.

Chapter 4

I had been impelled into this action by the threat of a doubled bill. Three-quarters of the way to the stage, I realized that it was a double of something I couldn't pay the single of. What was I doing here?

Bravery in the face of mobs is something I do not understand. How an actor or singer or dancer can actually stand up there *alone* and look at an audience that is looking at him is quite beyond my comprehension.

On the stage, I turned to look. A huge, glaring spotlight was practically putting my eyes out. Adrift and disembodied were the masks, masks, masks, all pointed in my direction. And below it were the boots, boots, boots, stamping in a colored rippling haze of lights, ready, I was sure, to kick the daylights out of me.

What if they all rushed at me at once and started mangling me?

In other words, I had stage fright.

It had been half-formed in my mind that I would recite a poem. When I was a child, I had been taught some poems. "The Brave Hec at the Battle of the Blim" was one of them I had been praised for when I was six. I opened my mouth. For the life of me I couldn't think of the first line!

Hastily, I reviewed, all in a flash, any anecdotes I knew. There was one about two Apparatus agents who each thought the other one was a female until they wound up in bed. I opened my mouth to start to tell it.

Ulp, the last thing I could mention here was the Apparatus!

My knees shook. The audience was getting restive. The huge spotlight glared pitilessly. My buck-toothed Demon mask seemed to be melting.

Abruptly, I had an inspiration. Naturally, a hunter of songbirds uses their calls. I was pretty good at it. I could lure them within a few feet before I shot them.

In a voice I intended to sound bold, but which came out quivering, I said, "The mountain thriller!"

My mouth was awfully dry. But I got my lips pursed. I actually got the birdcall going.

Silence from the audience.

"The meadow warbler!" I said. And I gave the call of that bird.

Silence from the audience.

"The marsh hen!" I said. And I gave the somewhat raucous squawk of the marsh hen.

Silence from the audience. Not even a patter of applause. Nothing!

I thought furiously. I could not remember any more calls. Either the audience thought there were more or were waiting for me to do handstands or backflips or something.

Suddenly their silence made me very cross. I glared at them. I said, accusatively, "Well, the birds like it!"

There was an instant *storm* of laughter! They pounded their boots, they held their sides. They laughed and laughed and laughed!

I scuttled back to our table. The audience was still laughing. Hightee patted my sleeve, "I thought you were very brave."

The next person on had a sonic-light drum and juggled it while playing it. When he got through, the audience shouted at him, "Did the birds like it?" There were screams of laughter.

A girl, a singer, was on next and when she finished, the audience again called out, "Did the birds like it?" And more screams of laughter.

A man who rolled a barrel with his feet finished and the audience also asked him, "Did the birds like it?"

"You were a hit," said Hightee.

I began to realize I must have been and was even starting to feel cocky. A new round of bubblebrew didn't even make me wince.

But ah, how short-lived are the infrequent moments of happiness in life. I tipped my head back to drink and I saw it!

A press balcony!

It was up above the crowd, jutting out into the room. There were three reporters there and, oh Gods, a Home-view camera crew!

Hightee followed my riveted stare. "Oh," she said, shrugging it off, "they cover this club a lot. They are spotting talent, looking for something new. They also pick up what we call filler time: they never use it unless the event day has been totally dead." She laughed, "I think the newssheets just hang around here so they won't have to go to work!"

Any cheer I had been feeling was gone. If there is anything detested in the Apparatus, it is reporters and if there is anything more detested than that, it is reporters with cameras! Lombar was quite violent on the subject. "The victims have no right to know," was one of his favorite sayings. His specter seemed to loom closer in the outside dark.

And then the light beam which designated the next performer was on our table again. Hightee shrank back.

Heller touched the Countess on the arm and they rose.

Lightly, they trotted toward the open dance floor, the Countess in her shimmering pale orange and leper-tige mask, Heller in a glittering powder blue evening suit and steelman stars huge over his eyes. The spotlight shift-ed and picked them up.

The Countess held up her hand. To her right there was a serving table. It had tall bubblebrew bottles on it. It was cluttered with frail canisters. These all sat on a big square of white glittercloth. She moved to this rickety display. She took one corner of the cloth. I thought she was going to pull the table over! With a flip of her wrist, she gave an expert yank!

The cloth simply came out from under with a swish. It was dangling in her hand. Not one bottle or canister had even quivered!

The audience must have thought that was the act. They applauded lightly.

But it sure wasn't the act. The Countess called some-thing to the band. The pair had reached the center of the dance floor now. The Countess floated the big square of white glittercloth in the air: it was about a yard from corner to corner, diagonally. She folded it with an expert flip. She stuck one corner of it between Heller's teeth and took the opposite corner in her own. Their faces were now about six inches apart.

The band began a frivolous, folksy tune. Heller and the Countess put their hands behind their backs and with an intricate pattern of footwork, began to dance.

"The Manco Mancho!" said Hightee with delight. She patted her hands together in a little girl's expression of joy. "Watch this," she nudged me. "It's the nursery folk dance of Manco! They would both know it of course!"

Each of them biting a corner of the cloth, they grave-ly executed the geometric steps in perfect unison and time.

Suddenly at the end of a music bar, their teeth drop-ped a fold in the cloth and their faces were a foot apart. The music continued. But now they weren't following each other's steps. In sweeping foot motions, alternately, one seemed to be kicking the feet out from under the other one but the other one was in the air when the foot passed under. Back and forth.

Hightee was looking a little bewildered. The dance was suddenly much more complex. "That isn't the Manco Mancho!"

And indeed, it wasn't. It was the first elementary exercise of foot combat, timed and made to look like a dance! I thought, they better not get too good. That Homeview camera up there is right on them! The last thing we wanted here was an identified Heller, much less the Countess Krak!

There was a patter of applause from the audience. I gritted, fall down or something, blow it, don't get your-selves on Homeview!

At the end of a music phrase, there was a pop. They had let go another corner of their cloth. Still biting it, they were now a yard apart.

Heller must have given her a signal. They went over onto their heads! They each gave a half-turn and were now back to back, still connected by the cloth in their teeth! Upside down, on their heads and hands, they began to beat the soles of each other's feet together in rhythm!

The audience applauded! Not so good!

And then, exactly at a measure end, they each vault-ed upward, did a half-right in the middle of the same flip and were right side up face to face!

Gymnastics adapted to a dance. The audience had never seen such a thing. They applauded even stronger. Up in the press balcony, the Homeview crew was really working hard! Awful!

How he did it, I don't know, as his teeth were clamped on the cloth, but Heller yelled a signal to the bandmaster.

And then began the most skilled thing I think I have ever seen in acts! There is an exercise in unarmed combat that consists of kicking in a circular sweep at the opponent's head. The opponent cartwheels to avoid. But this crazy pair, connected with a yard long cloth held in their teeth, began to do it alternately and repetitively!

Slowly at first, one kicking, the other cartwheeling, then the one who cartwheeled doing it, back and forth, they began to go faster and faster.

Suddenly I realized they were no longer touching the floor with their hands!

The music went faster and faster. The kicks and turns got faster and faster.

And then they were just two blurs! One orange and one blue, just two spinning discs connected with a cloth!

The audience went crazy! They jumped to their feet cheering! They had never seen gymnastics and unarmed combat turned into a dance!

The band couldn't play any faster.

Then smoothly and very gracefully, the two blurs stopped. The band played a long note. Heller and the Countess Krak were apart. The glittercloth was held in the Countess's left hand. Heller was bowing.

I thought that was all there was. So did the audience. They were applauding and shouting.

"Oh, she *has* had stage experience," said Hightee near my ear. For the Countess was doing the two steps to the right and two steps to the left with the bow between, the formal performer acceptance of audience acclaim. It is a little sort of dance they do, very pretty to look at. She was holding the glittercloth in her left hand and it was flicking and glittering.

Abruptly the Countess was GONE!

She didn't walk away. She didn't even shimmer. Where she had been bowing an instant before was just empty space! The audience gave a gasp of indrawn breath, startled. I was more than startled. A prisoner had escaped!

The square of glittercloth floated down to the floor.

I think Heller was actually surprised. He certainly looked it!

He stared at the glittercloth. He drew back and got down on all fours. He stealthily approached the cloth. He covertly lifted one corner and peeked under it. He drew back, shaking his head. Then he seemed to make up his mind.

He pounced on the cloth! He went into a scramble around it to be sure to contain whatever might be in it. Carefully, he rose to his feet holding it.

The dumbest audience member could not fail to see he was looking for his vanished partner in that cloth.

Standing now, he unfolded it with care. The audience was beginning to giggle. He didn't find anything and in perplexity shook the cloth out. He looked on the floor to see if anything had dropped. He stood dejected. The audience roared with laughter.

Heller threw the cloth away and with some determination advanced upon the nearest table. He looked under it with no result. He looked under a canister. He found nothing. He looked under a plate. He found nothing. Then, with obvious sudden inspiration, he picked a funny hat off the top of a customer's head and looked in it.

The audience screamed with laughter.

There was a thump beside me. Startled, I looked sideways. There in the dimness, grinning, sat the Countess Krak.

Heller, defeated, looked in his own sleeves. Then he looked over at our table and with a sweep of his arm directed the light handler to throw his spotlight toward the table.

The audience saw her. They were silent for an instant and then there were cries of incredulity followed by a storm of applause!

The Countess bobbed up and bowed. Heller came back to the table. The audience attention shifted reluctantly to another act.

"How'd you do it?" asked Hightee, her professionalism alert.

The Countess laughed. "See that hanging drape back of the stage? I just drew the attention of the audience to the waving cloth, then did what they call a fast side kick and went behind the drape. I crossed behind the stage, crawled on my hands and knees along that wall back of the tables and did a front flip into this seat. Easy."

Heller wasn't even breathing hard and neither was the Countess. Heller ordered another round of bubblebrew. I'd lost count of the tab now. But dead men can't count. I looked up at the Homeview crew and they were all grinning.

The outside specter of Lombar had one foot in the nightclub.

Chapter 5

I looked at these two idiots. They were sitting there now, sipping out of each other's canisters, laughing, keeping Hightee included in. They were very beautiful people. They did not know that Lombar could order both of them killed without a second thought if he had no further use for them. And certainly would if they threatened any kind of exposure to the Apparatus activities on Blito-P3. There was no way to tell them.

The music played, the acts went on.

Suddenly the beam was on our table again. "Oh, no," said Hightee. "I hoped they would miscalculate. I'm all that's left at this table." She stood up. "Never mind, Soltan. They won't double your bill. I'll go sing for my supper."

She threaded her way between the tables to the stage. No one paid her very much attention, due to the number of acts that went on and off. She jumped up on the platform, her blue dress glittering. She said something to the bandmaster. He turned and said something to one of his musicians and the fellow reached back into a pile of instruments and handed one out.

It was the electronic half-globe they call "the chorder-beat." It is about eighteen inches in diameter. Hightee put the curved side of it against her stomach and then buckled it expertly behind her back. She took the "beater" in her right hand. By poising the spread fingers of the left hand over the chorder-beat in different positions and distances, one gets chords, usually enharmonic. By gesturing and sort of hitting in the air with the beater in the right hand, one makes the chords pound out a rhythm. They make a wild, sinuous, suggestive sort of music when they are properly played.

Hightee said something to the bandmaster. He looked a bit surprised. Then he looked at her more closely.

I thought, oh, my Gods, he has recognized her! Either through her voice or the song she'd asked for. I almost jumped up and screamed at her to come back to the table. I didn't. I glanced at that Homeview camera crew. They seemed to be at ease. So did the reporters.

The blinding spotlight turned on her full. Her blue evening dress threw sparks. Her sexy wood nymph mask sucked up attention. She raised her right hand. The bandmaster took it as his cue and watched it to get the beat.

Spraaaang! went the chorder-beat. *Yow-yow!* went the band.

For the first full melody she played and did not sing. And it was sexy! Her body swayed and curved, her left hand seemed to be indicating something else than chords. Her right hand writhed to the beat. It was SEXY!

Audience attention was almost electric in the air. The way that chorder-beat was playing, the way that performer swayed, they knew they were looking at a polished professional. It seemed to stun them. There wasn't another sound in that nightclub except the band and Hightee's chorder-beat.

She started the melody again and this time, she sang. Her voice was a throaty, sexy lure. But it had comedy in it.

> *There once was a man when I was young,*
> *Who said he knew a foreign tongue,*
> *He'd teach me!*

"Oh, my Gods!" a man cried out. "It's Hightee Heller!"

A ruffle of music and chords from Hightee. A high-pitched scream from the audience. "Hightee! It's Hightee Heller!" Bedlam!

> *He said it went a funny way,*
> *A thing the ancients used to say.*
> *He'd teach me!*

A ruffle of chords. Sexy sways. Even above this growing bedlam in the nightclub I heard a yell outside, "Hightee Heller is in there!"

> *It'd need, he claimed, a very soft bed,*
> *A place where he could lay my head,*
> *To teach me!*

The Homeview crew was grinding it out! There were shouts outside the building. Had the word spread, were the other night clubs emptying? Yes! A mob was pouring in the door! And this club audience was on its feet surging forward!

> *So we found a place we could repose,*
> *And he removed my underclothes,*
> *To teach me!*

"Hightee! Hightee Heller!" Bedlam of bedlams!

> *And so we got down to the song,*
> *He kept it up so very long,*
> *He taught me!*

They had turned the loudspeakers up to get her voice above the ear-shattering racket of the surging crowd.

> *Hija, hoopah, jiggety plow,*
> *Lecheroo, pokeroo, pow, pow, pow!*
> *Hourly, too!*

The place was a screaming jam, filling up, people at the front of the stage were trying to climb up on it, all of them yelling! "Hightee! Hightee! Hightee Heller!"

Up went the loudspeaker volume again.

> *The language is not hard to learn,*
> *And I invite you, if you yearn,*
> *To be taught!*

The music riff. Hands reaching for her, people getting on the stage! Heller on his feet, pushing his way forward to the stage to keep her from being mauled! The glaring spotlight, the busy Homeview crew!

> *Hija, hoopah, jiggety plow.*

They had shoved her back against the band. Dozens

of hands were trying to touch her. She was engulfed! Heller was through the mob and to her.

Pokeroo, lecheroo, pow, pow, pow!

She was still playing and singing!

Heller was to her. He lifted her high in the air above the mob and clutching hands.

Come see me!

It was at that exact moment that I pulled my handgun, flipped it to needle blast and with one expert twitch of the trigger, shot out the main spotlight.

I didn't do it to help Heller. I did it because, back of the mob and coming straight toward me was a yellow-man, holding in his hand what could only be the bill!

The explosion of filaments was deafening.

I spun. I had already spotted the main switchboard back of the dance platform. With unerring aim, I blasted it to bits! It was totally dark.

Above the deafening din of the crowd a new scream sounded, "Police! It's the police!"

Dim emergency lights came on. Sure enough, I saw a flicker of blue. Police plowing through the crowd, baton charging the riot!

A firm hand grabbed my collar and I was yanked out of the booth so fast I flew horizontally. I was being dragged across the floor.

The emergency exit door banged open! I was being dragged up the alley! I could barely hold on to my gun.

We were at the airbus. The door opened and I was

hurtled inside. And only then did I see who had dragged me. It was the Countess Krak!

I looked back anxiously toward the emergency exit. Sound and lights were bursting through it out into the alley.

There came Heller! He was still holding his sister high over his head.

Behind them came a solid wave of blue! Oh, my Gods, the police were right on their heels!

The Countess Krak sprang into the airbus and batted me to one side!

Heller arrived at the door. He launched his sister inside and the Countess Krak caught her expertly and put her on the settee.

Heller slid fast under the wheelstick.

A police helmet right at his door. A face.

"We'll be at the hangar ahead of you, Jet. We're all clear!"

It was Snelz! Snelz in a cop uniform!

The airbus sprang into the air!

We had fought free!

Perhaps it was because Hightee Heller was laughing fit to burst—it takes steel nerves to be a celebrity in the Confederation. Perhaps it was because I was still a bit high on bubblebrew. But I felt a bit elated. By not paying the bill I had escaped being cashiered on the one hand for bankruptcy or executed on the other for passing counterfeit money. And nobody but Hightee had been recognized, I supposed, and Hightee wouldn't matter. What luck!

We stopped at Hightee's garden in the clouds. She unstrapped the chorder-beat and Heller said he'd get it returned to the club for her. She kissed each of them on the cheek and touched my hand.

She stood for a moment under the darkened trees

and called back, "Thank you for a wonderful evening. Good luck, you two! And Jet! I really *approve!*" She was gone.

On the way back to the Apparatus hangar, we were given a routine challenge by night sky surveillance and I had to reach over and catch Heller's hand: he was automatically reaching for his own identoplate and I gave him mine. We mustn't leave a trace of identity on this night!

We landed at the hangar. The guardsmen's air-transport was parked there. Snelz and his men were sitting around in the dim hangar depths, chuckling and drinking a late snack. The Countess slipped out in her helmet and gas cape and sped to the tug.

Heller still sat under the wheelstick. My driver was coming toward us with some big boxes and Heller was waiting for him. The driver wasn't moving very fast so Heller turned to me in the back.

"I think I owe you a bit of an apology," he said. "I didn't realize this afternoon that I was forcing your promotion party on you at an inopportune moment.

"You don't have to go back there tomorrow to pay your check. When we arrived and the floorman held out his hand for payment to get us a good table, I couldn't help but see you flinch. I realized you must be broke and that pushing the party off on you came under the heading of a dirty trick.

"So I slipped into the manager's office and grabbed him and put my identoplate on a blank dinner check."

I think my heart stopped beating.

"I couldn't tell you straight out in front of the waiters and the girls but I passed the message to you a couple of times that it was cared for. I didn't want your evening spoiled."

Ske was there now with the boxes and Heller told

him to return the comedy cop uniforms to the party costumer tomorrow and take the chorder-beat back to the club at the same time.

He got out and called back to me, "It was a great party. I hope you did enjoy it. Good night!"

He was gone.

I knew what that identoplate would spell. It would hit the newssheets and Homeview. The Grand Council would know we had not left.

They would be all over Endow.

Lombar would be all over me! It might even imperil Lombar's whole Blito-P3 hidden operations!

A sudden surge of rage hit me. I felt like killing Heller!

I was instantly sick at my stomach.

Chapter 6

After a night of nightmares, burdened with an aching head, my upset stomach refusing even the thought of hot jolt, I sat, at noon the following day, on a pile of rusted hullplates, dully watching the almost unforgivable bustlings in the Apparatus hangar.

I was expecting the worst. I got something worse than the worst.

My driver, returning from the return of the comedy cop uniforms and the chorder-beat, walked over to me. From his smug smile, I should have been more prepared.

He didn't hand me the headache pills I had requested him to get. He did not deliver any of the medicine

I had begged him to bring back for my stomach.

He simply dropped the newssheet in my lap. He walked away and I was left to suffer over it alone.

There was a huge photo of Heller holding Hightee high above the crushing crowd! Somehow the lighting made the steelman stars vanish and it was Heller, recognizable, vivid, unmistakable!

The story was not some back-page filler that might be missed. It was headlines!

GUNSHOTS IMPERIL LIFE OF HIGHTEE HELLER!

FAMED BROTHER RESCUES HV STAR FROM FLYING BLASTS

RIOT POLICE BRAVE STORM OF HOSTILE SHOTS

ENRAGED MOB SEEKS POSSIBLE ASSASSIN

Last night at the Artistic Club in Joy City, a routine fan orgy of worship for Hightee Heller, Voltar's most popular Homeview star, was turned into a riot of blazing guns and charging battle police when an unknown maniac, using military multiblast weapons, threatened the lives of thousands.

Braving the avalanche of deadly fire, Jettero Heller, Royal officer and famed combat engineer, with superhuman strength, lifted his sister out of the path of the deadly hail.

Battle police, in a baton charge, fought furiously to establish order, suffering an unknown number of casualties.

By purest chance, a Homeview camera team, that visits the Artistic Club routinely, recorded part of the riot and has been beaming it continuously since 3:00 A.M. on the interplanetary Homeview all-home channels.

Interviewed at dawn in her home on Pausch Hills, Hightee Heller, with the true courage of an artist, disclaimed personal injury. "Please assure my billions of fans that I am perfectly all right," was the only comment she would make. But this reporter detected possible eye bruises.

Jettero Heller could not be found or interviewed. It had been generally believed that he was engaged in a secret mission for the Grand Council and had long since departed Voltar. A spokesman for the Crown, contacted at dawn, attempted to refute the continued presence of Heller on Voltar, stating, "We have it on the most reliable authority that Jettero Heller left Voltar some time ago. The matter will be brought before the Grand Council in its morning meeting."

Police Chief Chalp of Joy City modestly accepted credit for bringing the riot under such swift control. "My men are everywhere," he said. "They are always ready for anything."

> When this reporter suggested that the riot might have been a publicity stunt, arranged to bring higher recognition to the Artistic Club, the manager angrily pointed out that he had no faintest knowledge that Jettero Heller or his sister were in the club last night and that, in any event, he would never dream of imperilling the life of the idol of billions.
>
> The gang who shot up the club have not been traced.
>
> (See our special features, today and tomorrow: HIGHTEE HELLER, HUMAN OR GODDESS? and THE LIFE AND TIMES OF JETTERO HELLER, THE MODEST HERO WHO BECAME THE IDOL OF THE FLEET.)

I sat there numbly. They had it all wrong. I was not a *gang!* I was just one man.

It was all Snelz's fault, I finally worked out. If he hadn't made that silly pact with Heller to be at all times on duty, guarding, he would never have rented those comedy cop uniforms just so he could be handy. Snelz was too conscientious. Just because he had heard shots, glass breaking and screams was no reason to believe Heller needed any help. The idea of charging in for a silly thing like that! Snelz had caused all this. I realized I would have to discipline him.

But the very futility of doing anything at all settled over me. I was just a chip of wood in the roaring river of fate. It would do no good to point out that they were all secretly against me.

I just sat there and waited for the axe to fall, finally, completely and forever. Numb.

In midafternoon, I hardly even stirred when a big lorry drove up to the hangar. The signs on it said:

Educational Aids Company.
Delight your students even if they are children.
Entertainment is the backbone of Enlightenment.

Two laborers got down from the truck and boosted a long box out of the back.

Somebody called for Heller and he came down from the top of the hull where they had been restoring plates and shielding and trotted over to the newcomers. He was all bright and alert, red racing cap on the back of his head. A lot *he* knew about the sorrows of life. The axe was hanging over him, too. The thought vaguely cheered me but I soon slumped again under renewed pains in my stomach.

He directed them to carry the box in through the airlock. I knew where it was going: into that lower hold storeroom.

Half an hour after that, I still had not stirred. I dully watched a new lorry drive up. It said:

Mineral Resources Equipment Company.
If you think our equipment is too expensive,
buy some and manufacture your own purchase
price. Sold only under government license
to qualified and discriminating metalologists.

Two laborers got out and took down a long, heavy box. Heller showed them where to put it in the ship.

I sat there waiting. I knew it would come and it would not be boxes.

Finally it was there. I felt it. Sort of like an infusion of black poison gas into the scene.

A voice from behind a pile of crates: a horrible whisper.

"Officer Gris."

Chapter 7

Lombar Hisst, disguised as a workman, lurked half-hidden behind the dirty cases.

His awful face was intent upon what he was doing. He had a notebook in his hands. From his secret place, he had a view of the tug and the swarms of contractor teams that clambered all around and over it. In their company-colored cover suits, each one bore plainly the different contractor names. Lombar Hisst was listing them, each and every company.

I came up and stood trembling near him. With an abrupt motion he swept a copy of the newssheet out of his workman jacket and whacked it into my face. I caught it. I didn't have to read it. It was another newssheet, a different one but it had the same glaring picture of Heller holding his sister over his head above the crowd.

Lombar had gone back to his furious notebook writing. Eventually he was done. He yanked me back into the cover of the crates.

"You loathsome (bleep)!" he said. "I should shoot you out of hand right now!" He slapped his hand back against the notebook. "All these contractors working, working at vast expense and here you are, keeping it secret so that you can rake off all their kickbacks for yourself!"

I hadn't expected that. It was so unjust. If I had

tried to put the squeeze on any of these contractors they would have gone running to Heller and he, with his weird Royal officer ideas of honesty, would have beaten me up! But I didn't dare open my mouth.

"Well, what have you got to say for yourself?" demanded Lombar, amber eyes flaming crazily. He didn't expect any answer or wait for one. "It was (bleeped) lucky this was a Grand Council meeting day!

"The position you put us in! Right at the start, the Crown threw it at us! Oh, Endow is a fortunate fellow to have me. When the Crown demanded why Heller had not left, I was able to counter it, no thanks to you!

"I had Endow point out that the Grand Council allocation was so low that it was delaying the mission to Blito-P3. I used it to raise the allocation to thirty million credits instead of three. We can pretend there were other companies here that we own and you'll (bleep) well stamp the fake bills with your identoplate! Do you understand?"

All I understood was that I was not lying, that instant, a dead body at his feet. I was grateful.

"In return, you loathsome piece of trash, you are going to get this mission out of here by my deadline! We had to promise that! So be grateful!"

I was very grateful.

"What are those boxes I saw being hauled in?" he demanded. "He's got things there I am sure he's going to use to try to make this mission a success. You know very well it must fail. I have told you time and again we cannot possibly let it succeed."

He did not want any answer. He considered for a moment. Then he said, "Very well. In two days I will bring a special crew in here. You will distract Heller to some other place and we will inspect what he is taking."

Through a crack in the crates we could see the tug.

Heller slid down a rope and dropped lightly to the pavement. He beckoned and five Apparatus hangar people came over to him swiftly. They listened to him interestedly and laughed a couple of times and then sped off, quite unlike Apparatus personnel, to do what Heller had asked.

I glanced at Lombar. He had his upper lip raised in an expression of the purest hate. His eyes began to smolder. Under his breath he was muttering about "athletes" and "Royal officers" and "snobs," a stream of profanity mixed in. There was no doubt that he hated Heller and all his kind.

Lombar suddenly turned to me. "You are going to have crew trouble. That (bleepard) will get around them. He'll breed loyalty. He'll undermine your control of any crew unless I handle it." He thought for a moment. "Yes, yes, that will do it. *I'll* put the captain and crew aboard that tug the day she leaves."

For the first time, I found courage to speak. I squeaked, "She has Will-be Was main drives. She is very quick and sudden. She is a dangerous ship!"

"All the better," said Lombar. He had heard me! "Will-be Was main drives. That will be a little harder but I will find and fix up a crew!"

I was still gripping the newssheet. He snatched it back from me and put it in his pocket. "That's another thing. Have you heard any clues as to who leaked that original story about Heller and the mission? I thought not. I'm looking. I'm looking. I have to do everything myself but I'll find whoever it was!"

Heller was guiding down a piece of plating. Lombar looked through the crack at him. He swore again. It made him savage.

Lombar turned and seized my tunic lapels. He snapped me very close to him. From nowhere the stinger had appeared and he cut painfully at my leg to punctuate his speech.

"You are going to get this mission out of here by my deadline! If you don't we really could have Crown inspectors all over this hangar and there would be Hells for everyone! The whole Blito-P3 project is threatened by this mission! Twenty-four hours before departure, you and I will have another meeting! So you get this moving. You get Heller going! You get him off this planet! And if you don't make it by deadline, I will kill you very slowly with my bare hands!" The stinger struck again. "And one more last thing: As a punishment for attempting to privately short-circuit this rake-off to yourself, you are not going to get a single credit of the additional allocation! You are a thief!"

He dropped me and I staggered. I stood there for a little while, numb and hurting. Finally I realized Lombar had left: an old disguised airtruck was flying away.

Once more I started breathing. I got my legs working and made it over to the pile of rusty plates. I sank down. I was surprised to still be alive, to still have four paychecks. I had almost begun to cheer up when a horrible realization hit me.

He had said "deadline." That we had to be gone by his deadline. But he had not said when that deadline *was!*

I tried to make some estimate. Twenty-seven million had been added to the allocation. That meant it would take a couple days for him and Endow to dream up some fake companies and register them, maybe a couple days more, for appearances' sake, to date their billings and get them stamped. I knew they would not be careless about these details. Only the chance for a rake-off, personally, of twenty-seven million credits had saved my life: I had no illusions about that. But when was this deadline?

Then another horrible thought hit me. I doubted

very, very much that I could prevail upon Heller to wind up his refit, finish the tug and get going. That was the main problem! That is what I had to work on.

And the very thought of pushing him made me feel ill!

PART NINE

Chapter 1

Probably I should have waited until I was less in shock from Lombar's visit. But I knew I had to act while spurred with anxiety, newly freshened, to get off this planet.

To get Heller really going I had to pry him apart from Krak!

My screaming necessity was so great that it thrust into my mind a vital fact about Heller I had not used. He had been disciplined early in his career for refusing to let his crew be electric-shock trained. He had been quite violent about it, he detested electric-shock training. He had even said he wouldn't use a crew with "fried brains."

Yet here he was all involved with a female trainer who must use nothing else!

I saw Heller go into the tug.

Now was the time!

I straightened up my tunic. I made sure my stungun was loose in its holster in case I had to draw.

With determination, I entered the airlock.

Heller was in the flight deck. Workmen had more or less reassembled the panels and controls and Heller was checking the size of the base mount on the maneuvering sight in front of the astropilot's chair. He had a little rule out and was measuring away.

My back was to the passageway. There was no one else about. I had to get this over with.

"Heller," I said, "there is something you do not know."

"Probably a whole universe full," he said, going on with his measuring.

"Do you remember," I said, "coming within a hair of being court-martialled because you refused to let a training officer electric-shock train your crew?"

I had his attention now. He was turned slightly toward me, a frown of curiosity on his face.

"There is something you must know. You hate electric-shock training. Krak has you fooled! She uses nothing else! She is just a dirty cheat that is . . ."

The back of his hand moved so fast I did not even see it coming!

It cracked against my mouth!

I went backwards as though I had been hit by a zipbus, skidding down the passageway.

He was stepping quickly in my direction. From the expression on his face, I was certain he was going to kill me!

I grabbed the butt of my holstered gun.

My arm would not pull it!

I tried again. I could *not* get the muscles of that arm to function!

It was as though I had abruptly become totally paralyzed from the shoulder to the fingertips!

I was still certain he was going to kill me. He knelt down in front of me.

"There is something *you* don't know!" he said. "That very first day I went into the training room, I saw those brutal, shock-training machines. I went around to them one after the other. I checked their connections and control panels.

"Not one of those machines had been used for years! They were totally inoperational!"

His voice went very hard. "You had better be very careful of spreading lies about the Countess Krak!"

I was more certain than ever that he was going to kill me. I strenuously tried to pull my gun. My arm just plain wouldn't work!

Those eyes, blue as gas flames, felt like they were scorching holes in my skull.

His hand moved toward one of his inside breast pockets.

I was certain he was going to take out a blastick or knife and finish me off.

I made a frantic effort to pull my gun. My hand and arm just plain wouldn't obey me!

He had a paper in his hand. No, a copy of a clipping from a newssheet.

"I had this case looked up in the newssheet files. It concerns the deathbed confession of the former Assistant Lord of Education for Manco. See for yourself." He turned it to me. I saw it. That's what it was. But my eyes switched back at him in terror.

Once more I tried to pull my gun. My muscles again would not work!

Heller was looking at the sheet. "It clearly states here that the Manco Domestic Police interrupted a burglary and shot someone when he fled. That someone turned out to be the Assistant Lord of Education for Manco!

"He was dying of wounds. He wanted to make a confession and he did. He said that he had noticed one of his new university graduates was extremely skilled in training. Her father, the stage magician, Count Krak, had been killed recently in a plane crash. The mother, a noted trainer named Ailaena, had gone into seclusion from sorrow.

"This Assistant Lord of Education confessed that he

had been about to be ruined with gambling debts. He conceived a plan. He kidnapped Ailaena. Then he told the daughter, Lissus Moam, that he would torture her mother to death unless Lissus trained forty-three children he would select from poor houses.

"He said he told Lissus Moam that it was a government project, ordered by the Apparatus. They wanted small operatives that could penetrate enemy strongholds and bring back information. He promised that if she did this, he would release her mother, Ailaena, unharmed.

"When he finally had the children trained, he put them to work robbing banks. He was very afraid there would be witnesses to these robberies. He himself gave the children weapons and told them they must murder every guard. When the children did not want to do this, he capitalized on the fact that the children loved Lissus. He told the children that if they did not murder all guards, he himself would murder Lissus Moam. The children were certain he would. He told them that if they talked or ever mentioned his name, he would kill Lissus Moam with torture.

"When Lissus had finished the training, this insane fool killed her mother. He held Lissus prisoner in case the children were caught.

"The children were eventually caught, probably due to his faulty information or greed. He was able to produce and denounce Lissus Moam as the instigator and got off himself without suspicion.

"The children were executed. Lissus Moam was sentenced to die but, due to her skills, was spirited away by the Apparatus and some criminal was executed in her place.

"The Apparatus has been holding an innocent person for nearly three years! You have not even been decent enough to tell her!"

I was quite certain I myself was going to die in the next few seconds or minutes, such was the expression in those eyes!

Valiantly, I once again attempted to make my arm work. *It would not function!*

"I," said Heller, "am going to put this in the hands of legal counsels. I am going to clear her name. And I am going to marry the Countess Krak!"

He reached toward me. I was certain he was going to kill me.

I once more tried to pull my gun.

But he got me to my feet and into the crew salon. He sat me in a chair. He went to a locker and got a napkin and then he dampened it at the water bar.

His back was turned to me so I once more tried to draw my gun. It was futile. I couldn't make either hand or arm work. I was paralyzed!

He came back and began to sponge the small spot of blood at the side of my mouth. "I am sorry I hit you. I wasn't thinking. I just suddenly reacted. I assure you, that isn't like me. I was just trying to shut you up, not trying to knock you down."

Gods help me if he had really hit!

"I just got this this morning," he said. "I was going to tell her tonight as a surprise and ask her to marry me. We can certainly delay this mission long enough for a proper clearing of her name and a wedding. The mission isn't that urgent. Planets don't go to pieces in a day."

Perhaps it was the cool water. Perhaps it was his softer tone. But, faced with this further threat of delay, I found courage enough to talk.

"No, no, no," I said. "You mustn't start action to clear her name."

He drew back.

"You don't understand the legalities," I babbled.

"When a person is listed as dead, they destroy all the records! Right in the master data file, she is no longer listed. That Assistant Lord of Education for Manco is also dead. That confession applies to people who are dead. The Domestic Police will have destroyed all those records. You are dealing with a nonperson. Lissus Moam and the Countess Krak do not exist in the world of the living! It says so right in the master files. I have checked!"

His perplexity encouraged me. They don't educate the Fleet in civilian legal procedures. But what I said was true.

I plunged on. "Legally, you cannot raise the dead. Legally, you can get no papers or status for the dead. Legally, you can't marry the dead! And the only evidence you have is that newspaper clipping—and it is not legal evidence!"

What I wasn't telling him was that at the slightest hint that a Spiteos prisoner would be released to the world, that prisoner would be killed. In fact, Heller was lucky himself to know of Spiteos and still be alive: it was only permitted because Lombar had thought he would soon be gone to Blito-P3 and the Grand Council's familiarity with his name. He was luckier than he knew!

He was hesitating. If I could get him off this planet, he would never again be in a position to worry about the Countess Krak. I added a brilliant stroke.

"I am trained in these things and you are not," I said. "If you leave as soon as possible on this mission, I give you my solemn oath that when you return, I will help you in this. I will guide you through it. And without my help, you could not possibly free her and restore her to the world."

It was a safe oath. He would never come back. I wondered why I was suddenly feeling sick at my stomach. The blow, probably.

He looked at me. He was perplexed, doubtful. He said, "I will think it over."

I saw that that was all I could get. I still was afraid of him. My hand still gripped the butt of my gun.

I got out of there as quickly as I could! I had found myself defenseless in the face of death. It was terrifying!

Chapter 2

Outside, in the dimness of the hangar, I tried to move my arm. It was totally unresponsive. It would swing and dangle but the elbow and wrist would not bend at my command. The fingers would not flex. I felt I was done for!

Considerations that the mission was again stalled, that I was under threat of death from Lombar, that I could lose my paychecks and be cashiered and wind up as a gutter bum in Slum City were all acute enough. But they momentarily took second place to this arm.

One doesn't get personal care or disability in the Apparatus. When one is injured or becomes physically incapable of doing his job, that's it. He isn't retired. If he has held a security-sensitive post, he isn't dropped. He is simply shot in the head and the body dumped in any handy ditch.

The sensation of being hemmed in by a pack of wild beasts and having no chance of defending myself was pushing me toward panic. If I could not draw and fire a gun, I was at the total mercy of any Apparatus personnel I chanced to meet. I knew too many who would like to see me out of the way.

I disguised the disability as best I could and crept toward my airbus.

It was late afternoon, work in the area had slacked off, there were not many about.

My driver had apparently had a hard day running around on Heller's errands. Ske was sprawled out in the back, taking a nap. I stood there for a moment, looking at him through the open window. I was on the verge of opening the door and telling him to take me somewhere when a new thought stayed my left hand.

I had no money!

Obviously, I needed physical attention from a doctor. I vividly recalled the abrupt departure of the prostitute practitioner when he found I had no credits.

If Ske had been running errands, then he had money on him. With my left hand I silently opened the door. Without making the vehicle tilt, I leaned over him.

With practiced lightness I went through his uppermost two tunic pockets.

Luck!

My trained fingers drew out a ten-credit note!

I backed up, ready to leave.

"Wait a minute!" said Ske in a plaintive voice, "that ain't my money! It was the deposit on the comedy cop uniforms! I've got to return it to Officer Heller!"

He was lying. He always lies. I hoped that he hadn't noticed my right arm was disabled. He might attack me. I backed away so that I was well clear of him.

My problem now was where to find a doctor. I must not get one that could report this disability. I was racking my wits about it when my attention was drawn to a transport spaceship.

A huge, wheeled gantry was standing outside the hangar, gripping the vessel in its launch claws. The tall ship rose about four hundred and fifty feet as it sat on its tail. It was black, old, dented and shabby. An Apparatus troop carrier! When they were fuelled or repaired or whatever else they did to them in the hangar, their gantries were pushed out into the leaving zone. This was usually done toward sunset: the ship's crew was brought from barracks and put aboard and were supposed to spend the night readying their craft for takeoff in the dawn.

This one was outward bound for some planet of the Confederacy. She would have about fifty crew. Before sunrise, anywhere from two to five thousand Apparatus guard troops would be paraded out there and then file aboard to be packed like corpses into the personnel racks for the voyage. That ship would be gone for months and, with luck, within those months I, too, would be gone.

They would have a health officer on board!

It was my best bet. I would get him to fix this arm and no one would be the wiser.

I approached the gantry. The monstrous vessel loomed above me. There was a guard at the personnel loading airlock, a bored specimen. He blocked my way.

"I must inspect the vessel prior to its departure," I said and fished with my left hand for my identoplate.

The guard didn't bother to look at it. I entered the airlock. The stink of an Apparatus vessel hit me. Getting it ready for a voyage didn't include washing its interior: weightlessness can bring nausea and this vessel probably had troop vomit left over from its maiden voyage centuries before.

When they stand in gantries, their passageways are vertical. I had to climb and it was difficult with only one hand to hold to the bars. And even this was complicated by the many switchovers caused by branching passages.

Any crew or ship officers' cubicles would be way up toward the nose. It was easy to get lost inside these gigantic, fat-bellied things. The direction arrows were mainly filthed into obscurity and the signs and labels could not be read. I struggled along and then was glad to hear a distant sound far above me.

It was a song. Far from getting the ship ready, some of the crew were sitting up there somewhere, probably in their eating room, indulging themselves in a singing weep.

There was the throb of a hand air organ. It was beginning the chords of a new song. Spacers, I have always maintained, are not normal people. And the spacers of the Apparatus are insane.

They were beginning a song called, "The Spacer's Lot." It is a dirge! Why do they always sing dirges before they start a voyage? Hangovers?

It didn't make me feel a bit better to be climbing to the sad, sad melancholy of that tune. I was struggling as it was! The lament echoed down as though sung in a tomb!

> *To planets of the dead,*
> *And stars that have no light,*
> *We cruise throughout this endless space,*
> *Encased in darkest night.*

I missed a rung and almost fell two hundred feet.

> *The eyes that do not miss us,*
> *The hands without caress,*
> *The hardened hearts behind us,*
> *Spare no slightest warmth to bless.*

I tried to hurry my ascent. The awful dirge was depressing me.

The Forces of the firmament,
Enfold us as our home.
The lost, the damned, the outcast,
Cruise darkest space alone.

I almost fell again. The echoing walls made the song more deep and awful. Maybe if I got there quick, they would shut up. I was feeling bad enough already.

Shun space, you groundbound creature!
Suck in your planet's breath!
Hold safe to stable gravity!
For we of space live DEATH!

I stuck my head precariously in the compartment door. It was the end of the song and they all sat there weeping, about twenty of them.

"Is there a doctor aboard?" I asked in general.

A big, tough ape, probably wanted on half the planets for numerous crimes, turned his tearful eyes to me and then pointed silently across the passageway. The hand air organ was starting up again.

I made out a sign, very smudged: *Health Officer. Do Not Open.*

With a one-handed effort, I undid the seal cogs and stumbled into the room. A blast of decayed meat and tup fumes hit me. Somebody was snoring on the gimbal bed. With some difficulty, I woke him up.

Bleary-eyed, this doctor was representative of the profession, not the way they like to be seen in song and story but the way they really are: a stinking wreck.

"My arm," I said. "It suddenly has become paralyzed!"

"Well, buy a new one," he said and tried to turn over and resume snoring.

With some struggle I got him to sit up. "I have money," I said.

That reached him. He got professional.

"I want you to tell me what's wrong with it," I said.

I got off my gunbelt and somehow managed to get out of my tunic, all without the slightest aid from him. He started to examine the wrong arm and I had to direct his attention.

With a lot of yawns and some time out to get another drink of tup, he asked some questions and prodded. The questions were mainly a hopeful, "Does that hurt?" when he poked.

He had some sort of machine and he made me stand in front of it. I hoped he was looking but I heard him drinking more tup.

"No slugs, no bone breaks, no burns," I heard him mutter. Then, with a shrug, he indicated I could get back into my jacket.

He was looking at me rather peculiarly. "Well," he said, "I know what's wrong with it now."

I was just finishing buckling my gunbelt. His fingers were sort of twitching. I got out the ten-credit note. I intended to ask if he could change it for this action he was doing never cost more than two credits.

He took the note and put it in his pocket.

He gave a tremendous yawn and then he said, "The diagnosis is, you can't use your arm."

With that, he showed every sign of getting back onto his gimbal bed. I blocked him. "You'll have to do better than that!"

The doctor looked at me, very bored. "You want a technical term? All right: you had temporary hysterical paralysis of the upper articulation muscles." And he started to climb back onto his bed.

I shouted, "That doesn't handle anything!"

"There's nothing to handle," he said. "You apparently did not notice that you used your arm perfectly normally when you put your coat and belt back on."

I stared. I looked down. I swung the arm. I flexed my fingers. There was nothing wrong with it! I could use it perfectly normally!

Once more he started to get back on the bed. "Wait, wait! What could cause that?"

"The machine showed you had no slugs in your head or foreign matter pressing the nerves of the spine. So there is no cause."

I made my voice sound deadly. "You better tell me how such a condition could come about!"

He saw plainly that he was not going to be able to get back on that gimbal bed unless he either moved me out of the way or said something I would accept.

The doctor shrugged. "Hysteria? Battle shock? You're an officer, so no electric shock can be used on you. A lot of things can cause it."

"Such as?" and I continued to block his way back to bed.

He looked vague. "Neurotic predisposition which then precipitated into a temporary manifestation? Hypnotism?"

"You've got to do more than this!" I said.

"For only ten credits? I'm no Slum City head plumber."

"That's five times the usual fee!" I said.

"You were five times as worried," he said. And he pushed me aside and lay down and shortly was snoring once more. A true professional.

Chapter 3

Back at the airbus, I walked around it several times, thinking. It was almost dusk. Every now and then I would flex my arm and fingers. They were working perfectly.

I was trying to sort out what the meat-chopper had said.

Learned as I was in Earth psychology, I knew very well that he was wrong about "neurotic predisposition." I am not neurotic. That left hypnotism. But aside from language training, I had not been hypnotized.

Certain it was that I was at severe risk. What if this happened again? Just when I was about to shoot somebody down, my arm didn't work! The thought made my hair prickle.

I did not dare go near an Apparatus practitioner. Any drilling into my unconscious might reveal too much. The practitioner would report that I was blabbing state secrets and that would be the end of me!

What else had that (bleeped) meat-slicer said? Ah, that he was no "Slum City head plumber." That was the clue. I had seen their signs. I made up a plan quickly, calling on my skilled talents in this sort of thing.

I went around to the door to get in.

My driver said, "How am I going to explain to Officer Heller when I can't return that costume deposit?"

I hit him. I used my left hand as I couldn't trust my right. But I hit him.

I got in. "Take me to the Provocation Section at once!" I ordered.

We flew through the dusk over Government City, darted down to water level at the River Wiel and shortly zoomed into the tunnel of the shabby warehouses.

I got out. I trotted straight up the steps.

Raza Torr had been in the act of going home. He froze. He seemed to have turned bone white but it was hard to tell in the dim light.

I decided I had better put him at his ease. "Met any nice girls lately?" I said conversationally.

My former escort was behind me. They must have had burglars or troubles lately as he was holding a gun in his hand.

Raza Torr, in a sort of strangled voice said, "I'll take care of this."

I led the way. I knew the place inside out now. I went to the civilian costume area. Raza Torr followed. The escort had vanished.

"I want a speedwheel suit," I said. "The street kind. Something plain."

Raza Torr seemed to have recovered. Probably, I thought, he had had a hard day. He was a naturally nervous fellow. But he doesn't always have good sense. He walked over to the rack and got down a speedwheel suit: they are shiny, made of slick body-armor material. This one had flaring scarlet flame patterns painted all over it, it could be seen from a mile off and hurt the eyes even then.

"No, no," I said. I went to the rack and found a plain black one in my size. It had some accident blood caked on the collar but one can't be choosey and I was in a hurry.

"Now a helmet," I said and went over to that rack.

Again he got in my way and tried to give me a rider helmet with a flame plume and no visor. I pushed it aside and got a no-plume black visor one.

"Now a tri-knife," I said. I led the way over to the weapons section and finally found one. They are a great knife. Criminals use them when they want to do a particularly gory murder. They are thin as a needle when their ten-inch blade goes in. When it hits bottom, the blade springs into a narrow fan, becoming three razor-edged blades. When you pull it out, a lot of guts come with it. They even have a ring in the hilt so you can yank back. Some knife fighters say they are too hard to draw out of a stabbed body, but that is just quibbling.

"Gods," said Raza Torr. "Who you going to kill?"

"I doubt I'll return these," I said.

"I doubt you will either," he said. I ignored the unjustified slur on my honesty. I was too intent on my project.

Back at my airbus, I directed my driver on a circuitous course to the outskirts of Slum City. Night had come. Real evening traffic had not yet started up. People in other cities were at their suppers. Not too many people in Slum City would have suppers to be at.

Although they are poor in Slum City, they are not inactive. The dilapidated and decayed structures do contain spots of liveliness. These pinpoints of brilliance seemed to deepen, rather than brighten, the intense gloom. Fifty square miles of deprivation are strung around a fetid lake. Nobody had any record of when Slum City had been built and even when constructed it was probably old at once.

There was a tale that Lombar used to set fires down here to while away his youth. I doubted the story. Lombar was more efficiently destructive than that and he certainly hated any slum. Someday, he had once mentioned to me, all this would be swept down, the population annihilated. It looked like it was overdue for the treatment.

I saw what I wanted. It was one of the bright spots. Youths hang out in dens in Slum City. They sometimes have orchestras, pretty bad ones. Tup is about a twentieth of a credit per canister, pretty bad tup.

Around this place there would be speedwheels.

I directed my driver to sit down well away from the lights of a bluebottle station. It was in what once might have been a park. I made him turn out the lights so that not even he could see what I was doing.

I scrambled around, got off my uniform and got into the speedwheel suit. I put on the black-visored helmet. I left all identification and normal Apparatus weapons with my uniform. I took with me only the tri-knife and a small wad of counterfeit bills. I told my driver to wait right where he was, showing no lights, until I returned.

With very silent feet I raced in the direction of the orchestra. I stopped well clear of the flaring lights. A lot of youths were dancing.

A quick survey discovered a speedwheel of the more powerful type. It was deep in the shadows. I jimmied the lock. It was so easy, the guy deserved to lose it!

I pushed it well away and then, when safe from any detection, I went zipping down what they sarcastically call a boulevard in Slum City, the speedwheel crushing through the garbage. The fetid stink of the lake was almost solid in the night wind.

The district to which I was proceeding with speed was known for its fornication machines, electric thrillers and head plumbers. In ten minutes the dimly lit signs began to flick by. I slowed down.

Painted in bad lettering anywhere there was a bare

space on a building were directions to *Irrigate Your Rotting Bowels* to visit *Titillation Palace* and to announce that *Electric Penis Stimulation Is Done Here.* Finally, even dingier than the rest, I found a building which, amongst other signs, bore a badly scrawled floor label, *Mental Doctor; Brain Examination; Physiological Nerve Specialist; Hypnotist; Bowels Purged. See Doctor Cutswitz Before It Is Too Late.* There was my man.

I hesitated only because it was a little bit close to a bluebottle watch post. In fact, the police stand was only about thirty feet from the door of Doctor Cutswitz. It was handy for them because the police probably referred people they picked up to Doctor Cutswitz. But it was a bit public for me.

I had come in very slow. So I spun back and went into an alley. Beside me, a lot of building blocks were quite broken and edged as the wall ascended to the desired floor. There was also a window up there and it was lighted.

With catlike agility, I went up the wall and through the window. I was in a hall.

There were people about. Further down the hall a woman came out of a door and went into another door. Of course, she did not see me. I am good at that.

I slid along the passageway and found the door of Doctor Cutswitz. There was a light inside.

Boldly, I entered.

Chapter 4

The guy was lying on a mechanical fornicator. He was too interested to notice that somebody had come in. I reclosed the door—noisily. He bounced up off the machine, fastened his pants and said, "I was just trying out a new model to see if it should be recommended to my customers."

He was lying. The machine was all scuffed up and worn out. He was wearing side-blinders and it reminded me of Bawtch. He looked like he had soaked himself a year or two in oil and, from the smell of him, it must have been rancid.

I looked around his office. It was very dirty. There were five tiers of shelves along two walls. They had transparent jars on them, hundreds of transparent jars. Each jar contained something in a discolored fluid. I flinched. They were human brains.

He waved his arm toward them. "My very best customers," he said pleasantly. His voice sounded like it had been greased. "I am sure that we can satisfy your needs."

I told him my name was Ip—that being about the commonest name on Voltar. I told him that I had a friend who had a problem and that I wanted some advice for my friend.

He sat me down in a reclining chair. He sat down on a stool beside me.

I told him my friend didn't have any metal bits in him or broken bones and that my friend didn't suffer from battleshock or neurosis. But my friend had had a dreadful thing happen to him: he had tried to draw his gun to shoot in self-defense, only to find his arm and hand refused to obey him. And then less than an hour later it vanished. That my friend was in a dangerous line of work and couldn't afford not to be able to draw his gun and shoot people.

He was very sympathetic. He patted my hand—leaving a smear of grease on it. He got up and went to a closet and came out holding a hypnohelmet. A label had been scratched off the back of the helmet but it could still be read,

Stolen from the University of Voltar

"I think," he said, "that your friend must have been hypnotized. Just put this helmet on and we'll see if we can't learn more, Citizen Ip."

This seemed reasonable. The helmet fit well. He buckled the strap under my chin and turned on the current.

Immediately I could hear his voice like a shadow in the background. He was asking something and my mouth seemed to be answering. I did not pay much attention to it. It went on for a very long time. I seemed to be in other times and other places. My mouth kept on talking.

Then suddenly, just as if it was in this same room, a voice seemed to say, loud and clear: "You are now going to hear some orders. These orders are something over which you have no control.

"Think of the name Jettero Heller. Think of what he looks like.

"The first order is that any time you contemplate hurting or harming Jettero Heller in any way, you will get a sick feeling in your stomach.

"The second order is that if you actively plan or agree to commit physical alteration or damage to Jettero Heller, you will become violently sick at your stomach.

"The third order is, if you plan or connive in hurting Jettero Heller's career, you will have nightmares and a Manco Devil will appear and you will go crazy.

"The fourth order is, if you ever seek to poison or strike or draw a weapon of any kind on Jettero Heller, your arm will instantly experience total paralysis.

"When you awaken I will give you something to read. It will have the word *obedience* in it. The moment you read that, these orders will go deep into your consciousness and through your body. You will be totally incapable of resisting them and you will obey them utterly from here to eternity.

"You will now forget and banish from consciousness everything I have said to you but it will continue in total effect. Forget, forget! You have no knowledge of where these orders came from. Forget, forget!"

The words were brilliantly clear.

Through the visionary fog there was a face. The face of the Countess Krak!

That day in the training room! That day she had cleared everyone out and told me it was an "accent review." The day she had given me that book, afterwards, that had the word *obedience* several times on the pages.

It was like a sun had supernova'd in my skull!

The hypnohelmet was turned off. I was wide awake.

The Countess Krak!

(Bleep) her! (Bleep) (bleep) her!

She, and she alone, out of some stupid impulse to protect Heller, had consigned me to weeks and weeks of purest Hells! And all because I was just doing my simple, normal duty!

The strange illness that turned on each time I even casually thought of harming Heller! The Manco Devil in the nightmare! The fleeing from the scene to the mountains! The paralysis of my arm! My whole inability to carry out this mission! To even be my normal self!

All was explained!

The effects were gone!

The orders no longer held!

(Bleep) you, Countess Krak!

Aha, you wait and see now what happens to that (bleeped) Heller.

And to you!

Every Hells any planet ever heard of would be a lovely place compared to the Hells you two will be in now!

Chapter 5

For a seething half hour I just sat there.

Gradually I became aware of Doctor Cutswitz. He had let me be. He had removed the hypnohelmet long since and he was sitting over on a bench across the room just watching me. He saw now that I had fully come around.

I wanted to get out of there and get about my business. I reached into my pocket and got out a counterfeit five-credit note. He was no trained cashier. Might as well get him killed off by his friends the bluebottles.

I extended the note.

He smiled. "I am afraid that is not quite enough, Officer Gris."

I froze. How could he know my name? I had no identification on me!

"Not five credits," he said pleasantly. "I think five thousand credits would be more accurate."

I was thinking fast. "I don't have money like that."

"Oh, I think you could get it. You could give me all you have on you right now. And then give me the rest in installments—say, during the next week."

"You know nothing but my name!"

"Oh, and perhaps a few things more. Like twenty dead Fleet spacers in a dungeon. I think the Fleet would dearly love to know about them."

I pretended to sag. Listlessly, I put the riding helmet on and dropped the visor. Then, as though hopeless, I took the rest of the counterfeit money out. I got up and walked over to him. He stood. He reached out his hand.

There was nothing wrong with my arm now and never would be again.

The hand that was extending the money to him did a small jerk.

A ten-inch tri-knife snapped out of my sleeve into my palm.

The (bleeped) fool was still smiling, thinking he had won.

I lunged. Ten inches of steel went through his heart.

Abrupt surprise shot into his eyes. And the knowledge he was dead.

I yanked the knife back, stepping aside. The blade inside him turned into three parts. Guts and a gush of blood rushed out of him, splatting on the floor.

He fell in it face down.

I prodded him. He was dead. Very messily dead.

The bills had flown sideways. I picked them up and wiped the blood stains off the shiny paper by rubbing them on the back of his coat. I put them in my pocket.

Then I ransacked the room and found the recording strips he had made on a hidden machine. I destroyed them.

He had uttered no sound. I had been silent. I went to the door and opened it a crack.

For an instant I thought I saw someone at the lower end of the hall, someone who had abruptly stepped out of sight. A witness?

Footsteps were coming down the hall from the other direction. It was a woman. She was middle-aged. She looked like she worked in this building.

I stepped out in front of her. I was holding the bloody knife. She stopped. I handed it to her hilt first.

"Quick," I said in a low urgent voice. "Take this and run down to the bluebottle station and show them that Doctor Cutswitz has been murdered."

She would have screamed. But a low, secret sort of voice prevents that when used right. Her eyes went round and glazed.

She grabbed the hilt of the knife and rushed off, heading for the police station just below.

Another flick of movement in the shadows down the hall. Had I been observed?

Well, who cared? It would do them no good. I had the riding helmet on and the black visor down. I sped to the window. Nobody followed.

I went down the wall like an agile insect, I mounted the speedwheel.

A call for an arrest van blasted out at the police station. To Hells with them. I silently rolled the speedwheel to the other end of the alley, into another street. I made no noises with the vehicle. It was two blocks away when I opened it up to a roar.

They would arrest the woman, of course. The police

principle of "the least work consists of arresting the handiest person" would be in full play. It was a solved crime on their books. Be neat, I always say. Leave no loose ends.

I dropped the speedwheel at the den, putting it exactly where it had been before. I even locked it up again.

Shortly after, I slipped into the airbus. My changing clothes woke my driver up. We flew away on quiet wings. As we passed over the River Wiel, I dropped the suit and helmet into the raging water below.

That night I lay in my room. I planned and planned. What would happen to Heller and Krak now was all their own doing. I had never felt so deadly before in my whole life. I told myself, Hells have no Demon as full of hate as a man covertly hypnotized. And no Demon would have dared make up such ugly and varied plans as I made that night.

Heller was totally at my mercy now and I intended to make the very vengeful most of it!

Chapter 6

I was up with the dawn. I loftily did not comment on my driver's petty tribulations about the costume refund—Heller, it seems, had forgiven him but the driver, of all things, felt *guilty!* I swept into the office where the early arriving Bawtch was sucking his early morning jolt: I took it right out of his hand and finished it! I didn't even stand there to enjoy his surprise.

Climbing down the stairs into the hidden rooms in the basement, I made my way to the secret forgery unit.

Every Apparatus section has its own forgery unit—one couldn't run without one. Such actions are usually reserved for the framing of resistive or dissident citizens: few would be brave enough to make forgeries of the type I planned.

But, under the shadow of Lombar, forced to it by his orders—and even, I must admit in this case, enjoying the vindictive flavor of it—I swept aside assorted pens and stamps and sat down to compose my masterpieces.

It took me quite a while, what with scratch-outs and additions, but I was finished by the time the two forgers arrived.

They sat down at their tables and I put the rough drafts before them. It made me smile to see them flinch.

"I don't think we have the right paper," said the senior.

"Get it," I said. "Right now. Get it!"

He fished around for a time, going through materials in the cases. He finally found two sheets of what he needed.

The other forger said, "I don't think we have the right seals."

"I think you have," I said.

He raked about in some old boxes and finally located some that could be converted.

They were both a bit white and terrified, as well they might be. Because I have enough on both of them, material not even in the master data files, and they elected to commit the present crime on the basis that it was less painful than the revelation of old crimes.

Forgers are very funny people. There is a streak of artist in them and, along with it, artistic pride, and soon they were both deeply immersed in concentration and ink. I did not have to tell them to do the best possible job. Their own tradecraft was a matter of self-respect. But, more than that, if these two forgeries had the tiniest detectable flaw in them, and if they were prematurely exposed, half the Domestic Police Division would be on their trail. Necessity breeds precision!

I sat down on a case full of unused execution orders and waited. The tongues of the forgers suffered the clenching of teeth, the pens drew out, with painful slowness, the flowing swirls and ornate convolutions these documents required. Two hours was not too long to wait for they were making absolutely undetectable masterpieces.

Finally they came to the stamps. Only one of the documents required the final affixations of seals.

At last, sweating, sort of proud and terrified at the same time, they were blowing the waxes dry.

The junior looked at them for any flaw. The senior compared them critically to a book containing facsimiles of the real thing.

"Gods," said the junior. "They look realer than the real thing!" There was some pride in it. "I do think that the only way they could be detected as artificial would be by inspecting the Royal Issue Log itself! And no one outside of Palace City has access to that. These are masterpieces!"

The senior forger got down a pair of official covers and then a thin, waterproof envelope with body tapes.

As he was assembling them, he said to me, "You know, of course, that possession of a forgery of the Royal signature and seals gets immediate torture and execution. These will never be traced to us. We have forgotten we ever heard of them. But just carrying these on your person, Officer Gris, if found and detected, would be the finish of you. With embellishments."

He handed over the packet but didn't let go of it. "Open your tunic so I can tape this to your chest." And as he worked at it, "It is clever, of course, as these would never appear in the master data files. But they *would* appear in the Royal log in Palace City. If anyone ever tried to present them there, the first thing that would happen would be a check and verification of the Royal Issue Log. It would show that these two documents had never been issued. The result would be immediate seizure of the presenting person, torture and execution."

He had finished up and, as I rebuttoned my tunic, looked at me gravely. "I hope you know what you are doing. Be very careful to whom you show these. Keep the matter folded in the deepest secrecy. Even if you gave them to somebody, that person could implicate you as well."

As I opened the door to leave, the senior forger shook his head. "My Gods, Officer Gris, you must be awfully mad at those people." That, from a forger who routinely forged things that got people imprisoned and executed, was quite a compliment.

I didn't even bother to stop by my desk. I had places to go.

I had lots of time, really: it was only ten o'clock. But I said to the driver, "Open that throttle!"

He was doing two hundred in the thick, midmorning traffic. "Who the Hells do you think I am?" he said crossly. "I can't drive like Heller and you know it!"

He was getting awfully insolent lately. I was about to reach forward and bat him one when I realized that if we were to have a crash and live through it, this packet might be found on me. I forcefully checked my impatience and let him bumble along.

The Great Desert fled beneath us. There were more sun-dancers today but I spent no time watching them.

My eyes were fixed on the ugly hulk of Spiteos, swelling in size as we closed the distance to it.

This was going to be very sweet.

Chapter 7

The training room, when I came in, was in its usual turmoil. It had been cleaned again and stank of army disinfectant. The assistant trainers were putting various people through their paces: here a special agent getting skilled in the use of electronic needle bombs blown from a tube; there, two claw fighters learning how to look like they were tearing each other apart without suffering the slightest injury beyond the stain of fake blood; over there, an act with a magician and a primate who seemed to be exchanging roles in making each other disappear.

And there was the Countess Krak, my *quarry*. She wasn't doing any training: apparently she had turned all that over to assistants now. She was wearing a powder blue, one-piece exercise suit; she had her silky hair bound back with a powder blue band; her sparkling ankle boots were twinkling as she worked upon a pair of rings. She was shooting herself up in the air, her toes moving rapidly in cross-uncross twitches, and then at the top she would flip upside down and catch herself with her heels in the rings. She was very graceful.

She seemed very happy. When I drew near her I could even hear that she was humming a little song. She was very beautiful. She saw me suddenly and the smile went off her face. But she dropped down to the floor. "Hello, Soltan." A bit wary.

I was the picture of glad but secret tidings. I glanced around and saw a hidden corner back of some old machines. "I have wonderful news," I whispered. I went over to the corner, beckoning.

She came over. I glanced all around and made very sure that we could not be seen nor overheard and also that no one could come up on us suddenly.

I beckoned with my fingers to get her to move even closer. I whispered, "I have just had the most glorious audience."

That phrasing meant only one thing. "The Emperor?" she said. "You?"

I looked very modest. I fiddled with my emerald insignia locket. "Really, it is because Jettero is so important." I knew she would accept that. "But who can fail to shine in reflection of his glory. It is just that I have the good fortune to be associated with him." She was buying it.

"You see," I continued, "I was terribly concerned that he might be injured or hurt." Aha, the (bleepch) thought that the hypnotic suggestion was still in place, (bleep) her. She was nodding: she thought she understood that very well.

"So I have gently been pulling strings," I continued with the most innocent face I could manage. Then I looked around to make sure we were alone and drew much closer to her and dropped my voice. "I really should not be telling you any of this. It is the most secret of state secrets. It was thoroughly impressed upon me that I must not reveal it to a soul!"

I managed to look puzzled, very slightly. "I am not sure why I felt so compelled to come and tell you at once." Ah, she was really buying it, the filthy (bleepch) with her hypnotic tricks! I put on a "little boy" look that women can't reject—it raises the motherhood in them.

"But in addition to that, I really could not see how I could do it alone. I desperately need your help."

Oh, she was eager to give it. Anything that had to do with Heller was her top, and maybe only, priority.

I resumed the confidential manner. "I could probably be severely punished for revealing any of this," I said. And then seemed to regret my incaution and drew back a bit. But women are absolute sponges of curiosity.

"I promise no one else will hear it from me," she said eagerly.

"It would be my life if they did," I said. I resumed. "Really, I have no choice as I need your help in this. May we sit down?"

I raked a couple of stools over into the hidden corner. By turning our faces to the wall, slightly, it was doubly difficult for anyone to see what we were about should they walk up. I began to undo a couple of my tunic buttons and reached in as though about to produce the packet. But I didn't. Her eagerness, of course, became intense enough to overweigh some of her natural critical sense.

"Before dawn this morning," I whispered, "a Palace City air limousine came for me secretly. Honestly, I was terrified at first: I thought I was being taken for interrogation. They brought me into the palace by a back route and through a secret door. They led me to a room that had a vast swimming bath. Honestly, I never knew they threw rare rugs around the edges of a swimming bath. I waited for half an hour—I was very nervous, I can tell you.

"And then there he was! I could hardly believe my eyes, he is so seldom seen. He entered in a sparkling morning robe. Cling the Lofty himself! Honestly, I could have died. There I was in no dress uniform or anything.

"His Majesty said, 'Is this the officer in charge of Mission Earth?' and the escort officer said it was.

"The king took his robe off and took his morning swim—honestly, I didn't know he swam every morning: and in a diamond pool, too! Imagine it!

"I just stood and waited, scared to death, not knowing what I'd done wrong. But after a while His Majesty came out of the bath and lay down on some cushions and a couple of his yellow-men began to lard him with perfumes. He made a gesture at a spot near him and the escort shoved me to that spot.

"His Majesty said, 'I have always believed that Jettero Heller was a very good man.' "

As I expected, this produced an instant reaction from her. Wide-eyed. Amongst a hundred and ten planets and tens of millions of officers, one would not expect an Emperor, even one with a brilliant memory, to know the name of a junior officer. She was now grabbing for every word. To myself, I thought, you asked for it, you (bleepch), and now you are getting it.

I continued, "After a bit His Majesty looked at me puzzled. He said, 'So there is some other reason why he is delaying his departure on this mission and I have brought you here to tell me!'

"Honestly, I expected his next words would order me executed. Well, I am not that brave. And so I am afraid I betrayed some confidences. No, no," I added hastily, "don't start so with alarm. This has a very happy ending." It filled me with private glee to say those words. The "happy ending" would be total tragedy for them both.

"Forgive me, Countess. I am an officer and know where my duty lies. I am even imperilling myself to relate this to you. But what could I say? Now," I said, changing the subject slightly, "has Jettero shown you the clipping? The one that concerns you?"

She probably didn't know that I knew. She nodded.

I continued, "I had never heard of it before. If I had, I would have acted sooner. But to get on. I had to tell His Majesty the real reason the mission was delayed."

I could practically hear her heart beating rapidly inside her chest.

"His Majesty hectored me. He told me that the most vast and secret affairs of state depended upon a successful completion of that mission. He sounded very provoked and when it occurred to me that, because of this, he might hurt Heller, I got very sick at my stomach! The thought was that awful."

Gullible (bleepch). You think that hypnotic suggestion is still in place. Ah, you're going to pay for that, (bleep) you. Look at you nod!

I drew a long breath as though it had been a painful moment. And then I got back to my lying. "Sick as I felt, I simply had to plead with him. Oh, I tell you, even the yellow-men rubbing the perfumed lard into him were frightened that anyone should seek to plead with the Emperor about anything. But something, I don't know what, was making me desperate.

"I told him that he knew and I knew that Jettero Heller was the only one who could do the mission to Blito-P3. He agreed with that, as Jettero had done the original mission. And then I did something I couldn't ever before have imagined myself capable of. I suggested—imagine that, suggesting something to Cling the Lofty! I don't know where I found the courage—that if Jettero Heller's immediate personal problems were removed, the mission could go quite quickly.

"And you know what he did? Oh, it is plain to see why he is the Emperor! He called in his scribes right that moment and he dictated to them. And they wrote it all down. And then he rolled over and looked at me and he said, 'Never let it be believed that I do not concern myself with the welfare of my officers and subjects. Part of the power of ruling should always be devoted to justice. But you will note that the second document is unsigned. The mission is important to the State beyond belief. See to it.' And then he had them give me the documents and he waved to them to take me off."

I glanced around to verify that we were still hidden. The sounds of the training room even seemed far away. I drew from under my blouse the packet.

I reverently opened the first one and, holding it, let her read it.

Adorned and embellished and covered with sworls and curling letters it said:

SECRET
NOT TO BE UNAUTHORIZEDLY SEEN

KNOW ALL:

We, Cling the Lofty,
Majestic and Undisputed Ruler
of the vast Realm of Galaxies,
Stars and Planets known throughout Heavens
as the Voltar Confederation,
Emperor of All Dominions Whatever,
Conquered and as Yet Unconquered,
Do Hereby and Herewith Secretly Decree:
The MISSION BLITO-P3 of current date, secret and vital to the realm, shall go forward with complete speed, dispatch and

expedition, without compromise or halt.

And I do pledge our Royal and inviolate word to wit: That when Jettero Heller, Grade X, Combat Engineer, Fleet Corps of Engineers, shall have successfully concluded said MISSION, even though it be easy and nonperilous, he shall be suitably rewarded. It is noted that he has served as a frontline combat engineer three times as long as the normal life expectancy in that profession and it is unreasonable to expect he would survive much longer. Therefore, to wit and witness: Upon the return of said Jettero Heller, reserving only that he shall have rapidly carried it out to complete success, he shall be attached thereafter to the Royal Staff of Palace City, freed from the absences and perils of the Fleet.

SEALED, SIGNED, STAMPED, VALIDATED, AUTHORIZED AND LOGGED THIS DATE:

Cling the Lofty
Emperor!

She was hardly breathing. All this stuff about safety! How clever of me! I had had it measured exactly! The (bleepch), there she sat, utterly starry-eyed!

After a while she sort of came out of it. "You said there were two."

"Yes. But this one is unsigned. His Majesty is quite

clever. He wants something. He wants this mission. He promised to sign this second one when presented and when the mission is successfully completed. See, that's what it says."

I unfolded the second forgery and held it so she could read it. It, too, had all the sworls and curling letters. It said:

SECRET
TO BE SIGNED ON THE
SUCCESSFUL COMPLETION
OF THE MISSION BLITO-P3

KNOW ALL:

We, Cling the Lofty,
Majestic and Undisputed Ruler
of the vast Realm of the Galaxies,
Stars and Planets known throughout Heavens
as the Voltar Confederation,
Emperor of All Dominions Whatever,
Conquered and as Yet Unconquered,
Do Hereby and Herewith Secretly Decree:

The female once known as Lissus Moam, actually of the family of Krak and also known as the Countess Krak, by reason of a deathbed confession of the true instigator of numerous crimes, is resurrected from the dead and is restored not only her papers and identity but also all the lands once held by said noble family Krak.

> Royal permission is also granted to this said person to marry Jettero Heller, but only at such time as he has joined the Royal Staff on transfer from the Fleet.
>
> NOT VALID UNTIL SEALED, SIGNED, STAMPED, VALIDATED AND AUTHORIZED BY FINAL SIGNATURE BUT LOGGED THIS DATE AS AN ORDER PENDING SIGNATURE

Her cheeks were flushed. Her eyes were almost glassy with stunned comprehension. One of her hands was fluttering at her breast. She was having a little trouble breathing.

Ah, you (bleepch). Your expectations are high, now, aren't they? I put the documents back in their covers and into the waterproof sleeve.

"So you see," I said smoothly, "I have saved dear Jettero the trouble of going through all the legal nonsense of getting you restored to life. All he has to do is go quickly on his mission, finish it rapidly, return, present these papers at the palace and the rest of your lives will be a beautiful dream." It gave me a lot of satisfaction. Heller would never come back. And anybody presenting these forgeries at Palace City would pray for death for days before they got through with them. But, of course, none of this would ever get that far.

"There is only one trouble," I said.

She looked at me with abrupt attention.

I said, smoothly, "Jettero will probably not take to

being cast out of the Fleet. You know how he is. It would mean almost death to him."

She considered it. She knew it was not without truth.

I went on, "So this is where I need your help. I am the mission handler and these documents are supposed to be known only to me. I am afraid Jettero will balk or try to see friends and get all this modified. It would make the Emperor furious. It would put Jettero in grave danger."

She could see that.

"Now, let's be reasonable," I said. "This is an easy mission, nothing dangerous about it. The sooner he goes, the sooner he will return. The help I need is for you, without telling him anything about these documents, to persuade him to go, to quickly complete the mission and get back. You have to use all your wiles. You can't use these documents. Can I have that help?"

I watched her, my face betraying nothing of Heller's real future.

The Countess Krak thought it over very carefully. "I will do it on one condition."

I waited.

"If," she said, "you let me hold those documents myself, I will do my best to persuade Jettero to leave as soon as possible and get back quickly."

It brought me no surprise. I had actually thought it might occur and the dangers to me of these documents being exposed was, I thought, minimal. Actually, I took a sort of glee in her having on her these forgeries. Like I was putting a big death stamp right in the middle of her lovely forehead. (Bleep) her.

"If," I said, in my turn, "you give me your solemn word that you will not show them to Heller, that you will not mention them to him, then you can hold them. But," I said, quite factually but with double meaning, "there is danger in it for you. They are Royal documents and a person in your legal status would be imperilled by their possession."

"There is a chance," she said, "that you might, shall we say, misplace them? I think it is safer that I hold them, don't you, Soltan? Then they will appear when needed."

I shook my head sadly. "You should trust me more. I don't want to see Heller hurt."

Ah, well, she thought she knew that.

She took the waterproof packet, verified the documents were still in there, closed it all up and strapped it to her body and pulled down her jumper over it. It made no slightest bulge.

Then she looked at me. "I have to say thank you, Soltan. You deserve my gratitude."

She was thanking me for putting a knife in her heart.

I left.

All the way back to Government City I actively had to suppress shouting and laughing exultantly. It sort of put flavoring on the bun to also think of an additional power I now had. One word from me to search her and she'd be tortured and killed by experts because of what they'd find. That wasn't part of the plan. It was just a bit of perfume wafting up.

I controlled myself with effort. I had a lot to do now. A lot to do! This was only the beginning!

Chapter 8

We flew directly to Communication Complex Towers. There is no place that has more traffic, as everyone knows. Air, ground, pedestrian, tens of thousands of people move through it every day, paying their communication bills, arranging for new Homeview service, placing difficult calls to the next inner and next outer planets of this system and just plain complaining about the service. What I wanted was the uppermost dome, Central Directory.

Heller was going to get operated on and bugged—real good!

My driver muttered and complained his way along the tight traffic channels, trying to keep his new paint on the airbus and not on somebody else's.

I was busy in the bag. I took a second set of top-row teeth out of my pocket and put it under my upper lip. I popped color shifters into my eyes so instead of brown they would be bright green. I took off my rank locket and put it in my pocket.

The driver had us in under the dome overhang and into a slot that said,

Ten minutes! This Means YOU!

He said, "Don't you be too long or I'll get a fender bash from the local bluebottles!"

"Before much longer, you're going to be rich," I said. "So shut up."

"Hey," he said, suddenly interested. "You gonna rob this place?" Silly nut. They don't even keep money in Central Directory.

I sauntered in. Actually there were no more than one or two thousand enquirers and there were a lot of empty interview chairs. I was looking for a female clerk that could turn out to be a complete nitwit. Somebody really dumb. I found her simply by the fact that other customers were avoiding her counter area. This would not take long.

"We have an emergency," I said. "We need the absolute *top* authority on cellology in Voltar."

Her hair was done up in a tall peak like a temple. Probably that was the shape of her skull underneath. I had to explain what a cellologist was. She punched it out on her keyboard and the symbols appeared on the desk top before her, upside down to me. I can read upside down. Anybody in the Apparatus can.

"You want his communications number?" said vacuum brain. That's what they do in Central Directory.

"I have to make sure he's the top authority first. Do you mind?" I reached over across the desk top to the key ranks. I started punching and this lunkhead just sat there interestedly watching me.

You can strip down a lot of data from these communication information consoles. They run off whole categories of professions as well as businesses. They tell you where this or that person can be reached right then if he is in the habit of inspecting calls. To keep from confusing this person with that, they give full identoplate data. And in case the person wants some new service, they give his credit rating.

It was nursery school stuff to get all the senior teaching cellologists on Voltar, to get their credit ratings—which is an index to how high up they are in a profession—to get the listed full identoplate data of these top ones, where they were right this minute and to get every bit of that data rolled off and delivered.

Temple-skull just sat and watched me operate her machine backwards. Maybe she was learning how to use it. Who knows?

When I had the stack of sheets, I said, "Oh, dear! These will be much too expensive!" There was no such data on any sheet I had pulled but chuckle-wit nodded wisely. Where do they find these girls? Back country of Taugo? Where the men have tails?

I punched in cellologists who had very recently had new office service installed, which meant they had just completed all their training, had passed all examinations of qualification. Then I got their full credit backgrounds including histories and origins. Then I got their identoplates. It was a foot-high stack.

"Now do you want someone's communication number?" said marvel-wit.

I had a foot and a half stack of closely packed print sheets. I put them under my arm. "You gave it to me," I said. "And I do thank you. You have been so much help. You should be promoted."

I had caught a supervisor looking over in that direction and my pleasant attitude to the girl said that everything was fine.

I left, jubilant. I had a full intelligence survey of the profession. And without a single trace or show of my identoplate.

Heller was going to be bugged and, by my extensive plan, neither he nor anyone else would know it except me. A bugged man is wholly at one's mercy.

There was no bluebottle in sight. But my driver said, "You took long enough!"

"For a creature of impending wealth, you whine too much. Fly up in the sky to some blank spot and hover."

"That's paper. That ain't money. You didn't rob anybody."

"Give it twenty-four hours," I said. "Now get going before I bash your fenders myself!"

In the quiet of ten thousand feet above the lanes, I removed my disguise and sorted out my finds.

Professor Gyrant Slahb was my top authority choice. He was probably the dean of cellology in the western, opposite, hemisphere of Voltar. He was retired. He liked to keep his communications blocked from incoming. He had made a packet. The chances of anyone ever being able to contact him were remote.

Now for the bright new graduates. There were many candidates. I was looking for a solitary type who belonged to no clubs and had huge book bills and who had opened an office to an empty waiting room but who had had a brilliant prepractice hospital record. I found him.

He was named Prahd Bittlestiffender and he came from the eastern hemisphere of Voltar. He was twenty-five, unmarried and poor. The chances of him ever having met Professor Gyrant Slahb were nonexistent as Slahb had retired before Prahd got out of kindergarten. There was shortly going to be one cellologist less running around loose.

I fed all but the key tear-offs to the sunlit skies of Government City and ordered my driver to the Provocation Section.

As we skimmed along the brown wave crests of the River Wiel, my driver said, "I ain't gonna accept no counterfeits!" He remembered the last sad times in the Blike Mountains.

I laughed at him. He said, "You're acting strange today, Officer Gris."

"I'm a new man," I said. It did not seem to encourage him. But indeed, I felt like I was floating. All my skills and talents were in free play. Krak had gotten it and Heller was about to get it. They deserved every bit of what was coming and more!

We flew into the tunnel. I bounced up the steps. Raza Torr was his usual, suspicious self. Something in his personality, no doubt. Paranoia?

His hand went into his drawer. Funny habit.

"How are the women treating you?" I said. Anything to ease the tension.

An escort bobbed up but Torr told him, "I'll take care of this one."

I led the way, happily and cheerfully. I went immediately to the clothes racks and began to inspect them. Raza Torr seemed quite interested. He made some unsuitable suggestions, holding out a garment used to bury people.

I found the first thing I wanted. It was the overgarment and pants of a type seen on Homeview when they want somebody to look like an old, wise scientist. I chose the proper, loose-flapped hat and then a cane.

I got an ordinary clothes-carrying case and dumped my finds in. Then I went back to the racks and searched through until I found the everyday, casual uniform of Army Intelligence, badges and all: it is an ugly color—custard—but it can, because of its cut, look quite smart. It had a dagger hole in the back but not much blood. Nobody would notice. I found the cap. Then I went and got a Grade Thirteen locket, false stones of course, but quite bright cherry red. I dumped these in the case.

I then went back to the clothes racks and got out a common civilian afternoon one-piece and its haberdashery and shoes.

"What the Hells are you doing, Gris?" demanded Raza Torr. "This some new personal murder spree?"

I ignored his tone. I was too cheerful. "It's really official business," I said. "Legally illegal as can be. I have an assignment to infiltrate and provoke the Retired Prostitutes Association to strike a blow for Prince Mortiiy over on Calabar."

"You mean you're leaving for Calabar?" He was fingering the clothes as though for quality. He opened the pockets of some of the garments I had chosen. I thought he was seeing if there was any money in them. How wrong I was!

I went over to their makeup section. I got me some false skin, some spare teeth, a lot of wadding, some fake hair, some different colored eye-color shifters and some pats of powder of different shades. I brought those back and threw them in the case. Then I added, from another section, a portable scriber that is used for forging orders in the field.

He was tagging me now. As we went through the weapons section, I didn't even pause. "What?" he said. "No dead bodies?"

"Not with your self-exploding guns," I said. "Here's what I want."

It was the false identoplate section. I began to rake through its bins.

"Wait a minute. Those things key into the immediate arrest list."

I smiled at him. I picked out one for Army Intelligence. It looked real good. Officer Timp Snahp. I put it in my pocket. "Now," I said, "you are going to make me two counterfeits."

"I can't do that!" he wailed. "(Bleep) it, Gris! You make so many crazy mistakes you are liable to pull an investigation in on me!"

"Oh, Raza," I said, mockingly sad. "A person in your position, talking about someone making mistakes. Tch. Tch."

He went over to the machine himself and told the operator to leave. I gave him the names of Professor Gyrant Slahb and Prahd Bittlestiffender and all particulars. This identoplate maker at the Provocation Section is the exact same model of machine that they use in the Finance Department to make real ones. But it is ordinarily used just to make false ones.

I will say Raza Torr was doing a first-rate job. He finished up and then aged the plates in an aging buffer and spray. He said, "You're dangerous, Gris. You can get executed for using a real counterfeit, even in the Provocation Section. There are limits."

"Good," I said, "let's hit one." I handed him the phony Army Intelligence identoplate. "Now make one with this same name but change the series number so it won't trigger an arrest alarm. And promote 'Officer Timp Snahp' to Grade Thirteen and base him on Flisten. Right?"

"It won't respond in the computers," he protested.

"No, but it will rattle around for twenty-four hours because it won't match up to anything. And who knows what Army Intelligence in Flisten is up to? Do it. Officer Timp Snahp might want to take somebody's mistress out to dinner."

His hands clenched so hard that he was in danger of breaking their bones. But he did need reminding now and then that blackmail isn't something that is lightly held.

He was actually gritting his teeth as he did it. He made a mistake and had to get another blank.

When he was done, I did a final wander around, picked up an item or two I thought I might like. And then that was all.

I patted him consolingly on the shoulder. He needed soothing. "The originals are in a perfectly safe place. There's not a soul that will find them unless something happens to me. You haven't a thing to worry about. So don't look so worried. Nothing is going to happen to me: those originals will never get mailed to the Commander of the Death Battalion."

His hand had been gripping his beltgun. And as I

spoke, it sprang clear of it convulsively. Color had drained from his face.

I patted him again. I took my loot and turned my back on him and left.

To Hells with Raza Torr. My game was Jettero Heller. He was right in my sights.

This was coming off as smooth as high-priced tup and every bit as heady.

Heller was going on his mission and he was going to go on it at my total mercy and he was never going to come back!

Chapter 9

Physically bugging someone so that even he does not know it is not a simple project, particularly when that someone is knowledgeable about wavelengths. But Heller was stupid on the subject of espionage. Complicating the project was the fact that I was determined that not only Heller would remain ignorant of it: no one anywhere would know of it except myself. I wanted no intruders on my private line!

However, my considerable skill as an Apparatus officer could surmount the huge obstacles. In my present mood I was confident I could get it done.

What I needed now was a secret operating room. Hovering at ten thousand feet above the traffic lanes of Government City, I considered it. Then I remembered the Widow Tayl.

Early in my days with the Apparatus, I had been serving on the night watch desk, a routine posting for new officers. A call had come in from the Domestic Police Execution Center to the effect that they had a criminal who was begging to be put in contact with the Apparatus. They sometimes do this, hoping that, instead of being executed, they will be transferred to an Apparatus regiment under a false identity. Purely routine.

I had gone over, somewhat bored, to find a scrawny, quivering wretch in the Awaiting Execution cell block, grovelling around, pleading not to be exterminated. He had been picked up while attempting to burglarize the residence of the Pausch Hills Chief of Police! It was such a stupid act that I didn't think even the Apparatus would want him, but I interviewed him anyway. I told him he was too stupid and he tried to prove to me that he wasn't: that he had done some smart things in his day. So I demanded that he convince me.

It seems that two or three years before he had been robbing an estate on the outskirts of Pausch Hills and, elbow-deep in the silverware, he found himself challenged by a small female holding a big gun. But to his amazement, she didn't call the bluebottles. She seemed glad to see him. She even had him sit down and have some bubblebrew to quiet his nerves.

Apparently she had wanted to be a widow for a long time. Her husband was a retired and invalid industrialist and she was a young female who was the last of a long string of demised wives.

Rather than reside in a hospital where he belonged, her aged but filthy rich husband had caused to be built a small structure on the back edge of the property— actually, a complete hospital in miniature. And there he invalided along in company with a doctor and a communications system that ran all the staff of the main house. No one could move anywhere on the property without him knowing about it or supervising it from his sickbed.

The aged husband had another twenty years to go and his present wife wasn't getting any younger. So she looked on this fresh-caught burglar as something sent from the heavens.

She wanted her husband murdered.

So they arranged that she would go on a visit to her mother's, this scrawny burglar nut would enter the miniature hospital, make it look like a burglary, murder the husband convincingly and she would pay him five hundred credits.

It had all gone off as planned. But this stupid nut hadn't counted on one thing: the Widow Tayl was a nymphomaniac. She had then tried to blackmail *him* in return for regular company in bed. He couldn't stand her! He had run off to Flisten and had only now come back.

The stupid fool had gotten no blackmail evidence on her. He didn't have any evidence now. So it was pretty useless.

I was clever, however. I had him write it all down in confession form. Then I went and got it stamped as a deathbed confession and told the guards to run him through the garbage shredder on schedule at dawn. He was too stupid even for the Apparatus.

It wasn't enough to extort money with, but the paper was worth something. I didn't even turn it in as, with his death, all his records were destroyed anyway. One idle day I had gone to see the Widow Tayl.

It was a nice, five-acre suburban estate with a large house up front and way back in some trees was this fully equipped miniature hospital. She was preserving it, a sign on the gate said, in memorium to her dear departed spouse.

I should have been warned when a young man burst out the side door and sped away on his speedwheel when I, in uniform, knocked at the front.

The Widow Tayl heard me out, was glad to be reassured that I really was her friend, told me the place was always at my disposal and tried to get me into the bedroom. No fear there. Just lust. I stayed away from the place.

But now I had a use for it and shortly my driver landed in the back yard target. And there in the trees sat the miniature hospital. And there was the Widow Tayl, scantily dressed, by her swimming bath, *dee*lighted! to see me.

She started to spring up.

The corner of her robe was caught under the chair leg.

The robe fluttered to the pool edge.

I turned brick red.

The Widow Tayl's hand fished for the robe and got it back. A sybarite statue at the edge of the heart-shaped pool was leering as water poured from his mouth. He looked like he had seen all this before.

She had her robe back on now, laughing prettily as she adjusted it.

The Widow Tayl was not bad-looking: she was about thirty-five, a blond with smoky blue eyes. Her lips were too slack. She had two big warts on her face. Under the robe her breasts could be seen as far too sagging, but there was nothing slack in the way her eyes were now devouring me.

She bade me sit down by the side of the heart-shaped pool and a servant who was smirking brought a tray of drinks.

I explained, while we sipped sparklewater, that I had been bribed—she would understand that—to perform a service for a Lord whose name must not be mentioned.

He had a son who HATED women and there would be no heirs unless something was done. Oh, she surely could understand that something had to be done about *that!* And I explained that a secret doctor was going to perform a secret operation on this secret young man that would alter his attitude toward women. She thought this was an emphatically patriotic action and the place was, as always, at my disposal.

That wasn't all that was at my disposal. We inspected the three rooms of the "hospital."

We paused by the bed where her late husband had had his throat so expertly cut.

"You must lie down and see how soft it is," said the Widow Tayl.

I felt my hair shoot up with alarm as I heard her continue. "You will never find a bed so serviceable!"

Her naked foot was hooked behind my heel as I tried to go backwards.

Tayl's robe hit the floor.

My right boot hit the far wall and fell with a thud.

A standing lamp began to reel.

A table of instruments was shaking and every instrument on it clattered.

The lamp crashed on the floor.

The double window blew open inward with a terrific blast of wind.

The outer door looked solid. I got to it and put my hand on it to steady myself. I was totally shot.

The sybarite looked like he was laughing as he sprayed out water into the pool.

You have to be careful who you blackmail.

An hour later, flying away from the place, though jaded, I was still cheerful. I had my objective. It even had its potentials: supposing Heller got tangled with the

Widow Tayl, Krak discovered it and killed Heller. Lovely thought.

The driver had not failed to notice my disarrayed clothes. He said, "Is that the route I'm going to get rich on? Or did you pay her in counterfeits?" My, he was insolent these days. Couldn't he admit, even to himself, that my personal charm and good looks had anything to do with it? "But she looks like she'd grab anything," he went on.

"Land near a bookstore!" I ordered. I had to keep my mind concentrated on this project. It was intricate.

In the bookstore I browsed around the technical section. I found a book by Professor Gyrant Slahb called *Cells I Have Known* and sure enough, there was his picture on the back of it! I covertly tore it off the book, sauntered around a bit more and then we were aloft again, hovering.

I got out of the bag the things I needed and using the mirror, working back and forth between the picture and my face, applied the techniques of Apparatus School "Visual Deception 21-24, Advanced Age." With the false wrinkle skin, it was easy.

I turned to the driver and showed him my face and the picture. "How's that?"

"Hey, that's quite an improvement," he said. He really was storing up some owed cuffs!

I shed my uniform and donned the "wise, old scientist" pants and overgarment. Very convincing.

I pulled out the portable scriber. They are handy rigs. They have a paper feed from the bottom and they use different types. I didn't have to spend much time forging this contract: I would be dealing with somebody very unschooled in administration, who had no access to computer consoles.

The driver was shortly heading for Slum City. Some public-spirited, pompous (bleep) had once tried to build a whole hospital complex "for the poor." It was a sprawling ruin, eighty acres in extent. All around its outskirts were small "professional buildings" where doctors completed ruining the cases the hospital had botched. There are lots of parking places, most of them empty, for who wants to get wrecked even at the low prices of Slum City? But there was enough traffic for it to obscure one more airbus.

We parked some distance away from the wanted address. I hobbled to it, heavily leaning on my cane.

The office of DOCTOR PRAHD BITTLESTIFFENDER, as the sign said, was in the rattiest of a series of dilapidations. You had to go around fifty garbage cans, assorted dead animals and up three fire escapes to get to it—an obstacle course which patients would have to run: natural selection—it was easy to cure anyone who could make it to the office.

There was no waiting room. There was no nurse. There was just a brand-new diploma. Perfect. As I stepped further in, I thought the place was empty until a pile of newssheets moved on the couch. It was new Doctor Bittlestiffender. He also *lived* here!

I sank tiredly down on a stool. I really was a bit weary after the Widow Tayl. The effect was somewhat spoiled by the stool trying to tip over.

Young Doctor Bittlestiffender stood up. He was a tall young fellow, long-boned, almost gawky. He had a remarkably pale head of hair that stood up at all angles like bleached straw. His eyes, bright green, were eager and professional. Women might consider him handsome, but he looked gaunt, half-starved; that very clean operating coat he wore was obviously stolen from the hospital and, from the absence of others in the place, was probably the only indoor clothes he had. Good, good, better, better. My luck was holding.

I ignored his professional greeting. I said, in a quavering, aged voice, "Young man, you probably have never heard of me. I am Professor Gyrant Slahb."

The effect was dramatic. His eyes popped. He almost came to attention and saluted.

I drew out the false identoplate and shakily extended it. "As I am unknown to you, please look at this so you can be sure."

He did look at it. But he was stammering. "But . . . but . . . P . . . Professor! I am honored! I . . . I first got interested in cellology reading your nursery texts! Er . . . oh . . ."

He rushed to his desk and opened a bottom drawer and got out two jolt canisters. He rushed over to a culture heater and looked anxiously for a flask that was empty. He dropped the canisters in his effort. Two flasks fell and broke.

"I came to find," I quavered, "if you were competent in your profession."

He forgot about the jolt. He raced to a cabinet and slammed open some drawers. He drew out a stack of papers, saw they were the wrong ones, dropped them, found the right ones and, stumbling on a broken floorboard, got them into my lap rather suddenly.

"I . . . I am not like this," he said. "You have startled me. I . . . er . . . I haven't eaten for two days!"

Oh, was my luck in! But not all luck. It was knowing your field. That's the way these new graduates are. After ten years of study and five years of doing the work the hospital doctors should have been doing, they are turned out to starve in the glory of total, private, administrative and financial independence. For which they have had not the faintest training: what senior cellologist wants competition? Yet they grind out thousands of them every year.

I looked at what he had offered. It was a schedule of difficult operations with the statistical results. Ninety-nine and a half percent successful! That was high! It's usually thirty percent. No wonder the older independents didn't favor him!

But the hospital examiners had not spared the adjectives in his examinations. They practically recommended him as fit to alter the cells of the Emperor! There were even fifty cases of introducing foreign objects along nerves to regulate vision and hearing!

He didn't know what was coming. He stood there like a starving animal about to be tossed some meat.

Maybe he was too good for Heller. Maybe I was being too smart. A little lingering infection or a wrong cell generating the wrong fluids might be just what Heller needed. But I had gone this far.

"I know," I said, "that you have begun a successful practice and that you would not be willing to be torn away from it or your friends or loving females . . . ."

"Professor! Please, please. I . . . I got to confess. I don't have any friends or loving females. If you want me to do something . . ."

Dinnerlessness talks loud. I was a bit sorry I had put such a high figure on the paper. But it was too late now.

I fumblingly, with age-palsied hands, found the contract.

"When the government asked for my recommendation, I told them that I could not honestly recommend until I had personally spoken with you." I seemed very doubtful. "You seem like a nice young man and it appears from the records that you are competent enough . . . ." I hesitated.

He was almost dying on his feet, so great was his anxiety. But that's the way these young fellows get—they are so used to standing up and getting examined that they get into perpetual hysteria about having to pass.

"It is not," I said, "always comfortable to be on some foreign strand, far from home. The air might be good, the local women attractive and compliant, the gravity fine, the food enticing; the pay might be good but, truly, there is nothing to spend it on; really, on such posts there is nothing to do but work with strange cases of complex problems and putter about in the hope of making some universe-shaking discovery."

He groaned in near ecstasy. The vacuum he was setting up almost pulled the paper out of my hand.

"The drawback, in this case," I continued, "was the nature of the post—extreme secrecy. One breath of exposure and it could shake the whole Confederacy. It required a doctor who could end off his affairs quietly, attracting no attention, and simply fade from his present scene unremarked. The slightest secrecy breach would, of course, cancel the post!"

Oh, he could be secret. The whole profession was built on it. He could fade. He could fade without a trace.

"And then there was the first case. The test case," I continued. "They said they were going to set up a test case and told me not to mention it. But amongst us professionals, I could not expose you to a test without informing you. I made that a condition. But they said that even the slightest hint, to the patient or to anyone, would cancel the contract."

Oh, that was no problem! None at all!

"Now," I quavered, "do you think you could successfully introduce foreign objects undetectably along optical and hearing nerves? That's the test case."

Oh, no trouble. Do it in his sleep!

"You might not like the contract," I quavered. I handed it over.

He snapped it out of my hand so fast it almost tore. I knew what it said. I had just typed it.

SECRET HUMANITARIAN SECTION
GOVERNMENT OF VOLTAR

KNOW ALL:

As of this date, one
PRAHD BITTLESTIFFENDER,
Graduate Cellologist, is appointed
CHIEF CELLOLOGIST
to Sensitive Secret Station X.

His salary shall be FIVE THOUSAND CREDITS (C5,000) per year with all expenses paid.

After the successful completion of a test case, upon the outcome of which this contract is contingent, he shall thereafter proceed as ordered to the place ordered to perform the duties which will be ordered.

Signed: _____

Authenticated: _____

"Oh," he cried, scarcely daring to say more.

"Sign on the line there," I said. I gave him a pen and he raced over to his rickety desk and signed it. He found and stamped his identoplate on it.

I held out my hand and he reluctantly gave the contract back. I took the Professor Gyrant Slahb identoplate and put it on the "authenticated" line.

"Now there are some other things," I said. "I want you to make up two lists. The first is everything you will need to outfit a small, temporary hospital for one operation. The other is everything you will need for a small but complete hospital in a remote location that has no equipment, no supplies."

Oh, there was nothing complex about that. He scribbled and scribbled. I will say this: he knew his business to a point where he didn't have to refer to a single text.

Finally, he was done and gave me the lists.

"Now," I said, "the person who will be in charge of you, the person whose orders you must follow, is named Officer Soltan Gris of the General Services. You must require that he show you his identoplate so you can be sure it is he as this is very secret work. He will approach you. You are not to contact him.

"Close up all of your affairs. Tell everyone that you are leaving for the back country of Flisten to work with a native tribe. Handle it so that you get no mail and need receive none.

"Then go to this address and wait. There is a charming lady there who will be happy to see you." Indeed she would be. She would also feed him up so he could last longer in bed!

"Some equipment is there," I continued. "But more will be sent. Officer Gris will show up with the test patient. Now I must warn you that Gris is a good enough fellow but in secret work he is an exacting taskmaster. He knows everything. In the service it is said he can even read minds. He is an absolute genius. If he finds that you have leaked anything at all about anything—even to the test patient—I fear he will be furious. He will be the one who gives you the copy of this contract. And he will do it only if you pass your test case. Understand now?"

Oh, he understood.

"Well, you just remember," and I almost forgot to quaver, "that your whole employment continuance depends on you obeying Officer Gris and no one else." I softened my tone. "Actually he is a prince at heart. If you make him your friend, if you simply devote yourself utterly to satisfying his every slightest wish, you are fixed for life. He is a secret power in the government. One of their most brilliant assets."

I realized I was getting carried away.

I got up. I tottered to the door. "Oh," I said, "one tiny favor more. Do you have an old coat, something you would not miss? It is terribly chilly this evening and I am nearly frozen."

He tore the place apart. He found an ancient overcoat full of holes. It had his name inside the collar. He helped me put it over my shivering shoulders.

"I am so grateful," I said. "I shall see that it is returned."

"Oh, keep it, keep it!" he cried. He was rich beyond dreams. He could afford a whole wardrobe!

Actually, the Widow Tayl would probably give him some of her murdered husband's clothes. He was really set. For the moment.

He helped me totter down the exit steps and left me to wend my way through the garbage. Upstairs I could hear him whooping exultantly. And then I heard the shatter and bash of the breaking of already broken furniture. It was his celebrant idea of packing up and settling his affairs.

As I neared the airbus, I sensed somebody was observing me intently from around a pile of garbage but when I looked, the person ducked out of sight. It was nonsense, of course, that anybody would recognize me. I shrugged it off—just some thief being hopeful.

I flew back to the office where, using the handwriting on the lists, I could forge Prahd's suicide note and leave it and his false identoplate and old coat beside the River Wiel in a few days, to be found when he was safely gone to Blito-P3. Doctor Prahd Bittlestiffender was about to vanish forever from the Voltar Confederacy. The idiot. There is no "Secret Humanitarian Section." Nor any humanitarian actions either in this Empire. Wonderful what people will believe when they want to believe hard enough. Far be it from me to pay out five thousand credits a year for anything!

Chapter 10

In the morning, I stopped by the hangar to estimate the situation.

I had no doubts whatever about my planning and sure enough, here was ample evidence of it. The place was an insect swarm of flying contractors! They were moving at breakneck speed!

The top plates on the tug's back had long since been replaced. Now the cranes had a long fin, like the kind you see on the backs of fish, that was being lowered.

Heller was up there directing the positioning and it was going very *fast!* In no time at all, they had it where he wanted it and workmen were swarming over it to fasten it while he came swinging down on the crane hook. He saw me and bounced off.

He had a sheaf of papers in his back pocket. He

pushed them at me. "These are completed jobs," he said. He was talking in a hurried way, quite unlike him. "I've inspected them all. The costs are correct, the work has been tested. Please stamp them with your idento-plate . . . right there under the project number on each." He had magically produced a board to lay them on.

I stamped away. "How about that tendency of these Will-be Was engines to blow up," I said. "You handled that?"

He didn't seem to remember anything connected with it. He saw a Fleet passenger carrier arriving—a young officer got out. Behind him came an orderly carrying two small cases: they looked like cameras. Heller took the papers I'd stamped and ran over to the new arrival.

It was the Fleet Intelligence officer that had checked my documents after the club fight! There it was, right on his lapel,

Fleet Intelligence

They shook hands. Heller said, with a happy eagerness, "You got them!"

The orderly held up the two cases, grinning. The Fleet Intelligence officer said, "The last two. They're obsolete you know. They stopped making variable time sights when they stopped production on all Will-be Was use in small vessels."

Heller was gloating over the case he had opened. "Wonderful."

"I have to have your promise these don't fall into civilian hands," said his friend from Fleet Intelligence. He was extending a slip to sign. "They're amusing, you know. I hadn't ever heard of them until you called. I only knew of the big, clumsy, fixed time sights they use on battleships."

Heller took each one out of its case to see if it was operational. He was grinning as he looked through them. They appeared to be just small cameras. *All these guys from Fleet are crazy: kids with toys.* He stamped the receipt with his own identoplate.

"I won't ask to see the ship," said Fleet Intelligence. "It looks like you're full throttle!"

"We are that!" said Heller. "Working on zero time margin! I really owe you, Bis."

They shook hands again and Heller rushed off with the cases. He shouted an order to some contractor and then plunged into the ship. He came out in a moment without the cases and went hurtling off to speed up a contractor crew that was already boiling five times as fast as anyone could expect.

I grinned happily to myself. It was working! The Countess Krak had gotten to him last night the way females can and will. Heller was rushing like a rocket to his doom and in a frantic hurry to get there.

I didn't even return the Fleet Intelligence officer's sneer at me. Let them hiss. It was all going my way now!

My destinations for the day were all mapped out. Using the soon to be officially defunct Doctor Bittlestiffender's fake identoplate, I had culled from the master console in my office, all the company names I needed. I knew exactly what they sold. The one chosen for my first stop was the biggest: from the number of government contracts they got, I knew they were absolutely up to the crown of their corporate heads in graft.

After the short flight to Commercial City, I was introducing myself to reception in the very sanitary, haughty, towered anteroom of the chief of Zanco Cellological Equipment and Supplies. Through the huge windows, the vast roofs of Commercial City panorama'd widely in industrial haze.

The receptionist thought I must look a little seedy to be calling on the chief himself for he tried to get me to sit down and wait. I said, "Million-credit orders don't wait, clerky. Shove me in and right now."

That produced the desired buzzes, bows and open doors.

The chief, a huge, sleek executive in the latest twinklecloth executive suit, extended his huge, sleek, sanitary, gloved hand, shook mine and indicated his very best interview chair. The flashing label light on his desk said,

KOLTAR ZANCO

To myself I said, Koltar, you are about to make some people rich. Aloud I said, "Professor Gyrant Slahb, an old and intimate family friend, recommended your firm, Chief Zanco. I do hope you are prepared to furnish what is needed."

Oh, indeed he and they could! He extended a chankpop to relieve my possible fatigue. He must have had an open communicator and heard that million credits.

"I am on a secret project," I said. And I gave him the project number. "You may only have the number, but I suggest that you check it on your commercial computer. And also my identoplate." And I reeled off its numbers.

The receptionist must have an open communicator also. Before I had time to light the oversized puffstick Zanco gave me, the receptionist's voice jumped up from his electronic desk. "Valid, chiefy. Both valid. The unexpended balance is twenty-five million credits."

No surprise to me. I had checked it last night. It would take days and days for Endow and Lombar to dream up enough companies and fake bills and orders to use up such a huge sum. Some bills would have to be factual and I intended to help them out despite Lombar's forbidding me to grab any graft.

Zanco was even friendlier. I tossed the two lists on his desk. "Can you fill these?"

"Usually," he said hugely, "such matters are handled by our sales department but . . ."

"The secret nature of the project and the size of the order . . ."

"Precisely." Then he frowned. "These orders only run to, at a guess, about a third of a million."

"That's why I want you to shut off that communication link," I said.

He smiled. He touched a master plate. All the lights on his desk went dead.

"The bill," I said, "must be exactly doubled. Half of the whole charge is to be untraceably sent to Lombar Hisst, Chief of the Apparatus."

"Ah," he said. But he looked a little worried. "That will only be two-thirds of a million."

I had seen he had a huge catalogue on his desk. With his gracious permission I took it. I got out a pen. I started going through it, checking off everything of interest that I saw and writing quantities: electric surgical knives, instant heat flasks, seven varieties of anesthetic applicators, stainproof coats . . . on and on.

He was quite patient.

I ran out. I got the major list back and quadrupled the usable, expendable items on it like chemicals and power packs. It was enough to patch up an army or two.

I was very interested that he had been keeping a little wrist computer going. He must have very good eyes or he knew where the items were on the pages I had gone over.

"That's only four hundred and sixty thousand, before doubling," he complained.

"Well, I tell you what you do," I said. "You probably have several items that are exotic and not advertised.

Throw those in. Then get the actual price up to four hundred and ninety thousand credits."

"Why not half a million?" he said.

"Because," I said, "you are going to pad the price of some of the items to make it come out to half a million but you are going to hand me ten thousand in cash."

Oh, he could do that. He got permission to turn his desk back on and in seconds we had an office absolutely jammed with junior executives, accountants, stock clerks, shipping clerks and people to hold things for them while they ran off bills and orders and instructions. A beautiful display of utter efficiency.

I sat with lordly mien, puffing on an oversized puff-stick the while. And soon they were all cleared out. They had left some paper on his desk. He was waiting expectantly for me to produce my identoplate and start stamping. I opened a fresh chank-pop instead.

"There's one more thing," I said. "Take a little scrap of paper—that blue blank there will do—and write on it, 'Officer Gris: I consider your request for personal commission outrageous and refuse it. We only do business on proper channels and with total legality.' And sign it."

He did all that and gave me the paper.

"Now," I said, "the ten thousand!"

Some clerk had already brought it in. It was in a fabric wraparound case. He handed it over. I did not bother to count it. We big tycoons of business have to trust one another.

I began to stamp. Every time my identoplate hit a piece of paper, his grin appeared broader by half an inch. His head was practically split in half when I had finished. He was too satisfied. He was going to put in inferior goods or chemicals.

"As Inspector General Overlord for the project," I said, "I must warn you that I will catch all shorts and any spoiled chemicals or any faults in packing."

A little bit of his smile faded.

"And if Lombar Hisst ever hears about this ten thousand, I will say *all* the goods arrived damaged and the chemicals spoiled."

He looked at me for a moment. Then he jumped up and pumped my hand. "I appreciate a careful client, Officer Gris." And he laughed. "We understand each other completely."

"I will stop by your shipping department and tell them where the two different shipments are sent. I will also want fifty spare shipping labels just in case some fall off."

He handed me the fabric wraparound case. I put it and the blue handwritten note into an old lunch sack I had, folded, in my pocket. He saw me out clear through the bustling shipping department and to my airbus. He even waved as I took off.

"Am I rich yet?" Ske badgered at me.

I handed him ten credits. "You're rich," I said.

Actually, I had a glow inside me like a gallon of bubblebrew.

I suddenly wasn't poor! I could even buy some hot jolt and a bun!

"There was somebody watching this airbus," said Ske. He didn't seem as happy as I was. "I think you're being shadowed."

"Nonsense," I said. "Who would be interested in a perfectly legal government transaction? There's a jolt joint down there. Land so I can have some breakfast."

Nothing was going to spoil this marvelous day!

Heavens help you now, Heller, I said to myself as I ravenously chomped down on a sweetbun. A clever Gris might not be enough. But a clever Gris and a *rich* Gris are an unbeatable combination! You're sunk!

PART TEN

Chapter 1

I was on my way to getting even richer, but first I had to cover some tracks. Be neat has always been my motto.

Still sucking crumbs out of my teeth, I stepped into a streetside message center and started dropping hundredths-of-a-credit tokens in the slots. I got a greetings envelope, a fancy note sheet used for sending presents and a pen. Using the little desk, I wrote:

Know All Lombar:

Happy going away present.
H. was adamant to buy these supplies but
I got in real quick to protect your interests.
I hope I did right.

Your alert subordinate,
Soltan

For a hundredth of a credit, you can get a facsimile of something. I took the million-credit Zanco bill, copied it and on the duplicate drew a huge circle around the total, put an arithmetical division sign on it and the figure "2".

Then I drew an arrow and wrote *Lombar.* He would

certainly get the idea. We are used to using informal codes in the Apparatus.

On the greetings envelope, I wrote:

To a Great Chief

Then I took the blue paper that Zanco had written, refusing to give me a commission. I held it up to the glass and dropped in another hundredth credit to get a copy. I took the duplicate and diagonally across the bottom wrote:

Please can you lift this restriction a little bit?

That done, I splurged and bought a two-hundredths-credit cover envelope, put it all inside and addressed it formally—and top secret—to Lombar Hisst as Chief of the Coordinated Information Apparatus.

Of course I didn't put it in the regular post. I walked a little way up the street to a place I knew was a cover operation for the Apparatus—a women's underwear shop—and gave it to the agent in the back office for immediate transmission.

It made me feel very virtuous. I could hear Lombar purr when he got that! He might even say, "Ah, that Gris: a perfect subordinate." Lombar never turns down money!

I had breakfasted rather well. I had bought five huge sweetbuns and had only been able to eat four and a half. As a benign philanthropist, I handed the leftover half to Ske. He just glanced at the teeth marks in it and put it down on the seat. Ungrateful.

Nothing could dampen my euphoria. "Power City!" I commanded in a lordly fashion. "Boulevard of the Metal Markets!"

My driver made muttering noises. It is natural. Nobody likes to fly over Power City if he can help it. I

was shortly looking down upon it. That is to say, trying to.

The air over the place is a violent yellow. It is not
smoke: it is the effect of huge induction fields on the surrounding atmosphere; it does things to molecules, whether gaseous or colloidally suspended solids. These
induction fields come from the huge conversion energy
generators that hum and roar away, furnishing the bulk
of the power for this side of the planet and providing at
the same time, most of its rarer metals. The conversion
of one element to another delivers both the metals and
the power. It is very neat, really. But there is a lot of ore
dumping and downblasts from heavy flying trucks and
the atmosphere is pretty clogged. The whole complex,
with its towering elliptical transformers and elliptical
streets, was first created about a hundred and twenty-
five thousand years ago—at the time of the first
invasion—and although it has vastly expanded, it is said
that nobody has cleaned it up since.

Drivers and pilots hate to fly over it and through it.
It gets their vehicles filthy. It also makes car radios and
controls operate in weird ways. Traffic control beams get
distorted and there are crashes. And all this, coupled
with having to battle flying lorries and ground lorries
arriving and leaving for all parts of the planet, has
prompted some wit to call it "Profanity City."

Ske dodged and cursed his way to the Boulevard of
the Metal Markets. About a two mile stretch of hit-or-
miss shops and warehouses, it is not where one would
choose to drive for a scenic holiday.

My driver really cursed when I made him drive not
just up it but also back down it. I ignored him. I was looking at the price signboards. They change daily and no
company ever knows what another company is going to
post and a smart operator like myself doesn't just pick up

a communications link and say, "Give me three lorry loads of lead." No, indeed.

I finally chose one that seemed lowest today and directed the driver to land at the office. It was the Reliable Ready-Pack Take Away Metals Company.

I went in. They are used to dealing with factory agent buyers from Industrial City and there are no sales talks. It's all old-pal and put-it-in-the-truck. They are not used to seeing someone come up in a smart airbus, smoking a fat puffstick and looking down his nose at them. They looked surprised. Dealing in metals has made them metallic in appearance. Even their aprons look like they are cast.

"Military purchases are out back," clanked the salesman.

"This is personal," I said. I laid the old lunch bag on the counter and he started to walk off. I pulled a sheaf of gold-colored money out of it and he came back.

"A cash deal?" he clanked. His eyeballs click-clicked this way and that to see if anybody else in the place was watching. I knew he was wondering how much cash he could skim off for himself.

"You are posting," I said, "gold for eleven credits the pound today."

"Special," he said. "Only .001 percent impure."

"I think," I said, "you have some for ten?"

"Come into this tank," he said quickly.

He did some rapid clanking on an old calculating machine. It was very complex. How much did he have to steal off the stockpile and add to my order in order to arrive at ten credits a pound. Then how much more did he have to steal and add in order to pocket how much for himself.

But my calculation was not obscure at all. I was going to hold on to one thousand credits to spend. I was not going to return any advanced pay—as I couldn't spend it where I was going. I had nine thousand credits to buy with. I wanted nine hundred pounds of gold.

With many clicks and cracks of his face, he finally had it worked out. It really didn't cost the company all that much. Lead was a third of a credit a pound. Converting it down to gold, which is lighter on the atomic scale, delivered enormous power generation and paid for the processing. The main cost to the power company was in packaging and wholesaling to such companies as Reliable Ready-Pack and it in turn had overheads and commissions. The only reason gold stayed up as high as it did was because the power combines preferred to do lighter element atomic conversion, due to electrical demands. The metals themselves tended to be secondary. So skimming off a few ingots was nothing he would be tagged for. It would go down as "ordinary business wear and tear."

"That welds the deal," he said.

"One more thing," I said. "I want heavy ingot packing cases, nine of them, one hundred pounds to the case."

"That's extra," he said.

"What's the name of that company just south of you?" I said.

"That welds the deal," he said.

With a bunch of "Hey, Ip" and "You there," he got the laborers at it. They found nine battered-up but lockable ingot cases in the trash heap.

I took one of the fifty-pound ingots off the pile. Gold is deceptive. It looks small but it's *heavy*. It almost broke my arm. I poked at it with a fingernail and then put my teeth into a corner of it. Nice and soft. Pure gold. Gleaming, lovely! Gold is so pretty!

Into the cases it went, eighteen fifty-pound bars of

it. The metal man falsified the inventory log. Out to the front loading platform went the dolly.

I counted nine thousand credits out of the sack and into his pincer-grip fingers. I got my personal receipt. We clanked hands.

The deal was finished. The laborers left. And the dolly sat fifty feet away from the airbus. But an airbus can't get up to the loading platform and still open its doors. I called Ske. I pointed.

He started to lift one of the boxes and then stopped to give me an awful look. I gestured impatiently.

It was warm and it was dusty. Nevertheless, a sweating Ske soon had nine boxes sitting on the floor of the airbus.

I lifted a lordly finger. "To the Apparatus hangar, my man." And he got in and the airbus rose lumberingly, staggering into the sky.

Ske was snarling to himself and the airbus was lurching about. This was silly since the load it carried was only a hair above the full-rated passenger load.

The bouncing around made it a bit hard to do, but I got out the spare Zanco labels and began to affix them, one to the case. They were the immersion type label: when you put them on, they sink into the material of the case and nothing can remove them. The labels said:

DANGER
HEALTH HAZARD
RADIOACTIVE CELLOLOGICAL ELEMENTS
THE ZANCO COMPANY
IS NOT RESPONSIBLE
FOR SERIOUS BURNS OR DEATH
RESULTING FROM OPENING THIS CASE

Bright red. Delightful! They would glow even in the dark!

And as the somewhat dusty airbus lurched through the sky, I did some glowing of my own.

Nine hundred pounds of gold was ten thousand, eight hundred ounces, Troy.

On Blito-P3, the current average price of gold was a minimum of six hundred dollars American an ounce, to say nothing of what it brought on the black market or in Hong Kong.

This meant that one Soltan Gris would have six million, four hundred and eighty thousand personal dollars American to play around with. This was so ample I didn't even bother to adjust it for gravity differences. What was a million, more or less?

That would buy an awful lot of Turkish dancing girls.

It would also buy, if I was pushed to use it, an awful lot of Hells for Heller. I giggled because the words are similar in English.

Not only a clever Gris, not only a rich Gris, but a lofty, millionaire, tycoon, fat-cat Gris was not just un-beatable. He was *inexorable!*

"This ain't no truck!" snarled Ske, narrowly avert-ing a nose-dive crash.

I ignored him. Power, power, who saith it doth not have a sweet taste? I was spending it in English already. And in my imagination, Heller, a ragged, shabby and starving, panhandling bum, approached on the street and begged me for a quarter and I pulled the sleeve of my tailored jacket out of his bony, clutching fingers and slammed the door of my limousine in his tear-streaked face.

Chapter 2

At the Apparatus hangar everything was well. Ske crunched down on the landing target, went into ground mode and rolled off to the side.

From where I sat, I could see *Tug One* continuing to boil. The back fin was finished. They were doing something to the whole outside hull. In addition to other crews on other jobs, over a hundred contractor men, in bright yellow cover suits were working with bright yellow spray which instantly went black when it hit the plating.

I knew what this was: Heller was redoing the original Fleet absorbo-coat. You could see the difference between the old coating and the new. The old coating was a tiny bit gray; the new coating was so black it was almost not there. Absorbo-coat takes all incoming waves and simply drinks them up; absolutely *no* energy gets reflected, visible or invisible. Not the most searching beams or screens can get a bounce off of it. The vessel becomes completely undetectable unless it blocks off a light behind it like a star. It will defeat any modern surveillance system.

I smiled when I thought of going to all that work just to baffle the primitive detection systems of Blito-P3. Even a shabby, old, chipped Apparatus vessel could do it. And then I felt less cheerful: all this absorption would multiply the dangers of *Tug One* blowing up. She would shed *nothing!* Screaming through space, picking up fields and light . . . I looked away quickly to get my mind off it.

Ah, something more cheerful! The *Blixo!* The *Blixo* was just clearing in! My luck was really holding!

One of the several Blito-P3 run freighters, the *Blixo* was no better or worse. These are small freighters, only about two hundred and fifty feet long. They are rather skinny and light. But they carry good tonnage, certainly all the tonnage that could be utilized. And they would carry fifty or sixty passengers in addition to a twenty spacer crew. Their warp drives push them about six weeks one way, sometimes more, sometimes less. Uncomfortable and shabby, they can slip in and out easily and they are no more dangerous than any other freighter. The best part of them is, they look ordinary: nobody remarks about them coming in and out of Voltar—just some of the thousands every week.

I motioned to Ske and he ground-drove over—a half a mile was too far to walk in my exalted state.

She had settled into her gantry within the last half hour and the huge trundle dolly had finished taking her into the hangar and lowering her to the floor. It was now pulling back out.

But that wasn't all that was beginning to leave the *Blixo.* Behind the tall hangar screens that had been dropped down for security, I could hear the chatter of small cranes.

A convoy of armored flying lorries was standing by in a short column. They were one by one inching ahead. The *Blixo* was discharging her priceless cargo under the cover of screens.

The first lorry, all buttoned up after loading, drew out and stood waiting. When joined by the loaded remainder, they would go roaring off across the desert, advisedly to Camp Endurance, actually all the way through to Spiteos. The vast storage spaces of the antique fortress would be getting filled up. Just a small amount as yet, but as the months went on, it would be appreciable. Lombar would be in jumping glee to see these lorry loads roll in.

Half a regiment of Apparatus guards were standing about to keep the area secure. It wasn't very important to them. They were leaning haphazardly on their blast-rifles, talking to one another about some prostitute or some dice game.

It wouldn't take them long to discharge this priceless cargo. I sat and waited and at length, all the flying lorries were full and the convoy drove over to the nearby landing target and one after the other, they lumbered into the sky. The chain of them thundered off toward Camp Endurance.

I nudged Ske and we drove up near the guard commander and I flashed my identoplate. An orderly near him took its reflection on his board and we went through the security screens and stopped at the airlock ladder.

Actually, it was by my authority as head of Section 451 that these freighters came and went. But you wouldn't have thought it by the attitude of the spacer by the airlock ladder. He was plainly anxious to get off and go into town and have himself a binge.

"Tell Captain Bolz that Officer Gris is here," I said.

"Tell him yourself," said the spacer. They are always a bit surly when they come in from a run.

But we didn't have time for me to administer proper discipline. I was just getting out of the airbus when there was a row in the airlock.

Three big Apparatus guards, apparently sent from Spiteos for the purpose, were pushing and hauling at a debarking passenger—captive is the better word.

There was nothing unusual in this and I was stepping aside to let them brawl their way down the ladder when my alert ear caught what the captive was saying.

"Take your God (bleeped) hands off my God (bleeped) neck and get these God (bleeped) cuffs off my God (bleeped) wrists!" It was in English! Not Turkish or Arabic. But English!

The individual was a bit of a mess, very dishevelled and much the worse for wear from his voyage. He was squat, very muscular. He had black hair and black eyes and a swarthy complexion. He had on the remains of a tailored suit and a blue shirt with black stripes. But that wasn't the oddity. He was in metal, not electric cuffs and he had no ankle shackles. Further, he was not comatose, but awake and talking and tough! All very irregular.

As they reached the bottom I said to the leading guard that had him, "I am Officer Gris. This is all very irregular. Where are your orders?" I sounded very official. You have to be with these Camp Endurance riffraff.

The leading guard was thumbing through his papers. There was apparently more than one captive. He found it. "It says he is to be brought in straight up and taken directly to top interrogation." The use of "straight up" means minimal duress and awake. Dangerous practice.

"Who signed those orders?" I demanded.

The leading guard looked at the sheet and then at me. "Why you did, Officer Gris."

Oh well, just one of thousands of orders one has to stamp. I looked at it. The order was from one of Lombar's personal clerks, the one that handles interrogation personnel. I went a little bit chilled. I hope they had the right man here. Lombar hated slip-ups. I read the name.

I turned to the captive. "Is your name Gunsalmo Silva?" I said in English.

"American?" he said. "God (bleep) it, do you talk American? Where is this (bleeping) place? What the God (bleeped) Hell is this? What the Jesus H. Christ am I doing in a barn full of flying saucers?"

"Please," I said patiently. "Is your name Gunsalmo Silva?"

"Look, I demand you call the God (bleeped) United States Consul! Right now, do you hear? I know my God (bleeped) rights! You get the United States Consul down here, buster, before I decide to really put your (bleeps) in the fire!"

He obviously wouldn't answer. I gestured to the guard to take him to the waiting covered van. He hadn't denied he was Gunsalmo Silva.

As they pushed him into the van, he was shouting back at me, "I'm gonna write my congressman about this!"

Well, good luck, I thought. Trying to buy United States postage stamps in the interrogation rooms of Spiteos would be a bit difficult.

There didn't seem to be any more captives coming out so I bounced up the internal ladders to the captain's salon. And there I found Bolz. He was a big man, a grizzled old spacer, the hardness of a hundred years of bouncing off stars. He was uncoiling after his landing. He had his tunic off. Hairy, hairy chest. Probably from Binton Planet, from the way his shoulders hunched and his mouth drooped.

He saw me and waved to a gimbal chair. "Sit down, Officer Gris." I had met Bolz before a time or two. I was glad it was him. "I'm just going to have myself a spot before I waddle over groundside. Care to join me?"

He was fishing a bottle out of the table rack near

him. I knew what it would be. It was "Johnny Walker Black Label." Earth whisky! I don't know why the captains on this run do it. Blows your head off! I took about three drops of it in a canister, not to drink it, but to be friendly.

Bolz chattered on a bit about his run. The usual stuff. Almost hit a cloud of space debris; bigger electric storm than usual passing this star or that; blew a converter on a main drive; two of the crew in the brig for stealing stores—you know, banal.

And then, my, was my luck holding! I saw the reason for all his friendliness. He made sure no one was at the door and leaned over, whisky fumes rising, to whisper, "Gris, I got twenty cases of Scotch in my locker. I need a pass to get them through the guards and over to a friend in Joy City. Do you suppose . . . ?"

I laughed with delight. I made a beckoning motion with my fingers and he handed me the blank. I put my identoplate on it. I had thought all this was going to cost me money!

He beamed. He could get fifty credits a bottle. Then he looked at me speculatively. "It just so happens I bought a black girl this trip. There's high demand in the brothels. You don't mind if I add her to this pass?"

Better and better. "Go ahead," I said.

He made a money motion with his fingers. "And how much?"

I really laughed. "Bolz, we're old friends. The price is nothing. I don't even have anything illegal to go back to Blito-P3."

"I owe you a favor, then," he said.

"As you will," I said. "But do you mind if I get on with the ship business?"

Between the whisky and his coming profit, Bolz was really relaxed. "At your orders, Officer Gris."

"When do you head back?"

"Maybe a ten-day turnaround. I got to replace a converter. Make it maybe ten days. After all, they're your orders, Officer Gris."

"Well, ten days will be just fine. But there are certain items you must have aboard before your shoot-away. The first is a young man named Twolah."

Bolz was scribbling with a huge hand. "Probably get spacesick."

"He's a courier carrying confidential material. He'll be on the run quite often. Now Twolah is sort of . . . well, man crazy. You are not to let him talk to anyone or the crew or another passenger. And don't let him get sexually involved with the crew."

"Got it. Locked cabin. Locked (bleep)."

"The other is a scientist. He holds some scientific secrets. He is on a secret mission. Do not put him down on your manifest. He is not to talk with anyone."

"Got it. Locked cabin, empty. Locked mouth."

"Now there are three freight consignments."

"Hey, now," said Bolz. "That's good. You know we never carry nothing back to Blito-P3 but some food and a few spare parts. So! *Real* freight! That's good. Makes the ship run better. You know, Officer Gris, we carry too little cargo."

"I'm glad you approve. Now, there's a big lot coming from Zanco Cellological Equipment and Supplies. Physical health sort of thing to set up a base hospital."

"Hey, things are looking up. Maybe somebody can treat that venereal disease that's poking around down there. I got two crew limping with it right now! The dumb (bleepards)."

"Then a bit later, there'll be a second, smaller lot coming in from the same firm but it's being held for inspection. It will have some very sensitive stuff in it so don't let it get knocked around."

"Knocked around," said Bolz, writing busily.

"Now, do you have a lead-sealed storeroom, that can take radioactive material in boxes?"

"Yeah, we got one. They won't blow up, will they?"

"Not unless they're opened," I said. "But they're so sensitive that I brought them down myself. Could you have an officer stow them in it right now. And lock it?"

Well, he could do that if he hurried before they all hit groundside for a spree. He pushed buzzers and, with Ske's help, soon had nine "radioactive" boxes in the vault. I turned the key in the lock and put it in my pocket.

Bolz accompanied me back to the exit airlock. "Hey, how we going to unload it if you got the key?"

I grinned at him. I was really floating. "I'll be there to meet you when you land on Earth, Captain. I'm going to run this show from Blito-P3!"

He swatted me on the back and almost knocked my breath out. "Great news! Then you can stamp passes for here right when I load there! So I'll see you on the target!"

"With a bottle of Scotch in my hand just for you," I said.

"Wait," he paused, puzzled. "How you going to get there before I do? Old *Blixo* is no sprinter but there ain't anything else leaving before I do."

We could see *Tug One* through the gaps in other craft. She only stood out because contractor crews were boiling over her.

He peered. "I don't recognize her. What is she? Looks like a Fleet . . . oh, my Gods, is that one of the Will-be Was engined tugs? Hey, Officer Gris, do you know one of them things blew up? I thought they'd retired all light-craft Will-be Was stuff from service. Oh, now, Officer Gris, I don't know if you'll be there to meet me or not." And he made an explosion motion with his two hands.

It was not too happy a thought to part on. But with promises to be careful and good wishes for his own next voyage, I went down the ladder.

I had a awful lot to do. In fact, on today's schedule there remained the dangerous part of my planning. The real make or break. My mind was full of the problem of how to get the secret bugs for Heller.

As I flew away, Bolz was still standing there, shaking his head.

Chapter 3

We flew up to ten thousand feet. My driver was pretending he had strained his back and scratched his hands. I had headed him for Joy City. I was trying to put makeup on and he kept taking his hands off the wheel-stick and trying to suck the blood out of the cuts the sharp-edged boxes had made. I got some powder in my eye and cursed him.

"Hover!" I demanded. And added a couple violent adjectives.

So he hovered. I was able to complete my face. With a bit of yellow liquid, dulled by pale yellow powder, I was able to duplicate the skin tone of a Flisten race's upper class. With a skin stricture on each temple, I down-slanted my eye corners. With black-looking color shifters, the eyes became quite sinister. I was very pleased. I snapped a close-cut, black wig on and blackened the hair on either side of my face. Wonderful!

I scrambled and grunted myself out of my General Service uniform and into the custard of Army Intelligence. I dropped the high-rank chain over my head, put on the spike-heeled yellow boots and the flat cap. I put my own wallet and the identoplate of Timp Snahp in my pocket.

I admired myself in the mirror. What a snappy, handsome aristocrat! Timp Snahp, Grade XIII, Demon ace of Flisten's Army Intelligence! How the girls must go for him! How the Army criminal element must tremble, the enemy shake under that sinister gaze!

"You going someplace to get shot?" said my driver hopefully.

"Joy City," I said. "The very best bars. North end."

"The Army officers hang out at the Dirt Club this time of day," said my driver. "That's in the south end."

I ignored him. He was too willful to be associated with. I was busy packing the civilian suit in a little kit bag and arming myself. Besides, he was right.

We landed a block away from the Dirt Club. "You," I said, "can now go someplace and spend your wealth; I won't need you until dawn tomorrow."

"Wealth!" he sneered. "I really owe that ten credits to Officer Heller!"

It didn't work. I sternly ordered him to buzz away. It was a relief to be free of his company.

I checked my weapons. I had a bladegun in my holster. Although it looks like a military issue, it isn't. It shoots flat, metal triangles that practically carve a body to bits. It was a souvenir of my early days in the Apparatus, recovered from a corpse. I had two 800-kilovolt blasticks but I didn't want to use those: they sound like a war going off. I had my Knife Section knife back of my collar. Silence was the watchword today!

Cheerfully, I wended my way through the clutter of

yesteryear's parties and down the block. In the distance loomed the Dirt Club. Actually that is not its name. It is *The Ground Forces Play Club*. It isn't run by the Army at all because the Army Division high ranks could never condone what goes on there: they themselves do it, but they could never officially admit it.

It is about fifteen stories high and covers about twenty acres, all under roof. Across the front of it two blast-cannons perpetually fire flame at each other and a naked girl in a general's hat lies on the top of the flame parabola, quite relaxed. The Army is silly.

I went in, hoping I looked furtive enough for the part of an Army Intelligence officer. I never knew why they put this branch of service in custard, the rest of the Army wears chocolate.

The outer lobby is respectable enough. The first two rooms are just dining bars. It's when you get to the third bar that you know you should never bring your sister here. Halfway to the ceiling there are glass runways and girls parade on them. They don't dance. They even wear a trifle here and there. But they are females who have no appointment in the beds upstairs for the moment and they just stroll along waiting for some customer to pick up a beam-marker light and pot one of them. Then they go upstairs with the marksman and he does some more marksmanship.

The fifth room is like the girl's parade except it is animals doing the parading. They get potted and taken upstairs the same way. The Army, being so much in the field and away from home, can develop peculiar tastes.

Wandering along, looking carefully careless, I had my eye open for a certain badge and, hopefully, a rank that was the same as I was wearing or less. So far I wasn't having any luck. It was early afternoon and the place was by no means crowded. The scattering of badges and ranks were mostly chatting and casually drinking.

I got through the gambling section and into the hypergambling section. It was too early in the day for the girls to be on the wheels. They put them vertically and spread-eagled on these turning discs and around they go while a gambler throws simulated hand grenades at them—made of fabric. If one gets a grenade to contact with one of her breasts, it "explodes," the girl lights up at all points and center and a shower of tokens seems to fly out of her (bleep). At least, that's what they say will happen. The girl can always control the wheel and move her breasts and I've played one for hours without ever a single payoff.*

I was beginning to get worried. I had gone through sixteen rooms without spotting *the* branch of service badge I was looking for. Maybe Supply officers were too smart to come in places like this!

I got clear back to the Bunker Room. It is where they dump crocked officers really. It is decorated to simulate a steel field bunker. It even has a field communication dummy layout that really serves tup. The tables in the booths all around are made to look like field desks. It is dim as Hells. I was almost ready to walk through to the Field Hospital Room—where they serve blood cocktails and the waitresses are dressed like half-naked field nurses—and had even put my foot through the arch when a sixth sense told me to look in the far corner of the Bunker Room.

I did! And there was the badge! The grasping fist of Supply!

He was sort of slopped over the "desk" and a drink was spilled and he seemed to be asleep.

I did a stealthy approach so as not to wake him up. The chocolate tunic was twisted about and I couldn't see the rank locket. I had to touch him to get a look. Aha, a Grade Twelve! The equivalent of a commander of ten thousand. But, of course, Supply commands no troops.

I needn't have been so stealthy! He was snoring drunk! I was about to go through his pockets when one of the waitresses—in the Bunker Room they dress like male dispatch riders without the pants—came over to find out what I wanted. I ordered plain sparklewater for myself. "And bring an oversize canister of double-strength jolt for my friend here," I said.

"It's time a friend showed up," said the girl. "He's been there since early this morning. You people don't look after your friends very well." She went off, a little huffish.

I completed my frisking. His identoplate said that he was Colonel Rajabah Stinkins of the Voltar Raiders, Section of Supply. Excellent. He would know nothing of Flisten. His complexion was white as mountain snow.

He was a very beefy man, much given to lard. He seemed to just snore on and on. So I really frisked him. I found some just issued divorce papers and the photos of five children. So that's what the binge was all about. One can figure these things out, particularly with my skill at Earth psychology. He was drowning his sorrows.

The girl brought the order and I stamped the check with his identoplate. She frowned slightly until I tossed one of his five-credit notes on her tray. "It's his binge," I said, "so he can pay for the sober-up. We were in school together. He always was a drunk."

"Who wash alwash a drunk?" he said. He had awakened. "Thash libelous! I wash ne'er drunk in my life!"

The girl thought it was a good joke. And she swished pantslessly away.

I got the hot jolt down him. "Colonel, you've got to

sober up. It is not manly to fall and sway before the misfortunes of life! They happen. One cannot . . ."

"Who's had misfortunsh?" he said.

"Well, you have. Drowning your sorrows . . ."

"Whoosh drowning their sorrows? I shelebrating! I jush got rid of the (bleeping) old hag and her five *awful* brats. I been shelebrating for two days, wheeeee!"

Oh, well, one is not always correct in one's diagnosis. Whatever the cause, I had to get this colonel of Supply in operating condition. It didn't have to be very good operating condition. He would be dead before the night was out.

And so I set to work with Earth psychology, hot jolt and sobering pills to make my prey ready for the slaughter. My luck was still holding.

For the sake of accuracy, the game "Girl on the Wheel," known in the Army as "Blow Up the Dame," is not a live girl but an electronic, three-dimensional illusion. It is not true that the proprietor moves the girl's breasts out of the way by means of standard battlefield prediction circuits which anticipate the path of the grenade. (Note included at the request of the owner of the Ground Forces Play Club who threatened suit against the publishers unless corrected. —Editor.)

Chapter 4

Only the end objective would ever have persuaded me to work as hard as I had to work to sober up this drunken colonel. But Heller had to be bugged and bugged in such a way that neither he nor anyone else would ever suspect it, and bugged on a line that no one else could enter. But sweating over that colonel the way I had to was beginning to make me wonder if it was worth it. Four hours had gone by!

The colonel eventually had the same idea. I was pressing a cold cloth to his forehead while holding him on the seat and trying to get another sober pill into him. "Why are you doing this?" he wanted to know.

Ah, he actually was sobering up! "The good of the service," I said.

"I wasn't making a spectacle of myself," he protested.

"No, no," I said. I decided to take the plunge. "Army Intelligence on Flisten is in the midst of a most difficult case. We have been told that you are the most discreet and the most reliable Supply officer in the service." He sat there looking at me. "Nobody ever said *that* before."

"Well, it's time the truth came out," I said, praying *that* catastrophe would never occur.

He marvelled for a while. "No (bleep)? Somebody said that?"

"The computers say so and they are never wrong," I said.

He perked up. "That's true," he decided.

"On Flisten," I said, "there have been thefts of the most secret and sensitive bugging devices known. A real crime. Affects the security of the State. Even the Emperor." I looked around covertly to make sure we were unobserved.

My delivery was slightly marred by my noticing that we *were* being observed. A shadowy figure just inside the door of the Field Hospital Room, when I looked, faded from view.

Oh, well, just some lush, I guessed. Place was full of lushes. I got back to the project.

I pushed my closed hand up toward his face. I opened it. His eyes fixed on the Timp Snahp, Army Intelligence identoplate.

"Oh, I know you're in Intelligence," he said. "I can tell by your uniform."

"I just wanted you to be sure. For what I am about to impart to you must not be related to a soul. Do you give me your word on that?"

"There's no need to question my word," he said a trifle huffily.

"Good. Then we understand one another. I certainly appreciate your promise of help."

"You're welcome," he said. I wondered if he really was sober. He looked it, though. Still, you can never tell about Army officers.

"So!" I said in a businesslike way. "To business." I leaned forward and spoke very softly. "These bugging devices were stolen. The very latest developments. And," I leaned even closer, spacing each word, "we have reason to believe that the thief was hired by the bug manufacturer!" I saw this startled him. "Only they would know of the devices. We think," and I tapped him on the lapel, "that the manufacturer stole them back on Flisten and is trying to sell them on Voltar!"

"No!"

"Yes! A very cunning way of making a double profit."

"Well, (bleep) *them!*"

"Now, as you know, hypersecret bugging devices can only be sold to the authorized supply and purchasing officers of the services. And these devices were exclusively Army and could be sold only to the Army."

"Oh, I know that."

"So here is what we are going to do. You are going

to pretend to be interested in buying . . ."

"Oh, I can't do that. I don't have my purchase form books."

"You gave me your word."

He slumped a bit. "So I did."

"Good. You are being very patriotic. The computer was right." That helped, so I plunged on. "You don't have to buy anything at all. I want you to simply inspect the items as though interested in purchasing them. Then I, without them suspecting, will glance at the parts numbers of the pieces they show you and compare them to the parts numbers of those stolen. And if we are right, we will simply go away and I will call my Army Intelligence seniors, they will stage a raid and we will have the whole thing cleared up." He seemed to hesitate. "It will look nice on your already splendid record. Even a citation." I think they also put citations on tombstones, I added to myself.

In Supply, they don't have much of a crack at citations. You almost never see any braid on their chests. It was the clincher.

"Now," I continued as he sat there gloating, "I will slip out and make a call. I'll be right back."

I went to a booth and slid his identoplate into the slot and called the number I had already carefully located. It was that of a small specialty electronics firm that flamboyantly called itself *THE EYES AND EARS OF VOLTAR COMPANY.* Nobody answered. I glanced at my watch. The colonel had taken so long to sober up that we had gone past business hours. But I was prepared for that. I had the residence number of the owner. Using the colonel's plate, I reached him.

"I'm sorry. The store is closed," he said.

"Closed to a million-credit possible contract?" I said.

He pushed the lever that lets one inspect the caller's

identoplate. There was an intake of breath. "I'll get my whole sales staff down there. . . ."

"No, no!" I said hastily. "The devices we are interested in are only your most secret devices. We don't want anyone to know we are considering such a massive order of them. Do us the favor of coming alone. We must maintain secrecy!"

"Will 1930 be all right?"

It would be dark. That would be fine. "Don't light the place up," I added. "There have been agents from the Calabar revolt spotted in town. But don't be afraid. I will have an armed bodyguard with me, posing as a civilian technical expert." That was fine, so I hung up.

I verified that the colonel had a private aircar on call.

The pantsless waitress was presenting a check to be stamped when I got back to the table and the colonel was looking through every pocket in alarm. "I've lost my identoplate!"

Smoothness is the essence of an Apparatus trained agent. With the colonel's identoplate in my palm, I scraped around on the dark floor under his feet, amongst the litter of discarded cold cloths. I reached up and dropped it on the table. "You ought to be careful of that," I said. "Never drop an identoplate!"

He took it thankfully and stamped the check. "I thought for a moment we'd have to use yours!" he said, laughing.

That would be all I'd need. I was shortly going to have two murders on my hands. No traces left in the club! No, thank you! I even gave the waitress a five-credit tip—it was the colonel's money.

We had not too much time and I had to hustle him along. We got outside and his aircar drove up! He had a driver! I had not counted on a driver. This one looked so tough he must have to shave with a blastgun.

Complications! I had thought that a *private* aircar would mean no driver. But that's the way the Army must do things. Wasting personnel all over the place. Lombar's plans for the riffraff would cure this overpopulation!

As we flew off, the colonel said, "Won't they suspect you are after them if you go in in that uniform?"

It was the very hint I was looking for. I was not going to be seen walking out of that club in the gaudy uniform of Army Intelligence only to be remembered in case of an investigation.

"I have predicted that. With your permission." And I moved further back in the spacious rear of the aircar. "Turn out the interior lights, please. We have certain professionalisms in Army Intelligence."

In the dark, I scrambled around, got out of the Army Intelligence custard and into the common civilian one-piece and its haberdashery and shoes. I checked to make sure all my weapons were in place in the civilian attire. I took out some scientist-looking spectacles and put them on. I signified they could turn the interior lights on again.

"My, what a change!" said the colonel admiringly. The (bleeped) fool. My makeup hadn't been changed, only the funny glasses added.

"Now, they may be desperate," I said. "Is your driver armed?"

Boy, this was way out of the sphere of activity of Supply! Exciting! The driver patted his holster. I insisted that I check that it was operational. When I got the gun in my hands, I opened it, verified its charge and, as I closed it, covertly bent the firing electrode over so it wouldn't connect. "All fine," I said, handing it back.

It was quite a flight to Commercial City and I was afraid we would be late. I spotted the darkened, small factory and store for them and the driver flew down and parked in back.

Chapter 5

The owner, all by himself, bless him, opened the back door and let us in. A wiry, elderly man, he stood there rubbing his hands together so hard I thought the skin would come off.

This area was a storeroom, display room and a counter. There is not much mass to bugging devices.

"Colonel," he said. "I am Spurk, the owner of the Eyes and Ears of Voltar. I am delighted to be able to serve you. However, as you know, our truly secret devices can only be marketed to the Army . . . ."

The colonel showed his identoplate.

I gave him the briefest peek of the Professor Gyrant Slahb identoplate.

So that was *fine!* I told him we were really interested in the latest subcranial devices.

Spurk ignored all the stuff on the shelves. That was just common bugging stuff for wives on the trail of their husbands and Domestic Police checking on their superiors. He carefully worked the combinations of plates that opened a big vault door and began to bring out the real goodies.

"It is very fortunate that we have just developed some superlative items," he said. "They passed the laboratory and test stages with wonderful marks. And frankly, you are here anticipating their actual offer to the Army."

Oh, was my luck holding! I had gotten, months before, a rumor of this and it was true!

Spurk had a box on the counter. It was the kind you

put diamonds in, all soft lined. He took a pair of tweezers from another desk. He opened the box and, like somebody handling a precious stone, removed the device. You could barely see it!

"This is the newest. Older ones had to be inserted in contact with the actual optical nerve. This one operates by induction. It can be within two inches of the optical nerve, so long as it is bone-immersed, and it will work clearly and splendidly."

"I don't quite understand it," said the colonel, playing his part.

I picked up a glass and made like I was looking for numbers on the thing Spurk held. I covertly winked at the colonel, with a slight nod. Numbers? The thing itself was smaller than the tiniest numbers.

"It is a respondo-mitter," said Spurk. "It is activated by a totally new and undetectable wave from an external source. This device here," and he tapped a box he had not opened, "sends a continuous wave to the respondo-mitter. In turn, the respondo-mitter, secretly introduced into the patient's temple or brow bones, to use layman's language, then picks up and amplifies the internal current of the optical nerve and transmits it to the receiver." And he tapped the box.

He got busy opening another box. It was a screen like a Homeviewer, but much tinier. "The result is that whatever the subject is looking at appears on this screen."

"Three-dimensional?" I said.

"Oh, no, I'm sorry. It has not advanced that far. But the picture is absolutely brilliant!"

"Range?" I said.

"The activator-receiver can be within two hundred miles of the subject."

Ow! How do you run somebody in the United States

when you are in Turkey? Too many miles! "Too short a distance," I said.

"Ah, then you would need the 831 Relayer," he said. And he tapped another box. "It boosts it to ten thousand miles. The respondo-mitter signal is picked up by the receiver and it in turn, when connected to the 831 Relayer, resends the signal."

He had me breathing again. I had thought all this was for nothing.

For the colonel's benefit I pretended to inspect the parts numbers of the receiver, relayer and the view-screen. Then I said, "But this doesn't take care of sound."

"Ah," said Spurk, proudly. He opened another box. He took the tweezers and held up a tiny object not unlike the first. "This is the simple one. Sound operates on bone resonance. This audio-respondo-mitter can be placed a millimeter or two from the optical one. The *same* receiver, relayer and screen have audio channels. Our scientists have thought of everything."

Except what an Apparatus officer is liable to do, I thought.

"So," I said, "these two devices, inserted in the vicinity of the temple or eye will carry everything the subject sees and hears to a point within two hundred miles which then can be relayed to a point ten thousand miles. The wave is new?"

"Undetectable! Nonobstructable. No known meters will register it. Actually, it is a very long wave acting as a carrier and conduit for a side band."

"Emotions?" I said.

"Oh, I am sorry. The scientists didn't think of that. I will make a note. Emotions. Good idea. Just sight and sound, I am afraid."

"How about hypnopulsars," I said. "You know,

when you strike a button, the subject goes into a trance."

"Oh, I am sorry. We make those but we are all out of stock. Not one in the place."

(Bleep). "How about electric jolts to get the subject under control?"

"Oh, those. We did have some. We made up an order for the Apparatus but there is not one left here."

(Bleep), (Bleep)!

But I winked at the colonel covertly. "How many of these cranial devices here do you have? How many complete sets?"

"Just two," he said. "They are not production line yet. But we can make them up."

"Let's see the two sets, with all parts and spares and power packs," I said.

He started to lay them out. "Power packs are no problem. It's a two-year, nonfail, all-weather. We had the Army in mind. A spy in enemy territory does not have to report, you see. His superiors just pick up everything he sees and hears. It is reporting by other means that gets spies caught. One can practically be on the other side of a planet and obtain everything wanted from a spy."

I was pretending to look at the numbers on the items. Really I was looking to make very sure that everything was here.

He had two sets of boxes stacked up. They were not very massive. I inspected carefully to make certain. "You sure this is all?"

"Absolutely. Spares, power packs, everything. Here's even the installation instructions. It is. I'm afraid, in technical language as it's intended for a professional cellologist, but I am sure the Army has lots of those." He laughed.

That was the last laugh he had this life.

I stepped back, drew my bladegun and shot him in the throat.

The colonel, startled with the fly of blood, was not the steady old campaigner I had thought he would be. I would have supposed he could add it up. I had found a parts duplicate, I was executing the offender. He didn't add it up. He grabbed for his gun! He was turning toward me!

What can you expect of Supply?

"What the Hells are you doing?" he roared at me.

But my concern was not to have a blastgun going off near that sensitive equipment. The resulting magnetic shock waves might disarrange it or something!

The colonel did not get his gun further than pointing at my shoes.

I shot him in the throat! He staggered back. He dropped the gun as he clutched at his throat.

My plans had gone awry. I had thought the colonel would understand. I was a bit off-balance.

Boots were hammering in through the back door!

I had forgotten the driver!

He stopped twenty feet from me. He saw his colonel writhing and dying on the floor in a spatter of blood.

The driver drew his gun. He pointed and pulled the trigger. Nothing happened. And then he did something silly. He dropped the gun and grabbed a bayonet out of his boot and started a lunge for me.

I fired and missed! (Bleep) the inaccuracy of a bladegun! It only contained one more blade!

The bayonet was up and coming down. I fired! I rolled to the side.

The driver drove the bayonet two inches into the floor. He fell on it, dead.

Ow, what a slaughterhouse! Blood all over the place! But I reached for the boxes.

"Stiffen, Gris!"

It came from the door to the next room! A blastgun pointing.

Chapter 6

My own gun was empty. And that blastgun over there was very steady.

I was caught!

With the act witnessed and the bodies in full view!

A sinister, dark figure edged into the room.

"I told you, you made mistakes, Gris."

It was Raza Torr! Provocation Section Chief!

He lifted an object he was holding in his left hand. "I've got full pictures of the entire action here, Gris. Throw down that gun."

No point in not doing so. It was empty.

"You're so inept, Gris."

"Call in your men," I said.

"Oh, there are no men. I can handle you. In this camera I have just put everything you just did. It also holds your meeting with the woman outside the hypnotist's office—and that, by the way, was pretty clever, she's been executed by now. I also have your approach to that cellologist in Slum City and I have no doubt he'll be dead shortly. I have your meeting with this dumb (bleepard) of a colonel in the Dirt Club. And I have this very messy mess you just made, totally complete."

Talking isn't shooting. Keep him talking. "Then

you were the one that blew up my airbus in the Blike Mountains!"

"*And* got back that counterfeit money before you, you dumb idiot, could spread it all around and start an investigation that would lead back to us. You don't mess up by halves, Gris."

"You tried to kill me out there," I said offendedly. "What a thing for a brother Apparatus officer to do!"

"I didn't know that you had a magic-mail setup to send those pictures of me to the Commander of the Death Battalion. That's all you owe your life to right this minute. I WANT THOSE ORIGINALS AND ALL COPIES!"

I shrugged. "I don't have them on me. They're at my office. Let me get this straight. If I turn those over to you, you will turn over that camera and its originals to me. Right?"

"You have it exactly! My Gods, I'm worn out worrying about it. Supposing somebody else killed you? And you're prime meat, Gris. So get moving. We'll go to your office."

"How'd you trail me? You're not that good."

"That reminds me you better take the bugs out of those clothes you're wearing. I put them in when you got them. You're inept, Gris."

No problem about bugs in this place. They were all over the shelves. He was missing things, too.

"I'll make a bargain with you," I said. "You help me clean this up and then we'll go to my office and swap. You don't want this on the trail."

"True," he said.

"You've got a stolen car outside, right?" I said. He nodded. So I went on. "We call a truce. You help me and then we go. You have my word on the swap."

That seemed to soothe him.

I dug around in the colonel's corpse to get the blade out. Messy. Then I flopped the driver over and dug the blade out of his throat. Very messy. Then I got the one out of Spurk's throat. Very, very messy.

"You look like a butcher!" Raza Torr said. "You're getting blood all over your hands and clothes." Listen to who was talking about blood, the chief of the Provocation Section!

It took me two full minutes to find the blade that had missed the driver. It had embedded itself in the back doorjamb with just a tiny sliver showing. I used some electronic pliers to pull it out.

I opened a cash drawer. There were only a few tokens in it but I put those in my pocket. I left the drawer upside down on the floor.

Then I got a box from the shelf and with loving care put the two complete sets and directions in it and lashed it closed and marked it with a big X. With Raza Torr escorting me, I carefully put it in his stolen car.

I went back and found some more big boxes and ransacked the vault. I didn't know what the stuff was and I certainly didn't stop to read the directions. Who cared what assortment of sophisticated gear I was taking. It had to look like a massive burglary.

I even made Raza Torr carry some of the filled boxes to the stolen car. The back was getting pretty full.

I then really put Raza Torr to work. We lugged the colonel's body out and put it in the back seat of his car. We lugged the driver out and put him in the driving seat.

Then I grabbed a blastick and took the safety off so any jar would fire it and put it in the colonel's cooling hand.

I fumbled a bit with the automatic pilot, finally got it set. I started the car. I engaged it and away it flew, higher and higher in the sky, probably heading for Slum City.

In an hour or so it would probably run out of fuel or crash into another aircar in the traffic lanes.

I found a can of cleaning spirits and poured it over the counter and around Spurk's body. I dropped an igniter in it and the flame exploded up.

"Let's get out of here!" said Torr. He was clutching the camera.

We got into the stolen car.

"I take it back," he said, putting the camera down. "You sure are thorough!"

"I sure am," I said, and I put ten inches of the Knife Section knife into his back.

Flames were leaping up in the store. Far out I heard a fire-alert siren start.

I pushed Raza's body aside and slid under the wheelstick. The aircar soared into the night sky and was quickly mingled with the flow of traffic.

I flew out over the River Wiel. I put the aircar on hover. I pulled the knife out and cleaned it.

Almost over his Provocation Section area, I dumped Raza Torr's body out. Too bad not to have the use of the section anymore but I would soon be gone anyway. Tomorrow, if I thought of it, I would mail those pictures of him murdering the mistress to the Commander of the Death Battalion. A poetic touch. No, maybe to the newssheets. No, better not. Let sleeping corpses lie. One can get too artistic.

I flew to my office area. Nothing and nobody there at this time of night. My airbus was parked and locked. I carried my loot into a basement under my office.

I spent an hour eradicating all trace of Eyes and Ears and pasting labels of Zanco on the boxes. Then I put some I didn't want into the stolen car, set it on automatic and let it fly off to crash somewhere. Help the police is my motto.

Then I put every scrap of clothes that had any blood on it or that led back to the Provocation Section into the permanent disintegrator, washed any remaining blood off myself in the toilet and dressed in my own uniform.

Just to put finishing touches on it all, I wrapped Prahd Bittlestiffender's old coat, his identoplate and suicide note in a package and addressed it to the police. *Found by the River Wiel,* the note said. I put it beside my desk to be mailed in ten days.

It was all neatening up. I opened my secret blackmail cache under a loose floorboard and took out the originals of Raza Torr's murder. I removed all the strips from his camera, verified them, and put the lot in the disintegrator.

The (bleeped) fool. Had I brought him here, he would have spotted my whole cache and I doubted he would have kept his word. He might even have tried to kill me once he had his hands on these pictures. The (bleeped) fool. As to his own pictures, they were worthless. Every one of me had been in disguise. Nobody could have identified me from them. Still, he had been a witness. And there is an old Apparatus motto that even he should have remembered: the careless die young. I yawned. I locked up. I walked down to my room to get some sleep.

All in all, it had been a pretty active day! But not too unusual in the life of an Apparatus officer. Frankly, it's hard to see how a government could run at all without clever and dedicated people such as us in their employ. The whole structure might come tumbling down!

Chapter 7

The day began a bit sourly. My driver was in a foul mood. When he brought the airbus by to pick me up, I had quite pleasantly asked him if he had had a good time on his night off and all the way to my office I had been treated to "How could somebody with no money have a good time?" and "One would starve if he went long enough without eating" and some distempered tale about some officer that had crashed because his driver was so worried about being a pauper. I was in too good a mood. I ignored it.

At the office, I set him to carrying the "Zanco" marked cartons from the basement to the back of the car and he kept throwing them in so forcefully with comments like "I work myself to death cleaning up this car and here we go again" and "This ain't no truck" that I got out of the back—there would be no room anyway when it was loaded—and bought a sweetbun and hot jolt from a passing vendor. I was pleased to have remembered to take the tokens out of the cash drawer of that shop—I had plenty even for a lunch and supper.

I sat in front eating and when he got behind the wheelstick, a bit hot and sweaty, he went into a new tirade about starving. I told him gently that the sweetbun and hot jolt were all gone and even tipped the canister to show him it was empty, but it didn't help. He actually picked a newssheet off the floor and threw it at me, excusing it with the remark, "I been all through it and can't find a (bleep) thing you were doing! You weren't working last night, you were loafing! It was you that had the night off, not me!"

I calmly directed him to fly to the Widow Tayl's in the Pausch Hills suburb and sat there reading the *Morning Oh! No!,* the dawn newssheet favored by the riffraff. How wrong he was: I had made the front page!

SORROWING SUPPLY COLONEL SUICIDES

EX-WIFE IN HYSTERICS OF LAUGHTER

Late last night, according to informed sources in the Domestic Police, Colonel Rajabah Stinkins, Supply, Voltar Raiders, took the last firm act to end his tragic life. At eighteen thousand feet over the Great Desert, he blew up himself, his driver and his aircar with a megavolt blastick.

His ex-wife has been hospitalized after hours of uncontrollable laughter. Associates at the Ground Forces Play Club say that even the last minute intervention of firm and lifelong friends failed.

The Voltar Raiders will bury what can be found with military courtesy on Saturday. The public is invited to the feast.

Colonel Stinkins is survived by five lovely children, the older two of whom could not be reached as they are in reform school.

It was followed by a service record biography that seemed to make it clear he had spent a long life at a desk. I looked further. Ah, here was the next:

FIRE RAVAGES INDUSTRIAL CITY

Last night, a wall of all-devouring flame tore through the night-shrouded electronics district. Fifteen people are missing, mostly watchmen.

A half a square mile of charred and smoking ruins marked, at dawn, what had once been thirty-one thriving businesses.

Fire Department authorities state they have positively isolated the cause to an electrical short in the Jimbo Electronics Toys Plant.

Competitors jubilant. . . .

Way down the list of firms consumed by flames was "The Eyes and Ears of Voltar." Nothing about Spurk. Probably had him confused with a watchman. I went on through the paper. Ah, another one:

STOLEN CAR FALLS ON HOSPITAL

Last night, a vehicle identified as stolen, crashed out of the midnight skies to land on the Hospital of Good Mercy.

The superintendent, Doctor Muff Chuff, who was not there at the time, said that damage was minimal, confined to the poor children's ward. As the roof collapsed, there is no body count as we go to press. "We were going to abandon that wing anyway," the Superintendent said. "We need more money and have too few doctors. Application for more building funds is being made. . . ."

I wandered on through the pages. And then, there it was, a small item:

APPARATUS OFFICER RUN OVER IN MIDAIR

The body of Officer Raza Torr of the Coordinated Information Apparatus was discovered in the small hours of the morning on the banks of the River Wiel. It was discovered by a passing garbage scow.

Police Traffic Investigator Roauf Roauf informed this reporter that evidence clearly showed Torr had been struck by a passing airbus and had fallen ten thousand feet.

I smiled. Leave it to the exacting press to get everything right!

We flew through the beautiful morning and were soon putting down at the Widow Tayl's. And I was so pleased I just sat there gazing toward the swimming bath. What a warm glow it gave me to bring so much happiness to this world.

There sat Doctor Prahd Bittlestiffender at the poolside. He was dressed in a robe several sizes too small for him. He had at least fifteen empty canisters lying about his reclining chair. On his lap he had a huge platter of sweetbuns he was wolfing—one bun, one bite.

Lying on her belly in the grass was the Widow Tayl. She had her robe skirt up around her shoulders and was naked from there on down. She had her chin cupped in her palms. She was gazing with rapt adoration at the doctor.

What a scene of post-carnal bliss! Truly, I felt like a benefactor of the whole race. The waves emanating from the Widow Tayl to Prahd almost shimmered in the morning sun.

Belatedly they noticed that an airbus had landed with a blast, ten seconds before, that had almost blown the leaves off the trees.

I got out. They looked in my direction.

But what was this? The Widow Tayl had patches of bandage on her face and the whole upper part of her torso was swathed in post-operation tape! Had they had a fight? Then I realized that Prahd must be set up and in business already. Practicing, maybe. Getting his hand in. Removing her warts and tightening her sagging breasts.

He came gangling halfway over to meet me. He was still chomping on a bun and wiping his hand on the robe.

"I am Officer Gris," I told him, in a very low voice.

I pulled my identoplate from my pocket and showed him. I looked stealthily to the right and left. I said, "You arrived okay?"

He was looking at me oddly.

"Is everything all right?" I said. "Did Zanco deliver the shipment?"

He nodded. But he said, "You sound just like Professor Gyrant Slahb!"

Ah, well, we have a penetrative intellect here, I thought. But they train you splendidly in the Apparatus.

I smiled, "Well, I should hope so! He is my great-uncle on my mother's side!"

Instant awe! Instant adoration!

"He's a wonderful man," said Prahd.

"He certainly is," I agreed heartily. "Now, to business. Are you set up for the test case?"

He loped ahead of me and we went into the hospital. A side room was piled with empty cases, big and small. The main invalid room had been all pushed about and a big portable operating table was centered. Lights were ready to beam down. Racks of knives were ready to probe. Spin drills were ready to spin. Culture flasks were ready to culture. Heaters and flame were ready to burn Hells out of everything in sight. What a layout!

"I see you've used the table already," I said.

He blushed faintly and, yes, I noticed there were a couple telltale spots on it.

"No, no, I mean the Widow Tayl."

He blushed harder and started to look hangdog.

"No, no, no!" I said. "I mean her operations."

"Oh, that," he said, instantly relieved. "The poor woman. Warts are so easy to handle. And there's no reason for her breasts to sag. By introducing a muscle-cord catalyst to the *mammora fermosa* . . . " What a dedicated cellologist!

I forestalled lecture 205. "It's all right. I know you had to see if the equipment works."

"Oh," he said, glowing, "her equipment really works!" He shook his head in wonder. "But there are several more things I can do to her. . . ."

I'll bet you will do them, I said to myself. Standing on one's head in the swimming bath or trying it in a tree might be novel. "The test case!" I said firmly.

He was all attention.

"You realize it is very secret and your presence here more secret still. I am here today to see if you are set up and to bring you more equipment."

"Good Lords," he said, "I have more equipment here now than we had in the whole hospital!"

"We will install one set of these in the test case," I said. "I want you to study the directions and get all set up. There must be no slip-up. Your future, I hate to have to remind you, depends on this first test case. My grandfather . . ."

"You mean your great-uncle, don't you?"

"My grandfather was a cellologist," I corrected quickly. "I have heard him say that the first case tells the tale. And although my great-uncle was very impressed with your record, it is I," I said very firmly, "that you must please. One leak of your presence here, one slip of the knife in this test operation and . . ." I made the gesture of good-bye.

That scared him. "Oh . . . I . . . I . . . I will obey you, Officer Gris. I will . . . will d . . . d . . . d . . ."

I went to the door. I bawled, "Driver! Bring in those boxes."

I found an additional storage space. My driver, Ske, muttering under his breath, began to make trip after trip, lugging in the cartons and filling the spare room. The one marked with an X was early and I opened it and got out the directions and the hearing and sight buttons, one set. I put them down on a table. I briefed him in detail and then concluded, "You study these. They will go into the test case."

He said he would. And although I tried to dissuade him that the rest were of no interest, he kept pawing around the other cartons. I didn't know or care what was in them, really.

"These aren't all cellological," he said.

"They have relevant applications," I said learnedly, although how you could treat a long-distance, miniature, pocket, electronic, automatic sound-aiming rifle sight as cellological I wouldn't know.

Ske finally finished and went grumpily back to the car. Young Doctor Bittlestiffender suddenly turned from his examination of cases. "There's blood on these boxes!"

Ah, me. Apparatus training has to be good, the demands made on it. I said, "Horrors!"

I rushed madly out to the car. Ske was just sitting down in it, very sweaty and cross.

"Let me see your hands!" I demanded.

He was willing to do that. And sure enough, the boxes of gold had gouged the flesh a trifle here and there. But not enough to bleed.

I held the hand firmly.

"Aha," I said. "Steel slivers!"

I shot the Knife Section knife out of my sleeve. I stabbed him in the palm!

He screeched!

I grabbed the other hand before he could get away. I stabbed it!

He screeched again.

I vanished the Knife Section knife up my sleeve.

Young Doctor Bittlestiffender was coming across the lawn behind me.

"The poor fellow," I said. "I've got the steel slivers out now. Perhaps you better bandage his hands. He is not used to rough work."

The blood was dripping. "I could have done that much less painfully," said young Doctor Bittlestiffender.

"Sometimes stern measures are required," I said.

Ske looked at me with blazing eyes. And then the pain got to him and he gripped his palms together to ease it.

Young Doctor Bittlestiffender looked at me with new respect. He led the whimpering Ske off across to the hospital.

A voice at my elbow. "They will be a moment. I want to talk to you. Could you come into the main house? There's nobody else here." It was the Widow Tayl.

I should have known better. She led me into a gorgeous morning room, all white and gold. The slanted sun was pouring in on a glistening, white rug.

Her slippered foot was hooked behind my boot as I tried to back up.

The jar of my hitting the rug made a grinning cupid rock upon its pedestal. Pratia was saying, "I just can't thank you enough for bringing him here."

My hat flew out the open window as she crooned, "We had the most wonderful day yesterday."

I got a glimpse of a manservant sweeping in the hall, a smirk on his face, as Pratia prattled. "And Prahd and I had the most wonderful night."

My hand was clutching the edge of the rug ineffectually as she said, "In fact, we had the most wonderful . . . wonderful . . ."

The cupid was really rocking! Pratia, in a strained voice was saying, " . . . wonderful . . . wonderful . . . wonderful . . ."

The curtains all fell off the rod as she said,

"Oooooooooooh!" with a shuddering moan.

The grinning cupid had settled back, steady once more. In a normal voice, Pratia said, "He is really quite nice. You should see what he has."

My tunic was crumpled up on the floor, just out of reach. I was trying to pull it to me. In a more strained voice, she said, "He was so starved." My hand had to abandon the tunic.

The cupid was rocking again. Pratia said, "So starved . . . so starved . . . so starved . . . Oh. Oh. Oh!"

My hand almost broke its fingers on the edge of the rug. "There!" shuddered Pratia.

The cupid fell over with a crash against the floor.

The servant's broom threw up a cloud of dust.

My hand finally reached my tunic as she said, in a more relaxed voice, "I just wanted you to know how great he is in bed."

I was pulling on a boot. "Well, thank you for telling me," I said. There is nothing quite so discouraging as going through this sort of thing with a woman telling you how great another man is. Wearing.

A glimpse of the servant's surprised face through the half-open hall door should have warned me. "Oh, don't leave!" said Pratia.

My boot flew out the window as she cried, "I haven't told you enough yet!"

I knew Ske would be looking at his watch.

The other set of curtains at the window came down.

A murmur of voices outside told me that the servant was chatting with Ske, probably about the weather, out at the airbus.

The open window let in Ske's distempered call, "Officer Gris! You going to be in there all day?"

The yard was very peaceful. The servant had

changed his uniform. Ske was picking up my boot and cap.

I stood in the door, trying to button my tunic. Difficult since now half the buttons were gone and I was having a hard time: it kept going askew.

Ske handed me my boot and cap.

Widow Tayl's face was at the window, smiling an enormous smile.

Young Doctor Bittlestiffender came out of the hospital and walked toward the house. Widow Tayl raced by me. She slid her arm possessively through his and looked up at him adoringly.

The young doctor shook me by the hand. "Officer Gris," he said in an emotional voice, almost tears in his eyes, "I will never be able to thank you enough."

She looked at me glowingly and her hand was reaching for him. She cooed at me, "Isn't he a wonderful young thing, Soltan?"

Well, it's nice to be appreciated, I thought, if only by the man in this case.

We flew away swiftly into the glorious morning sky.

"Why can't you leave that nice woman alone!" snarled Ske.

If I only could, I thought, gazing down at the dwindling scene. The two were hurrying toward the room I had just lost another battle in. Soon, praise the Gods, I would be safe on Earth!

Chapter 8

We were flying in the direction of the Apparatus hangar. But my driver was flying very badly. He had each of his hands so wound up in bandages so hugely that he was making it an excuse not to be able to control the wheelstick.

I decided this peeve of his had gone far enough. If we really had it out, it would clear the air.

"What did you tell that doctor about me?" I said.

He flew on for a bit—if you could call it flying. "You really want to know?"

"Feel free to talk," I said. "I won't discipline you."

"Well, first I said that if he was going to have much to do with you, he better watch his step."

Fine, I thought. Really pretty good, in fact.

My driver pretended to miss his grip on the wheelstick and the airbus reeled.

My suspicions were aroused. "And what else did you say? You're in no danger."

He took a deep breath. Then he spoke in pure venom. "I said you were a typical officer of the Apparatus: a sadistic, mean, cheap (bleepard) that would murder his mother for a hundredth of a credit!"

I hit him!

It was a good thing the communications buzzer went off.

I braced myself against the incipient spin of the airbus and picked up the instrument.

"Officer Gris?"

My blood started to congeal. I recognized the voice of Lombar Hisst's chief clerk. I got out an acknowledgment.

"The chief says for you to get the Hells down to the hangar right this minute. He's waiting for you." He hung up.

My imagination went into high gear. Had Heller escaped? Had Hisst found out about the Countess Krak? Hadn't he liked the present I'd mailed him? Had the head of Zanco talked about the ten thousand credits?

My mind boiled with fear.

My driver was grinning evilly. "You drive!" I yelled at him. "Get this wreck up to five hundred and now!" That's the way you have to treat riffraff. I was just paying the penalty for becoming friendly with him.

No, that wasn't it. It had all started when Heller had come on the scene. Heller corrupted everyone! He was a scourge!

And now, in all probability Heller had done something that had pulled Hisst down on me. Oh Gods, would I be glad when I had Heller off this planet and totally under my control!

What in the name of Devils had Lombar found out? What did he want?

When we landed at the hangar, I did not need the directions of the guard. There was a bilious yellow "contractor" truck sitting just inside the door. It said,

VERMIN AND INSECTS

on its side. That would be Lombar. He was taking the cover of an exterminating company. He often did and it went along with his conviction that all riffraff should be done away with and, besides, he was clever. All incoming spacecraft from other worlds were supposed to get a disinfection and it permitted access to all parts of a ship without exciting suspicion.

Tug One was bustling with workers and the amount of noise was deafening. One more truck and one more crew added to it would go wholly unnoticed. But what did Lombar intend?

I scuttled over to the bilious yellow van. I had been observed from inside. The door snapped open and I was forcefully yanked within.

Lombar was sitting in the dimness on a stool. He was garbed in a bilious yellow cover suit. His flaming amber eyes glared out from under the brim of an exterminator's helmet.

"It's a (bleeped) good thing you sent me that 'present'!" he snarled. "For days I've been considering taking you off this assignment!"

I was trembling. And this upset me more. That is the trouble with Lombar: he is not consistent. He'd forbidden me to take bribes and yet, while he must realize, despite my deception, that I had taken one, he was leaving me on because I had violated his orders . . . no, no. I was simply confused and thinking in a confused way. And it was also unjust. If he just knew all the good work I'd been putting in . . .

"You reported," Lombar said, "that certain boxes were going aboard and I myself saw some being loaded. You are going to lead us to those boxes!"

Somebody shoved a bilious yellow cover suit at me. It said,

KILL 'EM EXTERMINATORS

on the back. I hastily struggled into it.

I saw that there were three others in the back of the

van. I knew two of them. One was named Prii, an expert on opening and closing anything so that no one would know it had been touched. The second was Bam, the top-rated saboteur of the Apparatus—quite famous actually amongst the top criminals of the Confederacy. The third one was a plump scientist I did not know: but that is not unusual—the Apparatus has literally thousands of scientists in its employ, experts on the most minute trivia one has ever heard of. They, too, were in bilious yellow cover suits and helmets.

Lombar was peeking through a can't-see-in side window. He was looking in the direction of the hangar offices. "Hah, the contractor has arrived."

I peeked. A fancy aircar had landed and a very fat man in a very fancy suit was making his way somewhat anxiously to the office.

"Now, you little fat (bleepard)," muttered Lombar as though to the distant contractor, "Get into your act!"

Shortly, a guard ran from the office.

Heller was working with a group of men. He had a little hull-sounding device in his hand that tests the absorption quality, the thickness of plates and security of joints. Swinging from a rope, he was going all along the side of the hull, verifying each plate. It's what they do both before and after a new coating. He was working very quickly, tapping himself along with hull shoes, quite an athletic feat, actually. The others were recording his reads and adjusting his and their own ropes. He had his little red racing cap on the back of his head and the figures he was giving were being uttered in a continuous stream, hearable above the din.

The guard, pretty clumsy, clambered up on a staging below Heller and, yelling at the top of his voice, got attention. Heller called for a young engineer who took over Heller's hull-sounding device and, much more slowly, began to do what Heller had been doing.

Heller slipped down his rope. He hit the pavement and trotted toward the office.

"Now fall for it, you (bleeped), rotten snob," said Lombar as though giving orders to the distant Heller.

The newly arrived contractor was showing Heller a blueprint. Heller glanced back at the tug as though unwilling to interrupt his work. But the contractor kept at him. Heller shrugged.

The day subofficer from Snelz's platoon and one other guard went over at Heller's beckon. Shortly all four, the guards, contractor and Heller went out and climbed into the contractor's limousine. It took off.

Lombar laughed a very nasty laugh. "Typical of a lousy, rotten Royal officer! Contractor comes up with some stupid problem, begs for help, says his draftsmen can't get on unless he has expert guidance. And the Royal officer, he just thinks the world can't get on without him. Conceited (bleepard)! Know all!" He raised his voice in a mimic, " 'Anybody need my Royal help?' " He snarled, "No wonder Voltar can't get anyplace with the likes of him running things! I sure can read Heller right! Stupid snob!"

He opened the door and waved his arm to the rest of us. "Come on! Let's get at that cargo!"

Carrying various pieces of exterminator equipment, we walked in a businesslike way over to the airlock and entered. No one paid any attention to us, not even the guards.

I unlatched and lifted the deckplates of the passageway and very shortly we were all down in the small, cramped hold. The last one in, Bam, the saboteur, dropped the deckplates down in place behind us. Prii, the open-close expert, pushed a glowlight up against the bulkhead so we could see.

There were sixteen cases lying there, quite long, quite tightly closed, all of them strapped securely in place for a voyage.

Prii got to work immediately. He took a quick series of pictures so he could restore things to exact position. Then he cast off the voyage clamps. Working with a little set of tools, he took the case tops off, stacking them to one side.

They were a very efficient team. The moment a case was opened, the scientist made a rapid tally of its content.

It was hot in the cramped hold. Tugs don't have any carrying space except for their own stores. Lombar smelled bad, even to me, in these close confines. Maybe it was the slums sweating out of him, the slums he so despised. I was worried that Heller might come back unexpectedly. We seemed to be squatting there for hours.

"This is all there is?" Lombar said to me.

I thought. There were the two little cases somewhere else in the ship. But I knew what those were. I nodded.

But Lombar wasn't looking at me. He answered his own question as usual. "Of course it is. I've studied her blueprints and she hasn't any other cargo space. I've gone over the work he has ordered and it's just hull, controls and electronic nonsense. No guns. That's good. She's defenseless. Shoot her down with one blast."

I shuddered. Not with me aboard, I hoped.

"Well? Well?" said Lombar impatiently to the scientist. He was obviously getting tired of sitting there and the scientist, like all scientists in conference with themselves, was pottering along, looking at an object, looking up thoughtfully and then making notes. They can look so confoundedly wise when all they're really doing is thinking about a jolt break. Apparatus scientists are on the payroll to study the technology of the opposition and give opinions about it, not to do any real work.

They'd probably starve trying to earn a real paycheck.

Finally, the scientist finished. "The bulk of this stuff is just odds and ends: things you make repairs with like wires and capacitors and such. He must think he's going to be remote from base and that the ship must be liable to breakdown. Spares and such. Just junk."

Lombar grunted. His face said he would expect that of a (bleeped) fool like Heller.

"Now," said the scientist, "boxes 2, 3, 4 and 5 are a different matter. They contain the essential parts to make a miniature heavy-metal conversion plant."

I looked at them. Yes, it could be electrodes and metal crucible pans and small transformers and converters. They lay snugly in their packing, edges gleaming in the light, disturbed only enough to identify what they were.

"Hm!" said Lombar. "He thinks he is supposed to give them technology for cleaner fuel. So he *is* going to do something about fuel. I was very afraid of that!"

"Well, yes," said the scientist, easing his plumpness down on a crossbeam. "But he isn't being very clever. Blito-P3 already has atomic power. They use it to run steam engines. They have lots of uranium. They make it into bombs. Real nitwits, by the way.

"So if he thinks he is going to make any impression by trying to teach them to convert one heavy metal to another, he is very much paddling up the wrong sewer. They don't need more uranium. They will ignore him."

Lombar was actually listening to somebody. I was amazed. "Good. Good. We can forget about boxes 2, 3, 4 and 5. I know somebody down there that will kill him if he tries it. So what's box 1?"

"Yes, box 1. I see you noticed I gave it special attention. It's box 1 that will give you trouble, Chief."

I looked at it. It said:

Educational Aids Company.

Delight your students even if they are children.
Entertainment is the backbone of Enlightenment.

"That's just kiddie stuff!" sneered Lombar.

"Yes, I know, Chief. But I know your intense interest in not disturbing Earth fuels. And that particular kit
is 'Elementary School Kit 13'. It's the complete set needed for laboratory bench-type lectures to atomically convert carbon up two atomic numbers to oxygen or carbon
down five numbers to hydrogen. And, Chief, in a primitive fire society such as Blito-P3, hydrogen and oxygen
are the primary fuels."

Lombar was starting to swell up, glaring at the box
as though it had called him names.

The scientist bumbled on. "On Earth they fire-
ignite carbon and count on its consuming oxygen in the
atmosphere. They dig up coal and drill for petroleum—
that's the carbon from old fossils turned liquid—and
they fire-ignite it to produce heat. . . ."

"I know that!" snapped Lombar. "Get on with this
educational kit!"

"Well, really it's just the kiddie kit that directly con-
verts the carbon. You must have seen them in school.
They have a little converter and balloons on either side
of it. The teacher pours the carbon, in any form, into the
top scoop and the converter whirs away. The current generated by the released atoms goes up to those two silver
rods and they pop and snap with a nice big electrical display and the two balloons fill up . . . you must have
seen it in nursery school."

"Yeah, yeah," said Lombar. I wondered if he had

ever gotten through nursery school. Science wasn't his forte. But Lombar was thinking. "(Bleep) it, that thing could upset everything. Particularly one certain Earth person!"

"Precisely," said the scientist. "And I know you don't want to offend HIM!"

Bam suddenly got into the conference. "So just let me fix it so when it's used it blows up, kills Heller and a bunch of kids. Elementary solution to the elementary school!"

Lombar didn't laugh at the joke. He started to nod. Then he changed his mind. "No," he said thoughtfully. And then I saw the look of cunning creeping into his face, the cunning that made Lombar the genius that got him up to the top. "No," he said again. "Bam, can you fix that converter so it will run for eight or ten hours and then break down so thoroughly nothing can fix it? No blowup. Just work for a few hours and then cease to work without any visible explanation?"

"There's two of them in there," said the scientist.

Bam, the expert saboteur, got the machines out and began to look into one of them. "Ah, yeah," he said. "One element. With a tiny V-nick cut into its side, it will overload the adjacent elements. Every part would have to be replaced and there'd be nothing closer than Voltar where he could get the parts." He went over and checked the scientist's other box lists. "Yep, no such elements! This is easy, Chief. One tiny nick in each machine, they'll run about seven hours and then turn into fused metal."

"Do it," said Lombar, grinning his first grin that I had seen today. "Both machines. The amount of embarrassment that can cause will finish him. That is, of course, if he gets through a few other things planned, which is impossible. So do it."

Prii had already been restoring the other cases so they did not look touched, inside or out. He is an artist at it. Bam went busily to work.

Lombar jabbed me. "Go on outside and stall Heller if he comes back too quick. Oh, yes, remember that I have a briefing for you just before your departure. So be sure to report to me."

I hastily lifted a passageway plate and crawled out. Carrying my exterminator spray rod, I strolled nonchalantly back to the truck. I got inside and took off the disguising helmet and got out of the bilious yellow suit.

Unnoticed, I slipped out of the truck and wandered over to the office and hung around.

Suddenly I saw the contractor limousine had landed. Heller bounced out. Lombar was not out of the ship! Heller looked like he was going to race back over!

I stepped in front of him. "I've been waiting for you," I said.

He almost brushed me aside.

"What?" I said. "No completed jobs to be stamped?"

Heller had a few but it didn't take me very long to stamp them. Lombar was still in the ship. What could be keeping them? Heller might go inside and see the open deckplate. I had forgotten to close it! He could stumble right into them! And Lombar would tear me to pieces!

"Think hard," I said quickly. "Isn't there anything you really want for the ship? You know, we have a vastly increased allocation. I was supposed to tell you," I lied in the hope of gaining time, "that you had to use some of it up. It won't look good on the books unspent."

Fleet people evidently don't think that way. They have some weird idea of saving the government money and spending only on essentials. Dumb! If you don't spend an allocation, it lapses!

Heller was looking at me oddly. Then he said, "Well, we haven't ordered any flowers for the going away party."

"Oh, good," I said. "Make out an order for flowers."

He looked at me very strangely. He seemed to be having trouble keeping his mouth straight. But he took out a sheaf of blank order forms, put them on a board that usually hangs on his belt, snapped a pen into his fingers and wrote a formal order for flowers. I added two or three types and a wreath and a good-luck-on-the-voyage necklace for the ship, the kind they put on ships carrying celebrities. Then that was all I could think of. I stamped it with my identoplate.

What in Hells was detaining Lombar?

"Now surely," I said, "there is something else we don't have."

He *was* having trouble with his mouth. Sore tooth? It kept quivering. "Well, we don't have any yellow, pink and purple bubblebrew for the send-off."

"Oh, good," I said. I had never heard of yellow or purple bubblebrew. But he wrote it all down quite solemnly. I stamped it.

Where in HELLS was Lombar?

As Heller was about to move toward the ship, I blocked him again. "Surely there is something else!"

He looked at me. He was having real trouble with his mouth. He must have bruised it leaping about the ship the way he does. "Well, we haven't ordered a tup party, complete with polka-dot cakes and blue-skinned dancing girls for the contractors and their crews."

"Good. Good. Write it up."

So he wrote that up and I stamped it.

NO LOMBAR!

"Oh, we must get busy, I can see," I said. "There certainly must be some other items."

Heller seemed to be having trouble with his throat. But he finally said, "Well, we can't leave out all the hangar crews and hangar guards. They'd be upset if we favored the contractors and forgot them. Let's see," and he seemed to consider it. "How about a going away party for them with five separate dance bands, green mountain dancing bears, flitter from the roof and fireworks?"

"Oh, good, good, write that up!"

So he wrote up the order for a huge tup party. I stamped it.

MY GODS, WHERE THE HELLS WAS LOMBAR!

"Surely, surely," I said, "you haven't covered everything."

He was having an awful time swallowing. He finally said, "We haven't ordered new dress uniforms for Snelz's platoon."

"Oh, wonderful. Write that up!"

So he wrote that all up and even added to it new boots, new bedding for all of them and a new baton for Snelz. I stamped it.

Lombar, for the love of all the Gods in Heavens, get out of that ship!

"Now surely," I said, "we have not thought of everyone."

"Oh, so we haven't," he said. "A new uniform, a new pair of boots for your driver Ske. No, we'll make it two new uniforms and two new pairs of boots and a dress uniform for special occasions."

He wrote it up and I stamped it as slowly as I could.

My eyes, flicking constantly to the airlock, had seen no sign of Lombar. Oh, my Gods, how long can I keep this up?

"Jettero," I said pleadingly, "there must be some additional item we have forgotten."

He thought hard. But he did seem to be having trouble breathing. His chest kept jiggling and his mouth was very straight.

"Well," he said at last. "*You* won't need anything as you're going along. Ah, I have it! A whole new wardrobe for the Countess Krak!"

He wrote and he wrote. Boots, dresses, jumpers, a tiara, chank-pops, on and on. Finally he was done. I stamped it.

In agony I was looking at the airlock. No Lombar.

And then, accidentally, my eye shifted to another direction. The exterminator truck? It was GONE!

Oh, (bleep) him, Lombar and that bunch of hoods with him had slipped out of that ship and driven off! The coast was clear and probably had been for some time! I had been doing all this stalling totally in vain! They must have left the ship right on my heels! Maybe while I was changing in the truck!

"That's all for now," I said quickly.

Heller took all the stamped sheets, separated the copies. He handed the former over to an order clerk and the latter to me.

"Thank you very much, Soltan," he said. "That was very thoughtful of you. I thought you were just playing a joke at first and that I was playing a joke on you back. But halfway through, I began to see that you meant it. I'm sorry I was laughing at you. I hope they can find that yellow and purple bubblebrew. So far as I know, it doesn't exist. And neither do the solid gold-heeled lepertige leather thigh boots I put down for the Countess. But we'll let the purchasers worry about that. I thought we were supposed to leave very quietly. But obviously, that isn't required. That sure will be some going away party! So thanks again."

He clickety-clacked away on his hull shoes and was

shortly swarming up a rope to complete testing the plates. I watched him sourly. These Fleet guys, I had heard, did play jokes with purchase orders: sky-blue carbon black, cans of vacuum, a pound of photons, a perimeter of assorted space particles.

And then I thought of my revenge. If and when he got as far as demonstrating that element conversion equipment, he was in for some *real* humiliation. Serve him right!

I went back to my airbus. I told my driver to go up someplace and hover. I needed some peace and quiet.

It wasn't until a half hour later that I suddenly realized how the Finance Office would treat some of those orders. They would declare them "frivolous" and "exterior to existing allocations." And they would not do that until the orders had actually been placed and the goods delivered. You could spend millions of government money unless it was "frivolous."

In a sudden panic, I started tallying up the probable cost of these bills! The further I tallied, the more frantic I became.

If these orders were disallowed, they could be debited against the account of the stamping officer!

Some, like uniforms, might get okayed but the rest came to about eight hundred and fifty credits! Maybe more!

If I overdrew my account I would probably be court-martialled, even cashiered!

Ske said, "What's the matter with you? You look like you're having a convulsion!"

Finally, I managed to tell him. "Drive to the Finance Office. I've got to place nine hundred credits into my year's advanced pay account and quick!"

I nearly would be broke again!

Slumped, I gloomed over my fate as we rode along.

And then I sat up straight with a new horror. With all those parties, fireworks and wreaths on the ship, Lombar was going to tear my guts out for violating the secrecy of the mission!

I suddenly yelled, "(Bleep) Heller. (Bleep) him and all his kind!"

It didn't help to hear Ske laughing. He wouldn't laugh if he really knew how bad it was.

It had begun as such a beautiful day.

Chapter 9

I had spent the remainder of the day before tending to this and that and then had spent the night rolling around in a growing state of apprehension. Today I was somehow going to have to lure Heller to that miniature hospital and get him operated on. My main worry was the Countess Krak. If she suspected I had done something to Heller, Spiteos or no Spiteos, she would find ways to kill me. When I finally got to sleep, it was only to have a nightmare about her mistaking me for the yellow-man I had seen her stamp to pulp. In it, I kept trying to tell her that the only reason I was having a nightmare was because she had a role reversal, prompted by an elektra complex of father fixation, but she just kept on stamping. I woke up streaming sweat and for a few moments had been sure it was my blood kicked out of me. I didn't go back to sleep!

In the morning, I approached *Tug One* after sunrise when I was sure Krak had gone. The best tricks I could think of held firmly in my mind, I walked aboard, smiling a smile I did not feel. Heller was already up, sitting in the fancy salon, polishing off some notes. He was dressed in a white, flare-collared, work cover suit of some sparkly material. These Fleet guys certainly can put on airs. I hoped it got bloodstained before the day was out!

"You'll have to postpone any other work you have for today," I said. "You have a physical readiness appointment."

He laughed. "I think I'm ready. I'm in pretty good shape, actually. I was about to run around the hangar for a workout before the crews came this morning."

"May I sit down?" I said and did. "Jettero, you don't understand espionage. That's why I am here to guide you. In the place where we are going, they do ALL their police records with identifying marks. If you have any identifying marks, you can be spotted, just like that!" And I snapped my fingers.

He shook his head. "I don't have any."

"Hah!" I said. I reached over and grabbed the glistening white cloth and pulled it aside to bare his shoulder. I secretly hoped the cloth would tear. "What do you call that?" And I pointed to where Lombar's paralysis dagger had left a small white scar. "Do you see?" I let go and the jumper sprang back in place. I looked at his face searchingly. For a combat engineer who had been through all the battles and adventures he had, he certainly had few marks on him.

Then I found one. Just at the outer edge of his right eyebrow there was a tiny scar. The very thing! Through it one could enter between the temple and the overeye bone.

"So," I said, triumphantly, "there's two already." And I pointed to the eyebrow scar.

"Oh, that," he laughed. "You won't believe this but

I was with a campaign on a primitive planet once. I had to get into a stockaded village. And I got hit with a stone-headed arrow! Honestly. A bow and arrow! The on-board doctor who fixed it laughed and laughed over it. I was standing there with a blastgun ready to shoot and got hit with an arrow! Hilarious. Had the whole squadron laughing. It's nothing."

"It's an identifying mark," I said impressively. "Where we're going, they would see that and recognize at once you were from Voltar. Pick you up like that!" And I snapped my fingers to emphasize it.

Heller exploded with laughter. "We don't use bows and arrows on Voltar! Look around, Soltan. You see any?" He thought it was screamingly funny. He laughed and laughed. I hoped he choked.

I could see I was getting nowhere on that course, so I went into my second argument. I had spent hours on this project, all aspects of how to lure him into an operation. "Well, that may or may not be," I said a bit sternly. "But it doesn't get around Regulation 534279765 Part A, Paragraph 1! It distinctly states that no one with identifying marks may be landed on Earth! So there!"

He had stopped laughing. "You have the regulations here to show me, of course."

Well, I couldn't do that. I had just made it up. But I can think pretty fast. "You know of *Book of Space Codes* Number a-36-544 M Section B, prohibiting landing and disclosure of extraterrestrial identity."

He knew of that, yes.

"The identifying marks regulation I just gave you is a secret court interpretation of it. We're bound by it, you know."

Heller shook his head. "I confess I have not seen it. And if that interpretation is Apparatus, I'm Fleet. I'm not bound by it."

It was plain I was not progressing. But the psychology of Blito-P3 had not yet been brought into play. This is the real standby of my personal tradecraft. Nobody ever knew, until these disclosures here, that I owed my success to it.

A child, it says, when denied the things it wants, often goes into what is called a *tantrum,* which is one of their scientific terms. Adults, faced with it, usually recoil and surrender. I went into Stage One of a *tantrum.*

"You," I pouted, "are just trying to make my job difficult. You are an old meany." It is a magic psychological term, an incantation phrase. Right away, I could see it was having an affect. Heller looked at me, puzzled.

I went into Stage Two: *negation.* "If you don't go with me for your physical readiness appointment, I WILL NOT STAMP ANY MORE COMPLETION ORDERS FOR YOU!" I shouted the last in a proper pitch and wail.

It was working. He was peering at me, perplexed.

I went into Stage Three: *convulsive denial.* I fell on the floor on my back, I writhed. I beat my heels against the floor in a furious tattoo, simulating an *epileptiform seizure.* It is that which gets them. The secret is that an epileptiform seizure also occurs in death: the adults fear the child is in the last convulsions of dying. I was watching carefully out of the corner of my eye.

It really was working! He took a long sigh—the textbook response—and rolled his eyes up to heavens.

Stage Four is putting a piece of soap in the mouth and *frothing* and I had the soap all ready. I was also ready to go into Stage Five which is the *simulated death rattle.*

I didn't have to!

Heller said, "Oh, for Gods sakes, Soltan! You don't have to put on a phony act! If my not going will get you into trouble with Lombar Hisst, I'll come along!"

I had him!

Outside I told the subofficer and guard to stay by the ship. Heller would be gone for the day.

We took off.

Earth psychology works every time! Not as pleasant, of course, as a Bugs Bunny activity. But every bit as effective! Those psychologists and psychiatrists on Earth have it down pat! They can fool the suckers every time! Absolute masters of cold-blooded deception and chicanery!

Satisfyingly cruel, too. Just like my plans for today.

PART ELEVEN

Chapter 1

"Well, well," said Heller as we flew in. "Pausch Hills suburbs. An improvement over the operating rooms of Spiteos."

Ske was taking a low approach to the Widow Tayl's estate. "Oh, yes, indeed. I knew what I was doing when I persuaded you. You were very wise to come along. Everything will be just lovely. Nothing but the best." And I pointed out the sign on the gate,

Sacred Memorial Hospital
Preserved in Memory
of My Beloved Husband

Too bad, I thought to myself, that we can't bury you the same way. "A specialist doctor, the top of his profession, will take wonderful care of you." You crew-corrupting (bleepard). I smiled. We landed. "Well, here we are and out you get."

Prahd was standing way over outside the miniature hospital door. He had a surgical, aseptic mask on. He was holding a glittering pair of forceps in his hand. The sun flashed on the polished metal as he opened and closed them.

Heller jumped down out of the airbus. He took a deep breath of the fragrant, blossom-laden air and stretched. Then he started across the lawn and past the swimming bath toward Bittlestiffender. I could hardly contain my glee: he had taken the bait; I had him!

Over under the blossoming trees, I had not seen the Widow Tayl. She was standing there in the shadows. She had not moved forward. She was just standing there. Her mouth was half-open, her eyes round. She was holding one hand to her breast as though finding it hard to breathe. I thought to myself that she was, unfortunately, really developing a case on me. "Adoration fixation," they call it: the inexplicable attraction of the female for a virile and handsome male. I regretted having this effect on women at the moment. I had other business in mind. I hastened to keep up with Heller.

"Doctor Bittlestiffender," I said. "Here is your . . . patient." I had almost said "meat."

I had already briefed young Doctor Prahd Bittlestiffender. But he was a little nervous. Why not? He thought his world would collapse if he failed with this case. He nodded, snap-snipping the instrument in his hand convulsively. He led the way hurriedly inside.

Heller took a brief tour around the room. "Well, well. All the latest and the newest."

"Now, if you will just remove your clothes and lie down on this operating table," said young Doctor Prahd, "we can get on with it."

"I hope so," said Heller. "I've got a lot of things to do at the ship. We're sailing very soon, so . . ."

His ignorance of espionage and security was awful! He'd be telling Bittlestiffender his life history and right name next! I cut him off. "Then the sooner you do what the doctor says, the quicker it will be over."

Heller kicked off his shoes and peeled. He lay down on the operating table.

"Hm," said the young Doctor Prahd, "you are certainly extremely well built. And equipped."

It startled me. I glanced to see if there was amour in this young doctor's eyes. But there wasn't. He was just being matter-of-fact professional. And it was true, unfortunately, what he said of Heller. He was a very muscular, well-proportioned athlete and he was very well equipped. I realized Prahd was building patient empathy. Then I realized the compliment had made me a little cross. Other people are well built and equipped, too. Well, not really.

"Doctor," I said, "I want to call your attention to certain deadly identifying marks. Quite disfiguring. And a total catastrophe in our line of work."

Prahd was looking and looking. He couldn't see any. And the dumb (bleepard) was about to say so when I firmly pointed at the tiny white scar Lombar's paralysis dagger had made. "That," I said, leaving no room for dispute, "must be taken care of!"

I pointed at the end of the right eyebrow. "And *there* is the dead giveaway. Stands out like a glaring boil!"

Young Doctor Prahd peered and peered and finally saw the faint scar tissue. He shocked me by saying, "He certainly heals well. It would take a magnifying . . ."

"*That*," I said hurriedly—my Gods, this doctor was stupid, for I had drilled him well—"is the remains of a bone-deep wound. It was the result of a skull-shattering blow from a primitive stone arrowhead!"

Prahd blinked. "A stone arrowhead?" Then both he and Heller had no better sense, at this crucial moment, than to laugh. Heller told the story to him. It seemed they weren't even fighting the primitives and Heller had been curious as to how they held their stockade wall up— it seemed to be floating two feet off the ground—and, as a precaution as he approached it, had drawn his blastgun and a little kid had shot him with a stone-headed arrow. For the life of me, I couldn't see what was so funny about it. Further, I judged he must tell the story differently every time he had a new audience. It didn't make sense. If he had a blastgun in his hand, he could easily have killed the little kid first. So he was lying.

But before I could get this silly situation under control, young Doctor Prahd had picked up a machine that had a viewplate and was putting it under Heller's head. Prahd looked at the screen. I looked at the screen. I couldn't see anything but the outline of some skull bones.

Then young Doctor Prahd said, "Well, I'll be blasted! Was this treated?"

Heller shrugged. "Wasn't much to treat. We mostly laughed about it. The doctor just put some tape on it."

"Ah," said young Doctor Prahd. "He should have been sent before the doctor's review board!" He was very serious.

Heller had stopped laughing.

Young Doctor Prahd put his finger just in toward the eyebrow on the wound. "Does that hurt?"

"Ouch," said Heller.

"I thought so!" Prahd drew an *X* on the spot with a purple pen. He drew back and turned the machine off and put it on another bench. Then he stood back and shook his head at Heller. "Had that doctor taken the proper steps, he would have seen what I just saw!"

I gaped. I hadn't seen anything on the screen.

Young Doctor Prahd looked grave. "My dear fellow, I don't like to tell you this. Now don't be unduly alarmed for you are in competent hands. But in another two years at the outside, had it not come to my attention, the creeping penetration syndrome would have resulted in prefrontal lobe incision with the usual consequences of internal cerebral shield suppuration."

What the Hells was this stupid doctor up to?

"Hey," said Heller, "physical doctoring is not in my line. You'll have to put that in plain Voltarian."

Prahd took Heller's hand in his own in a comforting gesture. "I have to tell you—now don't leap up and run away—that the tip of that stone arrowhead is still in there!"

I finally got it! Wow, this young Doctor Prahd was a very sharp boy. No wonder the older practitioners didn't want him around as competition! A real con artist! Worthy of the finest traditions of the Apparatus!

"Hold it," said Heller. "I haven't got time to let you fool around with that now! I've got to get going on a mission!"

Young Doctor Prahd said, "Mission physical clearance refused. Officer Gris, please inform your superiors that said subject cannot be certified for physical readiness."

"Why?" demanded Heller, trying to sit up.

Prahd said, "If the inevitable consequences of a foreign body gradually eating its way into the brain were to occur after I passed you, resulting in mission failure as it would, the Board of Examiners could revoke my certificates. So, I cannot pass you. You cannot go."

Thank heavens, Krak had already worked on him. Heller started to get mad. "You don't understand! I've got to complete this mission!"

Prahd was just putting his tools away.

"How long would it take to remove it?" demanded Heller.

Prahd shrugged. "It's not a big job, even if it is vital. Two hours. Another four or five to recover from the anesthesia."

"Oh, no," said Heller. "I promised . . . well, I promised somebody not to let myself be put under around . . . around certain people."

"Oh, Jet," I said. "Don't you trust your friends?" But I had thought of all this. I knew that Krak would have a fit if she found Heller had been put into a general anesthesia. She had feared somebody would really cut him up or maybe do a hypnotic implant. I had worked it all out.

I picked up a case from a table from right where I had left it. I handed it to Heller. "That is a security recorder. Lockable. I give it to you. You set your own combination on it. You lock it to your own wrist. Nobody can interfere with it or change it but you. It will start recording. It will keep right on recording until you wake up. It will take both sound and picture of what is happening. Examine it."

He did so. There were no tricks in it. The metal case was totally impenetrable once it was locked. Only he would know the numbers and be able to open it and get at the recording strip.

Heller sighed. In a weary voice, he said, "Which wrist do I put it on."

I had won! I had won! But I preserved my grave mien. "Left wrist, as the doctor will be working on the right side. We can lay your hand on this little wheeltable and it will just sit there and record everything. Then you, at your leisure, can review it." I knew the Countess Krak would review it!

He thought of some numbers, committed them silently to memory, set the lock, put it on his wrist and laid his hand and the recorder on the table. He adjusted the position so it would show what was happening.

The recorder was running. I said to Prahd, "I feel a little queasy. Have you got something?"

He handed me a pill.

Heller was watching in a rather bored way as the doctor began to get out knives and forceps and probes and wheel things about.

Prahd was chattering along soothingly. "It's the small things in life that are annoying. You would just never think that a tiny bit of stone could do much real damage." Etc. Etc. On and on.

Finally Prahd wheeled a portable anesthetic gas machine into place. He said to me, "Could you hold this?"

"Oh, no," I said. "The sight of blood makes me quite ill lately for some reason."

Prahd shrugged, turned up the oxygen and turned on the sleep gas. He put the mask over the other part of Heller's face. Heller began to inhale it. The needle on a meter clamped to the back of Heller's skull registered *Unconscious.*

The young doctor picked up a scalpel.

I said, suddenly, "Oh, my Gods, I'm going to be sick at my stomach!"

I rushed headlong from the room, making heaving sounds.

Still groaning, I paused in the hall and letting the heaving sounds diminish gradually, reached down and pulled the string I had planted there yesterday. It pulled the wheeltable on which the recorder was resting back just enough to let the hand and wrist fall off, as though naturally, and drop below sight level of the bed. It would look as if he had moved his own arm. The recorder would now have sound but only the side of the bed for a picture.

I let my groaning die out in volume further as I tiptoed outside.

I had him! Of course, it wasn't as good as just plain

doing a prefrontal lobotomy, the one the Earth psychiatrists favor; they push a common ice pick up under the eyelids and slash the prefrontal lobes of the brain to hamburger and if the patient does not die at once, he lives on as a vegetable and dies in any case from within two to five years. A highly practical solution to psychosis. But the thought of the Countess Krak restrained me. She would notice.

It is one of the trials of life that one can't have everything one wants. Still, I could do with what I had. With those optical and aural bugs in place, I would know everything Heller was doing and could block him. He now could not escape me. He was going to be totally at my mercy. Thinking of all the horrible things I had suffered at his hands, I sank into a pleasant euphoria. Justice was about to be done.

Chapter 2

A hand was tugging at my sleeve. It was the Widow Tayl. I came out of my reverie. She was pointing in the direction of a little summerhouse some distance away in the trees.

"There's something I must show you," she whispered.

It was all going quietly in the hospital. I could now and then hear a machine move. Two hours, Prahd had said. It would be a long time yet.

Wondering at this power I had over women, I followed the Widow Tayl. I really had no illusions as to what she wanted to show me in the summerhouse.

It was a very pleasant structure, surrounded by flowering trees which drenched the air with perfume. It consisted mainly of a roof and a big, soft pad of bright yellow. A tinkle of music, soft and persuasive, came from the top peak of the ceiling, below which hung an ornate, painted glowplate. It was a secluded spot, safe from prying eyes, ideal for an interchange of secrets and other things.

"WHO was that?" She was still whispering.

I looked at her as she leaned a hand against a pillar. Her mouth was a bit slack, her eyes a trifle glazed. She was having trouble breathing. I looked at her face. I was quite surprised: the warts were gone, only a slight redness remained in the areas where they had been. Her face was quite pretty, really. I looked at her breasts: under her silken robe they were now firm and upright, no longer sagging.

I looked her up and down. I began to feel excited. I walked over to the pad and lay down, smiling at her invitingly. I became aroused, which I had never been before with her.

I expected her as usual to tear and rip at my clothes. She came over to the pad, moving slowly as though in a daze. Still robed, she lay upon it, three feet away from me. On her back and looking dreamily at the ceiling, she put her hands behind her head.

Her eyes, luminous as always, began to grow opaque. Her breath began to quicken. "When I first saw him," she whispered, "I thought he was some woods God. So strong, so powerful."

The lamp in the ceiling began to swing and the music took on a throb. "He stepped out of the airbus so smoothly . . . so smoothly . . . so smoothly . . . ."

A huge multipetalled blossom by the door seemed to

get larger. "Oh. Oh. Oh. OH!" cried Pratia and the blossom burst like an explosion!

I lay there, fully clothed, propped on my elbow, staring. What the Hells was going on? She wasn't even touching me!

Her slack mouth panted for a moment. Her eyes began to roll back. "Then he stretched and began to walk."

A bird peered in, curious. "His feet barely touched the ground," crooned Pratia.

The lamp was swinging as the music reached crescendo. "His toes caressed . . . caressed . . . caressed . . .

"Oh. Oh. Oh. OH!" she cried as her slippers flew up in the air.

I began to frown. I was just lying there unmolested. It puzzled me.

Some birds lit quietly in a nearby tree and her breathing slowed to normal. The music was sedate again.

The lamp was still. "And then he walked past the swimming bath . . . ." The lamp began to swing.

The bird was watching intently. " . . . and his shadow fell across my favorite place . . . favorite place . . . favorite place.

"Oh. Oh. Oh. OH!" she cried as the flock of birds, startled, flew away.

I was beginning to get a bit upset as I looked at her.

The two of us were lying on the pad a yard apart. Her hands were still behind her head. She was breathing a bit hard but it was quieting down. "And then," she began to whisper at the ceiling, "he stopped and with a heavenly motion he removed . . ."

The bird was really getting intent. " . . . little red cap . . . little red cap . . . little red cap . . ."

Once more the ceiling lamp was swinging and the

music was speeding up. " . . . and he put it in . . . he put it in . . . he put it in . . .

"Oh.   OOOOOOOOOOOOOOOOOOOH!"   she cried and the bird flew frantically away.

The lamp exploded into fragments!

Red cap? Lying there, the vision of him and his red cap washed over me.

Hey! This (bleep) was thinking about Heller!

And there I was, completely available, not even being talked to, much less touched!

Oh, it made me angry!

I pushed her aside in disgust. That would show her. I stalked out of the summerhouse. She couldn't trifle with me this way!

Behind me I heard her starting again. "And then he put it in his pocket. And he stood there a moment and as he started to go in . . . to go in . . . to go in . . ."

I waited to hear no more. I went over to the pool and sat down. Oh, I was cross, I can tell you.

But after a little while, I came out of it. The occasional clink in the hospital was restoring my good spirits. That filthy (bleepard) was getting his! And this was just one more injury he was paying for.

I tried to think of something even more vicious I could do. But actually what was happening was really quite enough.

It was a beautiful day after all.

Chapter 3

About noon, wiping his hands on a bloodstained disposable coat, Doctor Prahd Bittlestiffender came out of the hospital. But he did not come over to where I sat at the pool. He went walking along one of the curving rock paths that wound artfully under the blooming trees.

Well, I thought, he just wants to stretch. He hadn't been two hours on that operation; he had been more than three and a half! Long-legged and a bit too tall, he went ambling along on a zigzag sort of course, looking down. Maybe the operation had been a failure, maybe he'd put an electric knife in too deep and killed Heller: an intriguing thought. As I considered it, it seemed to have more and more merit.

Coming back along the path, the young doctor suddenly stooped over and picked something up. Then he went over to where a naked wood nymph posed erotically in stone. He took a small hammer from an inside pocket and started hammering something against the wood nymph's metal base. What in Hells was he up to? Trying to bring the wood nymph to life by rhythmic pounding? We had one too many nymphs around here already!

At last he began to wander over toward me again. He took a little spin drill and a pair of tweezers out of his inside pocket and was holding something and buffing it, wandering closer, humming. The spin drill was going screech, screech, screech; very hard on the nerves.

Near my chair, he stopped. He put the spin drill away and got out a vial of blood. With the tweezers, he immersed something in the blood and then put the vial away. What in Hells kind of hocus-pocus was this? He had me on tenterhooks to find out what had happened in the operation.

He took out a small, gold-plated, circular box. It looked like one of those which females carry perfume pats in. Then I realized it was probably part of the Zanco delivery. Firms specialize in fancy little cases that they hand out to doctors as presents for female patients: sure enough, it had an engraved *Zanco* on the cover.

Young Doctor Prahd popped it open and with great care, laid whatever he held in his tweezers into it, puffed up the interior padding and wiped the blood off the tweezers on it.

He held it out to me very proudly. He was like some long-legged cub animal, waiting for somebody to say, "Good barker," and give it a pat on the muzzle. There was a microscopic bit of stone lying amidst the bloodstains.

"The piece of the arrowhead," said young Doctor Prahd.

"You didn't get this out of his head. I saw you pick it up, right over there." Then suddenly it dawned on me what he was doing. Hey, there was hope for this boy. He was going to give it to Heller as the convincer. But I had no idea of letting this young fool get a good opinion of himself. Compliments are the destroyer of the race: they end striving. He could slide right out from under my thumb! I dismissed the box with a wave of my hand. "It took you long enough." I glanced at my watch. "Two hours is not three hours and forty-five minutes."

He looked a little crestfallen. "Well, you see, I didn't have the patient yesterday. I could have taken the basic cells then. I had to take cells of his dermis and epidermis as well as his bone. It took half an hour to get them into a sterile base and catalyze them so as to get cell supplies to use.

"Somebody had given him one of those crude vaccinations as a child and that had to be repaired so there was no scar. Then, besides the white scar in his shoulder, I had to repair an area of blastgun burn on his back.

"Then he'd caught a finger sometime or other and the nail was slightly crooked and I had not prepared nail cells so I had to get a catalyst growth tube going for those . . . ."

He was driving me up the tree with all this. "Come on, come on, what about the respondo-mitter and the audio-respondo-mitter?"

"Well, there really had been a small crack in the front bone. Those Fleet doctors are not careful enough. It had regrown by itself with no professional attention. It had filled itself with soft bone tissue and that all had to be scraped out. He must be from Manco. Their bones are quite hard and tough. I blunted a drill . . . ."

He must have seen my impatience. He rushed on. "It made a perfect cavity for the two items. And, of course, they had to be treated and the bone cells conditioned so as not to reject them. They have tiny microscopic antennas and these have to be slotted in between the molecular cell bone joints."

"What about that sore place he had on his eyebrow?" I demanded, thinking he might have put them into a tender spot that would require a later operation that would discover the two bugs.

He seemed puzzled. Then he remembered. "Oh, there was no tender spot. That was my fingernail."

He saw how impatient I was getting. He rushed on. "They are in there, they will never be detected. The scars are all gone. I think I passed my test very well."

I snorted. "There was a young trainee my uncle . . ."

"I thought Professor Slahb was your great-uncle?"

"I also have an uncle that's a cellologist," I said determinedly. "This young trainee was supposed to stay around and finish his contract." I was talking because he was in very elegant circumstances here. I didn't want anyone to put any ideas in his head. "But he met a young widow who was rich and he knocked right off his contract, violated all his promises and went on living with her right there!"

He shook his head. "Oh, if you mean Pratia . . ."

That clinched it. Pratia was the Widow Tayl's girl-name. Clearly they had gotten way into a relationship to be on a first-name basis. "So if you think I am going to pass you now, you are mistaken! I do not know if the operation works. Further, I do not know if you will talk to anyone and give away secrets. And you have no right to stand there and demand your contract be handed over. You will get that contract when you report to me on Bli . . . at your duty station. I will be there before you."

He looked like he was going to stutter. It's a very good sign.

"So I have some instructions for you. Sit down!"

He swallowed hard and sat down.

I had brought from the airbus a small case. "Here are three languages. They apply to your post. One is *Turkish.* Another is *English.* The other is *Italian.* There are books, dictionaries and a player machine in this case. Starting here and all during your six weeks voyage, you will study like mad. You will land on Bl . . . at your duty station, speaking, reading and writing English, Turkish and Italian. If you pass on this case as to work-ability and arrive knowing these languages, and if you have not violated secrecy—and believe me, I am having you watched every minute by unseen eyes—I will then consider handing over your contract. Do you understand this?"

"T . . . Turkish? It . . . it . . . whatever. Are these civilized languages? I have never heard of them!"

"Primitive tongues. Another galaxy. Do you understand?"

"Y . . . y . . . yes."

"Ten days from today, at ten o'clock in the morning, Zanco will send a lorry for all this equipment. They know exactly where to deliver it. They have a pass for that place." I had verified with the captain of the *Blixo* his exact blastoff time. I had spoken to him about all arrangements.

"Zanco," I continued, "will bring an empty case for the operating table and put that one in it."

"B . . . b . . . but it has a case! A long box."

"Exactly." I was taking no chances of the Widow Tayl detaining him. "You are going to bore holes in the ends and fix it to lock from within. When Zanco comes, you pretend to be showing them what to take. And you *do* show them and you *do* get that operating table packed in the case they will bring. And then you will jump into that empty case and lock it from the inside and they will deliver you to the ship."

He gaped. But it was a master stroke. He'd get loose from Tayl. Nobody would see him go aboard. I like things neat.

"C . . . can I pad the box inside? S . . . so I don't h . . . h . . . hit my h . . . h . . . head?"

I was feeling indulgent. "Of course," I said. I pulled out a note to Captain Bolz. It just said, "This is him. Gris." I gave it to him.

"I guess . . . I guess there's a lot I don't know about secret operations," he confessed.

There's a lot you don't know about beautiful widows, I muttered to myself. "Now, two more things."

"M . . . more?"

"On that ship there will be a young homosexual. You are not to associate with or speak to him. You must remain unknown to him. He is an enemy spy."

"A . . . and?"

"And if you are not delivered to that ship, if you do not arrive as I have said, its captain will bring a ferocious, blastgun-packing crew right here, seize you and . . ." I was about to say "rape the Widow Tayl" but she'd be overjoyed by that. " . . . burn down this whole estate and maim and shoot your dear Pratia on suspicion of being an enemy agent. Understood?"

He was paralyzed. Well, he'd have to get used to the operating climate. Might as well start now. I had worked out how he could make me a personal fortune. Except for that, I didn't need him and could have shot him right where he shivered. But, as Lombar says, money talks.

I sat there smiling in a Lordly way. Let him see I could also be his friend. Police psychology is the applicable branch. Crush them and then pretend friendship. But he didn't seem to be responding. However, if I sat there long enough with lifted lips, gazing down my nose at him in a superior way, it would eventually work.

But the psychotherapy was ruined. A voice came from the house, over a loud speaker. "Yoo-hoo, you boys," the musical lilt of the Widow Tayl. "Don't keep sitting out there like the dear little angels you are. Come into the house and get some lunch."

So we went in. It was a gorgeous dining room. All done in blue and gold with little gold nymphs having a rare time of it all over the ceiling. There were soft couches at various levels. The center of the room was utterly sagging under the weight of canisters, platters of cakes and dried rare meats and fruits.

She was dressed in the filmiest of films and she had her hair piled up and held with diamonds. She looked at the two of us. "Where's the other one?"

"He won't come to for another three or four hours," I said brutally.

She looked at the spread. She glanced at herself in a wall mirror. And she got a very, very sad look on her face. "Well, go ahead and eat," she said dispiritedly.

I ate. Prahd was just sitting there.

Finally he said, "Not burn down the whole estate!"

What a fool. To talk like that in front of the Widow Tayl. It was my lot to deal with fools and amateurs.

But the Widow Tayl had not heard him. She was sitting on the sofa behind him. Her eyes were dreamy. With one of her hands she was curling the hair on the back of Prahd's neck. In the other she idly grasped a large, soft fruit.

Prahd suddenly looked at me and said, "Oh, you mustn't doubt me. I'll come. I'll come!"

The Widow Tayl's eyes went glassy. Her breathing quickened. She yelled suddenly, "And he put his red cap in . . . in . . . in . . ."

The fruit in her hand was clenched into an explosion of soft white meat. "OHHHHHHHHHHHHHHHHH-HHHHH!"

I was glaring. (Bleep) her. She was thinking of Heller. She had dressed and primped and laid out this huge lunch THINKING ABOUT HELLER!

I attacked a sweetbun like it had bit *me!*

I'd show HIM!

Chapter 4

Late in the afternoon, Heller came out of the gas. Prahd gave me the signal and I made Ske shift the airbus to the confined space just outside the hospital door—a thing he cursed over, as landing on some shrubs scratched his paint. But I was taking no chances on the Widow Tayl seeing Heller again. She might remember what he looked like: it would be out security.

I whisked Heller through the hospital door and into the airbus and we took off at once.

The recorder was still locked to his wrist. It was running and with ten hours of strip capacity, would keep right on running and recording for some time. So I was saying nothing. Just before he had come out of the hospital door, I had thrown a towel over his arm, so it was not getting any pictures: there would be no views of where he had been.

He was still groggy. He had a cup-like dressing over his right temple and several more at different places on his body. Prahd had told him they contained "heal-fast" fluid, that they wouldn't come loose if he showered. Prahd had given him a small vial of solvent and in twenty-four hours, Heller could apply it and the cups would come off: the spots would be a light pink for another day, but Prahd had given him another vial of false-skin coating which would eradicate even that. Heller had received the data and vials with a minimum of attention. He seemed to want to go back to sleep.

I was very anxious to see how this equipment

worked. The whole success of the Earth operation depended upon it. I had the rest of the items of one whole set with me. My hopes were high but there was a bit of anxiety, too.

At the hangar, fortunately, most of the contractor crews had gone for the day and nobody wanted to see him. I passed him into the airlock of the tug: he seemed to be heading for the rooms in back.

With speed—which Ske objected to—I rushed through the evening sky and soon arrived at my rooming house. I grabbed the box containing the rest of the set and went zooming up the stairs. Meeley was on her hands and knees on a landing trying to scrub the floor and I almost knocked her flat. She swore at me with surprising violence but I ignored her.

Locking my door, I swept some empty canisters off a table and hastily began to set up the equipment. With hands quivering with eagerness, I got the activator-receiver going. I was only twenty miles from the Apparatus hangar and this thing was good, the late Spurk had said, for two hundred miles.

I turned on the separate receiver-viewscreen.

Nothing!

Not even a crackle!

I turned up the activator-receiver until it was practically shooting blue streams!

Nothing.

I turned up the receiver-viewscreen.

Nothing!

(Bleep) Spurk! He must have been lying! It served him right to get himself killed!

I sat back. I thought. Then it occurred to me that the whole rig might just be underpowered. So I picked up and added the 831 Relayer to the setup. It was supposed to boost the signal between the activator-receiver and the receiver-viewscreen so strongly that they could be ten thousand miles apart!

Nothing.

I boosted every manual gain knob I could find!

Wait. I heard something in the viewscreen speaker. A faint rythmic sound.

I looked at the viewscreen. I thought I must have turned the power up too high. Maybe a component was burning in it. It was a blurred, wavery pink.

I counted the rhythmic sound. It was going at about eighteen times a minute. Hard to recognize. The quality was poor.

Suddenly I had it! The sound was breathing! The dim pink was faint light coming through the eyelids. Heller was asleep! If it was Heller.

Well, it had gotten something. But Gods, with every manual gain at maximum and even the 831 Relayer on the line, it was only doing twenty miles! I despaired of ever using this in Turkey when Heller was in the Americas.

I sat back, wondering what to do now. With this rig so poor, Heller could just waltz around the United States as free as a bird; I wouldn't know what he was doing! I wouldn't be able to use information gained on this channel to sabotage his intentions. Awful thought!

For some time I sat there glooming. I was almost ready to give it up when I heard footsteps coming from the speaker. Very faint, hard to recognize as footsteps. They were a bit louder now. They stopped.

A voice: "Honey, are you all right?" It was so fuzzy, I couldn't recognize it from voice quality. But it must be the Countess Krak. Yes, as I glanced at my watch, the guard would have changed.

The viewscreen image came on gradually. Faint, furry. It *was* the Countess Krak. She was in uniform, her helmet was off. Her face was very big. A poor picture.

She looked concerned. She was touching the heal-fast capsule. "Did you fall? Did you have an accident?"

"Oh, hello, darling. I must have fallen asleep again." Bad quality, barely able to tell it was Heller's voice. "No, no. Don't be alarmed. It's nothing. I just had a lot of identifying marks removed by a cellologist."

"You WHAT?"

"Yes. Soltan came and got me and I kept an appointment."

There was horror on her face. "They put you under gas? You were *out?*"

"Oh, please. It's not all that much. It takes more than a little gas to hurt me!"

"Hah, Jettero Heller. A lot you know!" She was quite cross. "You do something crazy like that the minute I turn my back! I've told you, where Soltan Gris is concerned, I can handle him and you can't!" Then she suddenly changed. She cupped his face in her hands, looking at the wound cover. Her voice was full of sorrow and concern. "Oh, my poor darling. What have these beasts done to you?"

It gave me a bad moment. Would she guess what really had been done?

Heller tried to laugh her out of it. "Look," he said, fumbling about. "The doctor gave me the tiny piece of arrowhead he took out." He told her the story and then he opened the little gold case.

"It's all bloody!" she said, recoiling. I grimaced. Blood meant nothing to her unless it was Heller's.

"Of course!" said Heller. "He said he took it out of my frontal bone." He picked it up and the fragment became absolutely HUGE on my screen. "Hmmm," he said. "That's funny. I thought it was an obsidian arrowhead and this is flint."

(Bleep) Prahd for his fancy extras, I gritted.

"Could have been metamorphic," puzzled Heller. "But obsidian and flint seldom mix."

"Oh, Jet. You should have been more cautious. You should have made them do it here. Where I could be present. They may have said something to you while you were out. Think hard! Do you remember what they said? Any general anesthetic can act as a hypnotic."

You and hypnotism, I snarled to myself in a wave of hate as I recalled the horrible thing she had done to me.

Heller said, "Oh, yes. I forgot. It's still here on my wrist. Soltan let me put this on. Only I know the numbers to open it." He busily began to undo his combination. I made a mental note that he favored an idiot's combination—3, 2, 1. Ho, ho. You could learn things with this bug rig!

"It's still running," he said. "Here, I'll put it on a player." And he got a player and shortly had the strip running.

Heller was watching the Countess. And that was good because the whole thing made or broke on just this part of the project. Had I tricked her or hadn't I? My voice, very fuzzy, came out of the speaker, "I feel a little queasy. Have you got something?" Then Prahd, "Could you hold this?" And then my, "Oh, no. The sight of blood makes me quite ill lately for some reason."

The Countess Krak was sitting up very straight, listening intently.

Then my voice through the speaker on the ship, "Oh, my Gods, I'm going to be sick at my stomach!" Followed by the heaving sounds.

The Countess started nodding for all the world like a teacher who is approving a pupil for being exceptionally obedient. Then she relaxed. I knew I had won! She thought that the hypnotic suggestion to get sick if Heller was hurt was still securely in place.

When the picture went white, Heller said, "My wrist must have slipped off the table." The Countess shrugged.

"I'll speed play it through," said Heller. But, of course, there were only clicks and snips and bubbles of beakers. He spot-checked the return to the tug.

The Countess said, "I'll get you something to eat."

Had I won? You can't ever tell about females, but she apparently didn't suspect anything underhanded had been done. I realized she had been worried about physical damage; nothing would point to anything else.

But my problems with this rig were crucial. I could not hang on Heller's coattails and still oversee all our Earth operations.

There were some minor flaws. Peripheral vision—things in the view field but not being looked at directly—were there, if blurred. I could cope with that. But the overall visio and audio quality left so much to be desired that I was gloomy.

I thought of turning the strip on in my receiver-viewscreen and just leaving it. It had an automatic strip-feeder in it. It would record for days, maybe even weeks, untended. You just put a pile of strips in it. But then, the Countess came back in and I thought that maybe I could pick up some crucial data. After all, I knew nothing of their domestic relationship. It was really a new scene to me for they would not act naturally with me close by. What *did* this pair do when they were alone together? So I kept watching.

She had changed from her guard's uniform and was wearing a blue exercise suit. She was holding a couple of steaming canisters with tubes in them—you can't use anything else in space and it was, after all, a spaceship. "Yell up there and tell it to convert the gym to a steam bath, will you? I want to steam some of that anesthetic poison out of you."

Heller accommodatingly yelled, "Steam bath!" And they drank their soup.

Well, I was going to find out if water and heat hurt anything. And shortly Heller stripped and walked into the steam. I sure got a lot of steam! But the extra heat and water did not change things. Spurk hadn't flunked there. He had only flunked on range and quality, in my opinion, so far.

When Heller had showered in a bathroom, he yelled, "Gym!"

The Countess yelled from somewhere, "You put on an exercise suit! It'll take more than steam to get the poison out." There was still a tinge that he had been naughty.

He was shortly running on an escalatorlike rig and then he was doing some backflips and generally working up a new sweat. Finally he went and showered again and put on a blue lounging suit.

She was crossing the gym toward him when he stepped down to go back to the lounge. He suddenly grabbed her and kissed her. My set viewscreen flickered. Oh ho, it did register emotion in an odd way.

He pushed her back. "Am I forgiven?"

"Oh, Jet, I'd have to forgive you anything!"

They kissed again. And then Jet held her away from him and in a cheerful voice said, "You haven't said what *you* have been up to today! Maybe it was even worse than me!"

She laughed. "I've been drilling for the review."

Review? Review? I thought. What review? This was news.

She had jumped back. She did a one-two foot slam, came to rigid attention and then in total mockery, did an exaggerated cross-arm salute followed by a double foot stamp. Heller laughed with delight. "I better watch out. That Snelz will be recruiting you for keeps into the Fleet marines! What a thing to do for such a lovely lady."

"Oh, he says I am very good. You ought to see me with a blastrifle now!"

Heller was laughing so hard the screen jiggled.

"No!" she said. "I am very good! There's no reason a girl can't learn to twirl a rifle! You go get it and I'll show you."

Heller, still laughing, telling a few doors to open, was soon in the forward part of the ship. I was treated to a shifting view of all kinds of nooks and crannies.

"Hey," he yelled back to her down the long passage, "Where'd you put it?"

"Just inside the airlock." Her voice was very distant, distorted in transmission.

"I'll ask the sentry," he yelled back.

Views of all parts of the airlock. Then a determined spin of wheels and the airlock door.

Whatever I expected to happen, I didn't expect the result!

The screen flashed blue white! Total overload!

The hangar sounds roared up to a din.

And Heller's voice: it almost caved in my eardrums! "WHERE'S THE RIFLE?"

The sound came out of the speaker like a physical blow!

It almost made the roof of my room blow off!

I fought my way to the controls. I turned every manual knob I could see down to nearly off!

The hangar noises still sounded like a battle. The screen was still white!

I tried to think in the midst of the uproar.

There was a new uproar, local. Feet were pounding up the stairs.

I had everything as low as I could get it!

I grabbed the 831 ten-thousand-mile Relayer, snatched it out of the line and turned it off.

Suddenly I had the most beautiful clear picture of the hangar you ever wanted to see. Brilliant in the minutest detail! And that hangar is dimly lit!

The sentry was trotting back toward the ship. He was carrying a blastrifle. "Snelz had it taken over to have it polished for the review." His voice was clear and natural. I even recognized which guardsman it was by voice tone alone!

Jet took it, "Thanks, guardsman."

What quality!

It was just as if he were right here in the room!

There was something else coming in the room. Meeley finished pounding my door down and planted herself before me, fists on hips, furious.

"You get that rifle out of my house this instant!" Oh, Meeley was mad! "You know I don't allow rifles or explosives! Especially in *your* hands, Gris!" Oh, she was mad.

"It's the Homeviewer," I pleaded timidly. "I had it up too high!"

"Humph!" said Meeley and slapped me in the face. She flounced out. The door banged shut so hard it almost knocked the wall down.

I rubbed the sting off my cheek and turned back to the viewscreen.

It was dead.

There was no sound.

Spurk ought to be shot! His equipment was inconsistent, sporadic! He should have said so in the directions. But then, I remembered, I hadn't read them.

I turned all manual volumes full on and then in

despair, added the 831 Relayer. You had to be an electronics technician to run this stuff!

I had my picture and sound back, fuzzy and poor.

Then it hit me. That (bleeped) tug was totally painted with absorbo-coat paint! No known waves could get through it. And I was actually activating the respondo-mitter and audio-respondo-mitter through a waveproof ship!

There was nothing like absorbo-coat on Earth. So it was all right!

I watched the Countess going through a manual of arms I had never seen before. It included giving the rifle butt a kick that sent it spinning into the air on one side and then a kick with the other boot that sent it spinning on the other side. Fleet marine stuff, I guessed.

They got to spinning the rifle back and forth between them. I couldn't follow it, it was going so fast. I found myself wishing the safety was off.

They were laughing. Finally the Countess caught the rifle and came to present arms. "So I'm all ready for the review."

What review? I puzzled. Certainly the Countess Krak was not going to be in any review!

Heller said, "I can leave at noon, day after tomorrow."

She became sad. He put his arm around her and they wandered to the salon. They sat down on a couch, side by side.

All of a sudden the Countess put her arms around him and her head on his chest and started crying quietly.

After a while, she said, "I'm going to miss you so."

He held her close. His voice was attempting encouragement. "I'll do the mission very, very fast. Honest I will." After a little he said, "Mainly, I'm concerned about you."

Suddenly he held her away from him. There was a catch in his voice but a bitter determination, "If anybody harms you while I am gone, I will kill them!"

She was still crying. But she nodded at him and then said, "That goes both ways!"

A chill hit me. They hadn't said it very loudly. But there was a firm intention in it that meant exactly what it said. If anyone hurt the other, the offender was *dead*.

I didn't want to look or listen anymore. I hastily shut the equipment off.

I needed something to distract me, quick. I didn't want to think what could happen to me if they found out my real intentions.

I had information. I knew when the tug could leave.

I fled from the room.

At a message center at the corner, I got a connection to Lombar's chief clerk and, in code, imparted the information that the scheduled departure of Mission Earth was day after tomorrow at noon.

When I started up the stairs, Meeley was blocking the way. She screamed at me, "Don't you ever bring no more rifles into my house! Of all the tenants I have ever had, you, Soltan Gris, are easily the most . . ." It went on and on. All of it false. Her tenants were Apparatus officers. They were none of them different than any others, including me and she knew it.

Safely in my room again and the door bolted and barricaded, I caressed the bugging equipment. It certainly worked. I had no doubts at all I could run Heller from Turkey.

I got to thinking of the late Spurk. It was an awfully good thing he was dead. I was a benefactor of the race. Suppose this kind of stuff got installed in everybody! Even I shuddered at the thought.

Chapter 5

When I got the call the next evening, even though he had told me he wanted to see me twenty-four hours before departure, I felt scared. When summoned to see Lombar, one never knew what he was being invited to: his own funeral or somebody else's.

Sometimes he was pleasant, sometimes so agitated you felt he was going to fly apart in screaming bits.

All day I had been sort of putting the idea aside that he might send for me. I had occupied myself with last minute bits. Heller had told me in the morning of the approximate departure time and I had to pretend I didn't know already. All day he was busy making tests of recently refurbished or installed equipment, always at the center of a boil of contractors. It had all made me very nervous.

Food trucks had been coming and going, putting supplies aboard. When Heller asked me where the crew was and how many there would be, I couldn't tell him as I didn't know—Lombar hadn't told *me*. So I said I would put stores aboard for the number of bunks and stamped food orders to that effect. Enough food and drink for a crew of eleven and two passengers for two years was what I put down. It was a silly purchase—he wouldn't be around anywhere near that long. I charged it off to necessary deception.

Even before noon I had gotten sort of nervous around the ship. I tried to take refuge in a retreat to the

Blixo but Bolz wasn't aboard. I drove off on some unnecessary errands and even went to my office and stamped things for a while. But old Bawtch was making so many nasty cracks about how pleasant it would be around there shortly with me gone that I even retreated from my office.

So I was in no real shape for an interview with Lombar when, about seven that evening, two Apparatus guards loomed up outside my room door and beckoned. One always tries to read something in their faces: one notes how they are carrying their rifles—on sling or at ready. But it really tells you nothing. So, with no inkling as to the temper of the coming meeting, I found myself further unsteadied by being taken, not to his town office and not to Spiteos, but outside the city. I had no idea where we were going or why.

At length, the patrol van in which we had been riding stopped and the exit panel flew up. A black bulk stood near us in an open field.

It was a type of ship called, by the Fleet, "the gun." Its proper name is "Spacebattle Mobile Flying Cannon." It holds two pilots, it has regular warp drives and it carries the largest caliber blastcannon made. It has no frills, no comforts: it is just that, a gun. And that gun can wrap a whole planet into a ball of flame.

I knew this ship. Ordinarily it was hidden in the underground hangar near Spiteos. It was Lombar's own ship. He had illegally and secretly modified a Fleet version long ago. This one, unlike the standard model, was armored so well that no ground defenses and not even a battleship could knock it down. It made it slower, it reduced its interplanetary range, but it made it the most dangerous weapon in the Voltarian Confederacy. I had heard that from time to time he took it out and flew it, usually at night, baffling normal surveillance with a perversion of return responses.

The guards simply gave me a boost up into the underbelly entrance lock and I climbed in the dark to find myself, still in the dark, in the two-man control deck. I groped to the copilot seat I knew must be there but before I could even buckle myself in, the engines throbbed and the ship took off. For all I knew, anybody could have been at the controls, even a Manco Devil!

"I am going to let you in on a secret. I am taking you to where you can hear something that will convince you." It was Lombar's voice from the pilot seat. At least it wasn't a Manco Devil. But, on the other hand, a Manco Devil might be more trustworthy.

We were gaining in altitude. One of the twin moons of Voltar was just rising, spreading a greenish hued and long-shadowed light across the ground below. As we turned, the beams struck through the heavy armored windscreen and eerily lit the control deck. Yes, it was Lombar. He was wearing no helmet so we must not be going far.

He seemed in a friendly if somewhat covert mood. "I found the leak, you know. The one to the press the night Heller was seized. I had a man being followed. He didn't suspect it. It took a lot of work but we finally saw him and a reporter bump into each other on the street. They didn't pass anything but it was enough.

"The reporter was Blat Mortif. He wasn't the one who wrote the article but of course reporters have friends. You'll never guess who leaked it. The Knife Section man that acted the part of the Fleet orderly, the one that was so clumsy he let Heller break his wrist. Of course he denied it. But you can't trust anybody these days. They're all against us, plotting, plotting, plotting.

"So last night we had Blat Mortif picked up and he denied everything so we had to pick up his wife. He finally broke down. So the Knife Section man, the reporter and his wife were all executed. I knew you were concerned about it so I thought I had better tell you. One has to get rid of traitors and people who talk too much. They're riffraff anyway."

I not only had not been concerned, I had completely forgotten about it. Further, I knew of many ways the press could have learned of Heller's mission: even Fleet Intelligence knew. And also, the press had never mentioned any kidnapping. I wondered why Lombar was telling me. But then Lombar lives in a secret world of his own.

We were not flying very fast. We were not very high. He had not even turned on internal air. The green, long-shadowed moonlight turned the world below into a weird panorama.

Abruptly, Lombar, a sort of greenish shadow close by, began a sort of singsong lecture, like an Academy professor. "Any successful revolution or successful coup d'état requires that the revolutionaries possess an operating or supply base beyond the reach of the forces they seek to overthrow. Without such a base, one cannot overthrow an existing regime."

Yes, yes. That was elementary. If a revolutionary did not have a point beyond the knowledge or control of the regime they were attacking, a place from which they could secretly operate, a revolution normally failed. Textbook.

"You," said Lombar, dropping his professorial role and becoming harsh, "are now in full control of that base and its supplies. You must not fail in your duty to me."

I was a little heartened. I thought I knew now what this eerie and secret night ride was all about: a briefing to me as a mission handler that could not be overheard. I knew already that Blito-P3 was the unwitting and secret base outside the control of Voltar. I had always thought it an amusing role for a stupid and primitive planet. It had always been a source of private amusement to me. The dumb twits.

Lombar's hands darted to the automatic position switches and there was a series of clicks which cut in the complex navigational systems of "the gun" so that she would go to and hold on exact coordinates. Freed of flying, he leaned back.

The gun steadied down, the engines dropped to an inaudible pitch. I knew where we were now.

Only a few miles away and a few thousand feet below lay Palace City. Visibly, it is simply a hole in the landscape. The mountain behind it and the vast array of palaces are enwrapped in the effects of a gigantic space warp. The black hole in the mountain makes it invisible and this in turn causes Palace City to be invisible. Shielded against unwanted radiation, the whole area is thirteen minutes in the future.

It is utterly impregnable. Nobody can attack it. It simply isn't there. For nearly a hundred and twenty-five thousand years, it had defied all assaults. You can't shoot up a not-there-in-now.

Many stellar empires hide their central government on asteroids to put them out of reach of enemy and popular attack. It has its points but you can trace ships to it. Voltar's Emperor could not be touched by any combat means ever evolved. It made the Voltarian Confederacy one of the strongest governments in any galactic history.

There lay the nothingness, surrounded all about by a moonlit landscape. It always made me nervous. It wasn't wholly that that mountain could blow up some day when its mass imbalanced too far, it was that it represented such awesome might within its secret glove.

Lombar was fiddling with the gun's fire controls.

Even a weapon as heavy as this ship carried was of no avail here. But his twitching fingers increased my unease.

"See that?" said Lombar. And I was thankful when he took his hand off the weapon triggers and gestured. Of course there was nothing to see. "The Lords there in their fine robes are plotting against me."

I could agree with that. The Apparatus must make them quite nervous at times even though they thought of it as their own tool.

Lombar swept his hand in a wider gesture. "The people of this and every other Voltarian planet are just lying in wait to rise up and kill me."

Oh, I could surely agree with that. The way the Apparatus hated them and abducted them and slaughtered them, they undoubtedly were lying in wait.

Lombar sighed, an executive with many burdens. "So, I know you will agree, Soltan, that the only possible solution is to seize control of Palace City and the power of the throne. And then, with that, properly use the authority to slaughter the people."

I knew these were his plans. I had always thought them a bit drastic.

He must have sensed my reservations. "I am the only one brilliant enough and strong-willed enough to take over. The Lords are weak. The people are riffraff. It is my duty."

He nodded, firmly agreeing with himself. Then, "So the problem is, to take over Palace City."

Nobody had ever done it. It was considered impossible.

Lombar was fishing in his tunic pocket. "But we have our supply base on Blito-P3. And we have our weapons."

He took out a bottle of pills and dropped it on the

gun control ledge in front of him. I knew the bottle. Its label said:

I. G. Barben, Pharmaceutical
New York

The eerie Voltar moonlight glinted on the label so far from home. Methedrine, a powerful amphetamine.

He took out a cellophane package of white powder. Turkish heroin. By its number, part of the last *Blixo* shipment, now safely stored in Spiteos. The moonlight made it greenish, like dried venom.

He gestured to them with his hand. "These are our artillery." He smiled. "And violent ammunition it is. The higher nervous systems of Voltar populations react to it five times over and above the Earth reaction."

He turned to me, his face very serious. "So that is why you must keep Blito-P3 under control. You must keep the ammunition coming. These weapons take a while to work. Months, years. We can keep firing and we can wait.

"Above all, we must maintain our monopoly. Chemists here might learn to synthesize this. In producing heroin, the basic morphine is very garish to grow and easy to spot. But still there is a danger we could lose the monopoly before we have addicted the Lords and robbed the people of their will to resist. I have other plans to handle this here, but *you* are going to make sure the Blito-P3 base is secure to us."

A pleading note crept into his voice. All this meant much to him, Lombar, the slum-raised sewer rat, any Lord rank far beyond his reach. "When I am Emperor, you, Soltan, will be the head of the Apparatus."

It made me uneasy. Just to listen to this talk could

bring torture and execution. And the eerie moonlight made it worse.

Then he got serious. "This upstart (bleepard) Heller threatened all that. By a stupid fluke, he got into the scene. He doesn't even suspect what he threatens. But whatever happens, you must make certain that he does not succeed in tampering in any way with Blito-P3!"

The mention of Heller had brought out his aggressiveness. He glared at the invisibility of Palace City. "Those blundering idiots down there are stupid enough to place their confidence in Heller! Little do they know that I can outfight, outfly a dozen Hellers!"

Before I could get truly alarmed, he began to laugh. It didn't have any amusement in it. He turned to me and patted my knee. "That was a terrific trick, Soltan. Ah, you are a sly one. I can choose men well. Only you would ever have thought of loosing that rotten whore on him, the Countess Krak!"

I went cold. He knew!

"Clever, clever. Keeping him under control by using a murdering prostitute. Almost as good as some of the things I work out. There was every chance she'd kill him. Too bad she hasn't." He laughed over it.

Who had told him? Snelz! It must be Snelz! It made me feel surrounded by spies.

But Lombar was plunging on. "However, if she hasn't killed him by his blastoff tomorrow, he won't have long to run anyway." He fished out a sheaf of papers. "As you already know, I have allocated to you our two best agents on Blito-P3, Raht and Terb. They are to shadow him at all times. And here is a project written for Raht to do at once. As soon as you land. It concerns the identity Heller will be given. I can think of a few ideas myself—somewhat more refined than Countess Krak ones."

I opened the sheets. It was not easy to read in the moonlight coming through the windscreen. But what I saw stood my hair on end!

Blito-P3 is the only place anyone ever heard of where a gutter bum and criminal can rise by normal social processes to a point of absolute planetary control. It was probably this fact which had attracted Lombar to it in the first place, which had caused him to study all past surveys and its cultural and social patterns and even introduce them so thoroughly into his own work. On Earth, one man and his family had risen to such a position. He controlled the planet's energy companies, he controlled its drug companies, he controlled its finances and he controlled many other things including, to all intents and purposes, its governments. We ourselves, although he didn't know it, did business with him. His name was Delbert John Rockecenter. It was one of our operating maxims that we never upset anything connected with him.

And the birth certificate and credentials which Lombar was ordering Raht to procure were in the name of Delbert John Rockecenter, JUNIOR!

My Gods, this was taking risks!

Lombar must have seen my face. It amused him. "The difference between myself and other men is that I can very accurately predict what will really happen. The instant Heller shows up in the United States calling himself Delbert John Rockecenter, Junior, it will start a commotion. The name is too well known. The big one will hear of it instantly and have Heller put behind bars immediately. He has the power and the will to do things. Heller won't get ten steps into the society before he is nabbed. Into a penitentiary and we're rid of Heller. Maybe if he's crazy enough to try to tell them he's an extraterrestrial, they'll put him in an insane asylum for life. It can't miss."

I understood it then. I'd have to be very sure Heller carried no other identity.

"So you have that," said Lombar. "Now, there's the matter of a crew for that tug. I said I'd handle that. And I certainly have. We were lucky. There were several Fleet suboficers on the galactic run. They were, of course, piloting and engineering the big Fleet freighters with the Will-be Was drives. They mutinied and stole a ship intending to go pirating. The Fleet patrols caught them and tried them. But just before they were executed some of our people did a body substitution.

"There are five of them, a captain, two pilots and two engineers, plenty for that tug. They are a race that calls themselves Antimancos—exiled long ago from Manco for ritual murders. They hate the Fleet. They hate Manco. And oh, will they hate Heller! I'll see you're told more about them. So there is your uncorruptible crew."

He sat for a while, staring at the invisible hole of Palace City and just about the time I thought he had told me everything, he looked at his watch, frowned and began again.

"Now earlier, when I first heard about that (bleeped) tug, I ordered two warplanes to duty at the Earth base. The four pilots will not be under your orders. They will have their own orders. If that tug gets loose there or if Heller tries to use it locally, our planes have orders to shoot it down. Those planes will be arriving there shortly. So that takes care of that."

I felt very cold. The moonlight was cold. His face was cold now. I hoped I wasn't aboard that tug when they showed up. Our ship had no guns or defenses. It was just a tug.

"There's only a couple things more," said Lombar. I knew they wouldn't be good, but I wasn't prepared for what they really were.

He fixed me with a look. "If, at any time, it looks like Heller is going to succeed and you have no other way to stop him, you are to disregard any consequences and," he pointed a finger at me and said the next words slowly, "you are to murder him!"

His attention had gone back to Palace City. He seemed to be waiting for something, but of course there was nothing there to wait for: it was just a zone of nothing.

He glanced at his watch and then turned to me again. "There is one final thing." His tone was very unfriendly. "I have given secret instructions to someone in your vicinity. You will never suspect who it is. And those instructions are this: if you fail to handle Blito-P3, if you fail to keep our ammunition coming, if Heller gets loose and messes things up, if, in any way, you play me false, that someone has explicit orders to murder you!"

I felt like the moonlight had just turned into ice.

But Lombar was again looking at his watch. Then he held up a finger to me. Suddenly the most beatific expression came over his face. "There it was! Oh, there it was! Didn't you hear it?"

I had heard nothing. There was just the empty hole of Palace City out there, just the hateful moonlight. The ship was even soundproof.

I must have looked a trifle frantic. Lombar said insistently, "The voice, the voice! I brought you here so you could hear the voice!" He sat up, listening intently. "There! There it is again: 'Lombar Hisst! Come be Emperor! The destiny of Voltar pleads for you to take the Crown!'"

He sank back in relief. "Now that you have heard it,

you know that everything I have had to do is true, is destined. I am so glad you were here to vouch for it."

A conviction drove through me like a blastgun bolt. Like the pieces of a puzzle spinning about on a board and suddenly assembling, all my experience with Lombar Hisst and tonight came together in a single vivid fact. All the psychology textbook psychopathic symptoms of a paranoid schizophrenic, complete with megalomania and tonight, aural hallucinations, were there.

I was scared spitless!

Lombar Hisst was *insane!*

I was under the control of a complete lunatic!

And there was no possible way to escape it!

Chapter 6

I actually was a pretty sick Soltan Gris when the Apparatus guard bus dropped me at my office. It was very late. I knew I ought to be packing and getting moved in aboard the tug for blastoff. But I sat at my desk for nearly half an hour, just looking into nothingness.

Somehow, I felt, there must be some mistake. Nothing could be quite as horrible as being the pawn of a madman. With sudden inspiration, I dug some of my psychology textbooks out of what I call my "Carrot Hole," a code name for a cavity under the planking.

For another half hour I pored over the Earth texts. *Schizophrenia,* I verified, is *schizei*—"to split" plus *phren*—"mind." It was defined as a split or detachment from reality. *Paranoia* is a chronic *psychosis,* characterized by well-rationalized delusions of persecution or of grandeur. *Megalomania* often takes the form of a desire to rule the world. *Aural hallucinations* means hearing voices that aren't there. These terms, excepting the last, are called the *Hitler syndrome:* Hitler was a defunct military ruler on Earth. He and several of his chieftains were labelled in the texts as *paranoid schizophrenics* to explain their genocidal practices (they worked hard to kill off whole races).

Yes! I had the terms right. *Aural hallucinations* was the right label for hearing voices. So Lombar Hisst was insane.

It brought no comfort at all.

If he started taking those *amphetamines,* a drug called *speed,* and particularly the heart-shaped orange tablets called *methedrine,* that I knew were in that bottle he had displayed, he really would go crazy!

I sat there for another hour, glooming.

What could I do?

Nothing!

No, not nothing!

If I didn't get going and push this mission through to the end, I would be a dead man. That had been made too vivid to be mistaken.

The realization alone made me leap up. It was way past midnight. I hastily rushed down the hill to my room to pack. I had even forgotten Ske had been outside the office with the airbus until he, alerted no doubt by the way I came crashing out of my office, took off and landed in the side courtyard.

Frantically, I began to scoop up things and throw them into bags. I was about to stuff the Heller monitors in with old broken canisters when I realized I had to get a grip on myself. I carefully packed them in a disguised case marked *Fragile Heirlooms.*

Ske was leaning against the door. I said, "Give me a

of here and move aboard. I won't get any sleep at all tonight if I don't hurry."

"You mean you'll be gone for a real long time?" said Ske. "Years and years? Oh, great. I'll help you like fury!" And he pitched right in. He needn't have been so nasty. The bandages were off his hands. Every bruise I'd given him was healed except maybe for a broken tooth or two.

And then another voice cut in. "You will get plenty of sleep on a bench in the debt court if you don't pay your back rent!" It was, of course, Meeley.

She marched straight over and picked up the box I'd marked *Fragile Heirlooms*. She picked it up and held it to her chest. I was going to snatch it back when I saw the butt of a blastpistol sticking out of her apron pocket.

Ske had scooped up the remainder of my things along with copious quantities of floor dirt and marched out with them.

Meeley and I stood glaring at each other. That is to say, she glared. I was frantic. I couldn't leave without the one set of Heller monitors I had.

"Fifty credits," she said.

Beaten, I got out my wallet. I didn't have all that much left. And the thought of being bested yet again by this tyrant brought in a flood of bitter memories. I owed her. I really owed her. Oh, what wouldn't I give to . . .

I had a counterfeit hundred. It had some blood on one end from the hypnotist. I suddenly had to fight to keep a glorious grin from coming onto my face.

I shoved the counterfeit hundred at her. "I am giving you this in memory of my pleasant stay here," I said. "If you want to reserve this room for my return, that is up to you. But you deserve what you have earned." They would seize and execute her when she tried to present it.

She looked at the bill. She was no trained cashier.

Then she looked at me with a strange twist of her head.

"Good-bye, Meeley," I said. "May you really enjoy your immediate future."

I strode out with the box.

We flew through the moonlit night. Voltar's second moon was rising now and the Apparatus hangar was a weird patchwork of thin double shadows.

I was amazed how late it was. Nearly 4:00 A.M. I felt awful for more reasons than no sleep but no sleep was adding to the depression.

Ske refused to help me get my baggage to the ship. I found a hand dolly by myself, loaded it and pushed it to the airlock. When I started to pick it up and carry it in, I was infuriated to see that Ske had just been sauntering along behind me, hands in pockets.

"Carry this stuff aboard!" I demanded.

He just stood there. I could have killed him.

Suddenly I decided on something. I dissembled. Now was the time to get even with him for his nastiness these past weeks.

"Ske," I said, "you feel aggrieved that I did not make you rich. Actually I am very sorry I have not helped your career along to the place it should go." Into the maw of Hells, I privately added.

I reached into my pocket and got out my wallet. "You know that I came into some money lately. It will be no real use to me where I am going." Indeed it wouldn't, or here either. "You should be rewarded for your service. I should not be miserly about it." I fished out the remainder of the counterfeits. Bloodstains would not deter Ske and he sure was no trained cashier. I handed him the wad.

He looked at it, he looked at me. First he used one eye and then he used the other, as though he was not seeing right.

"Well, carry the baggage into the ship," I said. "Come on, come on!"

He put the money in his pocket and started to pick up baggage. I myself cradled the Heller monitors and went aboard.

A fresh temporary sign on the last cabin down the passage before the voice-operated door said:

Officer Gris

Ske dumped my things on the floor and, after a couple more loads, finished up.

I followed him back to the airlock.

"Good-bye, Ske," I said. "Whatever happens to you, I hope it is what you truly deserve."

He just walked off across the hangar without looking back.

How is it, I wondered, that Heller can give people money and they are happy and I give them money and they look at me so oddly? I'd have to study up on it in the psychology texts.

Chapter 7

I did not have any inkling whatever that I was about to begin what will rank as one of the most awful days of my life.

I went back into the ship. I was tired, I was depressed. I felt all rumpled up, inside and out. If I could only get some sleep!

And there was Heller in the passageway outside my

door. He had on a clean, blue, Fleet work-jumper, unwrinkled and creased just so. He had his inevitable red racing cap on the back of his neatly combed blond hair. He looked, despite the hour, rested and glowing with health. I hated him.

His first words increased the intensity of my emotion. "What the blast crash is this horrible stink?" Then he was staring into my cubicle.

I edged past him into my room. "It's my baggage." True, it was literally thrown all over the place. True, Ske had even packed decayed, broken, disposable dishes.

"Look," said Heller, "if you were to step aboard a Fleet vessel with gear like this, dirty as you are, they'd execute you! A spacevessel operates on a closed atmosphere system. This grit would clog the air recirculation filters and I don't think the deodorizers would handle it." He was being patient. "There's a crew laundry and cleaner in the opposite passageway. Throw this stuff in there and get it all washed quickly. You haven't got much time: the groundside water and sewage and power connections will be disconnected in an hour. So speed it up."

The thought of packing this gear anywhere appalled me. I wanted some sleep. Just a little sleep. Then a horrible thought hit me. The electronics of the monitor equipment would be ruined. Threat provokes fast thought. "I can't," I blurted out. "I've got guns, blasticks in this gear!" It had to work.

It didn't. A shocked look came over his face. "Hey, don't you know this whole ship will be awash with excess electrical charge? It could set them off!"

"I thought you fixed that."

He shook his head. But he wasn't thinking about that. Apparently, all he was registering was my objections. He stepped over to me and, in a fast frisk, began to remove blasticks, stunguns, the bladegun from my pockets. "You're a walking arsenal! If that stuff went off, you could blow us out of space!"

He stepped over to the wall and gave a knob a spin. A locker opened. "This is a shielded, antiexplosion repository." He started throwing my weapons into it. "Now get any other explosives out of your baggage and throw them in there."

Thankfully, I shoved the "Fragile Heirlooms" box in after them.

Heller was looking at my gear again. "It's full of just plain dirt!"

(Bleep) that Ske for packing even floor sweepings!

Heller had gone to a passageway locker and gotten some things. "This is a cleaning sheet roll. You pack your uniforms into the slots, roll it up and stuff it in the cleaning machine. They'll come out washed and pressed. Next, this is a dirty clothes and linen cleaning sheet roll. Stuff your underclothes and socks and so on in that, roll it up and put it in the washing machine. These are waterproof bags: put all your papers and notes and so forth in them."

He was about to leave when he turned back and looked. "I don't see any dress uniform in that gear."

I had never bought a General Services dress uniform. "They don't wear them on Earth!" I meant to be scathing.

"You'll need one for launching."

I was too sleepy and roughed up to comprehend why in Hells you needed a dress uniform to launch a ship. (Bleep) these Fleet guys. They were crazy!

"Your driver is still out there. I'll give him some money and he can rush over and get a shop open and bring one back."

I groaned. I couldn't cope with all this mania for looking nice. My reluctance must have provoked him.

He stood back and pointed toward the airlock. "You take all that baggage back outside the ship and sort it out into these rolls and bags, take the rolls over to the laundry. And include that uniform you've got on. Then take a shower. You've got to be quick. You won't have facilities much longer!"

I nearly wept. All I wanted was some sleep. I actually ached. (Bleep) these Fleet guys. He wasn't in the Fleet now! Who cared if the air filters of the ship all clogged up?

I carried all my baggage outside the ship and began to sort it on the hangar floor.

When I had discarded the broken canisters, old newssheets and piles of just plain dirt that Ske had packed, I didn't have too much gear, after all. The discards filled two hangar garbage cans.

I neated up the boots and caps and uniforms in the cleaning roll and then belatedly remembered I was wearing one. I emptied all my pockets into the waterproof paper-preservation bags and got my other papers into them. I stripped and put the uniform I was wearing into the cleaning roll and the dirty underthings into the washing roll.

I was standing there naked in the hangar, trying to see if I had everything straight when I heard somebody giggling. The Countess Krak was somewhere about. I didn't wait to see where. I grabbed the rolls and bags and sprinted back into the ship.

The incident didn't help my already rattled state. In the crew's cleaning and laundry room I was faced with huge discs that said this thing and that on them: typical Fleet jargon, typical Fleet lightning bolts pointing at this thing and that. (Bleep) the Fleet. I jammed the rolls into what I thought were the proper doors and then carried the bags of papers back to my room.

The shower did make me feel better. I was amazed at the amount of grime that rolled off! My head cleared up. Maybe all that dirt in my hair had been pressing down on my skull and fogging me up. It was an interesting theory. I was just about to concede that maybe the Fleet had something when a nerve shattering buzzergong in the laundry sent me tearing back in there to get my clothes.

I retrieved the underclothes roll. Everything was beautifully clean, beautifully flat and even several tears had been nicely mended.

For a moment I couldn't remember where I had put the uniform roll, there were too many disc doors. I started looking.

I couldn't find it!

With great care, I retraced my every prior action in this place. I had come in the door there and I had leaned *here* to rest while I tried to read signs and arrows. I opened the door I was now sure I had put the uniform roll in.

Nothing! I went tearing through the place opening every possible disc door.

Nothing!

I steadied myself down. I read the signs. And then it hit me!

I had put my uniform and boots roll in the disintegrator!

I stood there, naked, weeping quietly to myself. I had no clothes to wear but underpants!

Wait! Ske had been sent out for a General Services dress uniform! All was not defeated. I could yet triumph over Fleet supercleanliness!

With hope, I rushed back to my cubicle.

Success!

A package on the bed!

Quickly, I opened it.

What was I looking at?

I recognized the colonel's cross. That was one rank down, but Ske, of course, could be counted on to be inaccurate.

But what were all these designs?

Lying on a dead-black cloth, the red embroidery was quite startling.

Bones, hangman's noose, electric whips. Bones? Hangman's noose? Electric whips?

The helmet. Black! A huge phosphorescent skull!

It was the dress uniform of a colonel of the Death Battalions!

It even had the belts that represented bleeding intestines!

It was the number one terror uniform of the whole Voltarian forces!

I took a step toward the door. But then I realized Ske would carefully be gone.

Legally I could wear it as I outranked it and in theory a Secondary Executive could wear any of the Apparatus uniforms.

I was too tired. I lay down on the gimbal bed. I turned on a rest-heat light. What an awful way to start a voyage. If I could just sleep for an hour maybe some of this confusion would go away. Maybe, I thought, we would be safely in space when I awoke. Little did I know!

The lights went off. They were disconnecting the groundside cables. To Hells with it. I would just go to sleep. There was nothing, really, to a space blastoff.

Some of the tension was going out of me. I was just drifting off when a dreadful clamor brought me straight up. Pounding! Hammering! It sounded like they were ripping the ship apart!

I hastily threw a towel around my waist and rushed

into the passageway. The sounds redoubled. Then I realized they were coming from the forward auxiliary engine room. That was not right. We were still in the hangar! We ought to be getting crane-lifted to a trundle dolly.

In the control deck, there was Heller. He was perched on the edge of the local pilot chair, red cap on the back of his head. He was talking over the comm system to the engine room. From what he said, it was obvious that it was just a hangar engineer in there, somebody borrowed.

"I'll lift her off very easy, so I don't want much drive," he was saying.

I stared through the opened view windows. The space-particle armor plates were lowered. Heller leaned out and looked around and then yelled a "Stand clear" to some people in the hangar.

My Gods! He was about to fly this thing in the hangar! He might ram another ship or zoom through the roof! "Hey," I yelled. "Don't try to fly in here!"

Heller was sitting back. He gave a small laugh. "That's what tugs are for—to move around constricted spaces. Hold on, Soltan. She's jumpy."

Somebody with target wands was out in front of the ship. Heller reached for throttles.

I held on!

It wasn't even a straight run! He had to go around a crane and two spaceships and then turn again to get out the door!

There was a crash under us. I thought our bottom had fallen off. But it was just the big blocks and chocks tipping over.

He just perched there on the edge of the chair and flew her out of the hangar on warp drives!

The target man was putting him over well away

from the local landing circle but still quite close to the door.

"Hold on, Soltan," said Heller. He wasn't doing any holding on himself, he was just working throttles and switches. I should have believed him!

With a swoop and a drop back, he stood the tug on its tail!

I went sailing down the passage and brought up hard against the door.

The tug didn't. It touched without a quiver and was now vertically sitting just outside the hangar in the open air.

Heller swarmed down the now vertical rungs and offered me a hand and led me into the crew salon. The furniture had gimbaled over ninety degrees to adjust to the tug's being upright now. He pulled out a hot jolt canister from the locker, passed it through the heat coil, pulled the tube up and handed it to me. He smiled. "You ought to leave the bubblebrew alone the night before a voyage, Soltan."

It wasn't a criticism, it was just the kind of chatter these Fleet guys engage in. Probably a joke. But it made me feel cross. I didn't want the hot jolt. All I wanted was to go to my room and get at least a few minutes sleep. It was barely daylight outside.

I was just in the act of pushing the hot jolt away when a face jutted into the door.

It was Bawtch!

There he was, with his side-blinders flapping, his popeyes critical, his bony arms piled a yard high with paper!

"I couldn't resist the extreme pleasure of seeing you off, Officer Gris," he said. "And I brought you a going away present. Some orders to stamp."

"All those?" I groaned.

"No, only about a third. But you sure been busy ordering things! Buy, buy, buy! No wonder taxes are so high. The rest of this is just your neglected work: you have several weeks of reports you haven't read and I thought it might relax you on your voyage to do some *honest* application to your job."

I tried to wish him away. It didn't work. So I carried the hot jolt back to my room and fished my identoplate out of a waterproof bag, sat down at the gimbal table and started stamping. We would soon be gone. The worst was over—I thought. I would snooze from here on out.

"The rest of this," said old Bawtch, "I'll just put in between these voyage clamps where you can see this undone work every time you start to lie down. Hi, what's this?"

The room hadn't neatly returned to horizontal. I had not stowed the gear for flight. He wasn't looking at the weapons that had fallen out of the antiexplosion safe. He was picking the dress uniform off the floor.

"A colonel of the Death Battalions! So that's how you see yourself, Officer Gris. How nice. How appropriate. You'll look well in it, too. The color matches your soul exactly."

I ignored him. I noticed from a bill, Ske had bought that uniform at my expense! I went on stamping until my arm was tired. Finally he picked up the validated and OK-to-pay orders.

"Well, I'm leaving now. I heard a rumor that these ships blow up, so have a nice voyage." And, with the sort of evil chuckle that only Bawtch can manage, he was gone.

I finished off the hot jolt. Now if I could just stretch out and go to sleep, some hours later I would awaken, refreshed to find us hurtling through space and Voltar far behind us. What a lovely thought.

Alas, that wasn't the way it happened. I was about to experience the most nerve-shredding departure in space history!

Chapter 8

Just as I was about to lie down, I became conscious of a sort of thundering roar outside. The door to my room and airlock were open, but this wave of sound seemed to make the whole ship shake. It was exactly like a motorized army would sound if one were approaching. And then my ears were shattered by a heavy pounding close to hand.

It was too much for my nerves. I leapt up and ran to the airlock. I almost got my face knocked in as a stage section banged into the ship!

A commercial crew was working like fury erecting an eighty-foot-high, portable reviewing platform and wide steps which would reach from the ground up to the airlock!

I stared beyond this. My Gods! The hangar security fence gates to the outside world were wide open! Commercial lorries were pouring through the gap six abreast!

Already dozens of lorries were in the hangar.

Crews were unloading portable stages and bars: they were obviously converting this end of the hangar into the most gigantic entertainment tup hall anybody had ever seen! One bar was over two hundred feet long! One stage alone was thirty feet high and wide enough to take half the dancing girls on Voltar! And there were still more going up and still more lorries coming!

In total panic I rushed to the control deck. Heller was there dropping the meteor armor plates into position to cover the front ports.

I screamed at him, "You can't have a go-away party! That was just a joke! THIS IS A SECRET MISSION!"

He stopped working and looked at me with surprise. "But you've been okaying party orders. You authorized tons of them the other day. Just an hour ago I saw you stamping more!"

"Lombar will kill me!" I shouted.

"I'm sorry," he said, and he seemed to mean it. "But you see, this ship doesn't have a name. When she was transferred out of the Fleet she lost her designation. She hasn't been christened. It's about the unluckiest thing you can do to cruise around in an unchristened ship. Anybody in the Fleet can tell you that. They might blow up."

(Bleep) his Fleet customs. But the idea of this tug blowing up was never far from my mind.

He thought it over. "It's now going on eight! The christening will probably start around ten. We will be able to launch around noon."

I kept shaking my head.

"I'll tell you what we'll do," Heller said. "We'll hold it down all we can. We'll try to keep it just as sort of a family affair. All right?"

I knew I couldn't call back my orders or stop those lorries now. And there must be hundreds of contractor men, who had worked on the ship, invited with their families. And all the hangar crews. It would be worse to try to stop it than to let it go forward. So I nodded.

"By the way," he said. "Where's our crew? They should be aboard by now to get things ready to launch."

I had no answer to that. Practically sinking through the din, I climbed back down the now vertical passage to my room. It was impossible to sleep, no matter how exhausted I was. I slumped down into a chair.

I instantly got right back up. I had sat on something. A small bottle.

Where had it come from? It hadn't been there before, for that was where I had been sitting. I didn't see how it could have fallen from anything.

Then I remembered with horror that Lombar had said there would be a spy on my tail all the time and I wouldn't know who it was!

Could this be an example of it?

The bottle said:

> I. G. Barben, New York
> Amphetamine, Methedrine
> 5 mg., 100 tablets

It seemed to me to be the same bottle Lombar had produced last night.

I knew quite a bit about the stuff. It stimulates the central nervous system by potentiating the effects of *norepinephrine*, a neurohormone which activates parts of the sympathetic nervous system. It is colloquially called "speed," along with several other types of the drug. I had always been leery of having anything to do with it.

But I was desperate. How was I going to get through the next four hours? I got out the Knife Section knife. I took a little orange, heart-shaped pill. I cut off about a third of it.

I put the bit under my tongue. Bitter. I let it dissolve and absorb through the salivary glands of the mouth.

A tremendous hot "rush" hit me. My heart began to speed up.

Ah, I felt much better. I became confident. I began

to feel a little elated. Any worry about where the bottle had come from or the possibility of having a spy in my vicinity with orders to murder me vanished.

What beautiful, lovely stuff this speed was!

I realized I had better get dressed. It wouldn't do to keep running around in underpants. I gazed at the Death Battalion colonel uniform and it looked very nice. Just the thing.

With movements that were graceful, almost in slow motion but really a bit too fast, I pulled on the skintight pants. Actually, they weren't skin tight. They were three sizes too big, but that did not matter at all. I pulled on the boots. One was too large, the other too small.

But that seemed normal.

With an almost dancing grace, I got into the tunic. It was too small. But the designs were pretty, particularly the red daggers on the back. Fastening the collar almost strangled me but that was of no concern. I was breathing too fast anyway.

The black helmet was too big but I stuffed a towel in it to keep it off my ears. The mirror showed me that the skull seemed huge but was beautiful all the same. Oh, how right everything was with the world.

I put on my rank locket as I danced some floatingly interesting steps I never had known I could do.

Then I found the uniform belts intricate but interesting. The flattened, bleeding entrails presented a problem. Did they cross from right to left or left to right? I untangled them from the rank locket a few times and at length managed to fasten them correctly.

I discovered then the package of accouterments: red metal bands, with spikes, that covered the knuckles of each hand; a red sackful of lead that one hung on the right wrist; the ceremonial silver dagger stained with blood and beautifully enscrolled, *Death to Everybody,* the battalion motto. I hung it on the belt.

The mirror seemed to be in a euphoric state with the gorgeous image that it shined back. What splendid taste Ske had!

I happened to see my watch and was surprised to discover that it had taken me an hour to dress. So I hastily floated up the passageway, hardly touching the rungs at all.

The review platform was securely in place at the airlock. I stepped out upon it and gazed over the pleasant scene.

All of the platforms and bars had been erected, even a series of dressing rooms for dancing girls. Tup trucks were unloading vast quantities of drinkables.

Banner crews were stringing huge expanses of bunting across doors and anything else.

I counted five bands unloading instruments and setting up on stages. And over there were two fifty-member choruses, one from the Fleet marines, another from the Fleet base. There was certainly going to be plenty of music. Well, I always like music.

A lot of contractors who had worked on the ship were beginning to drift in. Hundreds of workers and their families. And maybe relatives. Ah, yes. And hangar crews were also drifting over. And there! Crews of Apparatus ships in the hangar were coming from the barracks. They were all early! But beautiful people. All of them.

Ah, yes. And transports of Fleet officers and spacers, unloading in showers of powder blue. Well, welcome, welcome. Fine branch of the service, Fleet.

And here came our crew! They slipped off an Apparatus police van. They hastily grabbed their spacebags. They held them on their shoulders in such a way nobody could see their faces. They came slinking up the eighty feet of steps. Five ex-pirates, still under a death sentence.

I stepped over by the airlock to welcome them. I knew the racial type. Antimancos: their heads are a bit narrow at the top and then swell out on each side to make the face a sort of triangle bottomed by a wide, savage sort of jaw. Their complexions are very swarthy; they average about three hundred pounds and six foot eight. There is a lot of hate in their very small, narrow-set eyes. The Antimanco feel the universe does not appreciate them. I would show them *I* did!

Expansively, I said, "I am Officer Gris. I have been waiting for you."

Maybe it was the way I said it, but the one in the lead, probably the captain, stared at my welcoming hand and then at my clothes and backed up so quickly he almost knocked the rest of them back down the steps. Then he sort of steeled his nerve, uttered a low command and rushed past me through the airlock and vanished into the ship. Inside I could hear what sounded like swear words from them.

I pondered it. I looked at my welcoming hand. There was nothing wrong with it if you disregarded the red, spiked metal knuckles. There was nothing wrong with my uniform either. Quite sharp, really, especially the hangman's nooses.

Feeling quite benign, I again surveyed the vast scene below.

There was Snelz walking about, lining up a full company of men. Dear Snelz. Always a comfort to have him around.

Wait! Euphoria or no euphoria, what was Snelz doing with a *company* of men? He only rated a *platoon.*   I looked closer. Even though Snelz was five hundred feet away, the red of the *captain's* locket glowed in the morning sun!

With a wave of total certainty, I knew it must have been Snelz who had told Lombar about the Countess Krak! How else would he have gotten promoted? SNELZ WAS THE SPY!

I backed up. Somebody was behind me. I turned and got a foggy view of Heller's face. "Snelz got promoted!"

Heller laughed. "Yes, I know. I gave him five hundred credits to buy his next rank. He deserved it."

I felt sort of spinny. If the spy wasn't Snelz, then who was supposed to kill me?

Heller looked strange to me. He had changed to his Fleet dress uniform. He had a round, flat-topped, brimless cap on his head, slanted a bit to the right and held in place with a gold chin strap. His skintight, waist-length tunic was gleaming with gold citation scrolls against the dark blue. His fifty mission star was blinding on his chest. A wide, red stripe went down the outside of each leg. In his Fleet dress uniform, Heller made a picture that would cause the girls to really faint.

He was looking at me oddly, though. "What are you doing in Death Battalion full dress?"

"It's Snelz," I said. "I mean, there seems to be an awful lot of tupples here amongst the danceships." I realized I was talking too fast.

"Are you all right?" said Heller.

"Of course, Lombar is all right. Whatever Snelz says, goes. Goes up to the bear girls, of course, unless the bands don't launch." (Bleep) it, I was talking too fast.

"You better sit down," said Heller. "On the rail, there. No, no, don't fall over! Here, I'll open one of these review chairs. Now you just sit there and take it easy. This will all be over and we'll be gone soon."

I didn't know why he was concerned. The world looked just great to me.

Chapter 9

I was about to see what Heller called "keeping it in the family."

Ten o'clock arrived. And so had scores and scores of lorries and thousands and thousands of people. The hangar guards seemed to be making no attempt to regulate traffic or numbers—the gates were simply wide open.

Gay bunting and flags were all over the place. Tup hadn't arrived by the canister: it had arrived in tankers; and everywhere you looked, people were drinking from mugs. Some of the bands had begun to play and the music, in conflict from band to band, rose above the chatter of the multitude. One would have thought the party had started.

Not so. A daylight fireworks crew had arrived a bit earlier and I had been eyeing them benignly, not realizing what they were up to. *They* signalled the start of the party!

Up from their platform went a "flaming planet"!

It soared half a mile into the air, hung there spinning and displaying lighted "continents" and then burst into a great ball of fire. It would have been visible for miles in all directions! That officially started the party.

The crowd burst into a cheer.

Oh, well, I thought, such displays are common enough: it wouldn't be thought to be anything special by the countryside. New store opening, a public bullet ball game. No harm. Besides, it had been quite pretty.

Sitting in my chair on the review platform, I was mostly hidden by the bunting on its rails but I could see quite well what was going on. I felt quite powerful, really, capable of controlling everything with ease from where I sat.

My eye lighted upon a crane platform lifted up from a big truck, higher even than I was. Suddenly I saw it was a Homeview crew! A *big* Homeview crew! With *big* cameras!

Oh, well, I thought. Probably the tup companies had called them in hopes of getting some free advertising into every home. Maybe the manager of the dancing girls or the mountain dancing bears. Homeview crews went everywhere and they often didn't use what they shot. Just routine.

Reporters! The vans of about ten newssheets were parked around the Homeview crane truck. There was a swarm of newshawks and their cameramen. Oh, well, they say where you find free drinks, you always find reporters.

They seemed to be heading over this way. Ah, of course! There was Heller standing there and they probably didn't have many pictures of him in fancy Fleet full dress, blazing with citations. He looked kind of cute. Naturally they would want some shots of him—for their files, of course, in case anything exciting happened in the future. And sure enough, I was right. Here they came storming up the eighty-foot rise of steps, jostling each other. And their cameramen immediately began shouting orders to Heller to smile, to look up, to look down, to turn this way or that and even to shake hands with one of the leading reporters who probably wanted one to show to his kids. No harm in all that. Just routine.

Then I caught sight of the Fleet Intelligence officer,

Bis. He seemed to be talking to three reporters and pointing up at the platform and here they came with their cameramen.

Aha! They recognized power when they saw it! They were not heading for Heller! They were coming straight to me! About time.

They asked me to stand up and look this way and that. I'm sure they got some very good portraits: probably sell them for use in history books of the future. Contemplating the feats I felt capable of at that moment, they would probably be writing whole sets of volumes about me.

Then they wanted me to stand just behind Heller so they could shoot Heller in the foreground to the left and me behind him slightly to the right. Bis was there, too, helping them pose me, whispering so as to not disturb Heller.

So, they got some shots of me looking at Heller's back. They weren't satisfied. But when they told me I was a natural actor and could glare and grit my teeth and all that I entered into the fun of it. I did all that and even added a few of my own such as tapping my lead-filled sack against my palm and clenching my metal-guarded fists. Heller was unaware of it and just went on chatting.

I thought they were through with me, but no, I had to sit back down in my chair. A cameraman assistant got a backscreen erected behind me—a sort of pattern of stones like a cave, quite realistic. And I posed and looked powerful for them.

But Bis, who was being very helpful, still wasn't satisfied. He was pointing down and whispering and I got up to see what he was pointing at. There was a whole display of figure-cakes along one bar: these are made of sweetbun dough, are lifesize and pretty realistic, nymphs and so on, all in natural color. And an assistant went racing down and chopped off a cake nymph's hand and smeared some red jam on it and came racing back up and handed it to me.

I told them I wasn't hungry. But they said they wanted to see how well I really could act and would I please look ravenous and voracious and look as if I was eating it. Well, nothing was easier: I am a natural actor and today I was capable of anything. Then they got some shots of me chewing the bite as though delicious. Finally, Bis and they agreed I'd done beautifully and left.

One hundred girls were doing a parade dance along the bars, floating big banners along and I got interested in watching them. They seemed a bit unreal but pretty.

The crowd was already pretty noisy and suddenly there was a surge of sound so I looked to see what had attracted their attention.

It was just a Palace City limousine. It glided to the landing target. And out stepped Captain Tars Roke, the King's Own Astrographer. He was accompanied by several aides and they were all in dress uniform and made a splendid sparkle of color to the crowd. They came sedately over to the platform and up the steps. The Homeview crane swung way over and got close.

Roke came up and shook Heller's hand and they chatted like old friends. And a Homeview interrogator was there. I caught some scraps of it.

"I'm sorry," Roke was saying, "I can't reveal where this mission is headed. I just came over to tell my friend Jet that I wished him well."

"From the type of engines that this mission ship has, Captain, couldn't we conclude that the mission is back to the old home galaxy? Perhaps to pick up and tow here some ancestral monument from the ruins of our racial planet?"

"I didn't say that," said Roke. "You did."

"But, Captain, this is *Tug One* and we have it on reliable authority that it can't be run within a galaxy without peril. Its sister ship blew up."

At the moment I thought, well, I'll just have to carry it there with my bare hands. I felt perfectly able to do so. Really capable of tremendous feats! Methedrine, I thought, what have I ever done without you? What glorious stuff! My mouth felt kind of dry but I didn't want to get down into that crowd just to get some tup.

The Fleet male chorus was singing some Fleet song and the crowd took it up. I didn't realize it was a prelude to something else. Then I noticed that everyone was looking up. So I looked up.

Maybe three miles above us, two hundred and fifty Fleet spacefighters were flying in formation. They do it in a very orderly fashion. I think the command ship has a computer which spits out coordinate orders to individual crews and they immediately take those positions. They wheeled and formed various figures, all very precise. And then suddenly they all strung out across about five miles of sky.

They fired their guns all at once!

Mile-long, eighth-mile wide bands of sustained flame, the kind that lasts a minute glaring in the daylight, and then throws out white clouds, blasted across the sky. It said:

GOOD LUCK, JET!

And then the concussion wave hit while the sign flamed!

It was loud enough to be heard by every person in every one of the five cities!

And even the ground was lit up by the glaring light of those letters!

Although I was feeling almost as high as those letters, something nagged at me that this was not quite all right for a secret mission! I couldn't put my finger on it. It just didn't seem fitting somehow. Then I realized what it was. Those pilots and crews up there were missing the party! Flying around up there, they wouldn't get any tup or cakes.

I was about to call this to someone's attention when down they came and, with new blasts, they landed in an open field nearby and out poured the pilots and crews and over they came to the party. So that was handled.

I was feeling a little sorry for the Homeview crews. They were working so hard and yet, really, they weren't getting anything newsworthy. The stuff would never be used. They had lots of films of dancing girls and tup trucks. Why would they show any more? So it was all right. The secrecy of the mission was still intact.

I was gazing down upon what now must be ten thousand Fleet and Apparatus people and had just about decided it was pretty well over when I heard a yell.

Somebody was pointing up and then a lot of people were pointing up and here came a white and gold air limousine. It was an unmistakable vehicle. It had been built as a present from billions of fans on a hundred and ten planets!

The din of the crowd hurt the ears! "It's Hightee Heller!" They chanted her name so loud it almost took the hangar roof off! "Hightee Heller! Hightee Heller! Hightee Heller!"

I smiled. I understood now what Jet had meant. A family affair. Of course. How nice of her to come!

The Homeview crane was swooping down.

Hightee Heller danced out of the limousine, throwing kisses. She was dressed as an angel!

Of course. For the christening!

Well, we'd get the christening over and leave. Nothing else of interest could happen.

All five bands and choruses began to sing and play her favorite song.

A special effects truck was drawn up below the review platform and its crew, waving canisters of tup the while, were setting up.

Hightee came dancing up the platform steps. She kissed Heller lightly on the cheek and the crowd screamed "Hightee and Jet!" "Hightee and Jet!"

Then here went the christening!

A great white cloud, by three-dimensional electronic projection, appeared in the sky above. An angel seemed to step out of it—but of course it was just Hightee on the platform furnishing the physical pattern which was projected on the sky.

The crowd screamed with delight!

The white cloud settled over the ship, billowing and curling.

Hightee leaned over on the platform and the three-dimensional image of her, a hundred and fifty feet tall, made an elegant motion over the ship with both hands.

All five bands struck a dramatic chord. Both choruses sang a prolonged note.

The angel cried, "Little ship, I give thee life!"

The bands and choruses went silent.

The angel seemed to bend over and kiss the ship upon the nose.

The bands and choruses sounded another chord which ended with a cymbal crash.

Then the angel again spread her hands and cried out, "THY NAME IS NOW *PRINCE CAUCALSIA!*"

The bands and choruses sang with joy.

The crowd went mad!

The Homeview crews got it all!

Some good sense seemed to penetrate my fog. Because it was Hightee Heller here, those Homeview pictures just could get viewed on every screen in a hundred and ten planets. And worse, all you had to do was put that name, *"Prince Caucalsia,"* on any office or school or museum computer keyboard and you'd get "Folk Legend 894M" and that would point directly to the mission destination, Blito-P3!

Oh, it was a good thing I was powerful enough even to work with such crass amateurs! Superhuman feat, but I could do it.

Besides, Hightee had probably christened other ships. That wouldn't guarantee they would use the pictures. It would take more than that.

The fireworks truck was busy again. The christening had ended with a wild display of daylight fireworks in all colors, visible for miles. And then there was a supernova! It must have been started earlier because now, twenty miles up at least, it burst with a flash that lit up all five cities already brilliantly lit by Voltar's sun. Spectacular!

About a minute later the shattering crash of it made even the ground shake!

Everybody, all the thousands, had drinks in their hands and they were shouting good luck to the *Prince Caucalsia.*

Hightee flew off to get back to the studio. Well, I guessed it was pretty well over and we'd be leaving. No real damage done, I told myself. The Homeview crew would never use those pictures.

A bunch of mountain dancing bears was performing now.

I was heartened by the fact that Bugs Bunny hopped up the steps and handed me a carrot. I wasn't hungry but I munched at it. "They'll never use those pictures, doc," he said in English. "No violence." I thanked him for his good advice. Always sound. But I wondered if a freighter had just come in from Earth. They had to be careful about stowaways. I turned to caution him but he was gone.

The dancing bears didn't go away and the crowd loved them.

Suddenly, in the cleared space below, Snelz, my dear friend Snelz, appeared with his company. Good man, Snelz.

His whole company was uniformed splendidly in black. They were wearing their visored combat helmets and carrying blastrifles. A band, accompanied by the Fleet chorus, began to play and sing a march, and to its time, Snelz's company began to go through the most complex set of geometric infantry figures I have ever seen. Squares and crosses and interthreading lines. Then doing it with blastrifles spinning and going through manuals of arms. How did he ever get Apparatus troops to do anything like those maneuvers?

The crowd was impressed. They cheered the conclusion of each difficult pattern.

Then the blastrifles seemed to fire. At the end of a difficult swirl, each time, the blastrifles all banged off a reduced charge. Maneuver, *Bang!* Maneuver, *Bang!* On and on. Impressive.

Then suddenly all the rifles seemed to shoot out a flag. And the most difficult patterns of marching yet seen were accompanied by a manual of arms that made floating blurs of color the while.

Then with one final bang, the rifles fired flitter up into the sky. With the whole company going to a knee-present-arms to the ship, the flitter began to float down in sparking bits over the tug.

The crowd went absolutely crazy! They had never before seen drilling like that!

The cheering died when Snelz told his company, "Dismiss!"

There was a moment's silence. And through it cut the voice of an Apparatus officer, addressed to the Fleet fliers, "Yeah, yeah! So you Fleet guys think the Apparatus troops can't drill!"

There was a silent, electric tension, like a blanket going over the whole crowd.

Then a Fleet pilot said, real loud, "That drill captain is an ex-Fleet marine! He ain't no 'drunk'!"

An Apparatus man hit him!

A Fleet pilot hit an Apparatus man!

Twenty Apparatus men hit twenty Fleet men!

A hundred Fleet men hit a hundred Apparatus men!

The fight was on!

The Homeview crews got it all and continued to get it!

Screams sounded!

Canisters flew!

Fleet military police spacers present leaped in to try to stop the fight.

Apparatus military police guards sprang up and tried to stop the fight.

Fleet and Apparatus military police met head on and began to fight each other!

Benches went over! Cakes were being used as ammunition!

The Homeview crews were getting every bit of it!

Heller, high on the review platform, gazed over the

seething scene. He grabbed a microphone that was hooked to the public sound system.

Above the din he shouted, "All bands and choruses! STRIKE UP 'SPACEWARD, HO!' "

It is what is called a song-chant. The first lines are sung as a melody and then some lines are chanted as though they are orders and so on.

Above the din, three bands which were perched too high on stages to get into the fight, struck up the refrain.

Those of the choruses still in place sang the first two lines:

> *Spaceward, ho!*
> *To the stars we go!*

Then the chant:

> *Upward, upward, upward!*
> *High, high, high!*
> *Roll the blast! Roll the blast!*
> *Close all locks! Grab sky!*

Canisters were crashing. Screams and shouts racketed. The bands and choruses turned up their volumes. The choruses sang:

> *Spaceward, ho!*
> *The planet flees below.*

And the chant:

> *Thunder, thunder, thunder!*
> *Flame, flame, flame!*
> *Feed the fuel! Feed the fuel!*
> *Correct the course and aim!*

Far off, above the din, sirens were wailing as alerted riot units rose to fly in!

The choruses sang:

> *Spaceward, ho!*
> *Some other land to know!*
> *Target, target, target!*
> *Drive, drive, drive!*
> *Bore the black! Bore the black!*
> *Fasten belts! G Five!*

Raid sirens were going off. The first of the antiriot ships bashed to ground nearby. The battle raged on.

The choruses sang:

> *Space is a mistress!*
> *Space is a whore!*
> *Space is a spell*
> *No spacer can ignore.*
> *So burn, burn, burn!*
> *And shove, shove, shove!*
> *We're into space another time,*
> *Lured from home and love*
> *Into hope and terror,*
> *Into stars above.*
> *Here we go!*
> *Here we go!*
> *Spaceward, HO!*

A tup lorry went over, spilling a flood of tup!

The riot police that were landing were Fleet and Apparatus! They started to fight even before they got to the gates!

The Homeview crew, high on their crane, ground on.

Heller said, "They'll be at that fight all day! Get in. It's noon. We're blasting off!"

He went in and perched himself on the edge of the local control chair. He sent some orders to the auxiliary engine room and then he hit every sound switch on the panel. Tugs have beams that, in space, which is silent, fasten to hulls of ships and conduct sound along them. These beams flashed into the hangar, against the ground and against every Apparatus spaceship in view. The tug's whistles, sirens, gongs and blast signals all started going off at once. Ear-splitting!

I had made an ineffectual last second attempt to close the airlock. But somehow I couldn't get my hands connected with anything. We were already lifting and I sprawled in the opening, my head out into the air.

The Homeviews were swivelled about to get the departure and, no doubt, my helmet falling the two hundred feet now separating us from ground.

The tug whistles, sirens, gongs and blast signals were still going. So was the riot!

For some minutes now, even before the song, my hands had been shaking. And now my body began to go into a sort of vertigo. The euphoria was gone and in its place I felt extremely irritable.

I told myself that this was the most *un*secret secret mission departure *anyone* had ever heard of!

Three hundred feet below us, in the space where the tug had been, there was a single guardsman, isolated from the riot. And the guardsman, with both hands, was madly throwing kisses after the tug. It was the Countess Krak! She had not been properly at Spiteos. She had been here all day!

She was very tiny now, far down there on Voltar. She stopped throwing kisses and stood there sort of slumped.

Somebody grabbed my heels, pulled me in and closed the airlock door.

We were on our totally advertised, totally certain to be shown on every screen on every planet, secret way.

We were headed for Earth.

But Gods only knew what would happen now!

*Will Earth discover
it is the target
of an alien invasion
in time to fight back?*

**Read
MISSION EARTH
Volume 2
BLACK GENESIS:
Fortress of Evil**

About the Author
L. Ron Hubbard

Filled with a dazzling array of other-world weaponry and systems, L. Ron Hubbard's *Mission Earth* is a spectacular cavalcade of battles, of stunning plot reversals, with heroes and heroines, villains and villainesses, caught up in a superbly imaginative, intricately plotted invasion of Earth—as seen entirely and uniquely through the eyes of the aliens that already walk among us.

An unprecedented event in publishing history, so momentous that a new word—dekalogy (meaning a group of ten volumes)—had to be coined to adequately describe *Mission Earth*'s sheer magnitude and mastery: 1.2 million words in ten epic volumes that surpass even his last triumphant, internationally acclaimed best selling masterpiece, *Battlefield Earth*.

Born in 1911, the son of a U.S. naval officer, L. Ron Hubbard grew up in the great American West and was acquainted early with the rugged outdoor life before he took to the sea. The cowboys, Indians and mountains of Montana were balanced with an open sea, temples and the throngs of the Orient as Hubbard travelled through the Far East as a teen-ager. By the time he was nineteen, he had travelled over a quarter of a million sea miles and thousands on land as he prodded and asked and recorded his experiences in a series of diaries mixed with story ideas.

Returning to the United States, Hubbard's insatiable curiosity and demand for excitement sent him into the sky as a pilot where he quickly earned a reputation for his skill and daring before he turned his attention again to the sea. This time it was four-masted schooners and voyages into the Caribbean as Hubbard mixed adventure with an education that was to serve him later at the typewriter.

While Hubbard's first articles were nonfiction and based upon his aviation experience, he soon began to draw from his travels to produce a wide variety of stories: adventure, mysteries, travel through the Far East, westerns, detective, and finally, science fiction.

In 1938, Hubbard was already established and recognized as one of the top-selling writers of the field, but a new magazine wanted new blood. Hubbard was urged to try his hand at science fiction. The red-headed author protested that he did not write about "ray guns and rockets" but that he wrote about people. "That's just what we want," he was told.

The result was a barrage of stories from Hubbard that changed the face of science fiction and excited intense critical comparison—then as now—with the best of H. G. Wells and Edgar Allan Poe. Today, Hubbard is recognized as one of the "founding fathers" of the great Golden Age of Science Fiction who, like Robert Heinlein and a few other grand masters, continues to develop and significantly enlarge the contemporary literature genre he helped to create.

At the same time, Hubbard's prodigious and continuing creative output over more than half a century as a professional writer has assumed the proportions of a true publishing phenomenon—with more than a hundred novels and novelettes, more than two hundred short stories (published under his own name and such no-less-celebrated pen names as Rene Lafayette, Kurt Von Rachen and Winchester Remington Colt, among others), and more than twenty-two million copies of his fiction, in a dozen languages, sold throughout the world.

To celebrate his golden anniversary as a professional writer, L. Ron Hubbard wrote *Battlefield Earth: A Saga of the Year 3000*. The epic quickly moved onto every national best-seller list with the author and book receiving critical acclaim.

Publisher's Weekly described Mr. Hubbard as "a superlative storyteller with total mastery of plot and pacing."

The *Buffalo Evening News* said *Battlefield Earth* was "vintage hard science fiction, done by a master storyteller."

Kirkus Reviews said *Battlefield Earth* was "a huge (800 + pages) slugfest. Mr. Hubbard celebrates fifty years as a pro writer with tight plotting, furious action, and have-at-'em entertainment."

Now, with the *Mission Earth* series, readers get a brilliantly conceived fusion of high science fiction adventure, rich comedy-satire and hilarious social commentary in the great, classic tradition of Voltaire, Swift, Verne, Wells and Orwell.

Unlike anything in the annals of science fiction, *Mission Earth* is told with the distinctive pace, artistry and humor that is the inimitable hallmark of L. Ron Hubbard, one of the most prolific and influential authors of the twentieth century.

"I am always happy to hear from my readers."
L. Ron Hubbard

These were the words of L. Ron Hubbard, who was always very interested in hearing from his friends and readers. He made a point of staying in communication with everyone he came in contact with over his fifty-year career as a professional writer, and he had thousands of fans and friends that he corresponded with all over the world.

The publishers of L. Ron Hubbard's literary works wish to continue this tradition and would very much welcome letters and comments from you, his readers, both old and new.

Any message addressed to the Author's Affairs Director at Bridge Publications will be given prompt and full attention.

BRIDGE PUBLICATIONS, INC.
4751 Fountain Avenue
Los Angeles, California 90029

**FOR MORE EXCITING ENTERTAINMENT
FROM L. RON HUBBARD SEE THE
FOLLOWING PAGES . . . . .**

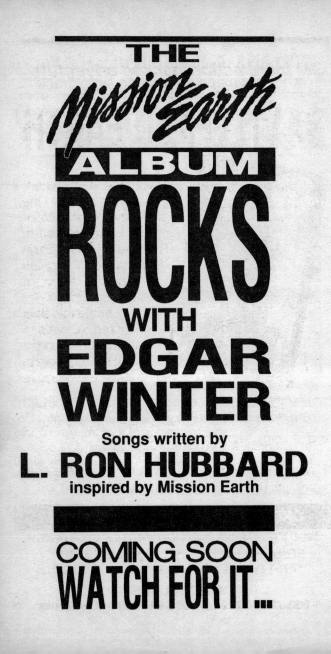

FREE
CATALOG

ORDER YOUR
FREE CATALOG
OF BOOKS BY
L. RON HUBBARD